Orby Shipley

Carmina Mariana

An English Anthology In Verse In Honour Of Or In Relation To The Blessed Virgin

Mary

Orby Shipley

Carmina Mariana
An English Anthology In Verse In Honour Of Or In Relation To The Blessed Virgin Mary

ISBN/EAN: 9783741100277

Manufactured in Europe, USA, Canada, Australia, Japa

Cover: Foto ©Andreas Hilbeck / pixelio.de

Manufactured and distributed by brebook publishing software
(www.brebook.com)

Orby Shipley

Carmina Mariana

Carmina Mariana

SECOND SERIES

AN ENGLISH ANTHOLOGY IN VERSE

IN HONOUR OF AND IN RELATION TO

The Blessed Virgin Mary

COLLECTED AND ARRANGED BY

ORBY SHIPLEY, M.A.

Editor of ' Annus Sanctus : Hymns of the Church for the Ecclesiastical Year '

SECOND EDITION

London & New York
SOLD FOR THE EDITOR BY
BURNS AND OATES, LIMITED
1902

SECOND HOMILY ON ST. LUKE I. 26.

ST. BERNARD, ABBOT OF CLAIRVAUX: XII. CENT.

From the VII. and VIII. Lessons, in the Third Nocturn of Mattins, for the Third Day within the Octave of the Immaculate Conception.

Translated (1879) by John, Marquess of Bute, in ' The Roman Breviary,' Vol. I. Winter.

'Rejoice, father Adam, and yet more thou mother Eve, ye that are the source of all, and the ruin of all, and the unhappy cause of their ruin before ye gave them birth. Be comforted both in your Daughter, and such a Daughter; but chiefly thou, O Woman, of whom the first evil came, and who has cast thy slur upon all women. The time is come for the slur to be taken away, and for the man to have nothing to say against the woman. . . . Wherefore, O Eve, betake thyself to Mary; mother betake thyself to thy Daughter; let the Daughter answer for the mother; let her take away her mother's reproach; let her make up to her father for her mother's fault; for if man be fallen by means of woman, it is by means of Woman that he is raised up again. What didst thou say, O Adam? "The woman whom thou gavest to be with me, she gave me of the tree, and I did eat." These are wrathful words by the which thou dost rather magnify than diminish thine offence. Nevertheless, Wisdom hath defeated thy malice. . . . One woman answereth for another: the Wise for the foolish; the Lowly for the proud; for her that gave thee of the tree of death, Another that giveth thee to taste of the Tree of Life. . . . Wherefore accuse the woman no more, but speak in thanksgiving, and say, "Lord, the Woman whom thou hast given me, she hath given me of the Tree of Life, and I have eaten." . . . Behold, it was for this that the Angel Gabriel was sent to the Virgin, to the most worshipful of Women, a Woman more wonderful than all women, the Restorer of them that went before, and the Quickener of them that come after her.'

IN MEMORY OF

JOHN, MARQUESS OF BUTE,

Who, in addition to giving poetical and literary help,

generously expressed during his mortal sickness a wish,

which has been loyally fulfilled by his Trustees, to

defray the cost of its publication,

THIS VOLUME IS GRATEFULLY DEDICATED

BY THE EDITOR.

HAIL, Holy Queen
Mother of Mercy, Hail
Our Life, Our Sweetness and our Hope
To thee do we cry
Poor banished Children of Eve
To thee do we send up our sighs
Mourning and weeping in this vale of tears
Turn then, most Gracious Advocate
Thine eyes of mercy towards us
And after this our exile, show unto us
The Blessed Fruit of thy Womb
JESUS
O Clement, O Loving, O Sweet Virgin Mary
Pray for us, Holy Mother of God
That we may be made worthy of the promises of Christ.

Preface.

A FULL and detailed statement of the object and intention of CARMINA MARIANA, of the plan and wish of the Editor, of the sources from which the collection of verse has been drawn and the materials which have been used, together with the methods and limitations adopted in the compilation, appeared in the Preface of the First Series. To this statement the reader of the Second Series is referred. It renders needless further discussion of such points, as the sources and materials in both volumes are similar, and the intention and plan which influenced the compiler are identical. The amount of English verse, however, whether old or new, whether original or translated, having our Lady for its august theme, which a quest pursued during nearly a score of years proves to be in existence, is far richer than had been anticipated, or indeed, than could be foreseen by one who had made no such search. A body of poetry —actually in extract or potentially in reference—was thus gradually collected by the Editor, larger than it was possible to reproduce in a single volume. This fact, emphasised by the sympathetic reception of the First Series both by reviewers and students, and the widespread interest evinced towards such a poetical tribute to the Blessed Virgin in the English tongue, encouraged an idea which had grown with the ever-increasing growth of the poetical excerpts—the idea, namely, of publishing another instalment of sacred song in Mary's praise. The generosity, moreover, of many

competent co-adjutors in aiding the compiler in various
ways with the literary production of the book—if he may
express his deep sense of individual obligations in vague
and impersonal, but not ungrateful terms—has been
very great, and has sensibly lightened his labours :
whilst the spontaneous and unconditioned liberality of
one munificent benefactor—offered after the MSS., in
course of issue by subscription, had been placed in the
hands of the printer—relieved the Editor from further
anxiety on the score of finance. The result of this many-
sided co-operative action, both mental and material, of
good and kind friends in honour of Mary may be found
in the following pages.

*   *   *

For the right appreciation by the reader of the
Allegorical and Mystical Poems, of the Love-Songs of
the Elizabethan Age, and of other verse reprinted in
the present volume, as well as on behalf of their
authors, a few words of apologia seem to be desirable.
The writers who have been consulted on the policy of
such an addition to the contents of the Carmina, at the
outset suggested some doubt as to the propriety of the
inclusion of these poems. But after discussion, they
either generously acquiesced in such inclusion, on the
Editor's responsibility, or declared themselves satisfied
with the explanation suggested. It is true, that more
than one author affirmed that our Lady was not con-
sciously contemplated during the creation of their work ;
or if present, that unique and indispensable Personality
in our holy Religion was present only with vagueness
and indefinitely. But it is also true that, in such verse,
thoughts were conceived and words were employed by
the writers which could hardly have been used if the

Blessed Virgin had not been prophetically anticipated, had not historically existed, or had not from the teaching of the Great Forty Days influenced the daily life, as well as the faith, the devotion and the intellect of Christendom.

The like may be said, perhaps, of the authors whose poetical inspirations survive them. Of these, one typical case only need be named. In pagan times, or in a modern civilization uninfluenced, not to say unimpregnated with the spirit and literature of Christianity, the magnificent Ode to Mary by the poet Shelley, quoted in the First Series of the Carmina (page 40), could not have been composed. This address to our Lady, which opens with the words 'Seraph of Heaven,' under a transparent veil of an earthly embodiment of them, describes with singular power, exactitude and beauty many of Mary's prerogatives, characteristics, gifts and graces, in terms which are distinctly based upon the thought and language of the Apocalyptic Vision. Neither is the argument affected by any proximate surroundings of the composition of the lines, nor by whatsoever may have been their human origin, nor to whomsoever they were first addressed, nor still less, by the popular verdict pronounced upon them. The poem owes something, owes much, perhaps owes all, to the Religion of Jesus Christ.

Here it may be permitted to the Editor to draw attention to a personal experience. Criticism is seldom trustworthy that leans upon negative evidence; yet negative evidence has sometimes a value of its own. It is a fact then to be estimated, in this relation, that in the past no adverse opinion was expressed by reviewers to the application of these same lines of Shelley to our Lady, in a book widely criticised at the time of its publication. In the year 1869, the 'Seraph of Heaven'

was quoted, as a modern instance, in the reprint of a
seventeenth century and Anglican Life of the Blessed
Virgin, called 'The Femall Glory,'[1] by Anthony Stafford :
and it may be added, that thirty years ago the literary and
religious world of England was less tolerant, or perhaps
less indifferent than now to any words of honour or
songs of praise addressed to the Mother of God.
Neither is the Editor aware that any hostile critical
estimate was formed on the occasion of his re-iterated
quotation of Shelley's lines, a generation later, in the
pages of Carmina Mariana, in 1893.   Indeed, the
reviewers of that volume—many of whom are quoted
at the end of this series—even if they felt an objection,
failed to object, though there was opportunity for protest.
They appear to have tacitly accepted the situation—that
the language of Shelley's address and the ideas which
produced it had connection, in some undefined but
real manner, with our Lady.   From this negative con-
cession, the Editor ventures to draw, inferentially, an
admission prompted by the same eloquent silence,
namely, that no undue strain was placed on the
author's words, and no insult was offered to the reader's
intelligence, by the application of Shelley's verses
to the Blessed Virgin.   Of course, such silence may
in some cases have had a different cause : but in
general, the reason assigned is believed by the Editor
to be valid.[2]

[1] The Editor's first offering made, as an Anglican, to our Lady.
The book, together with the Author's Apology, was printed, at
the expense of a friend, in 1860 ; was reprinted in 1869 ; and has
been long out of print.

[2] The above was written from memory. On again referring to
the reviews in question, after some years' interval, one critic
appears to suggest the facility of questioning the Editor's 'reasons

The principle involved, however, by the publication in a book dedicated to Mary, of Shelley's address to the Blessed Virgin, has been developed in the Second Series of the Carmina. Hence, it is deemed well to offer a short statement on the grounds of such expansion which, though it may fail to persuade the critical temper of others, will probably suffice for the literary conscience of 'men of good will.' The effort will be made without any attempt to be exhaustive, or to give more than a few illustrations in support of the contention. And the principle—if the term be allowed, apart from a definition of it—may be gathered from these considerations, which, from the nature of the case, will be suggestive rather than logical.[1]

First: Human faculties can seldom realise and never adequately express all, or even the larger part of that which fills the human mind ; still less can one convey to another human intelligence the larger part, or indeed more than a fragment of what fills the soul after contemplation. This is true of all kinds of literature ; but it becomes truer as the subject-matter of thought becomes more important, or the medium of communication becomes less simple. In subjects connected with religion and in conceptions created in a poetical

for permitting various fragments to appear.' But this marks the extent of his own expression of doubt, as may be seen in the review quoted from the 'Athenæum,' and printed in the Appendix. Another reviewer also considers that Shelley's lines are 'somewhat doubtfully assigned' to our Lady—in the 'St. James' Gazette.'

[1] This line of thought was finally adopted after consultation with the late Redemptorist Father, T. E. Bridgett—a priest of sound judgment and wide knowledge of English poetry, and of great kindness in imparting the fruit of such knowledge—and he supplied the illustrations which follow.

form, the difficulty of realisation and of expression is enhanced ; and when poetry and religion are combined, the difficulty of conveying thought definitely and fully reaches its highest point.

Secondly : Without invading the domain of divine inspiration, it is possible to believe in a secondary degree of inspiration granted to some minds, on certain subjects, in a certain way. Such partial inspiration may be given to elevated or purified minds—indeed, to any serious mind that contemplates high and holy themes— and still more, to minds which are both purified and elevated. In the abstract, religion is one such subject, and poetry is one such mode of communication between mind and mind ; whilst in the concrete, the union of both in the terms of sacred verse affords a medium for the influence and action of secondary inspiration here glanced at. Hence it is probable, that to those to whom it is given to write true poetry on lofty religious topics— and the great Mother of God and her transcendent office and work in the kingdom of grace is one such topic —are imparted thoughts which, from human incapacity, they cannot express in their entirety, and words insufficiently comprehensive and precise to transmit to others all they desire to convey.

Thirdly : Poets have often claimed for their words, and others have ever claimed for the words of poets a richer and fuller meaning than lies upon the surface of their work, or than the authors of their work were conscious of at the time of literary inception. Moreover, not unfrequently and in after years, writers of poetry have voluntarily acknowledged that they had become powerless to define the exact meaning of their verse at the moment of writing. They have owned that they can neither countenance, nor disallow, the inter-

pretation of their words which others believe they
perceive, and seeing, seek to enforce. Of course, such
a failure, first of memory and then of mental power on
the part of the poet affords neither excuse, nor en-
couragement to rash exegesis on the part of a student.
But it does honestly suggest to the latter the possibility
of a discreet rendering and translation of his work, if
not to the poet himself, at least to his reader.   Indeed,
the poet's candid avowal is almost equivalent to an
indirect permission, or even an appeal to competent and
sober criticism to take its share in the work of education.
Neither are these thoughts inapposite to prose compo-
sitions on deep themes, as many persons realise when
in sane old age they re-peruse the once self-written and
perhaps long-forgotten words of youth, at the authorship
and scope of which they feel surprise.

From these suggestions, crudely stated as they are,
comes the problem above alluded to, which may be
gathered from these inquiries, in regard to allegorical
and mystical poetry, and to verse of the character of the
Elizabethan songs, which have hypothetical and possible
relations to the Blessed Virgin Mary. Is it pardonable
for one who is and can be only partially cognisant of
what an author conceives and intends to convey, in the
order of poetry instinct with religious ideas, to assume
the rôle of the author's second self?   Is he at liberty to
act as if delegated to be the author's prophet and interpreter, to explain his meaning, supplement his words and
disclose his innermost intention? Is it permissible to
read into a poet's inspirations new and unexpected
meanings, whether lying below the surface or soaring
above it, which either were or might have been present
to the poet's mind at the supreme instant of conception?
Such exegesis is so commonly adopted in the field of

secular literature that little apology seems needed in defence of its application to the subject-matter of this book, viz., to some of the aspects in which the august Personality of the 'Perfect Woman' of Humanity may be viewed. The proposed questions, therefore, need be answered only by a general expression of opinion that, under conditions, this course is permissible; and the Editor, with feelings of mingled confidence and diffidence, accepts the principle and offers a selection of some noteworthy specimens of both classes of verse. The task, or the pleasure, however, of annotating the poems, or of explaining them, or of discovering their secondary and recondite meaning, and of finding real and deep analogies, whether or not intended by the several writers, has been left to the reader's poetical instinct and ability.

Some illustrations may here be given of the way in which authority, in the person of the Church and her divines, has dealt with inspired prose and poetry in relation to its allegorical and mystical interpretation. With these may be included testimonies from secular literature, in which authors of position have accepted the principle here pleaded for; among them one, in which an author on his own behalf has expressed himself content when his work has been independently subjected, at the hands of another, to the exegesis implied by such principle. The principle in question, says Father Bridgett, seems to be solid and is generally admitted. The citation and appropriation of a passage from a sacred or profane writer, because of an accidental resemblance in words only, would be a childish device. But when there exists analogy between the things represented and the words quoted, the use of the passage is legitimate and may be edifying. Sometimes there is found more than analogy ; there is discovered an extension of the primary meaning of the language, in one or other direction, either to what is higher, or to what is lower. Such an extension of the meaning of words in Holy Scripture is called, under varying conditions, the mystical meaning, or the pregnant sense. For instance: the Canticle of Canticles is an inspired allegory in which, under the similitude of the union of Solomon with a Royal Bride, the relations between our Divine Redeemer and his Holy Church are evolved. In the Introduction to this Book in the Douay Version, we read: 'The Spouse of Christ is the Church, more especially as to the happiest part of it, namely, perfect souls, every one of which is his Belovèd ; but above all others, the Immaculate and Ever-blessed Virgin Mother.'

In conformity with this system of interpretation, the Church adopts and adapts passages from the Canticle which she uses as lections both in the Holy Mass and in her Sacred Offices for the Immaculate Conception, the Nativity of our Lady, the Assumption, and other feasts. And in support of this law, a recent commentator, Father Geitmann, S.J. (in the 'New Cursus Completus,' 1890), has written thus: 'If what is said in Holy Scripture of Divine Wisdom is, with prudent moderation, transferred to the perfect Image of Divine Wisdom, the Blessed Mother of God, how still more fitting is it that the poetic Spouse in the Canticle should be piously identified with the dearest Bride of the Heavenly Solomon. For, what is that Spouse but the Church ? And what is the Virgin Mother of God but the most exquisitely perfect Flower of the Church ?' And the argument of the Jesuit Father is fairly applicable to the quoted specimens of the Elizabethan Love-Songs, as may

b

be seen from the Prefatory Note affixed to the selection
on page 140 of the present volume.

But the adoption of the principle of extension to the
primary meaning of an author's words need not be
confined in our estimate of it to the case of our Lady,
nor to the interpretation of Holy Writ. For example:
in the thoughtful Essays called 'Guesses at Truth, by
Two Brothers,' the late Augustus W. and Julius C. Hare,
published in 1827, we may read their conjoint testimony
on this subject: 'When a subtle critic has detected some
recondite beauty in Shakespeare, the vulgar are fain to
cry, that Shakespeare did not mean it. Well; what of
that? If there be, his genius meant it. This is the very
mark whereby to know a true poet. There will always
be a number of beauties in his works which he never
meant to put into them. This is one of the resemblances
between the works of genius and those of Nature, a
resemblance betokening that the powers which produced
them are akin. . . . The question, whether a great poet
meant such a particular beauty, comes to much the same
thing as the question, whether the Sun means that his
light should enter into such or such a flower. He who
works in unison with Nature and Truth is sure to be far
mightier and wiser than himself.' (I. Series, page 249.
Ed: 1838).

In substantial harmony with the tenour of these words,
may be quoted those of an eminent German author.
The 'Magic Ring,' of De la Motte Fouqué, had once
been interpreted as an allegory by a friendly, judicious
critic. Fouqué appears to have been not displeased with
the liberty thus taken with his work; rather, he was
gratified with the attempt to widen and deepen his words,
although he felt himself unable either to entirely accept,
or to entirely reject the proffered allegorical explanation.

In his preface to 'Undine' as translated in the Edition of James Burns, 1845, he says: 'With respect to the criticisms on the "Magic Ring," I willingly allude to one communicated to me without the name of its author. . . . It is clear that it proceeded from the pen of an earnest religious person. The author has erred in his view that the poet was self-conscious of laying as its foundation a designed allegory. Ingeniously, and as if inspired, has the critic interpreted the imagery; and the poet acknowledges that such also might in part lie within his vision, although till then in no wise, even to himself, had it arisen through the medium of the understanding. Similar phenomena often present themselves in poetic works, on account of the mysterious richness of the gift (of poesy) whereby the gifted one has much more imparted (to him) than he can evolve with his own intellectual power, if not excited thereto by some bright hint from another quarter.'

Perhaps this poetic fulness, attributed by the Brothers Hare and by Fouqué to works of imagination, may be illustrated also by what has been called above the 'pregnant sense' of Scripture. By this term is not so much meant, says Father Bridgett, the mystical sense by which what was written of the type has a higher sense, intended by the Holy Ghost, when applied to the ante-type: rather, the pregnant is the literal sense, though not its first and direct application. Thus, what is said of Wisdom may be applied, with certain limitations, to those who are guided by Wisdom, and in a still fuller sense to her who was the Seat of Wisdom. Such application is not only sanctioned but adopted by the Church, who directly refers to our Blessed Lady words and passages not originally written of her, in the primary sense of the quotations, which occur in the Sapiential

Books of the Old Testament. In the same way, it may
be added, what is said of our Divine Lord has a reflected
and modified application to his Saints. In his 'Essay
on the Development of Christian Doctrine,' Cardinal
Newman thus abridges the argument of St. Athanasius :
'Christ, in rising, raises his Saints with him to the Right
Hand of Power. They become instinct with his Life,
of one Body with his Flesh, Divine Sons, immortal
Kings, Gods. He is in them, because he is in nature ;
and he communicates to them that nature, deified by
becoming his, that them it may deify. He is in them
by the Presence of his Spirit, and in them he is seen.
They have those titles of honour by participation, which
are properly his' (Chap. IV : sect. 2 : part 6). And we
may add, the glorious things said by St. Paul, and others,
of ordinary Christian saints take a higher and fuller
meaning if considered in the light of the Model and
Queen of Saints—a thought learnedly and ingeniously
applied in detail to our Lady in ' Mary in the Epistles,'
by Father Livius, C.SS.R. (1891).

  Indeed, the Church has more than adopted the principle under consideration ; she has enforced it on her
children. In her use of and quotation from the eighth
chapter of the canonical Book of Proverbs, our Holy
Mother has directly applied to that marvellous prophecy
in the garb of history, or more truly, to that record
of an ever-present future, written in the divine decrees
and eternal foreknowledge of God, her sanction of the
principle here contended for—the principle which justifies
the interpretation of allegorical and mystical poetry so as
to include recondite meanings not actually, obviously
and avowedly present to the writer at the time of writing.
Cardinal Newman in his treatment of ' our Lord's Incarnation and of the dignity of his Mother,' discusses this

point in the same 'Essay on Development' (Chap. IV :
sect. 2 : part 8). Arius, he says, 'did all but confess
that Christ was the Almighty, (and) said much more
than St. Bernard or St. Alphonsus have since said of the
Blessed Mary; and yet (Arius) left (our Lord) a mere
creature, and (was) found wanting.' Thus, continues
the Cardinal, 'there was a Wonder in heaven'; a throne
was seen, far above all created powers, mediatorial,
intercessory; a title archetypal; a crown bright as the
morning star; a glory issuing from the Eternal Throne;
robes pure as the heavens; and a sceptre over all.' And
who, he asks, 'was the predestined heir of that Majesty?
Since it was not high enough for the Highest, who was
that Wisdom and what was her name,' of whom the
authors of the Proverbs and the Canticle wrote, the
Mother of Fair Love, and Fear, and holy Hope; exalted
like a Rose Plant in Engaddi, and a Palm Tree in
Jericho; created in the beginning before the world,
in God's counsels, and in Jerusalem was her power—
what was her name to whom these and many like words
were applied? The Cardinal supplies the answer to his
questions. They are to be found in the Apocalypse and
the Gospel: a 'Woman clothed with the sun, and the
moon under her feet, and upon her head a crown of
twelve stars;' and the 'Virgin's name was Mary.' The
votaries of Mary, he concludes, 'do not exceed the true
faith, unless the blasphemers of her Son come up to it :
the Church of Rome is not idolatrous unless Arianism is
orthodoxy.'

If there be truth in these propositions and thoughts,
they point to a high degree of probability that similar
'mysterious richness of the gift of poesy' may be found to
be a characteristic of much mystical and allegorical verse
outside the limits of the Holy Scriptures, more or less

clearly connected with, or suggestive of the Blessed Virgin Mary, as well as, perhaps in a larger degree, in the spirit and temper which produced the purer specimens of the Love-Songs of the Elizabethan age. And if this be so, a similar method of exegesis may be legitimately and profitably adopted in regard to both these classes of English poetry. Our own modern poets whether Christian, or Agnostic, in writing of Woman, of Womanhood, or of the Feminine Ideal, or of kindred subjects, must have been influenced by the traditions still pervading educated England, or perhaps were intellectually conscious of Catholic teaching, though they wrote not under the direct influence of the great Christian Ideal of Mary. There is no place for wonder, then, if writers like Goëthe, or Shelley, or Thomson, or others in the past, not to name authors of verse in the present day, fully acquainted as they were with the Ideal and Perfect Woman of our holy Religion in belief, in worship, in art, in literature, even if they were incredulous of Mary's historical existence, or did not realise the dogmatic attitude of the Church towards her, should have depicted her in their verse with more or less exactitude. Indeed, it would have been passing strange and almost unaccountable if, being what they were, living as they lived, and writing on the topic which they treated, such authors should not, all unconsciously perhaps, but to an extent inspired to this end, have described the supreme and unparalleled place Mary occupies in the Divine scheme of Redemption, or have written of her attributes, dignity, power and gifts, even vaguely, obscurely or tentatively, when they rose above themselves in the contemplation and description of the highest and most perfect type of Womanhood. It is in accordance with such deeper instincts and truer criticisms, be they natural or supernatural, be they antecedently conceived or subsequently interpreted, that such allegorical and mystical poems, and such pure Love-Songs are here presented to the reader in an Anthology of Marian verse.

*   *   *

On two subjects brief passages with advantage may be reproduced from the Preface of the First Series, that the reader may realise, and realising may be prepared for the scope and genius of the poetry to which his attention is directed in the Second Series, and the mode and manner of its quotation. (1) 'The principle on which the selection of verse has been made requires explanation. As differentiated from some collections, poetic merit has not been made the main, or sole qualification for the admittance of extracts into Carmina Mariana. Merit is only one of two factors which combinedly guided the choice of verse in honour of our Blessed Lady. The book professes to be a work of piety; it also may be regarded as a work of art : and the attempt to combine merit with edification constitutes its claim to existence.' And (2), the method of quotation which has been adopted is as follows : 'As a rule, the whole of each poem is quoted. In poems capable of contraction, the contents, or the length of which precluded the whole from being quoted, a portion only is given, and omissions are indicated in the usual manner. In cases where the subject-matter of any poem demanded a longer extract than one which contained a reference only to our Lady, another plan has been adopted. Here the context of the passage is quoted at greater or less length, on either or on both sides of the objective of the poem from the point of view of the Carmina, in order to

set before the reader's eye a picture, as it were, in
verse, wherein Mary stands as the central, supreme and
all-important figure.'

In regard to the selection of verse published in the
two Series, a certain amount of variation in choice
has been adopted in the Second. The new Volume
has been drawn to a large extent from books and
sources either not quoted, or but shortly quoted in
the older one. And though a few Authors, who
previously allowed their work to be utilised, again
enrich the Anthology, especially such as may be less
familiar to English readers—yet, new sources of poetry
have yielded the large proportion of contributors to
the present collection of poems.

Amongst other verse more or less freely employed
in the compilation of the Second Series—omitting the
two classes of poetry already named, the Allegorical
Poems and the Elizabethan Songs—the following may
be specified. 1. Early English religious poetry—the
amount and variety of which, when the theme has
reference to our Blessed Lady, is large. 2. Old
German poetry, and poetry from the same fatherland
of religious verse of a more modern date, in both
cases of Catholic origin or inspiration. 3. Some
unknown or unremembered verse, sonnets and lyrics,
from the Italian, Spanish and French, both late and
early — of course, only a fractional part of what
might have been enlisted into the service of our
Lady from the devotional poetry of the Latin races.
4. A small, a much too small number of new translations from the Greek of early Christianity, and from
hymns and sequences of the later and Mediæval sacred
tongue. And 5, amongst others, and in some cases
valuable and rare acquisitions for the Anthology, may

be mentioned certain religious songs and prayers from
the Ancient Irish, and one, a legend, from the old
Welsh; a long hymn, or series of hymns from the
Coptic 'Theotokia'; some Art-verses—'Poems on
Pictures,' and many other contributions from American
sources; a selection of seven Rhythms from a manuscript poem on the Mystical History of Mary—amongst
the first-fruits of its future publication as a whole,
under the title of 'the Perfect Woman'; and several
verses from Old English poetry, of varied character,
length and date, which may be indefinitely called
Elizabethan, and seem not unworthy of a fresh opportunity to escape from premature oblivion.

Neglecting, as not pertinent to this enumeration,
all reference to the works of living authors who have
enriched the present Series — which will far more
eloquently speak for themselves—it may be noted that
the following pages contain several single poems, or
series of poems which if familiar to some readers, or
even well-known, may be new to many. For instance:
a poem by John Ruskin, contained in his works;
another by Thomas Moore, not contained in his
works; another by W. C. Bryant, not found in all the
English editions of his poems; a fourth of Ben Jonson,
known only to readers of the 'Femall Glory'; a fifth
of Nahum Tate's, copied from a Christ Church MS.
in Oxford, and not reprinted since the seventeenth
century; a translation of Father Caswall's, made after
the collection of his 'Hymns and Poems'; the 'May
Songs' of Cardinal Newman; an excerpt from 'All's
Well that Ends Well,' which deserves the candid attention of those who still hesitate to admit Shakespeare's
claim to be a Catholic; a frankly Protestant 'Hymn
to the Virgin' from the dramatic poem of 'Anne

Boleyn,' by H. H. Milman; Scenes of 'Truth and Beauty
in Catholic Lands,' by Mrs. Maria Buckle; a 'Vision'
of historical Christianity by the late W. Chatterton Dix;
a charming Love-Song by the late Alfred Gurney, quite
in the manner and with more than the chaste purity
of the best specimens of the songs of the Tudor times;
and lastly, twelve fine 'Triolets' by Inigo P. Deane, a
vigorous theological lyric by Father Michael Mullins,
and a mystic verse 'Rosa Mystica' by Father Gerard
Hopkins, S.J.—all three poems preserved, it is hoped,
for posterity by the discriminating and fatherly patronage
to poets, young and old, of the 'Irish Monthly.'

A few sentences may be devoted to another author,
one of the seventeenth century, quoted in this Series, of
whom it may be safely predicted that with one poem
only from his pen the average reader will be acquainted.
This is John Brereley, whose real name is declared by
an expert to be Lawrence Anderton, S.J. The story of
his seven Sonnets which, whatever their poetical value,
it is the Editor's honour to re-introduce to Catholics in
the twentieth century, is long, and is difficult to tell in
brief. It must suffice to say that their manuscript
reached the Editor's hands, through the kindness of
the late A. B. Grosart, who has, perhaps, done more
for Elizabethan poetry, in the way of re-production, than
any other editor. The volume was bought at the sale of
the Phillipps' Library, with but a short pedigree from
the Library of Dolman, or that of another; and was
described as being of the 'early eighteenth century,'
a character hardly justified by the hand-writing, even
had not the water-marked paper disclosed a date in the
second quarter of the nineteenth. However, the book
was esteemed a prize by the present owner, and after
long and far-reaching inquiry, it proved to be a badly

written, altered copy of an original MS. in the possession of Mr. Joseph Gillow, who was so good as to collate
a copy of the seven Sonnets with the originals, and to
correct it in the form in which it now meets the reader's
eye. The forty-four Sonnets of which the MS. consists
appear to have been printed in the year 1632, under
the title of 'Virginalia'; and the volume was critically
described in Corser's 'Collectanea Anglo-Poetica,' in
1874; but no copy has hitherto been discovered by
the Editor. To this author we owe—in addition to the
'Song of Mary,' from which a quotation will be found
below—the well-known and beautiful hymn which begins,
'Jerusalem, my happy home,' and is signed J(ohn)
B(rereley) P(riest).

The arrangement of the poems follows the plan previously adopted. This plan is open to just criticism;
but is continued from the Editor's inability, under
existing conditions, to find a system, free from objec-
tions, which shall be more convenient. The arrangement, in regard to the author's name, or to the leading
word of the section containing the poem, is alphabetical, modified by circumstances over which, sometimes, the Editor could exercise no control—for example,
the arrival of a poem too late to be inserted in its proper
place, or a change in the signature of the writer. But
the Table of Contents, the Index of Authors and the
Index of First Lines will, it is hoped, supply all the
deficiencies caused by a faulty arrangement of the text.

The Index of Authors has been made more full than
in the First Series, by the addition of the titles of many
of the sections, and by references which show the
original language of the translations, the sources whence
many poems are taken, and the extent of indebtedness

to American authors by which the Carmina has been enriched. Of course, a statistical classification and tabulated view of the poems here reproduced would have been curious, and might not have been without interest. But in most cases, all needful information as to the history of each verse has been afforded in the text, in a brief form, either before or after the several quotations. It may be stated, however, in general terms, that each of the five 'Quarters' of the globe has contributed verse in praise of Mary to this Series of the Carmina ; that the Dominion of Canada, Cape Colony, and the Commonwealth of Australia are represented ; that all ages of Christian literature have been taxed, and most Christian tongues, living and dead ; and that, whilst the mother-land of the Anglo-Saxon race has supplied its fair quota of verse, the amount of poetic help received from the trans-Atlantic branch, as well as from the Irish nationality, has been very large.

An Appendix of critical extracts from some periodicals in review of the First Series has been added to the Second. This, to the extent here adopted, is unusual. In extenuation, it may be explained that mere laudatory opinions only have not been reproduced ; but, as the subject-matter of the volume in a collected form is comparatively new to English literature, the extracts, which exhibit estimates gathered from a wide sphere, have a value of their own, and may prove to be of interest as a contribution to comparative criticism. The Editor's task has been one of discovery and selection only ; and the reviews deal almost exclusively with opinions on the conception and execution of the Anthology, and with critical judgments on individual poems. Hence, the course adopted may be deemed excusable, even if the result fail to prove attractive to the reader.

The Editor takes this opportunity to avow, with a mixture of conflicting feelings, that he is still in possession of poetical materials, in manuscript and print, sufficient to make a third and final Volume of verse in honour of or in regard to the Blessed Virgin Mary. This superabundance of material will surprise no one who contemplates the unique and exalted position occupied by the Mother of God in the Divine scheme of the Christian Religion, or remembers the honour in which our Lady is held, the love which she inspires, and the devotion with which she is worshipped in the Catholic Church. In any case, the praise of Mary is a theme which, at one time or another, for twenty centuries, has inspired nearly all Catholic poets who have sung : and it requires only appreciation to make a collection of these spiritual songs. Should the present book be favoured with the welcome accorded to its predecessor, the last volume of the series will be produced as soon as may be possible ; and in common with the first volume, will be published by the disagreeable method of 'subscription.' And then, the Editor's absorbing work of many years in our Lady's service will, *Deo volente*, be completed.

Amongst many friends who have done good work for the present volume, and who are here thanked heartily for their pious service to our Lady, one friend has more than once read every word of the book with a view to secure textual accuracy, and another has considered every line from the stand-point of 'sound doctrine.' To many publishers also, and others, the Editor returns grateful thanks for permission to use their copyright poetry in praise of Mary. An acknowledgment of this generosity it is a pleasure to make, individually and definitely, to the following—to Mr. G.

Allen, for the use of Miss Francesca Alexander's Legend;
to Messrs. Bell and Sons, for the Carol by Mr. Ashe;
to Messrs. Chatto and Windus, for the extract from 'the
Outcast' of Mr. Buchanan; to Mr. Murphy, U.S.A., for
the reprint of one Quatrain by Father Tabb; to
Mr. Lane for many verses by the same Father Tabb; to
Mr. Elkin Mathews, for three excerpts from 'the Book
of the Rhymers' Club,' and also for the three contributions from Miss May Probyn; to Mr. Murray, for the
poem to 'Two Sisters,' by Arthur Hallam; to Mr. Nutt,
for an epigram, or motto by Tennyson; to their executors,
for the quotations from John Ruskin and John Adding-
ton Symonds respectively; to Mr. Reeves, for 'Villon's
Ballad,' by John Payne, and James (B.V.) Thomson's
'Our Lady of Beatitudes'; to Mr. Grant Richards, for
the use of two poems by Mr. Housman; perhaps to
others; and certainly to the editors of many periodicals
(all of which are named in the text) on both sides of
the Atlantic, and especially to those of the 'Ave Maria'
and the 'Irish Monthly,' whose generosity in granting
permission, knows no bounds. If any verse has been
republished without necessary leave, the Editor begs, on
behalf of a work of piety, to be pardoned for the omission
to secure the same; but to every poem is prefixed the
source from which it was derived, and such acknowledgment, it is hoped, will implicitly convey to all concerned,
both a petition to borrow and gratitude for consent
granted.

ORBY SHIPLEY.

39, THURLOE SQUARE, S.W.
   The Immaculate Conception, 1901.

Contents.

c

Index of Authors, Some Sources and Subjects, Translations, &c.

        d

NOTES AND ERRATA.

IT may interest the reader to know that, since these Notes were sent to the press, a beautiful volume has been published which has done for the Blessed Virgin in the domain of art, what has been here attempted in the realm of poetry. The similarity of aim between the two efforts, in different lines of treatment, may excuse a reference to the book which, unexpectedly, forms a complement to the idea of the present volume. 'The Madonna,' says the title-page, contains a pictorial representation of the ' Life and Death of our Lady, by the Painters and Sculptors of Christendom, in more than five hundred of their works.' One result attained is a series of plates from sacred pictures produced during a period of thirteen centuries, from the frescoes on the walls of the catacombs to the master-pieces of the middle ages, and dating from ' the close of the

second century' downwards. Of course, there is much common
ground in the subject-matter of the poems and pictures, severally,
in the two books. Many of the scenes and events sung in the pages
of the Carmina are represented by photography in the engravings of
the 'Madonna.' Indeed, nearly all the old Masters, and some of their
works, which are described in the one will be found depicted in the
other, especially works, amongst others, from the hand of Fra Angelico, of Botticelli, of Bellini, of Gaudenzio Ferrari, of Ghirlandajo,
of Francia, of Michael Angelo, and of Raphael. It only need be
added that the text of the ' Madonna ' is a translation from the
Italian of Adolfo Venturi, that the specimens are mainly taken
from the Italian Schools, and that the book is enriched by an Introduction from Mrs. Meynell, and is published by Burns and Oates.

PAGE 7. Line 3 : *for* than's *read* than is.
        5 : *for* than is *read* than's.

p. 12. No. VI. st. 1. l. 3 : *read* azure-arched.

p. 57. l. 16 : *add* full-stop *after* exiled.
     17 : *add* semi-colon *after* allay.

p. 64. l. 16 : *read* foretell.

p. 102. heading No. VI. : *read* John Gray, Priest.

p. 142. No. III. ll. 1 and 2 : If there be truth in the argument n the
    Preface, on the Tudor Love-Songs, and in the Note on
    p. 408, on the Religion of Shakespeare, the argument receives
    support from the first two lines of this Sonnet, in which the
    poet inferentially denies the popular opinion on the worship
    of our Lady by the Church.

p. 147. last line of prefatory Note : *after* 'my happy home,' *add*
    and ' Virginalia'; Sonnets, etc. (1632). Also title of No. 1 :
    read Sancta Dei Genitrix.

p. 164. Notes, l. 2 : *read* variant.

p. 180. Note in the text : *prefix* a bracket.

p. 227. Title of Verse : *read* Frederick George Lee : 1832—1902.

p. 324. Title ; and p. 326. page-heading : *read* Bryan O'Looney :
    and *add* to title, 1829—1901.

p. 348. Prefatory, l. 8 : *insert* comma *after* creatures.

p. 356. l. 10: *read* Each heightening the other, endlessly.

p. 366 : to the Author's name, T. J. de Powis, *add :* In all probability
    T(homas) J(ones) : *c.* 1825—1900.

p. 454. Title of Ode : *read* Aubrey de Vere : 1814—1902.

p. 478. l. 3 : *read* Egypt's.

p. 506. last line but 3 : *read* And light us o'er the ocean wild.

CARMINA MARIANA

SECOND SERIES

Anthology

THE BLESSED VIRGIN MARY.

SECOND SERIES.

Two Sequences of Adam of St. Victor:

XII. CENTURY.

TRANSLATED (1892—1894) *BY* '*A.*'

I. FOR THE ASSUMPTION.

Ave, Virgo Singularis.

MOTHER of our Great Salvation,
Excellent in exaltation
Over every constellation,
 Never-wandering Star of Sea;
While in this life's rolling surges
Many a wreck the storm submerges,
Where Salvation's love-wind urges
 With thy prayer our ship would flee.

Here the wind and sea are raging,
Here are billows doom presaging,
Here are foemen warfare waging
 With their fierce occurrent power;
Here with whirlpool-veiling measure
Sirens chant the song of pleasure,
Pirates wait to spoil of treasure,
 Monsters hunger to devour.

B

Now into the deep descending,
Now on wave-crest skyward tending,
Flaps the sail; the mast is bending;
   Ceases seamanship to be;
Hearts of men for fear are failing,
Ills so terrible assailing;
In the ghostly war prevailing,
   Us from perils, Mother, free.

Superfused with sacred Shower,
Wearing chastity's white Flower,
Newest Bud from newest Bower,
   Thou hast brought to earthly gloom;
Equal to the Sire Supernal,
Yet indwelling House Maternal,
God is Flesh, the Word Eternal
   Seeks the covert of thy womb.

He the universe directing,
Thee foreseeing, fore-electing,
Never stain thy white affecting,
   Found in Virgin-flesh a shrine,
Never pang, like Eve's, oppressed thee,
Ere the midnight heaven confessed thee,
And the generations blessed thee,
   Mother of the Child Divine.

Far above the ninefold stations,
Musical with adorations,
Without peer in exaltation's
   Excellence, sublimely throned;
On thy day of throning, Mary,
Sweet the risen luminary,
Sweet the vision angel-starry,
   So thy sons be blessed and owned.

Holy and immortal Mother,
Root, who barest God, our Brother,
Flower, Vine, Olive, whom not other
   Graft of time made fructify;
Lamp of earth and empyrean
Lit in mountains Galilean,
When the saints wake time's last pean,
   Mercy sweet the Judge be nigh.

Thou the little flock forget not,
Sinfulness their souls indebt not,
In the Great King's presence let not
   Hope of pardon hopeless be;
He, the Judge benign and tender,
Worthy ceaseless self-surrender,
Is the promise's true Sender
   From the Cross of Calvary.

Offspring of the womb unspotted,
O'er the water shipwreck-dotted,
To the gladness love-allotted,
   Way and Guide and Sign and Pass;
Grasp the helm, the vessel sway thou,
Each terrific tempest lay thou,
Through each breaker souls convey thou
   To the silent Sea of Glass.

II. FOR FEASTS OF OUR LADY.

Ante thorum Virginalem.

Now with concert universal
Let the Church make glad rehearsal
   Of a spiritual song,
Round the place where God is resting,
Mortal Motherhood attesting
   To pure Maidenhood no wrong.

Like a robe our nature wearing
And its every loss repairing,
  Loss upon the outward track
Of his love and of his pity,
To the sweet celestial City
  God the Word has brought us back.

Loving care and faith unerring
To the Written Word referring,
  This awhile our question be;
What is spoken of the Mother ?
What is spoken of that Other
  Word, in ancient prophecy ?

Hear Isaias sweetly singing—
Lo, a Rod from Jesse springing,
  From the ' Virga' springs the ' Flos ':
Virga, Virgo-like, is Mary,
Flos, the Victim Salutary,
  God in Manhood crowning Cross.

Stream from Prophecy's fair Fountain,
Daniel, speak of Stone from Mountain,
  Breaking image, world-wide Realm:
What the Mount ? the Mother-Maiden;
What the Stone ? the Word, Flesh-laden,
  Pride eternally to whelm.

Oh, the mighty-handed Prophet,
Who Goliath hurled to Tophet
  Wielding puny sling and stone;
Faith of David crushing, daunting
Power and perfidy and vaunting,
  Born of Gath and Ascalon.

Oh, the Might all might excelling,
Oh, the Word our flesh indwelling,
  As the stone was in the sling:
Verity, the Star, is glowing,
Chastity, the Lily, blowing—
  Listen, meekly marvelling.

Oh, how holy that Child-bearing;
Oh, how free from sorrow-sharing;
  Oh, how full of happiness:
Pangs of nature quenched in blessing,
Not the sentence Eve oppressing
  May the Second Eve oppress.

Earthward-tending Wings descending,
O'er that stainless, o'er that painless
  Birth came Grace's plenitude;
Through that portal Love Immortal,
God come nighest, man made highest
  Passed, in Jesus, to the Rood.

He the law of death out-blotting,
Nought in him our nature spotting,
In the place of God's allotting,
  Purest womb, all hidden lay:
Then with peace for fair donation
Crowning lowly self-oblation,
Dooming pride to degradation,
  Came, a Child, to mortal day.

Lit no more by lights that fable,
Led by star around the stable,
Seat of him who sole is able
  Seals to lose, sigilla seven,

Carol we a carol newest,
Praise we him with praises duest,
Worship we the Leader truest
    Who comes seeking us from Heaven.

Look thou then, with kind compassion,
On the race thou didst re-fashion;
Who the saved dost round thee gather
Likest children round their father;
    To their souls thy Light has come:
To the Kingdom long awaited
By the heirs predestinated,
To beatitude beseeming
Purchased peace with bounty teeming,
    Maker, Saviour, Sire, lead home.

Allegorical Verse.

PREFATORY: An explanation of the principle on which the following and other Allegorical poems are printed in the Anthology may be found in the Preface. Explanations of the Allegories, whether obvious or obscure, have been left to the reader.

I. SPRING: A TYPE OF THE BLESSED VIRGIN.

ROBERT BRIDGES, M.B.

FROM 'SHORTER POEMS,' 1890.

I SAW the Virgin-Mother clad in green
    Walking the sprinkled meadows at sundown;
While yet the moon's cold flame was hung between
    The day and night, above the dusky town:
I saw her brighter than the western gold
Whereto she faced in splendour to behold.

Her dress was greener than the tenderest leaf
   That trembled in the sunset glare aglow;
Herself more delicate than's the brief
   Pink apple-blossom, that May showers lay low,
And more delicious than is the earliest streak
The blushing rose shows of her crimson cheek.

As if to match the sight that did so please,
   A music entered making passion fain;
Three nightingales sat singing in the trees,
   And praised the goddess for the fallen rain;
Which yet their unseen motions did arouse,
Or parting Zephyrs shook out from the boughs.

And o'er the tree-tops, scattered in mid air,
   The exhausted clouds laden with crimson light
Floated, or seemed to sleep; and highest there,
   One planet broke the lingering ranks of night;
Daring day's company, so he might spy
The Virgin-Queen once with his watchful eye.

And when I saw her, then I worshipped her
   And said, ' O bounteous Spring, O beauteous Spring,
Mother of all my years, thou who dost stir
   My heart to adore thee and my tongue to sing,
Flower of my fruit, of my heart's blood the Fire,
Of all my satisfaction the Desire.

' How art thou every year more beautiful,
   Younger for all the winters thou hast cast;
And I, for all my love grows, grow more dull,
   Decaying with each season overpast:
In vain to teach him love must man employ thee,
The more he learns, the less he can enjoy thee.'

II. 'IF I LOSE THEE, I'M LOST.'
AN ALLEGORY ON THE CHRISTIAN'S STAR OF THE SEA.

J. J. CALLANAN: 1795—1829.

FROM 'POEMS,' 1861.

These stanzas were suggested by an engraving on a seal, representing a boat at sea, and a man at the helm looking up at a solitary star, with the motto, 'Si je te perds, je suis perdu ' (Author).

SHINE on, thou bright Beacon,
　Unclouded and free,
From thy high place of calmness
　O'er life's troubled sea ;
Its morning of promise,
　Its smooth waves are gone,
And the billows rave wildly—
　Then, bright One, shine on.

The wings of the tempest
　May rush o'er thy ray,
But tranquil thou smilest,
　Undimmed by its sway ;
High, high o'er the worlds
　Where storms are unknown
Thou dwellest all beauteous,
　All glorious—alone.

From the deep womb of darkness
　The lightning-flash leaps,
O'er the bark of my fortunes
　Each mad billow sweeps ;
From the port of her safety,
　By warring winds driven,
And no light o'er her course
　But yon lone One of Heaven.

Yet fear not, thou frail one,
　The hour may be near

When our own sunny head-land
  Far off shall appear;
When the voice of the storm
  Shall be silent and past,
In some island of heaven
  We may anchor at last.
But, Bark of eternity,
  Where art thou now ?
The wild waters shriek
  O'er each plunge of thy prow;
On the world's dreary ocean
  Thus shattered and tost;
Then, lone One, shine on—
  ' If I lose thee, I'm lost.'

III. CONCLUSION OF GOETHE'S FAUST.
ARCHER T. GURNEY: 1820—1877.
FROM 'TRANSLATION OF FAUST,' 1842.

Doctus Marianus.

UPWARDS gaze on her alone—
All can bear her splendour;
Kneel before her lofty throne,
Freely homage tender:
All our noblest feelings now,
Queen, for thee we cherish;
Virgin-Mother, we who bow
Must without thee perish.

Chorus Mysticus.

All earthly joy and woe
Like visions vanish;
Here heavenly starbeams glow
No shades can banish;

The nameless goal divine
Here it is won;
The Ever-feminine
Draweth us on.

IV. VIGIL OF RIZPAH : A FORESHADOW.

FELICIA D. HEMANS: 1793—1835.

Who watches on the mountain with the Dead,
  Alone before the awfulness of night?
  A seer awaiting the deep spirits' might?
A warrior guarding some dark pass of dread?
No—a lorn Woman. On her drooping head,
  Once proudly graceful, heavy beats the rain;
  She recks not—living for the unburied slain,
Only to scare the vulture from their bed.

So, night by night, her vigil hath she kept
With the pale stars, and with the dews hath wept:
  Oh, surely some bright Presence from above
On those wild rocks the lonely One must aid.
E'en so; a strengthener through all storm and shade,
  The unconquerable Angel, mightiest Love.

V. UNDERGLIMPSES : THE AWAKENING.

DENIS FLORENCE MacCARTHY:
1817—1882.

FROM 'BALLADS, POEMS, AND LYRICS,' 1850.

A Lady came to a snow-white bier,
  Where a youth lay pale and dead;
  She took the veil from her widowed head
And bending low, in his ear she said:
    ' Awaken, for I am here.'

She passed with a smile to a wild wood near
　　Where the bows were barren and bare;
　　She tapped on the bark with her fingers fair
　　And called to the leaves that were buried there:
　　　　' Awaken, for I am here.'

The birds beheld her without a fear
　　As she walked through the dank-mossed dells;
　　She breathed on their downy citadels
　　And whispered the young in their ivory shells:
　　　　' Awaken, for I am here.'

On the graves of the flowers she dropped a tear,
　　But with hope and with joy like us;
　　And even as the Lord to Lazarus
　　She called to the slumbering sweet flowers thus:
　　　　' Awaken, for I am here.'

To the lilies that lay in the silver mere,
　　To the reeds by the golden pond,
　　To the moss by the rounded marge beyond
　　She spoke with her voice so soft and fond:
　　　　' Awaken, for I am here.'

The violet peeped with its blue eye clear
　　From under its own gravestone;
　　For the blessed tidings around had flown,
　　And before she spoke the impulse was known:
　　　　' Awaken, for I am here.'

The pale grass lay with its long locks sere
　　On the breast of the open plain;
　　She loosened the matted hair of the slain,
　　And cried as she filled each juicy vein:
　　　　' Awaken, for I am here.'

The rush rose up with its pointed spear,
  The flag with its falchion broad,
  The dock uplifted its shield unawed,
  As her voice rang over the quickening sod:
    'Awaken, for I am here.'

The red blood ran through the clover near,
  And the heath on the hills o'erhead,
  The daisy's fingers were tipped with red
  As she started to life, when the Lady said:
    'Awaken, for I am here.'

And the young Year rose from his snow-white bier
  And the flowers from their green retreat;
  And they came and knelt at the Lady's feet
  Saying all, with their mingled voices sweet:
    'O Lady, behold us here.'

VI. MARY, THE LIGHT-HOUSE OF LIFE.
THOMAS MOORE: 1779—1852.

FROM 'THE LITERARY CLASS BOOK,' EDITED BY THE IRISH
CHRISTIAN BROTHERS, 1841.

THE scene was more beautiful far to my eye
  Than if day in its pride had arrayed it;
The land breeze blew mild, and the azure arched sky
  Looked pure as the Spirit that made it:
The murmur rose soft as I silently gazed
  On the shadowy waves' playful motion,
From the dim distant hill, till the Light-house fire blazed
  Like a Star in the midst of the ocean.

No longer the joy of the sailor-boy's breast
  Was heard in his wildly breathed numbers;
The sea-bird had flown to her wave-girdled nest,
. The fisherman sunk to his slumbers:

One moment I looked from the hill's gentle slope,
   All hushed was the billows' commotion,
And o'er them the Light-house looked lovely as hope,
   That Star of life's tremulous ocean.

The time is long passed and the scene is afar,
   Yet when my head rests on its pillow,
Will memory sometimes rekindle the Star
   That blazed on the breast of the billow:
In life's closing hour, when the trembling soul flies,
   And death stills the heart's last emotion;
Oh then, may the seraph of mercy arise
   Like a Star on Eternity's ocean.

VII. ESTHER, A TYPE OF MARY.

CHRISTINA G. ROSSETTI: 1830—1895.

FROM 'POEMS,' 1890.

'I, if I perish, perish,' Esther spake:
   And Bride of life or death, she made her fair
   In all the lustre of her perfumed hair
And smiles that kindle longing but to slake.
She put on pomp of loveliness, to take
   Her husband through his eyes at unaware;
   She spread abroad her beauty for a snare,
Harmless as doves and subtle as a snake.
She trapped him with one mesh of silken hair,
   She vanquished him by wisdom of her wit,
     And built her people's house that it should stand.

   If I might take my life so in my hand,
And for my Love to Love put up my prayer,
   And for Love's sake by Love be granted it.

VIII. ROSA MARIÆ.

SAMUEL WADDINGTON.

FROM 'A CENTURY OF SONNETS,' 1889.

RARE, mystic Symbol of the Life newborn,
Rejuvenescent to the dews of heaven;
Sweet Spirit-flower, by stormy wind-blast torn
Up by the root, and through dark regions driven
Far from the Eden of your home at morn,
Lo, dropt in peace, at the still hour of even
You bloom once more—once more by Love upborne
To your expanding boughs new grace is given.
　Pure, perfect Token of Life's deathless power,
From age to age—now here, now elsewhere seen:
Now gracing with its gift each vernal bower,
Now leaving desert tracts where it hath been;
For ever dying, yet for ever living—
New forms unfolding, and new beauty giving.

IX. PURISSIMA : A RONDELET.

MICHAEL WATSON, S.J.

FROM 'IN MADONNA'S PRAISE,' 1898.

MADONNA Blest,
All spotless art thou as a Snow-white Cloud—
Madonna Blest—
That thrones the Golden Sunshine on its breast,
And sails full swiftly, when the winds pipe loud,
Or floats in blue, a lone Isle, fair and proud,
Madonna Blest.

American Poetry.

I. THE ANNUNCIATION.

WILLIAM HARMAN VAN ALLEN.

SILENCE and sweetness in the flowery place;
The slender fingers that are skilled to guide
The whirling wheel are clasped; for by her side
There stands the great Archangel of the Face,
Bending before her, Maid of David's race,
Elect of God, the Holy Spirit's Bride,
Within whose womb Messiah should abide,
To whom he speaks: Hail, Mary, Full of Grace.
Daughter and Spouse of the Eternal King,
Blest among women thou art ever more:
All hail, the Mother-Maid of Nazareth;
The Burning Bush was thy prefiguring,
The prophets sang of thee in days of yore.
Pray for us now, and in the hour of death.

II. IMMACULATE.

'CASCIA,' SISTER MARY RITA, OF THE HOLY CROSS.

FROM 'THE AVE MARIA,' 1894.

From the beginning and before the world was I created, and unto the world to come I shall not cease to be (Ecclesiasticus).

FAR down the ages of eternity,
    Ere stars their vigil kept,
Within the bosom of the God Most High
    The thought of Mary slept:

And when the new-made stars gave praise to God
    On glad creation's morn,
They were but figures of a brighter Star—
    God's Mother yet unborn.

And when eternity gave unto time
    The Virgin preordained   .
To be the Mother of the God-made-Man,
    Her soul came forth unstained
By e'en the shadow that o'er earth was cast
    By Eden's fateful tree—
Her heart a crystal lily-vase that held
    The Flower of Purity.

III. MOTHER OF THE SACRED HEART.

HENRY COYLE.

FROM 'A GARLAND FOR MARY,' 1900.

THY sacred heart, dear Mother, was the shrine
    That held the precious Jewel—the Christ-Child ;
    No soul of mortal was found undefiled,
No other human breast was pure as thine,
A casket meet to hold the Gem Divine
    Brought by the angels to the Virgin mild,
    An Offering of Peace that reconciled
God and the sinner—sign of Love benign.

Mary, Mother of Jesus, look thou down
    On thy dear children, from heaven above,
    With pitying eyes of tenderest love ;
Our tears of repentance will gem thy crown ;
    Thy love and compassion will soothe pain's smart ;
    Pray for us, Mother of the Sacred Heart.

IV. ST. JOSEPH'S HOLY SPOUSE.

EUGENE DAVIS ('OWEN ROE'):
1857—1897.

FROM 'THE ROSARY,' 1897.

The Author was born at Baltimore, County Cork, Ireland, and died at Brooklyn, U.S.A. : and the following Sonnet, probably the last verses written by him, appeared in print almost at the very time of his death (W. D. Kelly).

A SPIRITUAL Essence, purer far
 Than the most gorgeous vision poets see
On dreamland's shores, was hers: nor sun, nor star
 Was nearer to God's firmament than she.
A Spirit in a frame of heavenly mould,
 Blurred by no stain, the Virgin reigned above
All womankind, transfigured by a love
Divinely wrought and full of grace untold.

Her smiles had more than human tenderness;
 Her eyes, the summer glory of the skies;
Her snow-white brow, crowned by each auburn tress,
 Enshrined a mind whose lustre never dies;
Her sacred Name all generations bless,
 In that she oped the gates of Paradise.

V. THE VISITATION.

MARY E. HENRY-RUFFIN.

FROM 'THE WEEKLY BOUQUET,' 1898.

' AND in those days '—what wondrous days they were
 To that meek Maiden, speeding o'er the hills
Of Judah's summer; and what reveries stir
 Within us, as that tender memory fills

c

The pictured past : O trusting Mother-Maid,
  Of thee and of thy thought, but scarce a word
Upon the silence of the scene is laid ;
  Only the echo of thy footsteps heard.

With the midsummer's blooms and breezes blent
  We see thy young joy, going forth to meet
The hope unto thy aged cousin sent ;
  Thine own, full of the promise dread and sweet.

' Magnificat ' : O little Maiden, sing
  Thy prophecy ; thy meekness now forget,
Only the world's great hope remembering,
  And all thy spirit to its music set.

' Magnificat ' : look down the stream of years ;
The generations' chorus shall not rest
From age to age ; the last, to-day, she hears
  Proclaiming her, above all women, Bless'd.

VI. CONSOLATRIX AFFLICTORUM.
ANGELIQUE DE LANDE.

FROM 'THE AVE MARIA,' 1887.

YOU say you're unhappy, that life is a burden,
  That sorrow aye sits at the door of your heart,
That the past holds no memories, the future no guerdon
  To sweeten her portion, or bid her depart ;
Has the voice of affection no power to console you,
  As sadly you bow 'neath the chastening rod ?
Has the fair realm of Nature no charms to allure you
  To seek in her labyrinths the foot-prints of God ?

Oh, come then with me, where a lamp dimly burning
  Reveals the sweet face of our Lady of Peace,
Where the hearts of her children for ever are turning.
  Where care finds a solace and pain a release.

Where the perfume of roses with incense is blending,
  Where sinner and saint bend a suppliant knee,
Where graces unnumbered are hourly descending—
  To Mary's dear altar, oh, hasten with me.

A heavenly stillness broods over the portals,
  And lowly we bend as we enter the door
Where the One Triune God, condescending to mortals,
  Has promised to dwell with his Church evermore;
'Tis the calm Vesper-hour, and the ' Salve Regina '
  In tremulous sweetness vibrates on the air,
And hearts wearied out in the world's great arena
  Are lulled to repose by the Angel of Prayer.

There, prone at the feet of God's own Blessed Mother,
  Unburden your soul of its anguish and pain;
She will bear it to Jesus, our dear Elder Brother,
  She will plead for you—she who ne'er pleaded in vain.
'Neath the folds of her mantle she will shelter and hide
        you
  From the tempest without and the tumult within;
At rest on her bosom no ill shall betide you,
  There your sorrow shall end and your joy shall begin.

VII. OUR LADY OF THE DAWN.

MARY E. MANNIX.

FROM ' THE AVE MARIA,' 1890.

TRANQUIL and fair are meadow, wood and sea;
  Folded the pink-cheeked rose and lily pale;
  Yet every one doth perfume sweet exhale,
As in the bosom of fast-fleeing night
It stirs expectant. Soon a line of light,
  Silvering the East, bids the dark hills grow bright

With dewy freshness, and a pearly cloud
Hides the moon's fading disc as in a shroud.
So thou above the soul's night dost arise
Like morning radiant, joy within thine eyes;
And in the heart sweet flowers of Paradise,
Patient, long-slumbering, bloom at sight of thee,
  Our Lady of the Dawn—more fitting name
  From poet's pen, or saint's lips never came.

VIII. TRANSFIGURED.

SARAH M. BRYAN PIATT.

FROM 'SCRIBNER'S MONTHLY,' 1879.
AND ' POEMS,' 1894.

Almost afraid they led her in—
  A dwarf more piteous none could find—
Withered as some weird leaf and thin
  The woman was, and wan and blind.

Into his mirror with a smile—
  Not vain to be so fair, but glad—
The South-born painter looked the while
  With eyes than Christ's alone less sad.

'Mother of God,' in pale surprise
  He whispered, 'What am I to paint?'
A voice that sounded from the skies
  Said to him: 'Raphael; a Saint.'

She sat before him in the sun;
  He scarce could look at her, and she
Was still and silent. . . . 'It is done,'
  He said: 'Oh, call the world to see.'

Ah, this was she in veriest truth—
   Transcendant face and haloed hair;
The beauty of divinest youth
   Divinely beautiful was there.

Herself into her picture passed—
   Herself and not her poor disguise,
Made up of time and dust. . . At last
   One saw her with the Master's eyes.

IX. WHILE MARY SLEPT.

ALICE ARCHER SEWALL.

FROM 'THE CENTURY MAGAZINE,' 1893.

THE Child-Christ watched sweet Mary's face
    The while she slept;
And for the woe that must claim his place
    The Child-Christ wept:

And on her breast laid kisses four,
    As a cross is made,
To heal those wounds which for evermore
    Should be on her laid.

And his little feet in her bosom pressed
    Where her soft hair trailed,
To comfort her with remembrance blessed
    When his feet were nailed:

And laid his face on her face in sleep
    To prevent the tears,
When the crown of thorns with his Blood should weep
    In the coming years.

X. ANNUNCIATION.

HARRIET PRESCOTT SPOFFORD.

FROM 'HARPER'S MAGAZINE,' 1897.

THOUGH seven of the tender maids
Of Nazareth cast lots to see
Who might be sped and set apart—
SING : 'Blue and purple and scarlet
      And fine-twined linen thread'—
To spin the smooth skein that should be
The Temple curtain, and should stir
To gust of frankincense and myrrh,
The happy fortune fell on her.
SING : 'Precious was the ointment
      Spilled on the high-priest's head.'

And as she sat and twirled her thread,
And sang, perchance, beneath her breath
Some sacred song of sweet content—
SING : 'Out of ivory palaces
      Hath music made thee glad'—
Only a Maid of Nazareth
She held herself within her thought,
Whose good-hap to the Temple brought
The royal purple that she wrought.
SING : 'With the wings of cherubim
      The mercy-seat was clad.'

And in such simple honour glad,
Serene in service moved the Maid,
And dreamed not if more honour were—
SING : 'Thou art fair, oh, thou art fair :
      Thou hast the eyes of a dove'—

Dreamed some time, spinning in the shade,
That the King said the house in vain
Would that High Presence hold, which fain
The Heaven of heavens could not contain.
SING : ' The covering of purple,
  The midst being paved with love.'

When suddenly what glorious stain
Dyed all the shadow of the room,
When the great Angel stooped and brought—
SING : ' Wondrous were the almond flowers
  Blossomed on Aaron's rod '—
All heaven in with him to the gloom,
Crying, ' Hail, Highly Favoured, now
The sun, the stars, before thee bow ;
The Lord is with thee, Blessed thou.'
SING : ' Yea, upon the harp will I
  Praise thee, O God, my God.'

XI. AD MARIAM.

CHARLES WARREN STODDARD

FROM ' THE AVE MARIA,' 1887.

As southward o'er the watery way
 The wanderer takes his aimless flight,
Thou art his Pilot-cloud by day,
   His Guiding-star by night.

Thy smile athwart the tempest's wrath
 Beguiles his spirit to repose ;
Thy tears compel his desert-path
   To blossom as the rose.

Yet false his life, as thou art Truth ;
 And sad his days, as thou art Sweet ;
Oh, be the Load-stone of his youth
   And draw him to thy feet.

To Our Lady of Loreto, and other Verse.

B. GIOVANNI GIOVENALE ANCINA,
OF THE ORATORY, ROME,
BISHOP OF SALUZZO: 1545—1604.

TRANSLATED (1895) FROM THE ITALIAN
BY E. M. CLERKE.

Copied from the Author's MS. in the Library of the Church of Santa Maria in Vallicella (of St. Philip Neri), Rome, by Orby Shipley, M.A.

I. TO OUR LADY OF LORETO.

BEHOLD, my heart, how fast
 The days and hours fly past,
 Swifter than stag or arrow they are gone,
 And thou, too, hastest on.

To death ye on do speed,
 And fly full fast indeed,
 Like sail, that spied at sea from distant land,
 Seems motionless to stand.

Five lustres have I spent
 In woe and banishment,
 Since from thy presence so divine and high,
 A pilgrim forth went I.

I went, Queen High and Sweet,
 Blindly, great loss to meet,
 Whither thou know'st; and in such guise return.
 To tell with shame I burn.

Snared had I been past cure,
   In myriad woes full sure,
   Had not thy might the snare of evil marred,
   That me from heaven debarred.

Hence lowly to thy shrine,
   Virgin of Heart Benign,
   I come, with thanks to thee and thy dear Son—
   Lily and Rose in one.

But if in years a score
   And three, to me once more,
   To come unto this fane it granted be
   Mine end approach I see.

And of life weary now,
   With silver threaded brow,
   Despise me not, nor my heart's living cry
   Rejected be on high.

If in grave woe, alas,
   My fiftieth year I pass,
   Thine aid in fate's dark hour do not deny,
   Else sure to fall were I.

Thou ever dost console,
   Maiden and Mother sole,
   My faith, my hope, my comfort are in thee,
   If live or dead I be.

II. TO THE BLESSED VIRGIN.

MOTHER and Maiden pure,
Who hast our mortal race in charge secure,
To me thy strong and helpful hand extend,
Ere death eternal make of me an end.

Mary, of Heaven's true Sun the blessed Dawn,
If at thy rising shadows flee away,
How glorious then will be that Sun's full day.

O Virgin, crowned with stars from heaven withdrawn,
Of God's great Son the Mother Blest and Bright,
The hordes of Tartarus put ye to flight.

III. THE ANNUNCIATION.

FROM heaven the Angel lit
To speak with white-veiled Maid, as had been writ,
He mighty Gabriel, and Mary she—
Oh, what a blest and holy company.

Never on earth was seen,
Since the sun tinged it with his radiance sheen,
An embassage like this at any time,
So great its aim, its import so sublime.

Not with vain splendours fraught,
Of gold, or gems, or things of value brought,
But of vast mystery and great event—
The Word is here by Truth Eternal sent.

To 'Hail' replies 'Behold,'
Which glad consent full plainly doth unfold,
And man to lift to heaven and save from doom,
The Eternal Word doth Mortal Veil assume.

IV. TO OUR LADY OF THE ANGELS IN ROME.

Written December 1st, 1597, on leaving the Oratory in order to fly the Episcopate.

IF thee I leave, O Mother, not alive
    Shall I depart, or if I still survive,
    Afar from thee, my wretched life will flow,
    In sighs and sobs, in weeping and in woe.

Ah, my sad fate, condition sorely tried,
    That only pricking thorns on every side
    I find. Alas, my heart seeks help in vain,
    Since flight is ill, and worse 'tis to remain.
But lesser evil, and more safe essay
    It were to fly when Heaven doth show the way,
    While to illume and darkness to divide,
    The sun's bright rays will shine on every side.
Thou Virgin-guide, on the good path to lead
    With angels round thee; O true Light indeed,
    Defend, I pray, 'gainst men of wrath and ire—
    My Hope, my Refuge, and my sole Desire.

Shepherds and Magi at Bethlehem.

SIR EDWIN ARNOLD.

FROM 'THE LIGHT OF THE WORLD,' 1891.

I. SHEPHERDS.

So when the angels were no more to see,
Re-entering those gates of space—whose key
Love keeps on that side, and on this side Death—
Each Shepherd to the other whispering saith,
Lest he should miss some lingering symphonies
Of that departing music, ' Let us rise
And go even now to Bethlehem, and spy
This which is come to pass, showed graciously
By the Lord's angels.' Therewith hastened they
By olive-yards and old walls mossed and grey
Where in close chinks the lizard and the snake,
Thinking the sunlight come, stirred, half-awake;
Across the terraced levels of the vines,
Under the pillared palms; along the lines
Of lance-leaved oleanders, scented sweet;
Through the pomegranate gardens sped their feet;

Over the causeway, up the slope they spring,
Breasting the path, with steps unslackening;
Past David's well, past the town-wall they ran.
Unto the house of Chimham, to the Khân:
Where mark them peering in, the posts between,
Questioning—out of breath—if birth had been
This night, in any guest-room, high or low?
The drowsy porter at the gate saith, ' No,'
Shooting the bars; while the packed camels shake
Their bells to listen, and the sleepers wake;
And to their feet the ponderous steers slow rise,
Lifting from trampled fodder large mild eyes.
' Nay, brothers; no such thing: yet there is gone
Yonder One nigh her time, a gentle One:
With him that seemed her spouse—of Galilee.
They toiled at sun-down to our doors: but see;
No nook was here.   Seek at the cave instead;
We shook some barley-straw to make their bed.'

Then to the cave they wended, and there spied
That which was more, if truth be testified,
Than all the pomp seen through proud Herod's porch,
Ablaze with brass and silk and scented torch,
High on Beth-Haccarem; more to behold,
If men had known, than all the glory told
Of splendid Cæsar in his marbled home
On the White Isle, or audience-hall at Rome
With trembling princes thronged.   A clay lamp swings
By twisted camel-cords, from blackened rings,
Showing, with flickering gleams, a Child new-born,
Wrapped in a cloth, laid where the beasts at morn
Will champ their bean-stalk; in the lamp's ray dim
A fresh-made Mother by him, fostering him
With face and mien to worship, speaking nought;

Close at hand Joseph, and the ass, hath brought
That precious two-fold burden to the gate;
With goats, sheep, oxen driven to shelter late.
No mightier sight; yet all sufficeth it—
If we will deem things be beyond our wit—
To prove heaven's music true, and show heaven's way;
How not by famous kings, nor with array
Of brazen letters on the boastful stone,
But, 'by the mouth of babes,' quiet, alone,
Little beginnings planning for large ends,
With other purpose than fond man attends,
Wisdom and Love in secret fellowship
Guide our world's wanderings with a finger-tip;
And how that night, as these did darkly see,
They sealed the first scrolls of Earth's history,
And opened what shall run till Death be dead.

Which Babe they reverenced, bending low the head,
First of all worshippers, and told the things
Done in the plain and played on angels' strings.
Then those around wondered and worshipped too,
And Mary heard—but wondered not—anew
Hiding this in her heart, the heart which beat
With Blood of Jesus Christ, holy and sweet.

II. MAGI.

THENCE came it those Three stood at entering
Before the door, and their rich gifts did bring:
Red gold from the Indian rocks, cunningly beat
To plate and chalice, with old fables sweet
Of Buddh's compassion, and dark Mara's powers
Round the brims glittering; and a riot of flowers
Done on the gold, with gold script to proclaim
The noble truths, and threefold mystic Name

OM, and the Swastika; and how man wins
Blessed Nirvâna's rest, being quit of sins,
And day and night reciting, 'Oh, the Gem
Upon the Lotus: oh, the Lotus-stem.'
Also, more precious than much gold, they poured
Rare spices forth, unknitting cord on cord;
And one by one, unwinding cloths, as though
The merchantmen had sought to shut in so
The breath of those distillings: in such kind
As when Nile's black embalming slaves would bind
Sindon o'er sindon, cere-cloth, cinglets, bands,
Roll after roll, on head, breast, feet and hands,
Round some dead king, whose cold and withered palm
Had dropped the sceptre; drenched with musk and
  balm
And natron, and what keeps from perishing;
So they might save, after long wandering,
The body for the spirit, and hold fast
Life's likeness, till the dead man lived at last.
Thus from their coats involved of leaves and silk,
Slowly they freed the odorous thorn-tree's milk,
The grey myrrh and the cassia and the spice,
Filling the wind with frankincense past price,
With hearts of blossoms from a hundred glens
And essence of a thousand rose-gardens;
Till the night's gloom like a royal curtain hung
Jewelled with stars, and rich with fragrance flung
Athwart the arch; and in the cavern there
The air around was as the breathing air
Of a queen's chamber, when she comes to bed,
And all that glad earth owns gives goodlihead.

Witness them entering, those Three from afar—
Who knew the skies, and had the strange white Star

To light their nightly lamp, through deserts wide
Of Bactria, and the Persic wastes, and tide
Of Tigris and Euphrates; past the snow
Of Ararat, and where the sand-winds blow
O'er Ituræa; and the crimson peaks
Of Moab, and the fierce, bright, barren reeks
From Asphaltites—to this hill, to thee,
Bethlehem-Ephrata. Witness how these Three
Gaze, hand in hand, with faces grave and mild,
Where, 'mid the gear and goats, Mother and Child
Make state and splendour for their eyes. Then lay
Each stranger on the earth, in th'Indian way,
Paying the 'eight prostrations'; and was heard
Saying softly in the Indian tongue, that word
Wherewith a prince is honoured. Nimbly ran,
On this, the people of their caravan
And fetched the gold, and, laid on gold, the spice,
Frankincense, myrrh; and next with reverence nice,
Foreheads in dust, they spread the precious things
At Mary's feet, and worship him who clings
To Mary's bosom, drinking soft life so
Who shall be Life and Light to all below.
'For now we see,' say they, departing, 'plain
The Star's word come to pass. The Buddh again
Appeareth, or some Boddhisat of might
Arising for the West, who shall set right,
And serve and reconcile, and maybe, teach
Knowledge to those who know. We, brothers, each
Have heard yon shepherds' prattling; if the sky
Speaketh with such, heaven's mercy is drawn nigh:
Well did we counsel, journeying to this place:
Yon hour-old Babe milking that Breast of Grace,
The world will praise and worship, well-content.'

On the Assumption.

I. OUR LADY UP-BORNE BY ANGELS.

FRAY LUIS PONCE DE LEON: 1527—1590.

TRANSLATED BY SIR JOHN BOWRING: 1792—1872.

FROM 'ANCIENT POETRY AND ROMANCES OF SPAIN,' 1824.

LADY, thou mountest slowly
O'er the bright cloud, while music sweetly plays;
Blest who thy mantle holy
With outstretched hand may seize,
And rise with thee to the Infinite of Days.

Around, behind, before thee
Bright angels wait, that watched thee from thy birth;
A crown of stars is o'er thee,
The pale moon of the earth,
Thou, Supernatural Queen, nearest in light and worth.

Turn, turn, thy mildened gaze,
Sweet Bird of Gentleness, on earth's dark vale;
What flowerets it displays,
Amidst time's twilight pale,
Where many a son of Eve in toils and darkness strays.

Oh, if thy vision see
The wandering spirits of this earthly sphere,
Virgin, to thee, to thee
Thy magnet voice will bear
Their steps, to dwell with bliss through all eternity.

II. TO OUR LADY, ON HER ASSUMPTION.

LADY CATHERINE PETRE: 1831—1882.

FROM 'THE MONTH,' 1875, AND 'HYMNS AND VERSES,' 1883.

HAIL, sacred living Ark,
Thine own Creator's loved abode ;
Pass on to-day thy joyous road,
    Pass from our world so dark.

Virgin of Virgins, rest ;
He who has laid his infant Head
Upon thy bosom for his bed,
    Will fold thee to his breast.

Not earth to earth—but heaven ;
If Adam's Daughter needs must die,
God's chosen Mother may not lie
    Where dust to dust is given.

O Queen, O Mother bright ;
Take to his feet our prayers and tears,
Carry our burdens and our fears ;
    They will not stop thy flight.

Dearest and Best and First ;
Place in his Heart our wants and woes ;
O Mother, plead as one who knows
    Life's anguish at its worst.

Plead for the sad at heart ;
That grief and pain may never dim
The weary eyes that strain for him
    While the hot tear-drops start

D

But let no thoughts to-day,
Save those of gladness, fill the breast;
Let not our trouble and unrest
    Darken our Mother's way.

On her triumphant car
Turn, turn the eager wistful gaze,
Where, mid the sun's most brilliant blaze,
    We still behold our Star.

Though gone from us, not lost;
With love yet stronger than of yore
Our soul's desire she will outpour
    To him who loves us most.

On with true hearts and strong;
Cast out the timid, doubting fear,
Light up the eye and dry the tear;
    Life's journey is not long.

Patience—for we must wait
Till self be conquered, heaven be won,
And Mary's prayers have drawn us on
    Safe to our Father's gate.

III. FEAST OF THE ASSUMPTION.

SARA TRAINER SMITH.

FROM 'THE AVE MARIA,' 1890.

WAS it dawn, sweet Mother, when they opened
                Thy sealèd tomb?
Or did the night of Syria o'ershadow
                Its sacred gloom?
Did the angels, through the azure sweeping
                Direct and swift,

Like splendid rays of light celestial breaking
        From dark cloud rift,
Float down into a radiant circle
        Around thy sleep?
Didst thou hear them—did their coming wake thee.
        No more to weep?
Or did they bear thee still all pale and pulseless
        Through boundless space,
Into heaven for that blissful wakening
        Before his face?
When thy long waiting after anguished watching,
        Love crowned with death, ·
Saints marked, with sinless envy, slow departing
        Thy gentle breath.
Then all reverent in their fulfilling
        Their Lord's bequest,
With tender hands they laid thee (oh, how softly)
        To perfect rest.
But lonely in their sorrow, soon returning
        To watch thy tomb,
Lo, they found it open, filled and fragrant
        With lily-bloom.
Not a vestige of thy presence left them,
        Except thy flower:
Was ever tomb before thus quickly altered
        To fairest bower?
Purest white in narrow cavern darkness,
        Those petal pearls:
Heaped high upon thy sculptured couch and pillow,
        Their fragrant whorls.
Not of earth their shining, stainless beauty,
        Their subtle breath:
Every curve and chalice spoke perfection
        Defying death.

Thou wert gone.   And they had passed the portal
                    In angel-hands :
It was as though a seraph-voice had answered
                    The saints' demands.
Thou wert gone whence they had come.   So, truly
                    They wrote it down,
And made the Feast of thy Assumption glorious,
                    Thy festal crown.

from Early Christian Hymnody and Drama.

TRANSLATED (1898) BY J. W. ATKINSON, S.J.

I. THIRTEENTH HYMN ; IN HONOUR OF OUR BLESSED LADY.

ST. EPHREM, THE SYRIAN : VI. CENT.

VIRGIN wholly marvellous,
Who didst bear God's Son for us,
Worthless is my tongue and weak
Of thy purity to speak.
Who can praise thee as he ought ?
Gifts with every blessing fraught,
Gifts that bring the gifted life
Thou didst grant us, Maiden-Wife.
God became thy lowly Son,
Made himself thy Little One,
Raising men to tell thy worth
High in heaven as here on earth.
Heaven and earth and all that is
Thrill to-day with ecstasies,
Chanting glory unto thee,
Singing praise with festal glee.

Cherubim with fourfold face
Are no peers of thine in grace ;
And the six-winged Seraphim
Shine amid thy splendour dim.
Purer thou art than are all
Heavenly hosts angelical,
Who with pomp about thee bear
The tiny Child, thy Son so fair.

II. MONOLOGUE FROM THE TRAGEDY OF 'CHRISTUS PATIENS.'

GREGORY, BISHOP of ANTIOCH, VI. CENT.

This early Christian drama has been attributed to St. Gregory Nazianzen (IV. Cent.), and is printed in the fourth volume of the Saint's work : it was, however, probably written two Centuries later.

AUGUST, most Reverend and All-happy Maid,
Thou dwellest in the blessed Court of Heaven,
Rid of what grossness clings to man on earth,
Stoled in the robe of immortality,
Untouched by years, and God-like in thy state.
Look down with kindness on the words I speak ;
Yea, Virgin Far-renowned, accept my words.
This grace is thine alone of all our race,
Thine, the Word's Mother, thine, beyond all words.
Therefore in trust I speak my words to thee,
And bring to thee the garland that I made,
Woven, my Lady, from a Virgin-field,
For many favours that thou grantest me.
Rescue me still from manifold distress,
From open foes—yet more from foes unseen.
So may I reach life's goal as I have prayed,
Rich e'er in thy protection all my life,

With thee to plead my cause before thy Son,
Welcomed amid his well-loved Virgin-band.
Let me not be to tortures given o'er,
Nor bring delight to man's destroying foe.
Guard me and save from darkness and from fire,
By faith that justifies and by thy grace.
For grace from God shone out to us in thee,
And unto thee this song of grace I weave.
Hail, Virgin, Full of Grace, hail, Mother-Maid,
Most beautiful beyond all virgins thou,
Exalted far above the hosts of heaven,
Mistress and highest Queen, the Joy of men—
Be thou for ever kindly to our race
And everywhere my sure deliverance.
Give me, O Lady, pardon of my faults,
And win for me salvation of my soul.

From '𝔐adonna's Child:' 1872 & 1895.

ALFRED AUSTIN, POET LAUREATE.

FROM 'THE HUMAN TRAGEDY,' 1876.

I. THE CHAPEL OF 'MARIA, STELLA MARIS,' SPIAGGIASCURA.

STANZAS IV, V AND XXII—XXV.

WITHIN, it is a lovelier little chapel
Than ever wealth ordained, or genius planned
For those famed shrines where art and splendour
        grapple,
Vainly, to blend the beautiful and grand:
No gold adorns it, and no jewels dapple,
No boastful words attest the builder's hand;
Sacred to prayer, but quite unknown to fame,
'Maria, Stella Maris' is its name.

Breaks not a morning, but its snow-white altar
With fragrant mountain flowers is newly dight;
Comes not a noon, but lowly murmured psalter
Again is said with unpretentious rite;
Its one sole lamp is never known to falter
In faithful watch through the long hush of night;
From dawn to gloaming, open to devotion
Its portal stands, and to the swell of ocean.

* * *

The little temple's door stood open wide,
And all the place by sunshine was possessed,
From the groined roof which time had slowly dyed,
Down to the inlaid altar whitely dressed:
But the smooth walls that rose on either side
Were marble; marble was the floor you pressed;
So that, withal, the spot seemed fresh and cool
Even as shady grove, or reedy pool.

Full on the left an antique pulpit rose
Of structure quaint, and it was marble too,
Where hands long numb had carven, as they chose,
Odd allegories, fair and foul to view:
Here virgins calm as newly fallen snows,
Bearing curved palms and singing hymns to you;
There long lank demons gnawing damnèd souls
And bastard animals and nightmare scrolls.

But from these fancies twain you turned full soon,
For on the right the Virgin Mother stood,
Down from her flowing hair to sandal-shoon
The mystic type of Maiden Motherhood:
Below her feet there curved a crescent moon,
And all the golden planets were her hood;
In comely folds her queenly garb was moulded,
And over her pure breast her hands were folded.

She looked the most Immortal Mortal-being
That ever yet descended from the skies,
As One who seemed to see all without seeing,
And without ears to hear man's smothered sighs;
With all our discords the one note agreeing,
'Mid death and hate a love that never dies;
A tranquil silence amid fretful din,
And still the sinless Confidant of Sin.

II.   EPISODE IN THE PILGRIMAGE OF
GODFRID AND OLYMPIA.

STANZAS XCVI—XCVIII AND C—CII.

WHEN for awhile the sea got lost to view,
Since landward now the hilly pathway wound,
By aromatic pine-slopes stern of hue,
Which shut the sunlight out, their gaze was bound:
Beyond their ken the shaggy summits grew;
Grimly below them yawned ravine profound,
Wherethro' swift torrent a rough pathway tore,
Filling the sombre silence with its roar.

But soon again the black pass broadened out,
On them once more the welcome sunshine streamed,
And budding larches, dotted sparse about
Among dark firs, like fairy foliage gleamed:
In valleys green they heard the shepherds shout
To flocks that browsed and herds that dozed and
        dreamed;
Torrent no more, the stream beneath them flowed,
Devious yet smooth, e'en as their mountain road,

Seeking a softly undulating plain
With trellised red-roofed villages bestrewed,
Whence, as the light of day began to wane,
'Ave, Maria' rang from belfries rude:

The air, the hills, the re-appearing main
Felt the soft touch of twilight's tender mood;
And every bosom in that region fair,
All, saving one alone, o'erflowed with prayer.

*　　*　　*

But when once more she rose up to her feet
Still at his side to bravely trudge along,
Her heart, he saw, with quicker pulses beat,
And lo, she burst unbidden into song:
It was a melody unearthly sweet
Which the fond ear for ever would prolong;
And with her voice, as ceased the belfries' clang,
The craggy hollows of the mountain rang.

O Mary Mother, Full of Grace,
Above all other women blest,
Through whose pure womb our erring race
Beholds its sin-born doom redressed,
　　　Pray for us.
Thou by the Holy Ghost that wert
With every heavenly gift begirt,
Thou that canst shield us from all hurt,
　　　Pray for us; pray for us.
Tower of David, Ivory Tower,
Vessel of Honour, House of Gold,
Mystical Rose, Unfading Flower,
Sure Refuge of the unconsoled,
　　　Pray for us.
Mirror of Justice, Wisdom's Seat,
Celestial shade for earthly heat,
The sinner's last and best Retreat,
　　　Pray for us; pray for us.
O thou of Heaven that art the Gate,
That to the feeble strength dost bear,

> To whom no outcast turns too late,
> E'en when thy Son is deaf to prayer,
>   Pray for us.
> O Morning Star, to chase the dark,
> Cause of our joy through care and cark,
> Thou of the Covenant the Ark,
>   Pray for us; pray for us.
> Bright Queen of the angelic choir,
> Of patriarchs, prophets, worshipped Queen,
> Queen of the martyrs proved by fire,
> And Queen of confessors serene,
>   Pray for us.
> Queen of the apostolic train,
> Queen that o'er all the saints doth reign,
> O Queen conceived without a stain,
>   Pray for us; pray for us.

So ceased the strain, and with it ceased the day;
The mountains slowly wrapped themselves in night;
Far off, the silent sea gloomed cold and gray,
Sky-sundered by one long low line of white:
Over the vale far down a flat mist lay,
Which for a phantom lake bewrayed the sight;
And louder now they heard the watch-dogs bark,
And cataracts dashing downwards through the dark.

Therefore with eager eye and quickened pace
Descried they twinkling lights not far ahead;
But many a zigzag yet had they to trace
Descending ever, ere their hopes were fed:
At length they heard the voices of the place,
Sought out the inn, and craved for board and bed,
Two little sleeping chambers side by side,
And what rude fare the mountains could provide.

Ballads and Legends.

I. MADONNA AND THE GIPSY.

A Translation.

FRANCESCA ALEXANDER.

FROM 'ROAD-SIDE SONGS OF TUSCANY,' EDITED BY JOHN
RUSKIN, 1885.

GIPSY. God be with thee, Lady dear,
Give thee comfort, give thee cheer.
Welcome, good Old Man, to thee,
With thy Child so fair to see.

MADONNA. Sister, in this lonely place
Glad I am to see thy face,
God forgive thee all thy sin,
Plant his grace thy soul within.

GIPSY. By your looks I understand
You are strangers in the land,
Seeking shelter for the night;
Lady, wilt thou please alight?

MADONNA. O my Sister, that kind word
Is the first that we have heard:
God reward thee from above,
For thy courtesy and love.

GIPSY. Oh, alight, dear Lady mine,
Something in thee seems divine:
Let me, for I long to bear
In my arms thy Infant fair.

MADONNA. We have come from Nazareth here,
All the way in haste and fear;
Weary, lost, on foreign ground,
We no shelter here have found.

GIPSY.   Though a Gipsy poor am I,
Yet to help you I would try;
This my house I offer free,
Though 'tis not a place for thee.

*   *   *

If 'tis not as you deserve,
Still I hope that it may serve:
How can I, so poor and mean,
Fitly entertain a Queen?
Here I have a little shed
Where the donkey can be led:
Straw there is; I'll bring some hay;
All can safely rest till day.

*   *   *

Lady, it would please me well
If I might thy fortune tell:
Ever since the days of old,
All my race have fortunes told.
Yet with all my art can do,
I may tell thee nothing new;
For in thy sweet face doth shine
Wisdom greater far than mine.
Ah, this joy is all too great—
Scarce my heart can bear the weight:
Wondrous things mine eyes behold—
God hath chosen thee of old:
God hath caused thee to endure,
Ever Holy, Spotless, Pure;
And on earth hath granted thee,
Mother of the Lord to be.

*   *   *

But, this Infant's birth had place
By the Holy Spirit's grace:
Thou art Mother—But I know
He no father hath below.

* * *

Now, my Lady, kind of heart,
Full of courtesy thou art;
Pray thee, let me look upon
My Redeemer, thy dear Son.

MADONNA. Pray thee, Husband, give me here,
From thine arms my Infant dear;
When the Gipsy shall him view,
She may tell his fortune too.
Here thy God, my Sister, see—
Heart and Soul and Life to me:
Look on this sweet face with care;
All of Heaven's joy lies there.

* * *

GIPSY. 'Tis enough—thou weary art,
Lady; but before we part
Unto this poor Gipsy, pray
Give an alms, if ask I may.
Silver ask I not, nor gold;
Though all wealth thy hand doth hold,
Star of Light: for on thy breast
Christ, the Omnipotent, doth rest.
Grant me, by thy prayers to win
True repentance for my sin;
That my soul may, soon or late,
Enter through the heavenly gate.

II. THE 'DARK GIRL' BY THE WELL OF ST. JOHN, AT KILKENNY.

JOHN KEEGAN: 1809—1849.

FROM 'THE BALLADS OF IRELAND,' EDITED BY E. HAYES, 1855.

' It is believed that when Heaven wills the performance of cures, the sky opens above the Holy Well at the hour of midnight, and Christ, the Virgin Mother and St. John descend in the form of three snow-whites, and with the rapidity of lightning into the fountain. No person but those destined to be cured can see this phenomenon, but every one can hear the musical sound of their wings as they rush into the well and agitate the water.' The poem was written in 1832, and is founded on an incident witnessed by the writer, in the anguish of a 'Sweet Wexford Girl' whose sight was not restored (From the Author's note).

' MOTHER, is that the passing-bell ?
　　Or yet the midnight chime?
Or rush of Angels' golden wings?
　　Or is it near the time—
The time when God, they say, comes down
　　This weary world upon,
With Holy Mary at his right,
　　And at his left, St. John?

' I'm dumb; my heart forgets to throb;
　　My blood forgets to run;
But vain my sighs, in vain I sob,
　　God's will must still be done.
I hear but tone of warning bell,
　　For holy priest or nun;
On earth, God's face I'll never see,
　　Nor Mary, nor St. John.

'Mother, my hopes are gone again;
  My heart is black as ever:
Mother, I say, look forth once more,
  And see can you discover
God's glory in the crimson clouds—
  See, does he ride upon
That perfumed breeze—or do you see
  The Virgin, or St. John?

'Ah, no; ah, no; well, God of Peace,
  Grant me thy blessing still;
Oh, make me patient with my doom,
  And happy at thy will:
And guide my footsteps so on earth
  That, when I'm dead and gone,
Mine eyes may catch thy shining light
  With Mary and St. John.

'Yet, Mother, could I see thy smile,
  Before we part below;
Or watch the silver moon and stars
  Where Slaney's ripples flow;
Oh, could I see the sweet sun shine
  My native hills upon,
I'd never love my God the less,
  Nor Mary, nor St. John.

'But no; ah, no; it cannot be;
  Yet, Mother, do not mourn—
Come, kneel again and pray to God,
  In peace let us return,
The "Dark Girl's" doom must aye be mine—
  But Heaven will light me on,
Until I find my way to God,
  And Mary and St. John.'

III. ROBES OF THE CHRIST CHILD :
AFTER THE FRENCH.

AGNES LEE (WATTS).

FROM 'THE HOLY CROSS MAGAZINE,' NEW YORK, 1891.

By Nazareth, in waters fair,
    The Virgin dipped the robes of white ;
A woman washed, beside her there,
    Her linen, in the rosy light.

' Sister,' the woman said, ' dost know
    . The story of this singing stream ?
At harvest time no waters flow ;
    No drink for bird ; no crystal gleam :

Yet now the lambs plunge deep their wool ;
    Bare-ankled boys its shallows ford—
Have angels stirred the mystic pool ? '
    The Virgin whispered, ' Praise the Lord.'

' Fair Edens rise along its way ;
    The trees, refreshed by its glad brim,
Bear fruit celestial, day by day.'
    The Virgin whispered, ' Praise to him.'

' But oh, most wonderful to tell,
    My babe lay dying : hitherward
I brought and bathed him—he is well.'
    The Virgin whispered, ' Praise the Lord.

' Know'st thou whence comes such blessedness
    To Galilee, such magic stored
That scribes and doctors may not guess ? '
    The Virgin whispered, ' Praise the Lord.'

And Mary smiled with secret thrill;
    Not yet the time: and dreamed her dream,
Sweet soul; and still she came, and still
    She dipped small garments in the stream.

IV. LEGEND OF THE REPENTANT THIEF.
MARION AMES TAGGART.

FROM 'THE AVE MARIA,' 1892.

WEARY and worn with desert and dust and heat,
    The Virgin-Mother vainly sighed for rest;
The burning sands had scorched her tender feet,
    The Babe moaned faintly on her sheltering breast;
St. Joseph placed her on his faithful beast,
Offering the pain as consecrated priest.

At last their eyes espy the sight they crave—
    A green oasis in the desert waste,
And kindly palm-trees that inviting wave;
    Thither renewed in strength and hope they haste,
And seek a shelter in the lowly spot—
By God remembered, though by man forgot.

Another mother there doth soothe her child,
    Whose tiny limbs with leprosy are white:
She looks upon the Stranger's beauty mild,
    And hopes for mercy in the gracious sight;
Quick brings she water, that her guest may lave
Her Blessed Babe, that hath the power to save.

Her child was but a robber's infant son;
    But mother-love knows not such thought to heed:
When the Maid-Mother's loving task was done,
    She seized the water, praying in her need:
She plunged her babe where Jesus had been laid,
And lo, her child was healed as she had prayed.

E

Their strength renewed, refreshed by food and rest,
  The Holy Family went on their way;
The burning sun, low sinking in the west,
  Enfolds the Mother in its last bright ray;
The robber-matron, with a grateful heart,
Holds her fair boy and watches them depart.

*   *   *

On Calvary, beneath a darkening sky,
  Once more the Mother stands beside her Son;
Upon his right hand, waiting too to die,
  Hangs a poor thief whose sands are almost run.
'Lord,' breaks his voice upon the heavy air,
'Entering thy Kingdom, oh, receive me there.'

Backward the thirty years then seem to roll:
  Mary once more doth see the desert isle;
Saved then in body, now he craves his soul—
  That robber's son.   And almost doth she smile
As Jesus speaks, 'Take heart; 'tis well with thee:
To-day thou enterest Paradise with me.'

Egyptian Traditions.

SIR JOHN CROKER BARROW, BART.

FROM 'MARY OF NAZARETH, A LEGENDARY POEM,' 1889.

To Egypt's land of mystery—that land
  Where Pyramid o'er-shadows Pyramid;
And where, half-hidden in eternal sand,
The ever-silent Sphinx, bereft of wings,
Seems thinking all unutterable things,
  Yet keeping all such secrets ever hid;
  And where, whilst other thrones and kingdoms waned,
  Had Pharoah after Pharoah ruled and reigned—

To Egypt's land, that land of world-wide fame,
Mary with Jesus and with Joseph came;
　And there, secure from Herod's lawless code,
　In midst of Egypt's sons in peace abode.

* * *

Tradition tells, how once at daily toil,
　Near golden-gated Heliopolis—
No water lying on the sun-burnt soil—
How sore athirst the Infant Jesus wept,
　Till Mary offered up her tears with his;
When on a sudden, from her feet there lept
　A spring of virgin-water from the ground;
　And as in showers the crystal drops fell round,
They wed themselves together in a well,
By side whereof she might with Jesus dwell—
　A well that sprang, the Arab still avers,
　From that same mingling of his tears with hers.

Tradition tells, moreover, how there stood
　A giant tree beside the golden gate
　Of that same city—tree of ancient date
And worshipped by the worshippers of wood—
　A tree which ever and anon, 'twas said,
　When men drew near bowed down its leaf-crowned
　　head;
And how, when Mary brought her Jesus there,
It bowed its branches downwards through the air
　Until they kissed the ground she trod—and then
　Uprose and never more bowed down to men.

Tradition further tells how, on the day
　When Mary in that golden gate-way stood
And Jesus sleeping on her bosom lay,
　The idols, gold and silver, stone and wood,

Which Egypt—all unmindful of her Lord,
The God of Abraham, of old adored—
  Had raised within her temples far and wide
  Fell down throughout her cities, side by side;
Whilst in one only scarce-permitted shrine
  In glory of the God of Israel,
The sacred lamp more brightly seemed to shine
  Soon as its light on her and Jesus fell.

*   *   *

Near there, where Mary wept, there that time lived—
Lived on, despite the sterile sand and thrived,
Still lives 'tis said, a giant sycamore,
  The Tree of Mary, named; by land so rich
In legends of traditionary lore—
  A tree well-leaved; beneath the shade of which,
As rose the sun upon its rising sap,
Would Mary sit, with Jesus on her lap;
  And there, beneath the shadow on her cast,
  Day-dream through all the legends of the past.

*   *   *

Thus musing often on the days gone by,
  Half-dreaming and half-thinking, with her hand
In Jesùs' hand, would Mary sit and sigh
  Made thus more mindful of her own loved land—
For were they not themselves in bondage there?
And would not God, in answer to her prayer,
Send down ere long, to save her Child and her,
Some angel or divine deliverer?
  Yes, surely, when the time of God had come,
  Would Raphael return to take them home.

Thus hoping on would Mary, night by night,
  Re-seek the shelter of her humble home;

Dreaming from hour to hour, from dark to light,
　Of shadows past and shadows yet to come—
Dreaming one while of Egypt's first-born slain,
　And childless mothers weeping out their loss ;
Another while, of Palestine again
　Fore-darkened by the shadow of the Cross.

To Mary Immaculate and other Verse.

DAVID BEARNE, S.J.

I. TO MARY IMMACULATE.

WHAT is the melody that I can bring to thee,
　　Queen of Creation, Empress of Heaven ?
Oh, for the psalm of a Seraph to sing to thee,
　　Oh, for the song of the Angel-Seven
　　　　Who stand in the marvellous mystery,
　　　　And chant of thy glorious history,
While garlands unfading they weave and they fling
　　　　to thee,
　　Rose-wreaths white as the snow wind-driven.

Thy beauty so God-like how shall man measure it ?
　　Oh, measureless mine of manifold gold ;
Immaculate purity, how doth God treasure it,
　　　　His one white Lily from earth's dark mould ;
　　　　　Oh, great and magnificent verity
　　　　　Of thy spotless, ineffable chastity ;
How may the Cherubim tell of the pleasure it
　　Gives to the Godhead, and glory untold.

Might of God's Mother, creation hath bowed to it
　　Nature hath owned its unceasing sway ;
Legions of Lucifer's angels have cowed to it,
　　The terrible army in battle array ;

O Earth, without measure or dysphony,
    Sing on in unending symphony.
Let the light of the noon and the night shout aloud to it—
    The midnight moon and the dawning day.

Let the riches of earth, sea and sky be unrolled to thee,
    Mother of Loveliness, Light and Song ;
Though the splendours of Paradise God doth unfold
        to thee,
    Earth's beauty and grace to thee belong ;
        And we bind and we bring and we give to thee
        All things in a sweet captivity ;
The wealth of the ends of the earth is all told to thee,
    And all to thy Majesty hasten and throng.

      ·

II. MATER GELU CONSTRICTA.

'Tears are the Soul's life-blood.'   St. Augustine.

I.

THE bitter chill, sweet Mother, on the way,
    The white and wintry way to Bethlehem ;
The chillier welcome as they say thee Nay—
    Spurning alike the Casket and the Gem

The withering winds that sweep within the cave
    And wrap the Royal Infant at thy breast,
Thy rain of joyful tears which warmly lave
    The crib as thou dost lay him to his rest.

II.

OH, chillier far the fair and frozen snow
    Of death-cold limbs upon thy trembling knee,
When from his Wounds the Blood had ceased to flow,
    And thou wert biding still on Calvary.

Again the Mother doth her Son embrace :
    But soon the chilly cave and swathing bands
Will hide the deep Heart-wound and furrowed Face,
    The ice-cold riven Feet and pierced Hands.

His cries upon the Rood's rough bed are hushed ;
    The stricken Mother waileth now ; and though
The Fount be dry from which his Life-stream gushed,
    The blood of Mary's soul doth freely flow.

III. THE VISITATION.

' And Mary abode with her about three months.'

    WHILE crimson roses blush
        Through summer's golden tides,
    Within that holy hush
        Our Blessed Lady 'bides ;
    Hostess, alike, and Guest
    Remain in prayerful rest
And glad thanksgiving for the secret each one hides.

    Within white, hallowed walls
        Our Lady dear remains
    While bird to birdie calls
        Through softly falling rains ;
    Hostess, alike, and Guest
    Awaiting God's behest,
Sing soft Magnificats with silver-sweet refrains.

    All heavenly the life
        That Maid and Matron know ;
    Such sacred fervours rife,
        Such graces overflow
    In Hostess and in Guest ;
    For oh, in Mary's breast
The lasting Life and Light and Love of Jesus glow.

IV. REGINA SÆCULORUM.

STREW sweetness for the passing of the Queen ;
    By the high hedgerows, white with bridal bloom
Woven of white-thorn, and the arras green
    Broidered with amber of the April loom,
        Our Lady passeth and will pass :
        Ah, nay ;
Falls the fruit blossom, fades the meadow grass,
    But Mary passeth not as doth the May.

Touch the white torches with a flake of flame,
    Sing honeyed psalmody from prime till noon,
Make stream and meadow murmur Mary's name
    Till floats upon the blue the May-night moon,
        The month is setting and will set :
        Ah, pray ;
The moon of May be far from waning yet,
    And Mary pass not with the passing May.

Ibymn, Laub, and Colloquy.

GONZALO DE BERCEO: XIII. CENTURY.

The Author was a Priest in the Monastery of San Millan
(St. Æmilianus).

TRANSLATED BY E. M. CLERKE.

I. HYMN.

HAIL, Holy Mary, Star of Ocean clear,
Mother of Glory's King, who hast no peer ;
Virgin for aye, whom sin could ne'er come near ;
The sinner's Gate to enter heaven's bright sphere.

To thee the Angel Gabriel ' Ave ' cried,
Word in which honey-sweetness is implied :
In thee, true Mother, we in peace abide,
Ave hath Abel's Mother's name belied.

Save sinners whom the toils of evil stay ;
Give light unto the blind who darkling stray ;
Take from us ills which heavy on us weigh,
And give that good in which we fail alway.

Our Mother show thee, moved to pity be ;
To the King's Majesty present our plea,
Grace for God's love, and for his charity,
Thy Son's, who took humanity from thee.

Maid-Mother glorious, sole and peerless styled,
All gentleness, than harmless sheep more mild,
True life thou givest, Mother Undefiled,
And art Heaven's Key to us when thence exiled

Thou rul'st our life, its fever to allay,
Thou, lest we stumble, art our Path and Way ;
When hence we go, thou, Lady, art our Stay ;
That we may see our God in joy alway.

II. LAUD.

On yonder mountain bold
    Thou seest a Fountain which doth ever play ;
Its rim is all of gold,
    Its pipe of massy silver past assay.
O thirsty soul, proceed,
    An thou wilt drink, thereto now take thy way,
No silver dost thou need,
    Or coinèd money for the draught to pay.
Whoe'er to drink hath will,
    Must strip his gown and mantle straight away ;

The soul that drinks its fill
  Becomes more lucid than the star of day.
O glorious Virgin bright,
  Who of good wine hast storage 'neath thy sway,
In grace give of thy might
  Unto the humble soul that thee doth pray.
Unto my soul ingrate
  Though sinful, give to drink, its thirst allay;
On Christ all blessings wait,
  Who deigned to die the purchase to defray:
And she, the Mother Great,
  And Sister of the Lord, be blest alway.

III. COLLOQUY BETWEEN THE SOUL AND
OUR LADY.

Soul.

TELL me, sweet Mary, what didst meditate
  When on thee did the Angelic Presence shine,
  And unto thee in lowly guise incline,
  In greeting which thy soul did perturbate?

Mary.

Thy question, Soul devout and loving well,
  Shall answered be:
  I, in my lowly cell,
  Intent was on Isaiah's prophecy,
  Which that a Virgin shall conceive and bear
  Doth wondrously declare,
  Emmanuel, who of heaven the keys shall hold.

Silent I mused, and said within my mind:
  'Sweet Lord, I do implore

The mortal Goddess to such part assigned
That I may see; the Virgin from of yore
By God elect to bear and to bring forth,
Let me but serve on earth,
Ere yet my limbs shall stiffen or grow cold.'

Such was my thought, and rapt in its delight
   Awhile was I;
And straight there shone unto me a new light
Round a pure Spirit, who said, 'God on High
   Is with thee, Full of Grace, and blest alway
   From women chosen this day.'
   Then did I fear his speech so sweet and fair,

Till spake the Angel, 'Cast all fear from thee,
   O Mary, fair and bright;
   I come to bid thee learn that thou shalt be
   Mother and Spouse, Rose fragrant and snow-
      white,
   That thou the Son of the Most High shall bear;
   Thine is the Lily fair,
   And thou art she to serve whom was thy prayer.'

Aware then what the angelic speech foretold,
   Thereto I thus replied:
   'In me the Handmaid of the Lord behold;
Be done as thou hast said.'
         Then homeward hied
God's Messenger, and full my heart did seem
   Of love and joy supreme;
   Fulfilled my utmost longing then and there.

Matri Absconditæ:

ON A HIDDEN SHRINE.

EMILY BOWLES.

FROM 'THE THREE KINGS,' 1874.

MOTHER, deep in shadow hidden,
  Thou standest with thy Child in arms,
Meek Handmaid of the Lord, still bidden
  To taste thy joy midst earth's alarms.
When Angel-warned by vision of the night,
So didst thou hurry in Egyptian flight,
While deeper glooms wrapt all thy soul in mute affright,
      Sweet ' Mother out of Sight.'

About thee falls no gilded vest,
  No stars bedeck thy gentle head,
Rich gifts around thee are not pressed,
  For thee no flowery carpet spread.
So, Mother, didst thou stand one long-past night
Unkissed, unwelcomed in thy Mother-right,
And pleading still, still left without, unheeded quite,
      Sweet ' Mother out of Sight.'

When the long-hidden life was done
  Whose sweetness man may never spell,
O Mother, none might hear the moan
  With which thou badst thy Son farewell.
From out the lattice with grape clusters dight,
Following with streaming eyes thy Soul's Delight,
Thou still didst watch and listen through the fading
    night,
      Loved ' Mother out of Sight.'

Thou wast not bidden to the Feast
   When the last Paschal Lamb was slain;
No Bread was given thee to taste,
   No Chalice strengthened thee for pain.
The words divine the Eleven shared that night,
The prayer which fills each new-born soul with light,
Were hid from thee, dear Mother, in thy woeful plight,
      Sad 'Mother out of Sight.'

Standing all tearless by the Cross—
   No 'Hidden Mother' then—
Thy boundless right to pain and loss
   Made known to angels and to men;
Thou yet was named not by thy Lord that night,
When Death and Hell were trampled in the fight,
And Heaven at his uprising sang with new delight,
      Meek 'Mother out of Sight.'

When smote thine ear those accents brief,
   'Woman, behold thy Son,' the sword
Pierced all thy soul with darkest grief,
   Exchanging man for God's Own Word.
Yet still unconquered in the silent fight—
For us the gift, for thee the sharp despite—
Thou didst in travail-throes then vanquish Satan's might,
      Great 'Mother out of Sight.'

And even when to Olivet
   He led his chosen band,
Sweet Mother, still thine eyes were wet,
   Barred from the Promised Land;
Thou fain wouldst cling to him with loving might,
Fain, fain wouldst stay with hands his upward flight,
Left on that lone hill-side when fled thy Life and Light,
      Still 'Mother out of Sight.'

When he whose new-born joy in grace
  First placed thee, lowly, in thy shrine,
He oft was here with buried face,
  Heart-thankful for faith's gift divine;
For this perchance, when thine own May shone
    bright
His earthly bonds were loosed to instant flight,
And thou wast with him, Mother, guiding through
    death's night,
          Then, Mother full in sight.

Thus, Mother of the Hidden Shrine,
  I love to bring thee prayers and tears;
All sad forsaken ones are thine,
  All lonely hearts, all doubts and fears:
Thy sheltering love shall aid our unwatched fight,
Thy pleading voice shall cheer our starless night,
And when our evening time shall dawn to heavenly
    light,
          Then, Mother bright,
          Thou shalt be ever in our sight.

NOTES.

The Image of the Blessed Virgin which suggested these lines was given to a church by the late Sir John Simeon, Bart., after his conversion.

St. II. l. 7 : Still left without ; *cf.* Thy Mother and thy brethren stand without.

St. VIII. : Sir John died, May 21, 1870, saying, 'Sub tuum præsidium.'

Song of Mary, the Mother of Christ:

CONTAINING THE STORY OF HIS LIFE AND PASSION : 1601.

JOHN BRERELEY, PRIEST (VERE LAWRENCE ANDERTON, S.J.) : 1575—1643.

'The Holy Childhood' is a cento taken from 'the Song of Mary,' a small, thin, printed volume in the British Museum Library, of which only a single copy can be found by the Editor. It was copied by him in the Library in 1893, and was reprinted in 'The Month.' The same book contains a few other poems, apparently by the same hand, one of which 'Jerusalem, my happy home,' well known to hymnographers, is signed in an existing MS. with the Author's initials J.B. : P(riest). These facts, in addition to other circumstantial evidence known to and collected by Mr. Joseph Gillow, warrant the attribution of authorship here made on his authority.

THE HOLY CHILDHOOD.

FAIN would I write, my mind ashamèd is,
  My verse doth fear to do the matter wrong :
No earthly music good enough for this,
    Not David's harp, nor Hierom's mourning song,
      Nor Esaie's lips are worthy once to move,
      Though Seraph's fire hath kindled them with love.

        *   *   *

Then sing, O Saints, O holy Heavenly Choir,
  And I shall strive to follow on your song ;
This sacred ditty is my chief desire,
    My soul to hear this music doth now long ;
      And longing thus, all whilst there was no din,
      They silent stood to see who should begin.

For none did think him worthy to be one,
  And every one to other there gave place ;
But bowing knees to Jesus every one,
  They him besought for to decide the case :
    Who said to me, ' Most fit for this appears
    My Mother's plaint, and sacred Virgin's tears.'

*   *   *

But yet in me, far more than all the rest,
  Thy love, O Lord, and glory doth appear ;
Extolling her that was the very least
  Thy only Son, our Saviour, for to bear ;
    And lodge within so low and straight a room,
    The Judge of all in dreadful Day of Doom.

This sacred message, Gabriel, thou didst bring
  From God's own mouth unto my silly cell,
How I, a Virgin, should conceive a King
  And Lord, whom all the prophets did foretel :
    Oh, what a message seemèd this to me,
    Unworthy once a Handmaid for to be.

*   *   *

The time expired ; in Bethlehem thou wert born,
  Where, in a crib upon a lock of hay
'Twixt ox and ass, thou, Lord, didst think no scorn,
  Swaddled in clouts, thy Mother should thee lay :
    O Sacred Lord, sweet Son, what should I call?
    My God, my Babe, my Bliss, and All in all.

*   *   *

Oh, lowly place for him that was so high ;
  Oh, happy stable, palace of the King ;
You angels there did make us melody ;
  The silly shepherds said they heard you sing ;
    The shining Star from th' East did go before,
    And shew the Kings the place for to adore.

They laid their sceptres at my Saviour's feet,
  And kissing them his God-head did adore ;
Offering their gifts, myrrh, gold and incense sweet,
  A present rich to them who seemed so poor ;
    But they inspired, these offerings did bring
    For Christ their Priest, their Saviour and their King.

*   *   *

After, my Lord, according to the Law
  Within the Temple I did thee present ;
Where Simeon, as soon as he us saw,
  And in his arms thy little Body hent,
    To bless our God within he did not cease,
    Desiring leave for to depart in peace.

' For now (quoth he) my aged eyes have seen
  The saving health most pleasant to my sight,
Which of thy Saints hath long expected been,
  The glory of the Jews and heathen nations light ;
    Who yet by malice shall be much gain-said,
    O worthy Babe, O happy Mother-Maid.'

All this was joy and comfort unto me,
  Who did confer these sayings in my mind ;
Wherein such truth and light I still did see,
  But Simeon added further : ' I do find
    That though thou Christ's elected Mother art,
    The sword of sorrow shall transpierce thy heart.'

Oh, saying true in me, full many an hour,
  Such is the way that God doth use with his ;
With comforts cross, with sweet to mix the sour,
  'Twixt weal and woe, to wield them unto bliss :
    The one doth show his goodness and his love ;
    The other doth our grateful patience prove.

*   *   *

F

Seven years in Egypt living in exile,
  Joseph his axe, my needle in my hand,
In poor estate we passèd all the while
  Amongst the simple people of the land :
     For all was heaven, for comfort we did sing
     To lull our Babe and reverence our King.

Oh, how my cross was ever mixed with sweet,
  My pain with joy, mine earth with heavenly bliss,
Who always might adore my Saviour's feet,
  Embrace my God, my loving Infant kiss ;
     And give him suck who gives the Angels food,
     And turn my milk into my Saviour's Blood.

Sometimes he cast his hand about my neck,
  And smiling looked his Mother in the face ;
Some joy, or skill I found in every beck, ·
  Each day discovered wisdom, love and grace :
     I cannot utter what I did espy
     When I beheld his little glorious eye.

At seven years' end we did return again,
  And brought the Ark into his wonted place ;
For he was dead that would my Lord have slain ;
  Thus worldly things do turn and change their face :
     But they which Jesus keep and do his will,
     In all events be one and happy still.

Yearly we went with others to adore
  Within the Temple, as the Law doth bid ;
A holy place, but how doth he much more
  Who being Lord, a subject's duty did :
     O Christians, then, how ought you for to live
     Obedient to the laws the Church doth give ?

And Christ my Son, now being twelve years old,
  Thou didst bewray thy heavenly Wisdom there :
And midst the Doctors treasures didst unfold,
  Joseph and I, meanwhile, affright with fear
    For either weening other had my Child,
    Each trusting other, either was beguiled.

My soul, remember what thy thoughts were then,
  What griefs and fears did lodge within my breast
Who now had lost the Joy of God and men,
  My sacred Son, in whom my soul was blest :
    What tears could serve to wail so great a loss ?
    Lo, thus we still approachèd to the Cross.

Thus three days spent in wailing, tears and woe,
  Behold, my Saviour in the Temple still :
Of whom I asked, ' My Son, why did you so ? '
  ' Must I not do (quoth he), my Father's will ? '
    And so, you see, I learnèd by my grief,
    Amongst all duties that to God is chief.

Till thirty years my Lord at home did dwell,
  Joseph and I enjoyed his presence still :
Where I myself abashèd am to tell,
  How he in all obeyèd to my will :
    How do you think I moved was to see
    The Prince of Angels subject unto me ?

Our Life, our Sweetness, and our Hope; and two Sonnets.

T. E. BRIDGETT, C.SS.R.: 1828—1898.

FROM 'SONNETS AND EPIGRAMS,' 1898.

I. OUR LIFE, OUR SWEETNESS, AND OUR HOPE.

'The very beauty of her body was an image of her soul, the type of sanctity. A good house should be known by its vestibule.' (St. Ambrose on the B.V.M.)

THE Church has taught both East and West
    That whatsoe'er is choice in grace,
In nature whatsoe'er is best,
    Unite in Mary's heart and face.
Her orators lack words to teach
    The thoughts that Mary's name imparts;
Her artists strive in vain to reach
    The ideal of their kindling hearts.

Then, Scoffer, babble not that she
    Was fashioned first in times obscure—
The dream of monks' credulity,
    The phantom of a faith impure.
For monkish legend half so bare
    Has never moved the critic's scorn
As that the very Type of Grace,
    From sordid ignorance was born.

Less grossly they from truth depart
    Who hold that Mary's image first
Was formed by the creative art
    Of men who great conceptions nursed.

And yet, not so: what Raphael sought
  In noblest lineaments to paint,
Was but a body to the thought
  Which peasants share with sage and saint.

Man may invent a Juno's pride,
  Of Venus paint the sensuous charms;
Not his that Holy Spirit's Bride,
  Whose beauty pride and lust disarms.
It was not dreaming piety,
  Creative art, nor bull of Pope—
'Twas God's great love made her to be
  'Our Life, our Sweetness, and our Hope.'

II. BETHLEHEM.

Our Lady, about to enter the Cave, speaks:

'My God and Father, Father of my Son,
  Thy Son and mine, oh, grace of the Most High,
  This is the place foretold, the hour is nigh
When men shall gaze upon our Blessed One.
Thy hand has led me hither; be it done
  To me according to thy word; thine eye
  Is on this lowly cave; thou wilt supply
A cradle for the Heir of David's throne.

The shades of eve are falling on the plain
  Where David led his sheep, his breast aflame
  With faith and prayer; and in thy mighty Name
He slew the bear and lion, and was fain
  To meet Goliath; Joseph too and I
  Await thy mercies under Bethlehem's sky.'

III.　NAZARETH.

The Child of Mary speaks :

'O MOTHER, hast thou heard the cruel deed?
　Thy Son, thy Jesus, thy Most Holy One,
　Of God Most High the Sole Begotten Son ;
The Flower which thou didst bear of heavenly seed,
The promised Flower to spring from Jesse's reed ;
　Which thou didst watch unfolding to the sun
　Its sacred petals, as the years did run,
And perfect Flower to perfect Bud succeed :

Him, from the synagogue where oft he prayed,
　The Nazarenes have dragged, and from the hill
Would fain have headlong cast, had he not stayed
　By his Almighty Power their ruthless will :
He would not let the horror of his death
Rest on his cherished home, his Mother's Nazareth.'

Truth and Beauty in Catholic Lands.

MARIA (MARTIN) BUCKLE :
1796—1878.

FROM 'THE PILGRIM,' 1853.

I.　TRIDUO AT SANT' ANDREA DELLE FRATTE, ROME.

OFT did the Pilgrim seek a church obscure,
Yet ever thronged ; and they who minister
Are monks, whose rugged gown and naked foot
And girdle of harsh rope are seen beneath
The gorgeous cope.　The snowy amice hides
The tonsure large which, like the crown of thorns,

The rigid Minims bear. There is no gold,
Nor much that strangers praise; it is not long
Since o'er that little altar they have placed
The bright Madonna.
              Now her festival
Decks the high Altar with a thousand lights
So skilfully arranged; the lambent flame,
In honour of St. Andrew's martyrdom,
Plays o'er it cruciform. The tapers burn
Like constellations figuring the nave,
And star-like sparkles to the roof. The eye
Wanders; yet ever to the centre turns,
The blaze of glory round the Incarnate God.
And yet the crowds that small side-altar throng,
And stoop to touch, to kiss the marble step,
And press, that from the friar's patient hand
They may receive Communion. See that boy:
His hands are clasped as, kneeling on the floor
To the Madonna, he uplifts his eyes,
And trusts the whispered prayer is borne by her
Safe to the courts of heaven. A slender alms
He offers then; and grasping with both hands
Her picture, prints on it a fervent kiss,
A cross on his own forehead, and departs.
That aged man: some boon his heart desires
Is on his lips; he pours out all his soul
And knows that he is heard. That high-born girl
Lifts her dark eyes and joins her slender hands;
Her veil conceals the movement of her lips,
But she has told her grief; with lightened heart
She rises; and with step more confident
Departs in hope.
             'How is it that such faith
Is found on earth?' Nay, marvel not, but read

That scroll beside the altar. As thou seest,
Thus borne upon the clouds, with sunny rays
Thus streaming from her hands, our Lady stood
Here, on this very spot, before the eyes
Of a proud scoffing Jew. But five years since
Before that altar as a Jew he fell,
Prostrate in unbelief : he rose, in faith
A perfect Christian. ' Nothing did she speak,'
He said; and yet he understood it all.
The learned would instruct him ; but they found
His knowledge faultless ; for his mind contained,
As by intuition, all the depths of truth
Without the intervention of the sense.
But when he stood within the thronged Gesù,
They bade him bow his lofty forehead down
To touch the pavement, ere they washed away
The sin which burdened him. One struggle passed
Across his haughty features ; prostrate then
His natural pride he laid for ever down ;
And meek thenceforth and gentle, he retired
Beyond the praises of the wondering world,
His very name forgotten in his cell.
Fame may not reach him ; but the miracle
Spreads o'er the world the glory of our God,
Still mighty in his wonders and still praised
In all his saints; still, through the Virgin-Queen,
His gifts of grace bestowing on mankind.

II. LITANY OF OUR LADY : VARENNA.

THE morn was bright as in the south. The sun
Rose like a giant in his strength and spread
Not light alone, but joyous life around.

The past was like a dark and gloomy dream;
And this was real.

                  So the Pilgrim thought,
As the gay peasants passed her on the road
Skirting the Lake of Como.   Here and there
The water laves the horse-hoofs; then aloft
The gallery long is hewn in living rock,
Dark, but for windows whence the waters blue
And Alps and woods and villas white appear—
All in the luxury of summer; all
With more than nature's delicacy glow.
The shrubs are all exotic; and the flowers
Bloom with no vulgar beauty.   In the north
They foster such in gardens; and by art
They strive to imitate Italian climes.
On the clear water's brink Varenna lies,
Beneath the rocks with coronella hung
And rich geraniums.

                  In the village church
They sang the Litany.   The joyous air
Came from their inmost heart—not less devout
Than it was joyous: and it breathed of love,
Love for a Creature beautiful and pure
Beyond angelic excellence, yet still
A Woman, and the Handmaid of her Lord.
It was a new affection.   Feelings strange
Rose with the deafening chorus.   Men and boys,
Women and aged ones their voices raised.
'Ora pro nobis,' seemed to pierce the skies,
Where sits the Queen of Heaven.   By one and two
They hailed her; then, 'the sinner's sweetest Hope,'
'Mother of Mercy,' 'Mother of our God.'
And then, again, the stirring chorus rose
All jubilant, and through the open door

The softened accents echoed up the lake.
Worn was the Pilgrim's heart with toil, and worn
With care and doubt: the sense of joy was new;
And as she watched the sunset on the Alps,
She marvelled at the change from cloudy skies
And gloomy studies, to the glorious earth
And smiling faces round her.
                              It grew dark:
But all were merry still; and sleep was chased
The live-long night with tinkling violin
And sounds of tripping feet.   She asked the cause:
And she was answered, ' This is Italy.'

NOTE.

No. I., l. 45: 'Scoffing Jew;' The future Père Ratisbonne,
whose miraculous conversion occurred on 20th of January, 1842,
and was described by himself, in his Narrative, written in the
month of April following.

The Sleeping Mother.

PASCAL DE BURY.

WHITE-WINGED, ethereal Sleep,
Come from the high Empyrean,
Where with harmonious pean
Angels their love-watches keep,
Answering one to another
Watchword of heavenly greeting:
Come where the Gentle Mother
        Fondles her Little One.

When the warm sun sets in gold,
Drawing his beams from the daisy,
Vexed and unwilling and hazy,
Thou dost the petals enfold:

Lo, now speed fleet to the Maiden
Bending in weariness downward,
Close to her heart calm-laden
    Pressing her Little One.

Bring with thee comrades of joy,
Music and Melody sweetest;
Chant as when Jahveh thou greetest—
God is this Innocent Boy:
Sing, to his Mother low murmur,
Lullaby low to her Darling—
Firmer in slumber, firmer
    Holds she her Little One.

Evenings mid the dulled flowers
Stayest thou, counting them stories,
Telling of graces and glories,
Flitting away the dusk hours;
Speak to this Heaven-loved Lily,
Fairer than lily of Sharon,
Whisper her softly, stilly,
    Tales of her Little One.

Borrow of Nature her hues,
Ask of frail Frost his light pencil,
Then on the eyelid faint stencil
Outlines of paradise views,
Visions of realms everlasting,
Scenes of the awful abode,
Splendour and godhead casting
    Over her Little One.

Breathe as the tenderest sigh
Down through her fair, drooping lashes—
Not as the wind that crashes—
Breathe as a god passing by:

Out on the meadow at gloaming,
Perfume around thou spreadest.
Sprinkle her fancies roaming.
　　After her Little One.

Pouring thy phial of dew,
Welcome restorer of beauty.
Blithe in thy pleasing duty
Colour the cowslip anew :
Pass not, however unthinking.
Mary, the Queen of God's Garden ;
Gratefully rest she is drinking.
　　Clasping her Little One.

Let no disparaging word
Causing the heart's contraction.
Nor the fierce war-sound of faction,
'Mid her sweet resting be heard :
Though gladsome journeyings taking
Distant in shadowy dreamland,
Ever her heart-eye waking
　　Watches her Little One.

━━━

The Annunciation and other Lyrics.

DOM BEDE CAMM, O.S.B.

I. THE ANNUNCIATION.

At Maredsous, 1893.

Not a breath stirs the midnight air
In the stilled streets of Nazareth,
But laden with perfumes rare
Sleep hovers, a vision of death

And eye hath not seen,
In his robe of sheen,
The Herald announce to the Angels' Queen ;
                    ' Ave, Maria.'

Not a light in the lowly home
    That hides the Pearl of Galilee ;
But set in the azure dome,
    Only the silent stars to see,
The Maiden who there,
In a rapture of prayer,
Sighs for his Face whom a Maiden shall bear ;
                    Gratia Plena.

Not a cry, as the ' Strength of God '
    Flames as of old on Daniel,
But the trembling of Jesse's Rod
    For Virginity's Citadel,
Till the ' How ' is said
That removes all dread,
Then the soft swift bowing of meekest head ;
                    Dominus tecum.

Not a whisper the silence broke
    As waiting knelt Saint Gabriel ;
But Heaven, till Mary spoke,
    Hung breathless as under a spell :
When the world to save
Her ' Fiat ' she gave,
God flowed o'er her heart like a spring-wave tide ;
                    Ave, Maria.

II. SANTA MARIA AD NIVES.

Lines written in Rome, May, 1894, on the picture of our Lady
ascribed to St. Luke, in the Basilica of Santa Maria Maggiore.

SILENT she standeth, spellbound ; in her eyes
As in a well's transparent depths, revealed
The dawning of profoundest thought ; her soul
Rapt in the Godhead, shines from out its veils,
While in her arms God's Glory sits enthroned.
With Baby hand upheld, the Incarnate Word,
Yet word-less, speaketh words unspeakable.
Silent she standeth, listening ; her heart
Drinking in waves of measureless content.
Mother of God, 'twas thus thy Luke would say,
'Twas thus thy tranquil beauty, like a star,
Dawned on those aged eyes, betwixt the lanes
Of sculptured columns in the golden Court.
Oh, mystery bitter-sweet, of sorrows first,
Amid the joy the destined anguish-thrust
Casting its shadow o'er thee.   Luke, alas,
Hath all too skilfully pourtrayed thy pain,
The sad presentiment of Cross and Tomb,
That veils with tears unshed the tender light
Of new-found Motherhood.   Ah, purest Maid,
Mother of Sorrows, Mother of my God,
Sweet Flower of Jesse, all Immaculate,
I know thee better, since I knew thee thus.

III. 'MARY, HELP.'

FROM THE GERMAN.

WHAT time to slay our God and Brother
The jealous tyrant madly strove,
The Infant flying to his Mother
Clung to her side with trembling love.

'O Mary help,' he crieth ever,
And weeps full loud and bitterly,
' Help, Mary, help : desert me never
O dearest Mother, rescue me.'

And as his arms so small and tender
More closely yet her neck enlace,
With piercèd heart his one defender
Locks him more fast in her embrace.

With fondest love her Boy caressing,
She seeks to soothe his childish pain,
And soon in hasty flight is pressing,
A refuge for her God to gain.

'O Mary, help,' he crieth ever,
As in her lap he seeks repose ;
' Help, Mary, help : desert me never,'
He pleadeth as his eyelids close.

'Tis thus so deeply is engraven
This cry for ever in her heart ;
'Tis thus that she is still our Haven,
Still holds a balm for every smart.

So often as this cry resoundeth
Against the bases of her throne,
She in all gracious help aboundeth,
Still mindful of her Little One.

This ready help and consolation,
Lo, thousands prove it day by day :
Wherefore from every clime and nation,
' Help, Mary, help,' shall sound for aye.

Triolet.

MARY, JOSEPH AND JOHN, EXEMPLARS TO MAN.

PATRICK CAREY: c. 1651.

FROM 'TRIVIAL POEMS,' EDITED BY SIR WALTER SCOTT, BART., 1820.

CHRIST IN THE CRADLE.

LOOK, how he shakes for cold:
How pale his lips are grown:
Wherein his limbs to fold
Yet mantle has he none.
His pretty feet and hands—
Of late more pure and white
Than is the snow that pains them so—
Have lost their candour quite.
His lips are blue—where roses grew—
He's frozen everywhere:
All th'heat he has, Joseph, alas,
Gives in a groan, or Mary in a tear.

CHRIST IN THE GARDEN.

Look, how he glows for heat:
What flames come from his eyes:
'Tis Blood that he does sweat,
Blood his bright forehead dyes.
See, see, it trickles down;
Look, how it showers amain:
Through every pore his Blood runs o'er,
And empty leaves each vein.
His very Heart burns in each part;
A fire his breast doth sear:

For all this flame to cool the same
He only breathes a sigh and weeps a tear.

CHRIST IN HIS PASSION.

What bruises do I see :
What hideous stripes are those :
Could any cruel be
Enough to give such blows?
Look, how they bind his arms
And vex his soul with scorns ;
Upon his hair they make him wear
A crown of piercing thorns.
Through hands and feet sharp nails they beat ;
And now the cross they rear :
Many look on ; but only John
Stands by to sigh, Mary to shed a tear.

MORAL TO MAN.

Why did he shake for cold?
Why did he glow for heat?
Dissolve that frost he could ;
He could call back that sweat.
Those bruises, stripes, bonds, taunts,
Those thorns which thou didst see,
Those nails, that cross, his own life's loss,
Why, oh why, suffered he?
'Twas for thy sake. Thou, thou didst make
Him all those torments bear :
If then his love do thy soul move,
Sigh out a groan, weep down a melting tear.

G

A Trio for Twelfth-Night.

HENRY BERNARD CARPENTER:
1840—1890.

FROM 'A POET'S LAST SONGS,' BOSTON, 1891.

The Author was born in Dublin, and died at Sorrento,
Maine, U.S.A.

WHO first brought man the morning dream
Of a world's hero? Whence the gleam
Which grew to glory full and sweet,
As the wide wealth of waving wheat
  Springs from one grain of corn?
What drew the spirits of earth's grey prime
To lean out from their tower of time
Tow'rd the small sound of Hope's far chime
  Heard betwixt night and morn?

First it was sung by heaven; then scrolled
By the scribe-stars on leaves of gold
In that long-buried book of Seth,
Which slept a secret deep as death,
  Unknown to men forlorn,
Till a seer touched a jasper lid
In a sand-sunken pyramid,
And out the oracular secret slid
  Betwixt the night and morn.

Zarathustra, Bactria's king, next said:
'When in the sky's blue garden-bed
A Lily-petalled Star shall fold
A Human Shape, the Gift foretold
  Shall blossom and be born:

Then shall the world-tides flow reversed,
New gods shall rise, the last be first,
And the best come from out the worst,
 As night gives birth to morn.'

So while the drowsed earth swooned and slept,
Mute holy men their vigils kept,
By twelve and twelve : as light decayed
They marked through evening's rosy shade
 The .curled moon's coming horn,
All stars that fed in silent flock
And each tossed meteor's back-blown lock :
So watched they from their wind-swept rock
 Betwixt the night and morn.

Slow centuries passed : at last there came
By night a dawn of Silver Flame,
Whose flower-like heart grew white and round
To a smooth perfect pearl, with sound
 Of music planet-born,
In whose clear disk a Fair Child lay,
And ' Follow Me,' was heard to say—
Round him the pale stars fled away
 As night before the morn.

Forthwith from morning's crimson gate
The Three Kings rode in morning state
Across Ulaï's storied stream ;
With westward wistful eyes agleam
 As pilgrims westward borne,
They left the tide to sing old deeds—
The stork to plash half-hid in reeds—
A thousand spears, a thousand steeds,
 They rode 'twixt night and morn.

   * * *

Twice fifty sennights o'er them bent
The fierce blue weight of firmament:
Through sea-like sands they still pursued
The unsetting Star until it stood
    Above where, travel-worn,
A new-made Mother smiled, whose head
Lay near the stalled ox, as she fed
Her Babe from her warm heart, on bed
    Of straw, 'twixt night and morn.

As day new-sprung from dropping day,
Near her in shrining light he lay
And made the darkness beautiful:
Couched on low straw and flakes of wool
    From Bethlehem's lambs late-shorn,
He seemed a Star which clouds enfold,
Swathed with soft fire and aureoled
With sun-born beams of tender gold,
    The Very Star of Morn.

At her Son's feet the Kingly Three
Laid, with bowed head and bended knee,
Their gold and frankincense and myrrh,
Nor tarried—so the interpreter
    Of God's dream once did warn—
But hied them home ere the day broke;
While without awe the neighbour folk
Flocked to the door and looked and spoke,
    Betwixt the night and morn.

    *   *   *

A shepherd spake: 'Behold the Lamb,
Who ere he reign as Heaven's I Am
Must undergo and overcome,
As sheep before the shearers dumb,
    Unfriended, faint, forlorn:

Him then as King the skies shall greet,
And with strewn stars beneath his feet
This Lamb shall couch in God's gold seat,
    And rule from night to morn.'

A woman of the city came,
Who said: ' In me hope conquers shame:
Four names in this Child's line shall be
As signs to all who love like me—
    God pities where men scorn:
Dame Rahab, Bethsabee, forsooth,
Tamar, whose love outloved man's truth,
And she cast out, sweet alien Ruth,
    Betwixt the night and morn.'

Next Joseph, Spouse of Mary, came—
Joseph Bar-Panther was his name—
Who said: ' This Babe, Lord God, is thine
Only-begotten Son Divine,
    As thou didst me forewarn;
And I will stand beside his throne,
And all the lands shall be his own,
Which the sun girds with burning zone
    And leads from night to morn.'

Said Zacharias: ' Love and will
With God make all things possible:
Shall God be childless? God unwed?
Nay; see God's First-Born in this bed
    Which Kings with gifts adorn:
I would this Babe might be at least
As I, an incense-burning Priest,
Till all man's incense-fires have ceased
    Betwixt the night and morn.'

Whereat his wife, Elizabeth:
' My thoughts are on the myrrh, since death
Shades my sere cheek, which as a shore
Is wrought with wrinkles o'er and o'er:
    Now be this Child new-born
A Prophet, like my Prophet-boy—
A Voice to shake down and destroy
Throne, shrine, each carved and painted toy
    Betwixt the night and morn.'

But Mary, God's pure Lily, smiled:
' Lord, with thy Manhood crown my Child—
More Man, more God; for they who shine
Most human shall be most divine:
    Of those I think no scorn,
King, Prophet, Priest, when worlds began;
But higher than these my prayer and plan—
Oh, make my Child the Perfect Man,
    The Star 'twixt night and morn.'

The Building and Pinnacle of the Temple; and Translations.

E. M. CLERKE.

I. THE BUILDING AND PINNACLE OF THE TEMPLE.

I.

Not made with hands, its walls began to climb
  From roots in Life's foundations deeply set,
  Far down amid primeval forms, where yet
Creation's Finger seemed to grope in slime.
Yet not in vain passed those first-born of Time,
    Since each some presage gave of structure met
    In higher types, lest these the bond forget

That links Earth's latest to the fore-world's prime.
  And living stone on living stone was laid,
  In scale ascending ever, grade on grade,
To that which in its Maker's eyes seemed good—
  The Human Form : and in that shrine of thought,
  By the long travail of the ages wrought,
The Temple of the Incarnation stood.

II.

THROUGH all the ages since the primal ray,
  Herald of life, first smote the abysmal night
  Of elemental Chaos, and the might
Of the Creative Spark informed the clay,
From worm to brute, from brute to man—its way
  The Shaping Thought took upward, flight on flight,
  By stages which Earth's loftiest unite
Unto her least, made kin to such as they.
  As living link, or prophecy, or type
  Of purpose for fulfilment yet unripe,
Each has its niche in the supreme design ;
  Converging to one Pinnacle, whereat
  Sole stands Creation's Masterpiece—and that
Which was through her—the Human made Divine.

II. AVE, MARIA : AN ODE ON THE CHURCH OF POLENTA. (*c.* 1896.)

GIOSUÈ CARDUCCI.

HAIL, Mary, when upon the breeze doth sigh
  The lowly greeting, lesser folk attend
  With heads uncovered, while their foreheads high
              Dante and Harold bend

A long-drawn strain, as of flutes heard afar
From earth to heaven doth pass, where none can see,
By spirits breathed perchance, that were—that are—
Or that shall be.

A soft oblivion of the toil and stress
Of life, a pensive calm that thought o'ershades,
Desire of tears that hath no bitterness
The soul invades.

And beast and man are hushed with all below,
The sunset's rose melts in the azure pale,
And thrilling heights of ether whisper low,
Hail, Mary, hail.

NOTE.

Stanza I. Harold : Lord Byron ; in allusion to the Ave Maria
stanzas in ' Don Juan,' which are quoted in page 263 of the First
Series of ' Carmina Mariana.'

III. MARY'S REWARD.

VITTORIA COLONNA : 1490—1547.

With love how tender hath thy Son Divine
His choicest secrets oft to thee disclosed,
Mother most high ; and how in faith disposed
Didst thou go forward in his laws benign.

That Love supreme first in God's thought did shine,
Ere yet in fleshly circuit hemmed and closed,
And now in heaven with bondage reimposed
Of tie more firm and close your hearts doth twine.

In birth and death, and in his heavenward flight,
As help and comfort, Handmaid, Mother, Friend,
In lowly love thee did he still descry.

Now the sweet Spouse, the Father Infinite,
And loving Son do unto thee extend
The full reward of zeal inflamed so high.

IV. MARIS STELLA.

JOSÉ-MARIA DE HÉRÉDIA,
OF THE FRENCH ACADEMY.

'NEATH linen coifs, with folded arms devout,
Their wear rude wool or cotton slight, in dole,
The women kneeling on the rocky mole,
The Isle of Batz see Ocean blanch and flout :
Men, fathers, husbands, lovers, sons gone out
With those from Cancale, Audière, Paimpole,
Have northward sailed—a distant port their goal,
Ne'er to return, alas, those fishers stout.
'Bove clang of surf and shore, from the sad crowd,
Doth rise the plaintive song, invoking loud
The Blessed Star, the sailor's Hope and Weal ;
While o'er bronzed foreheads bent in rhythmic close,
From Roscoff's towers to those of Sybiril,
The Angelus peals faint in heaven's faint rose

V. CORONATION OF OUR LADY.

DON JUAN DE JAUREGUI :
XVII. CENTURY.

THOU art, O Virgin, a new Sphere of Light,
Wherein the Eternal Wisdom is made known ;
As in the sun and moon and stars that throne
Upon the Orient's threshold silver white.
   And the Almighty Craftsman hath bedight
A radiant crown with twelve bright stars thick-strown,
Like the twelve signs of Heaven's resplendent zone,
To gird the empyrean of thy brow's pure height.

An orb art thou, whose aspect shining fair,
No ray of baleful augury doth send,
Nor good with evil presage alternate ;
　And to him born beneath its influence rare
In virtue, it doth promise and portend
Of bliss and glory everlasting state.

VI. TO THE VIRGIN MARY, THE SECRET INVIOLATE LILY.

JOHANN SCHEFFLER (ANGELUS SILESIUS): 1624—1677.

Thou glorious Lily, who thy like hath spied,
Though all the fields of Paradise were tried ?
Thou shows't like snow, when on it in the spring
The gold of Phæton high heaven doth fling.
The sun and stars and moon near thee grow pale ;
Thine aspect is more radiant than e'er shone
In all his pride, the robe of Solomon.
Near thee the Seraphim their lightnings veil ;
Thy fragrance doth the world refresh, and all
That at God's feet in adoration fall.
In thee alone doth maiden beauty shine,
The crown of saints, the martyr's constancy—
Then glorious Lily, so refresh thou me
That I behold thee with thy Seed Divine.

VII. TO THE MADONNA.

GIACOMO ZANELLA.

Improvised (1897) in passing a rustic tabernacle between
Passagno and Asolo.

From this bold crag, that steadfast to the sky
　Doth tower above the torrent's arid bed,

Where a far age's faith hath reared on high
A gleaming shrine 'mid wilds untenanted,
Hear, Lady sweet, the pious hymn whose sigh
Upward to thee from burning hearts is sped ;
The young hearts' vow fulfil, to thee that cry,
By trust in thy maternal succour led.
And as this lofty peak which nought can shake—
Where prostrate we adore thee—doth the pride
Of the flood's rage in April stem and break,
So be our faith unshaken to resist,
And like this torrent—which we now see dried—
Dispersed the clouds of error's darkening mist.

On Christopher Columbus:

1445—1506.

I. THE VOYAGE OF COLUMBUS:

CANTOS VII. VIII. AND IX.

SAMUEL ROGERS: 1763—1855.

FROM ' POEMS,' 1839.

ARGUMENT.

Columbus, a person of extraordinary virtue and piety, acting
under the sense of a divine impulse, having obtained three ships,
sets sail on the Atlantic. The compass alters from its ancient
direction : the wind becomes unremitting : night and day he
advances, until stopped by a mass of vegetation, assuming the
appearance of a country overwhelmed by the sea. Meanwhile, a
mutiny ; but Columbus restores order ; continues his voyage ; and
lands in a New World. (Author.)

SILENT with sorrow, long within his cloak
His face he muffled—then the Hero spoke :

*   *   *

'Grant but three days': he spoke not uninspired;
And each in silence to his watch retired.

*   *   *

Twice in the zenith blazed the orb of light;
No shade, all sun, insufferably bright:
Then the long line found rest—in coral groves
Silent and dark, where the sea-lion roves—
And all on deck, kindling to life again,
Sent forth their anxious spirits o'er the main.
'Oh, whence, as wafted from Elysium, whence
These perfumes, strangers to the raptured sense?
These boughs of gold and fruits of heavenly hue,
Tinging with vermeil light the billows blue?
And (thrice, thrice blessed is the eye that spied,
The hand that snatched it sparkling in the tide)
Whose cunning carved this vegetable bowl,
Symbol of social rites and intercourse of soul?'
Such to their grateful ear the gush of springs,
Who course the ostrich as away she wings.
Sons of the desert, who delight to dwell
'Mid kneeling camels round the sacred well;
Who, ere the terrors of his pomp he passed,
Fall to the demon in the reddening blast.

*   *   *

The sails were furled: with many a melting close,
Solemn and slow the evening-anthem rose—
'Salve, Regina, Mater misericordiæ;
Ad te clamamus, exules filiæ Hevæ'—
Rose to the Virgin.   'Twas the hour of day
When setting suns o'er summer-seas display
A path of glory, opening in the west
To golden climes and islands of the blest;

And human voices on the silent air
Went o'er the waves, in songs of gladness there.

Chosen of men, 'twas thine, at noon of night,
First from the prow to hail the glimmering light;
(Emblem of Truth divine, whose secret ray
Enters the soul and makes the darkness day)

'Piedro; Rodrigo; there, methought, it shone,
There—in the west; and now, alas, 'tis gone.
'Twas all a dream: we gaze and gaze in vain—
But mark and speak not, there it comes again:
It moves; what form unseen, what being there
With torch-like lustre fires the murky air?
His instincts, passions, say, how like our own?
Oh, when will day reveal a world unknown?'

*   *   *

Long on the deep the mists of morning lay,
Then rose, revealing as they rolled away
Half-circling hills, whose everlasting woods
Sweep with their sable skirts the shadowy floods;
And say, when all, to holy transport given,
Embraced and wept as at the gates of heaven,
When one and all of us, repentant, ran,
And, on our faces, blest the wondrous Man.
Say, was I then deceived, or from the skies
Burst on my ear seraphic harmonies?
'Glory to God,' unnumbered voices sung;
'Glory to God,' the vales and mountains rung—
Voices that hailed Creation's primal morn,
And to the shepherds sung a Saviour born.

*   *   *

Slowly, bare-headed, through the surf we bore
The sacred Cross, and kneeling, kissed the shore.

NOTES.

Line 24: The reddening blast: the Simoon.
Line 27: I remember one evening, says Oviedo, when the ship was in full sail, and all the men were on their knees, singing 'Salve, Regina.'

II. THREE SONNETS TO CHRISTOPHER COLUMBUS.

BENJAMIN D. HILL, C.P.
(FATHER EDMUND OF THE HEART OF MARY)

FROM 'MARIÆ COROLLA,' 1898.

I.

GOD chose thee out, O Man of faith and prayer,
    And sent thee o'er the deep—if truth be told.
    Neither ambition's greed nor lust of gold
Could make thy heart so confidently dare.
'The boldest steer,' the poet saith, 'but where
    Their ports invite.'   Yet thou, divinely bold,
    Didst little reck what wrathful billows rolled
'Twixt thee and shores imagined—havens fair
Which seemed to lesser minds the veriest 'stuff'
    That 'dreams are made of.'
                                  Into the vast unknown
Thou wentest forth—in steadfast hope, alone.
But God was with thee: for thy peace enough.
His breezes served thee; and when seas were dark,
His stars more surely led thy destined bark.

II.

AYE, and for thee a Star shone all the way
  Which others would not see—the Queen of Stars;
  Brighter than Venus, Jupiter and Mars
In one ; and clearest 'mid the blaze of day :
The Ocean Star, whose sweetly constant ray
  Smiled calmness on a brow no petty jars
  Could vex—a brow where pain had printed scars
Which told of vanquished self through years of fray.
Thy soul, uplifted ever to the light
  Of that true Guide whose name thy vessel bore,
Took her for pilot.   Morning, noon and night,
  To her thine 'Aves' rose : and more and more
Thy trust increased, the sullen crew despite—
  Their menace deadlier than the tempest's roar.

III.

BUT thou, Christ-Bringer to the new half-world,
  Christ-Bearer too, didst, with the Christ, his Cross
  Thy portion find.   Thy glory's earthly gloss
Scarce lasted till the home-bound sails were furled.
Ingratitude and envy swiftly hurled
  Their torches at thy fame.   But was it loss
  They wrought thee ? Nay, a merit purged of dross.
For this those lurid flames so fiercely curled.
And when had past the years that seemed so long,
  And came our Lady with a call to rest,
She led thy spirit through the sainted throng
  To where her Son reigns Monarch of the Blest ;
And he bestowed, in meed of suffered wrong,
  A richer realm than thy discovered West.

III. THE FATE OF COLUMBUS.

HENRY NUTCOMBE OXENHAM, M.A.:
1829—1888.

FROM 'THE SENTENCE OF KAÏRES,' 1854.

And was it all for this—
    to see his fondest hopes belied,
His name reviled, his every prayer denied
Himself an outcast from his new-found home,
His glory's meed a traitor's shameful doom. (Author.)

SUCH are the thoughts (might skill of mine presume
To read aright that sullen brow of gloom),
The musings such of anguish and unrest
That vex the captive Hero's fevered breast ;
Pressed through the lips, though pride enchain the
        tongue,
Words burn within to speak the spirit's wrong :
' Darkly, oh, darkly lowers the coming night,
From leaden skies fast fades the quivering light
Whose faithless dawn but now allured me on
To glorious deeds which cannot be undone.
Woe worth my country, since the sons of Spain
Guerdon Columbus with the felon's chain.
Woe worth the unequal law that matched in strife
The rival forces that divide our life,
Where love and hate alternate, good and ill,
Control the drift of man's ignoble will.
And what is man ?   Vile creature of a day,
Degenerate mass of animated clay,
Cursed with a soul that shall not, cannot die,
Heir of a hopeless immortality ?
Avaunt thee, Fiend.   Wild pangs my bosom tear,
Reels my sick brain all maddening with despair,

No kindly spell the agony to charm,
In heaven no ray, on earth no soothing balm.
To thee, Blest Maid, I turn.   When dark and drear
Fortune frowned on me, thou wast ever near,
With smile undimmed, with soft unclouded brow,
Mother of God, thou wilt not leave me now?
And One there is, one mild angelic form,
Seen through the mist-wreaths of the gathering storm
A Child of earth, of more than queenly grace,
More than a Queen, though sprung of queenly race ;
Her thought shall woo my angry tongue to bless
When it would curse men for their heartlessness.'

Dwells there a mystic spell, a power unseen
Shrined in the memory of that saintly Queen?
Or deigns the Virgin list her suppliant's prayer,
And lull to sleep the ravings of despair?
Lost in the dream of earlier, happier hours,
He roams once more through Genoa's myrtle bowers ;
Again he sports beneath the cypress shade,
Threads the dark grove, or high-arched colonnade,
Or rifles Nature's store for each bright gem
That helps to wreathe his flowery diadem,
Or prescient of the future, loves to guide
His mimic pinnace o'er the flashing tide,
Scanning even then with boyhood's eager glance
The rolling Ocean's infinite expanse,
No minstrel lay, no music half so dear
As the loud breakers to his listening ear.

NOTE.

Line 29 : And One there is ; Isabella of Castile.

H

Contemporary Poems.

I. LORETO PETITIONS.

ALEXANDER BAUMGARTNER, S.J.

TRANSLATED (1899) BY CHARLOTTE O'CONOR ECCLES.

FROM 'DIE LAURETEINISCHE LITANEI,' ROME, 1897.

I. HOLY MARY, PRAY FOR US.

OUR Mother's Name, more sweet than any singing,
Like heavenly music gently swelling, stealing
Upon our ears like Angels' voices, pealing,
Telling of joy, like Easter bells a-ringing.

Daily, nay hourly, that loved Name resounding,
That word of comfort will our spirits brighten ;
Midst life's fierce struggle will our courage heighten,
Like beacon set midst darkness all surrounding.

' Mary,' what treasures doth that word contain
Of love, of heavenly joy, eternal bliss,
Of song forth swelling like the boundless main :
What name of mortal hath such power as this ?
Upon the Angelic Greeting God might build
Whole worlds on worlds, all with thy praises filled.

II. COMFORT OF THE AFFLICTED, PRAY FOR US.

How many bitter tears are daily flowing
For faith betrayed, or poverty, or pain,
Or happiness outlived, repentance vain,
Or death : they run to swell a sea still growing.

Who pitying helps mankind their griefs to bear,
Griefs night and day bewailed by countless voices ?
Where is the heart that still in life rejoices,
Whose mirth is not out-balanced by its care ?

As thou didst fare towards Egypt once of old,
As thou with swords wast pierced the Cross beside
At Jesùs' grave thy hands in prayer didst fold,
Unlock the heavens, and pour thy pity's tide
On us 'gainst daily griefs for ever fighting,
With comfort's balsam all our souls delighting.

II. 'B.V.M. IN PURGATORIO.'

MATTHEW BRIDGES: 1800—1896.

Written by the Author in his eighty-eighth year.

I SAW our Lady on her Throne of Light,
  The Queen of Hades and the Queen of Heaven;
Ten thousand Seraphs, each a diamond bright,
  Moved at the voice of their archangels seven;
For Mary rose as God himself came down,
And placed upon her head a glorious Crown.

Then the pure pavement opened; and a Lake
  Of mingled love and fire its sheen displayed,
All full of souls, as yet who could not take
  Their rich reward till all the debt was paid;
Yet these too turned to Mary and the Lamb,
And praised the mercy of the Great I Am.

III. MADONNA: FOR A PICTURE BY 'FRANCESCA.'

WILLIAM P. COYNE.

FROM 'THE AVE MARIA,' 1890.

PENSIVE and sad, through sense of joy to be,
  Thine eyes full-flooded with the bliss of pain,
  And dawning on thy springtime lips the stain
Of those dear wounds that solved life's mystery;

O pure and Blessèd Maid, surely for thee
 The song of birds, the stream's sweet, wordless strain,
 The golden splendour of the ripening grain,
Brought thoughts of thy Divine Maternity.

So breaks the morn of days that never set,
 On lands untouched by Time's brief rhapsody,
  With flushes of a far-time sorrow in the sky,
 And dreamy drifts of clouds anear the sea,
  That ever pale, yet aye seem loth to die,
Like virgin hopes that know not sorrow yet.

IV. OUR LADY OF THE SACRED HEART.

AUGUSTA THEODOSIA DRANE,
(*MOTHER FRANCIS RAPHAEL, O.S.D.* 1823—1894).
FROM 'SONGS IN THE NIGHT,' 1876.

O Lily, budding from the root of Kings,
 Close well thy silver wings
 Upon their royal stem,
And keep with jealous care thy ruby Gem.

Choicest of Vines, thy Fruit of purple hue
 From thee its Life-blood drew ;
 Thy branches nearer give,
That we that ruddy Wine may taste and live.

Lady and Mother of the Sacred Heart,
 Wilt thou its love impart,
 As on the thornless Rose
In Sharon's vale the blushing buds unclose?

Kings once from Saba came thy Son to greet,
 And kneeling at thy feet,
 Adoring homage paid
To Jesus on his Mother's bosom laid.

Then to thy heart his Heart all trembling hold;
    He will to thee unfold
    His love's deep mystery,
And we will come and learn it all from thee.

O Sacred Heart, cleft Rock whence waters flow
    To the parched world below,
    Shelter when sin alarms;
We seek thee ever in thy Mother's arms.

When on the Cross the cruel spear pierced deep,
    Her station she would keep,
    And in those arms displayed
To a cold world the Wound that love had made.

Oh, ever be it thus. On Mary's breast
    Enthroned we see thee best:
    Still be they stretched to save,
Those blessed hands that first our Treasure gave.

V. THOUGHTS WHILE READING HISTORY.

FREDERICK WILLIAM FABER,
OF THE ORATORY, D.D.: 1814—1863.

FROM 'POEMS,' 1856.

I. CHIVALROUS TIMES.

BEAUTIFUL times, times past; when men were not
The smooth and formal things they are to-day;
When the world, travelling an uneven way,
Encountered greater truths in every lot,
And individual minds had power to force
An epoch, and divert its vassal course.
Beautiful times, times past; in whose deep art,
As in a field by angels furrowed, lay
The seeds of heavenly beauty, set apart
For altar-flowers and ritual display.

Beautiful times ; from whose calm bosom sprung
Abbeys and chantries, and a very host
Of quiet places upon every coast,
Where Christ was served and Blessed Mary sung.

II. OUR LADY IN THE MIDDLE AGES.

I LOOKED upon the earth : it was a floor
For noisy pageant and rude bravery—
Wassail and arms and chase among the high,
And burning hearts uncheered among the poor,
And gentleness from every land withdrew.
Methought that beds of whitest lilies grew
All suddenly upon the earth in bowers ;
And gentleness, that wandered like a wind,
And nowhere could meet sanctuary find
Passed like a dewy breath into the flowers.
Earth heeded not ; she still was tributary
To kings and knights, and man's heart well-nigh failed ;
Then were the natural charities exhaled
Afresh from out the blessed love of Mary.

VI.   SONNETS.

JOHN GRAY.

I.   OUR BLESSED LADY.

FROM THE PRIVATELY PRINTED 'BLUE CALENDAR,' 1897.

MOTHER of Sovereign Mercy, who didst bear
By faith the Pearl of Life, the Hope of Men,
The Conqueror, the Lily of the Glen,
The Rose of Beauty most exceeding fair.

Strengthen our prayers, who art Incarnate Prayer,
To him who answers prayer ; and even when
We think not of thee, have us in thy ken ;
Oh, shield us when we wander unaware.

Give us to love thy Son as thou didst love;
Assure us faith like thy faith; give us hope
In thy entreaties for us lest we fail.

We walk in darkness we know not of;
A bitter path is ours, in which we grope
Pitiable, unless thy prayers avail.

II. THE ASSUMPTION.

*TRANSLATED FROM THE SPANISH OF PEDRO
ESPINOSA.*

FROM 'SPIRITUAL POEMS,' 1896.

In turquoise-hued and sunset-coloured cloud,
Within the wide imperial palaces,
Where many a white torch and candle is,
The sovereign pages of the Emperor crowd.

Shafts of a thousand fragrances are proud
To mix with amaranth and lilies' fees,
Assyrian gums and Indian incenses,
On carpets deeply piled and furbelowed.

Her mantle is the sun; the moon between
Her feet, the Virgin greets the imperial hall.
(So hoped for, this, the coming of the Queen.)

Before her feet the mighty seraphs fall
Whom joyous chorals of the angels praise.
Beside the Holy Word she takes her place.

VII. SONG TO THE IMMACULATE VIRGIN.

HUGH HARKIN: 1791—1854.

FROM 'THE BULLETIN,' 1852.

Hail to thee, hail to thee, Queen of the Morning;
Hail to thee, hail to thee, Star of the Sea;
Graces conferred and repentance returning,
All owe their potence and virtue to thee;

Sitting apart on a throne ever-beaming,
Glory encircled—the Link that combines
Man with the Deity—Spring of all piety,
Spirit that softens and Love that refines.

Hail to thee, hail to thee, Ark of the Covenant,
Bearing the Manna from Heaven that came ;
Hail to thee, First in the Scheme of Redemption,
Brightest in Holiness, Highest in Name ;
Loved from Eternity, rendered Immaculate,
Sealed, set apart in the spring of thy youth ;
Honoured Virginity, Shrine of Divinity,
Mirror of Justice and Temple of Truth.

Hail to thee, hail to thee, Mother of Mercy ;
Hail to thee, hail to thee, Strength of the weak ;
Patience in trial and shrinking humility
Flow in our souls through thy spirit so meek ;
Wrapped in the blaze of his Love ever glowing,
Graces dispensing, abandoning none—
Sacred Maternity through all eternity—
Pray for the weak to thy merciful Son.

VIII. TWO SONNETS.

WILLIAM HENRY KENT, O.S.C.

I. TO MARY IMMACULATE. (1877.)

E'EN as a little child by darkness frightened
Feels in its helplessness a strange dismay ;
Its mother comes, and lo, its heart is lightened,
Her presence chases all its fear away :
So Mary, Mother, spotless in the night
Which sin and sorrow make this life of mine,
Let thy sweet face beam on me with its light,
And in my darkness like a beacon shine.

Oh, come, sweet Mother, come and dry my tears ;
In all my troubles, let me turn to thee ;
Free me from all vain doubts, all idle fears ;
Make me what Jesus wills that I should be.
Come, Mother, come, and make my sorrows cease,
And bring me confidence in thee, and peace.

II. OUR LADY OF PERPETUAL SUCCOUR. (1878.)

OH, ever help me, Mother mine,
And ask thine Infant Jesus for the grace
Which I do need : see, with a beaming face
He places both his little hands in thine ;
As while his eyes with tender mercy shine,
He gives all gifts and graces unto thee,
That with them thou mayst ever succour me,
And keep me ever his, and ever thine ;
And lead me onward, Mother, through the night
Of fear and sorrow, to that endless day
Where reign true peace and never fading light,
And love and happiness that ne'er decay.
Then, when the night is past, and then alone
Will all thy loving care for us be known.

IX. 'UNTO US A SON IS GIVEN.'
ALICE MEYNELL.

FROM THE 'WEEKLY REGISTER,' 1897.

GIVEN, not lent,
And not withdrawn—once sent—
This Infant of Mankind, this One,
Is still the little welcome Son.

New every year,
New born and newly dear,
He comes with tidings and a song,
The ages long, the ages long.

Even as the cold
Keen winter grows not old,
As childhood is so fresh, foreseen,
And spring in the familiar green.

Sudden as sweet
Come the expected feet ;
All joy is young, and new all art,
And he, too, whom we have by heart.

X. 'THERE WAS NO ROOM FOR THEM IN THE INN.'

AGNES REPPLIER.

FOOTSORE and weary, Mary tried
Some rest to find ; but was denied.
'There is no room,' the blind ones cried.

Meekly the Virgin turned away,
No voice entreating her to stay :
There was no room for God that day.

No room for her, round whose tired feet
Angels are bowed in transport sweet,
The Mother of their Lord to greet ;

No room for him, in whose small hand
The troubled sea and mighty land
Lie cradled like a grain of sand.

No room, O Babe Divine, for thee,
That Christmas night ; and even we
Dare shut our hearts and turn the key.

In vain thy pleading Baby-cry
Strikes our deaf souls : we pass thee by,
Unsheltered 'neath the wintry sky.

No room for God : O Christ, that we
Should bar our doors, nor ever see
The Saviour waiting patiently.

Fling wide the doors. Dear Christ, turn back :
The ashes on my hearth lie black :
Of light and warmth a total lack.

How can I bid thee enter here,
Amid the desolation drear
Of lukewarm love and craven fear ?

What bleaker shelter can there be
Than my poor heart's tepidity,
Chilled, wind-tossed as the winter sea ?

Dear Lord, I shrink from thy pure eye :
No home to offer thee have I :
Yet in thy mercy, pass not by.

XI. AVE, MARIA.

DORA SIGERSON SHORTER.

FROM 'VERSES,' 1893.

IN the darkness of night I toss and weep ;
Dread shapes crowd around me, I cannot sleep ;
       Ave, Maria, hear my cry.
Love that must separate, Death that takes all,
Come in the darkness with shuddering footfall ;
       Ave, Maria, hear my cry.
Stern seems the face of the Lord and turned away,
For my prayerless night and my deedless day ;
       Ave, Maria, hear my cry.
Thou art meek and full of mercy, pray for me ;
He will listen to my prayer for love of thee ;
       Ave, Maria, hear my cry.

Say that the world's dust was in my eyes ;
Say that my ears were deaf with city cries ;
  Ave, Maria, hear my cry.
Say that man and beast so questionèd,
That on the cross he hung beloved, but dead ;
  Ave, Maria, hear my cry.
In the darkness of night I toss and weep ;
All that I am not wakes my soul from sleep ;
  Ave, Maria, hear my cry.

XII. DOMUS AUREA.

ELINOR MARY SWEETMAN.

FROM 'THE IRISH MONTHLY,' 1897.

' O Lord of Hosts, how lovely are thy Tabernacles.'

I.

ALL beauty and all joy are tents of God
Spread in the wilderness. Love's sanctities
Embowering with lost leaves of Paradise
Brief days and sweet, a song, an April sod,
Make for the spirit heavenly abode
Wherein to rest—yea, often as he lies,
Come dreams of angels, and the pilgrim cries :
'The Lord of Hosts was in the place I trod ;
I knew it not.'
   But soon these wings of Heaven
Lift them and vanish from the cloudy stair ;
Sweet seasons wane, and love's dear roofs are riven,
Leaving all life uncanopied and bare ;
Earth hides no Eden whence we are not driven,
Nor apple boughs without a warder there.

II.

YET lovely are thy tabernacles, Lord ;
Not all unhoused thy people.   Lo, one Shrine
Enduring, incorruptible, divine,
Pure Ark on earth of thine Eternal Word,
Must ever sanctuary to our prayers afford.
Here all is heaven, and all of heaven is mine ;
Here thou, O Holy Christ, didst first recline
While angels sang, and shepherd hosts adored.

O Virgin Mary, earthly as I am,
How shall I kneel where viewless seraphs wait,
How plead for shelter in that stainless breast,
Yet how live banished?   Mother of the Lamb ;
Refuge of sinners ; O Immaculate—
Here will I set up my everlasting rest.

Translation of Verses upon the Blessed Virgin.

ABRAHAM COWLEY: 1618—1667.

FROM 'WORKS,' 1681.

Written in Latin by the Right Worshipful Dr. A. (Walter Aston,
of Tixall, County Stafford) : 1580—1639.

Ave Maria.

ONCE thou rejoicedst, and rejoice for ever,
Whose time of joy shall be expirèd never.
Who in her womb the Hive of Comfort bears,
Let her drink Comfort's Honey with her ears.

You brought the Word of Joy in; which was born
An Hail to all; let us an Hail return.
From you God-save into the world there came;
Our echo Hail is but an empty name.

Gratia plena.

How loaded hives are with their honey filled,
From divers flowers by Chymic bees distilled:
How full the collet with his jewel is,
Which, that it cannot take, by love doth kiss:
How full the moon is with her brother's ray,
When she drinks up with thirsty orb the day:
How full of grace the graces' dances are,
So full doth Mary of God's Light appear.
It is no wonder if with graces she
Be full, who was full with the Deity.

Dominus tecum.

The fall of mankind under death's extent
The choir of blessed angels did lament,
And wished a reparation to see
By him, who Manhood joined with Deity.
How grateful should man's safety then appear
T'himself, whose safety can the angels cheer.

Benedicta tu in mulieribus.

Death came, and troops of sad diseases led
To th'earth, by woman's hand solicited:
Life came so too; and troops of graces led
To th'earth, by Woman's faith solicited.
As our Life's spring came from thy blessed womb,
So from our mouths springs of thy praise shall come.
Who did Life's blessing give, 'tis fit that she
Above all women should thrice blessed be.

Et benedictus Fructus ventris tui.

With mouth divine the Father doth protest,
He a good Word sent from his storèd breast;
'Twas Christ—which Mary, without carnal thought,
From the unfathomed depth of goodness brought;
The Word of blessing a just cause affords,
To be oft blessèd with redoubled words.

Spiritus Sanctus superveniet in te.

As when soft west-winds fan the garden-rose,
A shower of sweeter air salutes the nose:
The breath gives sparing kisses, nor with power
Unlocks the virgin-bosom of the flower.
So th' Holy Spirit upon Mary blowed,
And from her sacred box whole rivers flowed:
Yet loosed not thine eternal chastity,
Thy roses' folds do still entangled lie.
Believe Christ born from an unbruised womb,
So from unbruised bark the odours come.

Et Virtus Altissimi obumbrabit tibi.

God his great Son begat ere time began;
Mary in time brought forth her little Son.
Of double substance, one life he began—
God, without mother; without father, Man.
Great is the birth; and 'tis a stranger deed
That she no man, that God no wife should need.
A shade delighted the Child-bearing Maid,
And God himself became to her a Shade.
Oh, strange descent: Who is Light's Author, he
Will to his creature thus a Shadow be.
As unseen light did from the Father flow;
So did seen Light from Virgin Mary grow.

When Moses sought God in a shade to see,
The Father's Shade was Christ, the Deity.
Let's seek for day; flee darkness; whilst our sight
In light finds darkness, and in darkness light.

NOTE.

The original Latin of these 'Meditationes,' signed 'W. A.,' was
published in the 'Femall Glory' of Anthony Stafford, 1635, and
reprinted by Orby Shipley, M.A., in 1860. The translation was
found in Cowley's 'Works,' by Mr. Charles T. Gatty, and sent to
the Editor, who, after consulting Mr. Gillow's 'Bibliographical
Dictionary of English Catholics,' was enabled to name the author
and to connect the translator with the original. It may be added that
Walter Aston was one of the first baronets created by James I.;
and that he was reconciled with the Church when acting as
Ambassador in Spain, and was made the first Lord Aston of Forfar,
on his return to England, in 1625.

Cynewulf's 'Christ.'

AN ENGLISH EPIC OF THE VIII CENTURY.

A MODERN RENDERING (1892) BY ISRAEL GOLLANCZ, M.A.

THE NATIVITY.

I.

'THOU art the Wall-stone that the workers once
Rejected from the work. It well beseemeth thee,
That thou shouldst be the head of this great hall
And shouldst unite, with fastening secure,
The spacious walls of adamantine rock,
That throughout earth all things with sight endowed
May wonder evermore. O Prince of Glory,
Show now thy skill; reveal thy handiwork
Firm set in sovran splendour. Yea, leave anon

The opposing walls erect.   The work hath need now
That the Craftsman and the King himself should come,
And should restore the house which lieth waste
Beneath the roof.   He formed the body erst,
The limbs of clay.   Now shall he, Lord of Life,
Deliver from their foes this abject throng,
These wretched ones from terror, as he oft did.
O thou Ruler, and thou righteous King,
Thou Keeper of the keys that open life,
Bless us with victory, with a bright career
Denied unto another if his work be worthless.'

*　　*　　*

Verily he may say it, who speaketh truth,
That when the race of man was all depraved,
He came and rescued it.   Young was the Maiden,
A Damsel sinless, whom he chose as Mother.
It came to pass, without the love of man,
That the Bride was great by Child-conception.
Never before or after in the world
Was any meed of woman like to that :
It was a secret mystery of the Lord.
All ghostly grace o'erspread the realm of earth,
And many a thing became illumined then
Through life's Creator, teachings of ancient day,
Which lay concealed beneath the veil of night,
The sages' songs prophetic, ere the Ruler came,
Who speedeth on its course their every prayer,
If mortals will but praise full earnestly
Their Maker's name, as Wisdom biddeth them.

II.

' O Sovran Lady of the blissful skies,
Thou noblest Maid through all the realm of earth,

I

Of whom the ocean-dwellers e'er have heard,
Unfold the mystery come to thee from heaven ;
How thou didst in some wise receive increase
By Child-conception, and yet thou knewest not
Communion after human fashion.
Truly we have not heard that ever yet,
In days of yore, the like hath come to pass,
Such as thou in special grace receivedst,
Nor may we hope that it will ever chance
In future time.   Lo, the faith that dwelt in thee
Was worshipful, since thou didst in thy bosom bear
The Flower of Glory, and thy great Maidenhood
Was not destroyed.   All the children of men
As they sow in sorrow, so afterwards they reap ;
They bring forth death.'
                    Spake the Blessed Maiden,
Ever full of triumph, the Holy Mary :

' What is this wonder which ye wonder at,
And grievously bemoan 'mid lamentations,
Thou son, and thou daughter of Salem.
Ye ask full anxiously how I preserved
My Maidenhood, my troth, and yet became
Great Mother of the Creator's Son.   To men
The mystery is not known ; but Christ revealed
In David's kinswoman, beloved of him,
That the guilt of Eve is all concluded now,
The curses overthrown, and the lowlier sex
Is now made glorious.   Hope is vouchsafed,
That now for men and women equally
Blessing may for evermore abide
 Amid the harmony of angels high above,
With the Father of Truth, to all eternity.'

III.

MARY.

'ALAS, now, Joseph mine, thou child of Jacob,
Scion of David's stock, the glorious king,
Must thou forthwith renounce thy plighted troth,
And leave my love?'

JOSEPH.

'Too soon am I o'erwhelmed
With grievous care; too soon bereft of honour.
Forsooth, through thee have I heard many a word,
Many an agonising bitter taunt,
Many an insult. They revile me now
With words of bitter wrath. My soul is sad;
I must shed tears. God may easily
Heal the grievous sorrow of my heart,
And comfort me, forlorn. Alas, young Damsel,
Mary, Maiden.'

MARY.

'Why bemoanest thou,
And criest aloud, lamenting? Ne'er found I
A fault in thee, or any cause of blame
For evil done; and yet, thou speak'st such words
As thou thyself wert filled with every sin
And all transgression.'

JOSEPH.

'Too much misery
Have I received from this Conception.
How can I escape the hateful words,
Or how can I find any answer now
Against mine angry foes? 'Tis widely known,
That from the glorious Temple of the Lord

I joyfully received a Maiden pure,
Immaculate ; and now all this is changed,
Through whom I know not.   Neither availeth me,
To speak or to be silent.   Speak I the truth,
Then must David's Daughter suffer death,
Slain with stones ; yet, 'tis a harder lot
To conceal the crime, and to be doomed to live
A perjurer, henceforth loathed by all the folk,
Accursèd 'mong men.'

MARY.

            Then did the Maid unravel
The mystery so true, and thus she spake :

' Truly I say, by the Son of the Creator,
The Saviour of Souls, that yet I know not
In conjugal communion any man,
Anywhere on earth.   But, 'twas granted me,
When still a damsel young and in my home,
That Gabriel, Heaven's Archangel, bade me Hail,
And said in very truth, that Heaven's Spirit
Should with his ray illume me, that I should bear
Life's Glory, an Illustrious Son, the mighty Child
Of God, the bright Creator.   Now, without guilt,
Am I become his Temple ; the Spirit of Comfort
Hath dwelt within me.   Wherefore dismiss thou now
All sorry care, and say eternal thanks
To the Lord's great Son, that I became his Mother,
Nathless a Maiden still ; and thou, I ween,
Art named his earthly Father, should the prophecy
Become fulfilled aright in him himself.'

Laus Reginae: in Twelve Triolets.

INIGO PATRICK DEANE: 1860—1894.

The Author was born in Dublin, and died at Yonkers-on-the-Hudson, U.S.A.

FROM 'THE IRISH MONTHLY,' 1897.

AN APOLOGY.

As a gleaming, white pearl in its shell,
　　Lies the thought or the wish in the triolet.
'Tis as slight—but 'tis precious as well,
As a gleaming, white pearl in its shell,
Or the note of a silvern bell,
　　Or the scent of a springing violet.
As a gleaming, white pearl in its shell,
　　Lies the thought or the wish in the triolet.

REGINA ANGELORUM.

O sweet, O strong, O glorious hymn
　　To the Queen of the Ninefold Choir.
Hark to the rich-toned Seraphim:
O sweet, O strong, O glorious hymn,
Thrilled with the love of the Cherubim,
　　With the Virtues' peace, with the Powers' desire
O sweet, O strong, O glorious hymn
　　To the Queen of the Ninefold Choir.

REGINA PATRIARCHARUM.

Grave and magnificent-souled,
　　They rejoice in the light of her face.
One thought in their hearts they enfold—
Grave and magnificent-souled—

She has held whom the world cannot hold
  In her womb, she, the Child of their race.
Grave and magnificent-souled,
  They rejoice in the light of her face.

REGINA PROPHETARUM.

O Singers of God, whose songs inspired
  Foretold your Queen in the dawn of time,
She has borne him at last, the Long-Desired.
O Singers of God, whose songs inspired
Thrilled the world's heart, are your hearts not fired
  To praise her anew, in new songs sublime ?
O Singers of God, whose songs inspired
  Foretold your Queen in the dawn of time.

REGINA APOSTOLORUM.

From twelve white thrones with hearts aflame
  They rise, and pay her homage meet.
They rise and bless her holy name
From twelve white thrones with hearts aflame,
Mindful that in their hour of shame
  She was their Strength, their Refuge sweet.
From twelve white thrones with hearts aflame
  They rise and pay her homage meet.

REGINA MARTYRUM.

Oh, the waving palms, and the burning faces,
  And shining robes of the martyr-band
Chanting thy praise from their lofty places.
Oh, the waving palms, and the burning faces
That turn to thee through whom all graces
  Flow to men from God's right hand—
Oh, the waving palms, and the burning faces,
  And shining robes of the martyr-band.

REGINA CONFESSORUM.

They live with thy love in their heart;
  They die with thy name on their lips.
Ah, theirs is the better part;
They live with thy love in their heart.
Thrust aside in the world's fierce mart,
  Torn with the world's red whips.
They live with thy love in their heart;
  They die with thy name on their lips.

REGINA VIRGINUM.

Sweet Virgins, aureoled, white,
  Surround thee, O Lily of God.
Who are nearest thee, left and right?
Sweet Virgins, aureoled, white,
Whose lamps from thine took light,
  Whose feet where thine went trod.
Sweet Virgins, aureoled, white,
  Surround thee, O Lily of God.

REGINA SANCTORUM OMNIUM.

Louder and fuller, till God's vast domain
  Throbs with the passion of the mighty pœan.
Sing—ye, to whom life's loss was glorious gain,
Louder and fuller, till God's vast domain
Trembles.   Oh, ye that sadly and in pain
  Fought out life's battle, fill the empyrean
Louder and fuller, till God's vast domain
  Throbs with the passion of the mighty pœan.

REGINA SINE LABE CONCEPTA.

Perfect, stainless as a star
  From the hand of God new-springing.
No faintest clouds thy pure light mar—
Perfect, stainless as a star—

Regent of these skies, that far
  And near with this rare grace are ringing ;
Perfect, stainless as a star
  From the hand of God new-springing.

REGINA SANCTISSIMI ROSARII.

With love's red roses, O Queen, thy ways are sweet,
  And a crown of roses is better than gold or bay.
For their buds one March were bright at thy virgin feet—
With love's red roses, O Queen, thy ways are sweet—
At Elizabeth's door they opened, thy coming to greet.
  And they burst into perfect flower on Ephesus' day.
With love's red roses, O Queen, thy ways are sweet,
  And a crown of roses is better than gold or bay.

REGINA SOCIETATIS JESU.

We are thine own, thy belted Knights,
  Thy champions, Queen of Beauty and Love.
Thy banner we've borne through a thousand fights ;
We are thine own, thy belted Knights.
Thy dear voice cheers, thy dear face lights
  Our path as we ride to the Court above.
We are thine own, thy belted Knights,
  Thy champions, Queen of Beauty and Love.

Mary at the Mass of St. John at Ephesus: a Vision.

W. CHATTERTON DIX : 1836—1898.

FROM 'DAYS OF FIRST LOVE,' 1870.

The following extracts are made from an *In Memoriam* reprint of
the poem (1900), edited by the Author's friend, Conrad P. Fry.

In Ephesus, where men were wont of old
With cries to greet Diana, Goddess great,
I saw, in vision, her whose feet are placed
By Christian art upon the crescent Moon,
With Stars of Heaven for glory round her head,
Crowned, for her rank in virginal estate
With queenly crown, only less bright than his,
Who, King o'er all, has pleasure in her grace.
She more than Goddess, yet not gross as that,
Material, yet supernatural,
In that, unlike all other matrons, she
In her great Motherhood was free from stain :
Clear as the moon, for her no silver shrine
Was reared by hands impure with curious arts :
Herself a Palace, Tower of Ivory
Whose pureness mirrowed back the Grace of God :
Herself the Flower of all Virginity ;
Lily whose snowy petals know no spot ;
The Sanctuary's Gate Ezekiel saw
Shut, and by which no man may enter in
Because the Lord, the God of Israel,
By it hath entered in his majesty ;
Star of the Sea—for thus Saint Isidore
Interprets her sweet Name of whom

Jesus was born, the very Light of Light,
Born of her substance, he the Uncreate.

*   *   *

But now, with measured step and solemn mien,
Vested in white as snowy as the locks
Which crown with silver sheen the Apostle's brows,
Saint John ascends the Altar's sacred height,
There in the bloodless Rite, with eyes uplift
And hands upraised, to intercede for souls,
To plead the all-sufficient Sacrifice,
To feed his flock, and with them, breaking Bread,
Deal forth to each the Body of the Lord.
Yes, he was celebrant ; he who had leaned
On Jesus' Breast to learn deep Mysteries :
He whose great words about the Sacrament,
Breathed in his own Evangel, burn with love ;
He to whom Jesus, dying, gave for charge,
That Holy Mother at whose breasts he hung :
Oh, wondrous thought, that in this sacred Feast
Back to that Mother John could give her Son.
Then I heard the holy Creed, and the shout
Of all the faithful as they made belief
In God the Father, Son and Holy Ghost,
And the great verities of Christ's dear Spouse—
For in my vision times were all confused.

*   *   *

When they confessed that God was born on earth,
Suddenly, Angels, where the Mother knelt,
Lit up the place with strange unearthly glow :
One on her pallid brow a bright crown placed ;
One in her hand, a sceptre, sign of rule ;
While others gave her robes meet for a Queen.
Then I said, They honour her thus, because
From her pure womb the Bridegroom deigned to come.

And I asked, Is this sweet, Maidenly Queen
She who with bowed head knelt a while ago?
Is this the Mother with the sword-pierced heart?
Yea; it is she who smiles upon her Babe,
Who hears him in the Temple judge the wise,
Who watches him, her God, play with the boys
About the streets of Nazareth, sees him
In Joseph's shed, planing the rough wood's face,
Or feels his soft, fair cheek against her own,
Or hears him call her Mother, calls him Son.
Then, when the Saint of Love the Eucharist
Had consecrated, she arose and stood,
Mother of Sorrows again, mourning him
Whose Flesh was pierced, e'en in her sight for me.
I saw her once again uncrowned; no more
The sceptre glittered in her hand; her robe
Of queenly splendour lay upon the ground:
But as she went to take the Mysteries,
I saw that Angels still kept watch around
The spot where her apparel lay, haply
To guard from touch, even of saint, what Christ
Had given his Blessed Mother at the Feast.
Thus it appeared that, when our Lady rose
To take the Holy Body of her Son,
All queenly attire left her, and she went
In simple dignity of Womanhood,
With sorrowful face and reverent tread,
Yet with sweet grace of Virgin-purity;
The lowly Handmaid to her Lord and God,
The Mother of Fair Love to Love Itself:
She, far above the others, went as they
To feed upon the Holy Mysteries.

✻   ✻   ✻

Ah, I have thought, what if that stricken soul
Was so pierced through on Calvary's dreadful height,
That there, beneath her dying Son, she died :
That as she saw him in her arms lie cold,
Her heart was broken, and natural life
Was wrenched away, and that she moved about
Thenceforward in life supernatural,
The Life of him whose Holy Flesh and Blood
By his own hands in love to her were given,
And thus from time to time to be renewed,
Until he sent what looked to men like death ;
Sleep which he gave to his beloved, ere
Forth from the tomb in dark Gethsemane,
Where Blood still trickled round the olive's roots,
He, Lord of all the Living and the Dead,
Called her with him in highest Heaven to reign.

The Holy Mother at the Cross.

RICHARD W. DIXON, M.A.: 1833—1900.

FROM 'CHRIST'S COMPANY,' 1861.

Of Mary's pains may now learn whoso will,
    When she stood underneath the groaning tree
Round which the True Vine clung : three hours the mill
    Of hours rolled round : she saw in visions three
The shadows walking underneath the sun,
    And these seemed all so very faint to be,
That she could scarcely tell how each begun
    And went its way, minuting each degree
That it existed on the dial-stone :
    For drop by drop of wine unfalteringly,
Not stroke by stroke in Blood, the three hours gone
        She seemed to see.

Three hours she stood beneath the Cross : it seemed
    To be a wondrous dial-stone ; for while
Upon the two long arms the sunbeams teemed,
    So was the head-piece like a centre stile ;
Like to the dial where the judges sat
    Upon the grades, and the King crowned the pile,
In Zion town, that most miraculous plat
    On which the shadow backward did defile ;
And now, towards the third hour, the sun enorme
    Dressed up all shadow to a bickering smile
I' the heat, and in its midst the Form of form
        Lay like an isle.

Because that time so heavily beat and slow,
    That fancy in each beat was come and gone ;
Because that light went singing to and fro,
    A blissful song in every beam that shone ;
Because that on the flesh a little tongue
    Instantly played, and spake in lurid tone ;
Because that saintly shapes with harp and gong
    Told the three hours, whose telling made them one;
Half hid, involved in alternating beams,
    Half mute, they held the plectrum to the zone,
Therefore, as God her senses shield, it seems
        A dial-stone.

Three hours she stood beside the Cross ; it seemed
    A splendid Flower ; for red dews on the edge
Stood dropping ; petals doubly four she deemed
    Shot out like steel knives from the central wedge,
Which quadranted their perfect circle so
    As if four anthers should a vast flower hedge
Into four parts, and in its bosom, lo,
    The Form lay, as the seed-heart holding pledge

Of future flowers ; yea, in the midst was borne
　The head low drooped upon the swollen ledge
Of the torn breast ; there was the ring of thorn ;
　　This Flower was fledge.

Because her woe stood all about her now,
　No longer like a stream as ran the hour ;
Because her cleft heart parted into two,
　No more a mill-wheel spinning to time's power ;
Because all motion seemed to be suspense ;
　Because one ray did other rays devour ;
Because the sum of things rose o'er her sense,
　She standing 'neath its dome as in a bower ;
Because from one thing all things seemed to spume,
　As from one mouth the fountain's hollow shower ;
Therefore it seemed his and her own heart's bloom,
　　A splendid Flower.

Now it was finished ; shrivelled were the leaves
　Of that Pain-flower, and wasted all its bloom ;
She felt what she had felt then ; as receives,
　When heaven is capable, the cloudy stroom
The edge of the white garment of the moon ;
　So felt she that she had received that doom ;
And as an outer circle spins in tune,
　Born of the inner on the sky's wide room,
Thinner and wider, that doom's memories,
　Broken and thin and wild, began to come
As soon as this : Saint John unwrapt his eyes
　　And led her home.

The Sole Witness and other Poems.

ELEANOR C. DONNELLY.

I. THE SOLE WITNESS.

FROM 'THE AVE MARIA,' 1890.

O VANQUISHER of hell and heresy,
  Immortal in thy loveliness and youth ;
  O fair, strong Witness, Morning-star of Truth,
Archangel and apostle hail in thee
The voucher for God's greatest mystery :
  For on thy word, thy simple word alone,
Rests for all time, rests for eternity,
  The Incarnation's grand foundation-stone.

What tongue save thine could tell the Angel's story,
  Grave Gabriel's message to thy virgin ear?
Could shed o'er rapt Evangelist the glory
  Of secret words not given men to hear?
O Mary, whoso seeks to cast thee from thy throne,
Seeks from its mighty base to hurl Faith's corner-stone.

NOTE.

' Humanly speaking, Mary is the only witness to the Incarnation. The Apostles, unaided by revelation, could have learned from Mary alone of the Angel's Salutation, of the Most High overshadowing her ; and that what was born of her was the Son of God.   The greatest mystery of the Christian religion, then, rests, historically, on the testimony of Mary.' (From a Sermon by the Rev. D. I. McDermott, at the laying of the corner-stone of the Church of the Nativity of the B.V.M., Philadelphia, U.S.A.)

II. 'OUR LADY OF O.'

FROM 'THE AVE MARIA,' 1894.

O SEAT of Wisdom, glowing with the light
  Of the Most High, which through all space doth reach :
Come and dispose all things with sweetest might,
  And to thy sons the way of prudence teach.

O Mother of the Chief of Israel's house,
　Of the Adonai seen by Moses grave
In Fiery Bush and on the Mount of Laws,
　Bid him with outstretched arm his people save.

O Earth Immaculate, whence Jesse's Root
　Brought forth its Flower, signal luminous,
To whom the Gentiles pray—while kings are mute—
　Let him delay not to deliver us.

O Keeper of thy father David's Key,
　Which heaven's gate doth shut at will, or ope,
Guardian of Israel's sceptre, come and free
　The imprisoned captive ; flood death's gloom with hope.

O Morning Star, preceding with thy rays
　The Orient brightness of Eternal Light,
Our Sun of Justice, come, illume the ways
　Of all who sit in death and darkest night.

O Mother of the long-desirèd One,
　The Gentiles' King, joining in God's good time,
The two walls with his mighty Corner-stone,
　Pray him save those he formed from earthly slime.

O Mother of Emmanuel, our King,
　Lawgiver, Expectation and Reward
Of Gentiles, and their Saviour—Mary, bring
　Thy Son to save us ; bring our God, our Lord.

NOTE.

The Mozarebs called Our Lady in the ardour of her desires for the Incarnation, 'Our Lady of O.' The seven anthems of the Magnificat, which the Church sings during the seven days before Christmas, and which all begin with ' O,' refer to this (St. Jure).

III. ERAT SUBDITUS ILLIS.

FROM 'POEMS,' 1892.

STRANGELY sweet and Ever-blessed Mother,
    And thou, Saint Joseph, chosen of the Lord,
Unto your sacred feet we come to ponder
    The mystic meaning of this wondrous word.

Floats through our hearts the breath of Faith's Evangel :
    'Erat subditus illis'; God Most High
Was subject to his creatures. O blest Angels,
    Shield us beneath your pinions lest we die.

For lo, before our spirits self-complacent,
    Our wilful hearts so proud and uncontrolled,
The great, great mystery of self-abasement,
    Of deep, divine abjection is unrolled.

Eternal Power, subject unto weakness ;
    Eternal Wisdom, hidden, shrouded, dumb—
The Godhead's Glory, all its radiant sweetness,
    Veiled in the lowly shrine of Mary's home.

Oh, with what trembling awe thou must have spoken
    Thy meek commands, dear Mother, to that Son—
Thy Spouse's heart with love and fear nigh broken,
    Marking th' appointed tasks so promptly done.

Never a murmur from those Lips majestic—
    Whose ' Fiat ' through creation's chaos pealed—
The Father's Word uttered from everlasting,
    Is here a Wordless Mystery revealed.

Hither, ye souls, so full of self-reliance,
    Come to the little cot in Galilee,
And from this Master learn the matchless science
    Of deep, unquestioning humility.

J

Look on your Love, your gracious Elder-Brother—
  The God whose glories earth and heaven fill—
He stands before Saint Joseph and his Mother,
  Submissive, silent, docile to their will.

No miracles or marvels : how it thrills us
  To read the record of those Thirty Years :
Three little words, ' Erat subditus illis,'
  Tell the whole story : ponder it with tears.

Fierce in our bosoms rage the storms of passion,
  Our stubborn wills 'gainst God and man rebel :
' Non serviam,' we cry—our heaven-born reason
  Dimmed by the lurid clouds that rise from hell.

' Erat subditus illis ' : downward flutter
  The magic words, as from an angel's lips ;
And oil descends upon the troubled water ;
  And heavenly light illumes our dark eclipse.

O Heart of Jesus, wisest of all teachers,
  Blest be this work of thine omnipotence :
Ruler of all, yet subject to thy creatures,
  Thou art the crown of our obedience.

IV.   AT THE NEW MOON.

FROM ' THE AVE MARIA,' 1894.

THE slender Lady Moon hath drawn
  A veil about her face,
And through her sapphire courts hath gone
  With chaste and dreamful grace.
And treading closely in her wake,
  One little handmaid star
Across the night its way doth take
  To sky-realms fair and far.

O Lady Mary, thee we hail,
  New Moon of earth's dark night ;
No cloud thy virgin face can veil,
  Nor dim its changeless light.
Shining in regions fair and far,
  With radiant purity,
Oh, would I were thy handmaid star,
  To follow close to thee.

V. OUR LADY OF THE LAMP.

FROM 'A TUSCAN MAGDALEN,' 1896.

HER maiden face so grave and sweet
  Is full of gentle majesty ;
From curl-crowned Head to dimpled Feet,
  The Infant Christ is fair to see :
And on the Mother's left—behold,
  A Lamp of bronze, antique and quaint,
Whose wind-blown flame of fiery gold
  Glows like a gem 'mid shadows faint.

Her virgin hand that Lamp hath trimmed ;
  Beside its lustre, pure and mild,
Oft hath she wrought ; with rays undimmed,
  Oft held it o'er her sleeping Child ;
Or in the window of the room
  Hath set it, trembling like a star,
To cheer St. Joseph through the gloom
  And guide his footsteps from afar.

O gracious Lady of the Lamp,
  We too, like Joseph, need thy light ;
Our path is dim with shadows damp,
  We grope towards thee through the night :

The World's True Light is in thine arms;
 Ah, lift him high, and let him shine
Upon our darkness; naught alarms
 The soul which hails that Lamp Divine.

And when along the vale of Death,
 We journey slowly to our home,
The 'Home, sweet Home' of Christian faith,
 Which rears afar its azure dome:
Ah, leaning from the window's height,
 Swing forth thy Lamp across the gloom,
And lead us, Lady of the Light,
 Safe through the shadows of the tomb.

Early English Poems of the Fifteenth Century.

FROM THE PUBLICATIONS OF THE EARLY ENGLISH TEXT
SOCIETY: EDITED, FROM THE LAMBETH MSS., BY
F. J. FURNIVALL, M.A., 1866 AND 1867.

The text of No. I. may be found in 'Political, Religious, and
Love Poems'; and the text of No. II. is printed in 'Hymns to the
Virgin and Christ.'

I. QUIA AMORE LANGUEO: c. 1430.

THE VIRGIN'S COMPLAINT BECAUSE MAN'S SOUL IS
WRAPPED IN SIN.

MODERNISED (1896) *BY E. M. CLERKE.*

WITHIN a chamber of a tower,
 As musing on the moon stood I,
A Queen with honour crowned and power
 Methought I saw, enthroned on high.
She made her plaint with bitter cry,
 For soul of man by sin brought low:
I may not leave mankind to die,
  Quia amore langueo.

I look for love of man my brother,
And plead for him in every guise,
His Mother I, who can no other,
Why should I my dear child despise?
Though he offend me divers wise
Through fleshly frailty falling so,
Yet must I rue until he rise,
     Quia amore langueo.

I wait and bide with longing great;
I love and look till man shall crave;
I plain for pity of his state;
Would he ask grace, 'twere his to have:
Call on me, Soul, thee will I save;
Child, bid me come, and I will go;
Thou ne'er didst pray, but I forgave,
     Quia amore langueo.

Mother of Mercy I was made,
For thee who need'st it to illume:
More fain am I to grant its aid
Than ye to ask; why mute in gloom?
When said I nay? tell me to whom?
Ne'er yet, indeed, to friend or foe;
When ye ask not I weep your doom,
     Quia amore langueo.

O wretch on earth, I look on thee
And see thee trespass day by day,
With sin against my purity,
With pride against my meek array:
My love thee waits, wrath is away;
My love thee calls; from me wilt go?
I prithee, sinner, to me pray,
     Quia amore langueo.

My Son was outlawed for thy sin,
And scourged for trespasses of thine ;
It pricks my heart so near my kin
Should be so used.   Ah, son of mine,
Thy Father is the Son benign
My breast hath fed ; he loved thee so,
He died for thee ; my heart is thine,
        Quia amore langueo.

My Son hath suffered for thy love ;
His heart was piercèd with a spear ;
To bring thy soul to Heaven above
For love of thee so died he here.
Therefore thou art to me most dear,
Since my dear Son hath loved thee so ;
Thou ne'er dost pray, but I thee hear,
        Quia amore langueo.

My Son hath granted for thy sake
Each grace that I to ask am fain,
For he no vengeance wills to take,
If I for thee crave grace amain :
Then mercy ask, thou shalt obtain,
I with such ruth look on thy woe ;
I long for mercy thou shouldst plain,
        Quia amore langueo.

II.   VENI, CORONABERIS : c. 1430.

A SONG OF GREAT SWEETNESS FROM CHRIST TO HIS DAINTIEST DAM.

MODERNISED (1898) *BY WILLIAM MICHAEL ROSSETTI.*

Surge, mea Sponsa, sweet to sight,
And see thy Son thou gave suck so sheen ;
Thou shalt abide with thy Babe so bright,
And in my glory be called a Queen :

Thy breasts, Mother, full well I meen,
I had to my food that I might not miss ;
Above all creatures, my Mother clean,
    Veni, coronaberis.

Cleaner than crystal, come to my cage ;
Columba mea, I thee call ;
And see thy Son that in servàge
For man his soul was made a thrall :
In thy palace so principal
Privily played I, without miss ;
Mine high cage, Mother, have thou shall ;
    Veni, coronaberis.

For macula, Mother, was never in thee ;
Filia Syon, thou art the Flower ;
Full sweetly shalt thou sit by me
And bear a crown with me in tower ;
And all my Saints to thine honour
Shall honour thee, Mother, in my bliss,
That blessèd body that bear me in bower ;
    Veni, coronaberis.

Tota pulchra art thou to my pleasing,
My Mother, Princess of Paradise,
Of thee a water-full well 'gan spring
That shall for all my righteous rise ;
The well of mercy in thee, Mother, lies
To bring thy blessed body to bliss ;
To thee my Saints shall do service ;
    Veni, coronaberis.

Veni, Electa mea, chosen meekly,
Holy Mother and Maiden mild
On throne to sit seemly by him on high,
By him thy Son and eke thy Child :

Here, Mother, with me to dwell
With thy sweet Babe that sitteth in bliss,
Here in joy and bliss that ne'er shall miss ;
  Veni, coronaberis.

Veni, Electa mea, my Mother sweet ;
When thou bade me, Babe, to be full still,
Full goodly our lips then 'gan to meet,
With bright branches as blossoms on hill :
Favus distillans, it went with will
Out of our lips when we did kiss ;
Therefore, dear Mother, now full still
  Veni, coronaberis.

Veni de Libano, thou lovely in lanch
That wrapped me lovely with pleasant song,
Thou shalt abide with a blessed Branch
That so seemly of thy body sprung :
Ego, Flos Campi, thy Flower, was sold,
That on Calvary to thee cried, I wis ;
Mother, thou know'st this is as I wold ;
  Veni, coronaberis.

Pulchra ut Luna, thou bearest the Lam
As the sun that shineth clear ;
Veni in Hortum meum, thou daintiest Dam,
To smell my spices that mingle here :
My palace is dight for thy pleasure,
Full of bright branches and blossoms of bliss ;
Come now, Mother, to thy Darling dear,
  Veni, coronaberis.

Quid est ista, so virtuous,
That is everlasting for her meekness?
Aurora consurgens, gracious,
So benign a Lady, of such brightness ;

This is the Banner of human cleanness,
Regina Cœli, that ne'er did amiss:
Thus endeth the Song of great sweetness;
Veni, coronaberis.

NOTES.

I. 2. gave: so, in the original, and grammatical according to the usage of the age.
sheen: related to the German schön, tenderly.
5. meen: remember.

II. 1. cage: an enclosed space, a domicile, home; or more probably, metaphorically, a cage in which dwells the Columba.
3. servàge: slavery.
6. without miss: a phrase inserted, probably, for the sake of the rhyme, as we say 'and no mistake.'

III. 4. in tower: possibly a French phrase, 'en tour.' or 'à l'entour,' 'encircling thy head.'

VI. 2. bade: in the original bad; see note on I. 2.

VII. 1. lanch: possibly, leafage.
7. wold: would.

VIII. 1. Lam: in the original lam me (as the final word in line 3 is dam me), probably a form of the old word leam, light, which survives in our word gleam.
4. spices: cf. Song of Solomon, vi. 1, 'My Beloved is gone down to the bed of aromatical spices.'

Ode to the Immaculate Conception.

MAURICE FRANCIS EGAN,
CATHOLIC UNIVERSITY, WASHINGTON.

FROM 'THE AVE MARIA,' 1895.

Sweet, pure and fair beyond the Morning Star
When fleeing darkness makes the heavens black—
All purple-black before the dawn of day—
Sweet, pure and fair
As none was fair before,
Thou from afar,
Out of the fulgence of the Eternal Ray,
To earth brought'st back
The Gift our primal parents' sin had torn away.

Oh, mystery of the Fall : oh, hopeless lore
Of that deep sinfulness that could so snare
All beauty in the soul,
And need that thou shouldst the pure Mother be
Of the Great God :
Oh, depthless mystery :
The seed that swelleth in the mother-sod,
The child that groweth in the mother-breast,
The force that makes the ceaseless ocean roll,
The power that gives no earthly atom rest—
Force, light and heat,
All worldly things that be,
Are clear—to this.

Sin stole our bliss,
And turned God's lap into a judgment-seat ;
Sin changed the world,
From Eden hurled
The two whose malice gained Jehovah's wrath,
And made our path
Stormy and weary through this vale of tears ;
Yet through the years
Thou, Morning Star,
Predicted from afar,
Wert the resplendent House of God to be ;
Oh, Grace's mystery—
No aftermath,
But Spring-time's Blossom ; he
From the beginning crownèd thee—
Thou who the joy of Eden didst repeat,
Thou seal upon the truth that man is free,
Thou of all beings unto our Christ most dear.

How vile the sin :
How dread a thing of fear :

How ulcerous, how vile, how black and base,
How occult—and how alien to him
Who, Love Itself, created us for Love.
He bade us enter in
The portal of Joy's home,
Where Peace was dome
And Grace the word that made his world our home;
His chosen Vase:
Into man's soul he poured,
From his deep Heart above,
Splendour and power—
The splendour and the power of a King—
Till all the heavens thundered, tone on tone,
The splendour and the power of man—Love's
      Flower.

Oh, power flown,
By angels once adored,
Greater we
Than they through God's Love-mystery:
Ah, power lost;
Ah, splendour, beauty gone;
And innocence, a lily burned by frost;
And strength, a battered oak by wild winds torn—
Wild winds of passion:
In serpent fashion
Was every hope of life by dark things crossed,
And all earth's joys are like the bells forlorn
Heard at the day's sad dawn
When in our household one we love lies dead.

Here with this earth
That waits the Second Coming of her Lord,
With sun aglow and stars upheld in space,
And fires auroral and the flaming sword

Of summer light reflected—to his face
His Bride will fulgent greet him :
Here with this earth we wait
In the sweet hope to meet him,
With lighted hearts and clean souls all aflame.
Mary has wed
Our body unto his,
And he that is
Is man's own Mate,
Through her from whom the Infant had his birth,
And by whose meekness the Redeemer came—
Immaculate, Immaculate.

Poems from the Love-Songs of the Elizabethan Age.

PREFATORY.

The following poems, taken from amongst the purer and more spiritual of the Love-Songs of the English Renaissance, have been chosen on a principle which may be thus shortly stated. In accordance with the teaching of ancient Philosophy, as developed by certain Fathers and Schoolmen, Love, abstractedly, is the beginning, sustaining power and end of all things. 'In that philosophy the object of Love is "the Good"; the act of Love is the tendency or movement towards its attainment ; and in its secure attainment (says Father Bowden in his "Religion of Shakespeare," 1899) Love is perfected.' Now, in the concrete, the Blessed Virgin is the highest, purest and most perfect exemplar known to man of both the existence and the practice of human Love, which is only not divine. The authors quoted and the poems reproduced, from the age immediately succeeding the era of the Reformation in England, are the legitimate products of the old Catholic tradition and teaching on this subject. To these writers, more or less according to their Catholic proclivities, education, or birth, and in their written works, Mary was the One, Sinless and Ideal Woman ; and the thoughts which they conceived, and the lines which they composed in relation to Love, or in honour and praise of their Beloved—the mundane and imperfect reflection of their Ideal—were based, even if all unconsciously, or with only partial consciousness, upon the pattern of the great Mother of God. It has been thought, then, not inappropriate in this volume to make choice of some noteworthy specimens of these poems, which were highly esteemed at their date of publication, and may prove edifying in the present day. And in order that the selection may be the more congruous, it will be convenient to restore these verses, by a harmless retrospective application, to the august source by which they were inspired, and to refer them directly to the Lady, above all Women, from the contemplation of whose natural characteristics and supernatural prerogatives they originated. Of course, opinions will vary upon the policy of such a treatment of the poems in question : but the plan here adopted admits of a valid defence, and the reader is referred to the preface for further explanations. The comparison and contrast, however, between the divine creation and the human copy must not be pressed too closely ; and poetical license must be allowed to thought and word, in the replica of a personality which cannot, in fact, be absolutely repeated.

I. OF HIS DIVINE MISTRESS.

SONNET IX.

HENRY CONSTABLE : 1562—1613.

FROM 'POEMS AND SONNETS,' EDITED BY JOHN GRAY, 1897.

My Ladie's presence makes the Roses red,
   Because to see her lips they blush for shame ;
   The Lyllies' leaves, for envie, pale became
And her white hands in them this envie bred.
The Marigold the leaves abroad doth spred,
   Because the sunne's and her power is the same ;
   The Violet of purple cullour came,
Di'd in the blood shee made my hart to shed.

In briefe—all flowers from her their vertue take ;
   From her sweet breath their sweet smels do proceede ;
The living heate which her eye-beames doth make
   Warmeth the grounde and quickeneth the seede :
The raine wherewith shee watereth the flowers
Falls from mine eyes, which she dissolves in showers.

II. TO THE QUEENE OF MY LOVE, PRAYING.

WILLIAM HABINGTON : 1605—1654.

FROM 'ENGLISH REPRINTS,' EDITED BY EDWARD ARBER, 1895.

I saw Castara pray ; and from the skie
A winged legion of bright angels flie
To catch her vowes, for feare her Virgin-prayer
Might chance to mingle with impurer aire.
To vulgar eyes, the sacred truth I write,
May seeme a fancie.   But the eagle's sight
Of saints and poets miracles oft view,
Which to dull heretikes appeare untrue.
Faire zeale begets such wonders.   O divine
And purest Beauty ; let me thee enshrine
In my devoted soule, and from thy praise,
To enrich my garland, pluck religious bayes.
　　Shine thou the starre by which my thoughts
　　　　shall move,
　　Best subject of my pen, Queene of my love.

III. MY BELOVED IS 'FAIR, KIND AND TRUE.'

SONNET CV.

WILLIAM SHAKESPEARE : 1564—1616.

FROM 'POEMS,' EDITED BY A. DYCE, 1832.

LET not my love be called idolatry,
Nor my Belovèd as an Idol show,
Since all alike my songs and praises be
To one, of one, still such and ever so.
Kind is my Love to-day, to-morrow kind,
Still constant in a wondrous excellence ;
Therefore my verse to constancy confined,
One thing expressing, leaves out difference.

'Fair, Kind and True,' is all my argument,
'Fair, Kind and True,' varying to other words;
And in this change is my invention spent,
Three themes in one, which wondrous scope affords.
    'Fair, Kind and True,' have often lived alone,
    Which three till now never kept seat in one.

IV. SPIRITUALLY FAIRE AND SWEETE.

SIR PHILIP SIDNEY: 1554—1586.

FROM 'POEMS,' EDITED BY A. B. GROSART, 1873.

O FAIRE, O Sweete, when I do looke on thee,
  In whome all ioyes so well agree,
Heart and soule do singe in me.
  This you heare is not my tongue,   •
Which once said what I conceaued,
For it was of vse beareaued,
  With a cruell answer strong.
No ; though tongue to roofe be cleaued
  Fearing lest he chastised be,
  Heart and soule do singe in me.

O Faire, O Sweete, when I do looke on thee,
  In whome all ioyes so well agree,
Heart and soule do singe in me.
  Iust accord all musicke makes ;
In thee iust accord excelleth,
Where each part in such peace dwelleth,
  One of other, beautie takes.
Since then, truth to all mindes telleth
  That in thee liues harmonie,
  Heart and soule do singe in me.

O Faire, O Sweete, when I do looke on thee,
  In whome all ioyes so well agree.

Heart and soule do singe in me.
  They that heauen haue knowne do say,
That whoso that grace obtaineth,
To see what faire sight there raigneth,
  Forcèd are to sing alway :
So then, since that heauen remaineth
  In thy face, I plainly see,
  Heart and soule do singe in me.

O Faire, O Sweete, when I do looke on thee,
  In whome all ioyes so well agree,
Heart and soule do singe in me.
  Sweete, think not I am at ease,
For because my cheefe part singeth ;
This song from deathe's sorrow springeth,
  As to swanne in last disease :
For no dumbnesse nor death bringeth
  Stay to true louve's melody ;
  Heart and soule do singe in me.

V. THE SOVERAYNE BEAUTY.

SONNET III.

EDMUND SPENSER: 1553—1599.

FROM 'WORKS,' EDITED BY JOHN MITFORD, 1839.

THE Soverayne Beauty which I doo admyre,
Witnesse the world how worthy to be prayzed ;
The light whereof hath kindled heavenly fyre
In my fraile spirit, by her from basenesse raysed ;
That being now with her huge brightnesse dazed,
Base thing I can no more endure to view ;
But looking still on her, I stand amazed
At wondrous sight of so celestiall hew.
So when my toung would speak her praises dew,
It stoppèd is with thoughts' astonishment ;

And when my pen would write her titles true,
It ravisht is with fancies' wonderment :
    Yet in my hart I then both speak and write
    The wonder that my wit cannot endite.

VI. A VOW TO LOVE FAITHFULLY, HOW-SOEVER HE BE REWARDED.

HENRY HOWARD, EARL OF SURREY: 1516—1547.

FROM 'POEMS,' ALDINE EDITION, 1831.

SET me whereas the sun doth parch the green,
Or where his beams do not dissolve the ice ;
In temperate heat where he is felt and seen ;
In presence prest of people, mad or wise ;
Set me in high, or yet in low degree ;
In longest night, or in the shortest day ;
In clearest sky, or where clouds thickest be ;
In lusty youth, or when my hairs are gray ;
Set me in heaven, in earth, or else in hell ;
In hill, or dale, or in the foaming flood ;
Thrall, or at large, alive whereso I dwell ;
Sick or in health, in evil fame or good—
    Her's will I be ; and only with this thought
    Content myself, although my chance be nought.

VII. THE FAITHFUL LOVER WISHETH ALL EVIL MAY BEFALL HIM IF HE FORSAKE HIS LADY.

SIR THOMAS WYATT: 1503—1554.

FROM 'WORKS,' ALDINE EDITION, 1831.

THE Knot which first my heart did strain,
When that your servant I became,
Doth bind me still for to remain
Always your own, as now I am ;

K

And if you find that I do feign,
With just judgment myself I damn
      To have disdain.

If other thought in me do grow
But still to love you steadfastly ;
If that the proof do not well shew
That I am yours assuredly ;
Let every wealth turn me to woe
And you to be continually
      My chiefest foe.

If other love, or new request
Do seize my heart, but only this ;
Or if within my wearied breast
Be hid one thought that means amiss,
I do desire that mine unrest
May still increase, and I to miss
      That I love best.

If in my love there be one spot
Of false deceit or doubleness ;
Or if I mind to slip this knot
By want of faith or steadfastness ;
Let all my service be forgot,
And when I would have chief redress
      Esteem me not.

But if that I consume in pain
Of burning sighs and fervent love ;
And daily seek none other gain
But with my deed these words to prove ;
Methink of right I should obtain
That ye would mind for to remove
      Your great disdain.

> And for the end of this my song,
> Unto your hands I do submit
> My deadly grief, and pains so strong
> Which in my heart be firmly shytt,
> And when ye list, redress my wrong :
> Since well ye know this painful fit
> Hath last too long.

Catholic Sonnets of the Elizabethan Age.

JOHN BRERELEY, PRIEST (VERE *LAWRENCE ANDERTON, S.J.*) : 1575—1643.

FROM AN ORIGINAL MS. IN THE POSSESSION OF MR. JOSEPH GILLOW, BY THE AUTHOR (J. B.: P.) OF 'JERUSALEM, MY HAPPY HOME,' ON THE LORETO TITLES OF OUR LADY.

I. SONNET II. : SANCTA DEI GENETRIX.

> MOTHER of God—oh, rare prerogative ;
> Oh, glorious title—what more special grace
> Could unto thee thy dear Son, dread God, give
> To show how far thou dost all creatures pass ?
> That mighty power within the narrow fold
> Did of thy ne'er polluted womb remain,
> Whom, whiles he doth th' all-ruling Sceptre hold.
> Not earth, nor yet the heavens can contain ;
> Thou in the springtide of thy age brought'st forth
> Him who before all matter, time and place,
> Begotten of th' Eternal Father was.
> Oh, be thou then, while we admire thy worth
> A means unto that Son not to proceed
> In rigour with us for each sinful deed.

II.   SONNET III.: SANCTA VIRGO VIRGINUM.

VIRGIN of Virgins, thou the first didst make
The sacred vow of spotless chastity,
Through which example many now forsake
The vain world's frail delights to follow thee ;
In the whole course of thy life's blessed race
All the perfections of virginity,
As in a clear unblemished looking glass,
In their true colours well reflected be.
Yet though a Virgin, thou a Mother wast
Whose fruitful Maiden-womb sent forth a Ray
Of sacred beams which all dim errors chased.
Deign then, pure Mother, to thy Son to pray
That he would grant, thy great Integrity
May be a salve for our impurity.

III.   SONNET VI.: MATER PURISSIMA.

MOTHER most Pure ; thou clear from any show
Didst ever live of any sinful stain,
Gainst all th' assaults of our accursed foe
Thy very thoughts did victors still remain.
From actual sins and from original
Thy soul alone, and none but thine, was free ;
Yea, the profoundest doctors, when they fall
To speak of sin, refuse to mention thee.
Thy soul and body now rejoined do shine
Next to thy greatest Son, by much more pure
Than Cherubins, or other Powers divine.
Endeavour, most pure Mother, to procure,
That when our souls with sins we taint, we may
With floods of tears wash all such spots away.

IV. SONNET VII. : MATER CASTISSIMA.

MOTHER most Chaste thou art, for thou alone
Of all thy sex a Virgin didst conceive ;
A pure chaste Virgin broughtest forth thy Son ;
A Virgin also this frail world didst leave.
Thou never didst (let hell storm, shift and lie)
After thy First-born Child a second bear ;
Thou still wert clearer than the world's bright eye,
Or all the lights which burn on every sphere.
Thy Chastity's strong bands no strength could cut ;
Thou art the Gate through which but Israel's God
Doth come and go, yet still remaineth shut.
Vouchsafe, chaste Mother, to divert the rod
Of thy great Son's just judgments from the head
Of those who serve him and his justice dread.

V. SONNET VIII. : MATER INVIOLATA.

MOTHER Inviolated, who can be
A perfect mother and yet undefiled ?
Did ever any age a woman see
A maid at once and mother of a child ?
None but thyself, great Mother, thou alone
Of all thy sex this title canst receive ;
Thou only free from all contagïon
Of lustful touch, a Body didst conceive.
Thy spotless chastity did not impeach
Thy wondrous Child-birth, nor that birth again
Make in thy virgin's fortress any breach.
Pray, I beseech thee, that I may refrain
From each lascivious, wanton, vain desire,
And to thy purity in part aspire.

VI.   SONNET IX.: MATER INTEMERATA.

MOTHER Unspotted, thou art Moses' Bush
Which flamed indeed, yet was not burnt at all ;
Thou art the Woman whose blest Seed should crush
The serpent's head, for to repair our fall.
As in hot furnace Israel's Three Young-men
Th' Almighty's praises did untouchèd sing ;
And as to Daniel in the lion's den,
The door shut, Abacuc did victuals bring ;
So to redeem the forfeit of the Tree,
Thy Virgin-womb True God, True Man did bear
Without all touch unto thy chastity.
Grant that I may, O spotless Mother, fear
To come before thee with a spotted soul,
A sin-infected, unprepparèd soul.

VII.   SONNET XLIII.: REGINA VIRGINUM.

O QUEEN of Virgins, thou the glorious crown
And chiefest grace art of that spotless state ;
Thy sacred womb to man was never known,
Yet he's thy Child, who doth hell's pride abate ;
Thou though a Mother, yet without compare
Than purest virgins wast by far more pure
From the deceits of each entrapping snare ;
Thy thoughts, words, deeds were ever all secure ;
None but thy greatest Son, whose wondrous birth
Did not at all thy virgin-bands untie,
Deservèd in thy virgin-womb to lie.
Vouchsafe, chaste Queen, that while we live on earth
Thou would'st be pleased with thy unspotted train
Before thy Son our Advocate t' remain.

Michael Angelo of his 'Madonna,'

NOW IN THE NATIONAL GALLERY.

SEBASTIAN EVANS.

FROM 'IN THE STUDIO,' 1875.

In the dawn not of earth ever looming
　　On the verge of the land untrod,
All alone in the infinite gloaming
　　Sat Mary, the Mother of God.

There I saw her, the Star of the Ages,
　　And alone as she sat I could see
The Book of the Prophet whose pages
　　Were open upon her knee.

She read therein, but the saying
　　Was dark as the noon's eclipse :
And I heard the voice of her praying
　　Going God-ward up from her lips.

'O God, that my prayer might win me
　　A gracious word in my need :
For my spirit is sad within me,
　　And thy Prophets are hard to read.

'Lord, how shall thy Handmaid gather
　　The wisdom thy seers declare?
The burden is heavy, O Father,
　　It is more than my soul can bear.'

And a Voice was heard there singing,
　　And a sound as of wheels that roll ;
A sound as of creatures winging,
　　And behold, a Hand with a scroll :

Like the scroll wherein was written
    Lamentations and mourning and woe,
Which the great Voice bade be eaten,
    When the Seer saw God in the bow.

And lo, it was spread before her,
    And she read there the doom of blood :
Of those who were hovering o'er her,
    Four folded their wings and stood.

And she cried, 'O Lord, for the Blossom
    That hath bloomed on Jesse's rod ;
The sword that hath pierced my bosom,
    Must it pierce his side, my God ?

'Oh, look down on thine own Handmaiden ;
    I prayed for a word in my need,
And behold, I am doubly laden,
    O Lord, are there two must bleed ?

'No hope ?   No shadow of turning ?
    O Father, thy will be done.'
But her head was bowed with yearning,
    And she groaned, 'O God : my Son.'

Yet ev'n as of old to the Prophet
    When he ate of that scathing scroll ;
Though bitter as reek of Tophet,
    'Twas as honey sweet to his soul.

So to her, but sweeter, oh, sweeter,
    As the words more bitter to eat :
A bitter beyond all bitter,
    And a sweet beyond all sweet.

The children came from their playing,
  Her own Boy, Jesus, and John :
Ah, what should they know of her praying?
  Of the secret that made her wan?

The Child touched the book of the Prophet,
  That lay on his Mother's knee ;
And he swept unheeded from off it
  That scroll of the dread to-be :

And one of the Four stooped lowly,
  Took the scroll as it lay at her feet,
Reading through in a whisper slowly
  The burden, so bitter; so sweet.

At his side, on his shoulder leaning,
  A second had bowed his head,
As he followed the terrible meaning
  On the scroll that his wing-mate read ;

Read, whispering low to his brother ;
  But the Little One took no heed—
'Oh, give me the Book, sweet Mother,'
  He cried, 'that I, too, may read.'

Ah, how earnest he waxed in his pleading,
  As she held the book from his hand :
'Mother mine, with thy help in my reading
  Indeed I shall understand.'

The fingers still clasped on the pages,
  How fainly he clung to the book,
Ah me, for thee, Star of the Ages,
  Thou, whose love forbad him to look.

What tenderness more than maternal ;
  What passion divine of regret ;
What yearning, what sorrow supernal :
  ' Not yet, O my Blessed, not yet.'

But that other, his playfellow, listened
  To the Angel's whisper the while :
What amaze in his wide eye glistened,
  And parted his lips with a smile.

For he heard, though an Angel's sighing
  Made fainter the whispered word,
Of a Voice in the wilderness crying,
  ' Prepare ye the way of the Lord.'

As he stood there, all ear, inly guessing,
  ' I, John, am that Herald, perchance,'
Two fingers half raised as in blessing,
  Half dreamily closed as in trance.

*   *   *

Thus I saw them, I, Michael, those seven
  In the Gardens, one morning in May :
They were neither on earth, nor in heaven,
  Yet I saw them clear as the day.

And I drew.   Ghirlandaio half-lauded
  My studies, and bade me work on.
Torregiano the Jealous applauded
  By filching my sketch for the John.

Till at last I set hand to my painting
  After Mass on Saint Michaelmas-day ;
I wrought with a fervour unfainting
  Till March in the Gardens was gay.

Then I lost my Lorenzo.   Ah, never
  Could I paint from that Vision agen :
I left it unfinished for ever,
  For how should I finish it then ?

Unfinished the work ; yet I wot, he
  Who searches may find if he will,
In mine own Casa Buonarotti,
  How the Vision abode with me still.

On the wall there in fresco far other
  The work and the symbol I wrought :
I, the Seer, I had changed ; but the Mother,
  The same, save the mood of the thought.

The same, too, my chisel discovered
  In the Florentine marble—the same :
The same ever o'er me she hovered
  When I mused, when I cried on her name.

In the brow, crowned with blessing, still human :
  In the breast, pierced through by the sword :
Mother-Maiden, the Hope of the Woman,
  The Woman through whom was the Word.

Virgo Præbicanba: Ronbeaux, Sonnets, anb Triolets.

JOHN FITZPATRICK, O.M.I.

FROM 'VIRGO PRÆDICANDA,' 1898.

PROLOGUE.

My Lady is a fragrant Rose,
And near to God my Lady grows;
And all my thoughts are murmuring bees
That haste, in silent ecstasies
Upon her beauty to repose.

Sweeter than any flower that blows,
Since all the scents her lips disclose
Are prayers upon the heavenly breeze,
My Lady is.

Her summer never comes and goes;
And for the sweetness she bestows,
My heart's the hive where by degrees
I hoard my golden memories;
For Mary, as my Angel knows,
My Lady is.

II.   ALMA MATER.

Sweet Mother-Maid, about thy knee
A bevy of sweet maids I see;
Thou shelterest 'neath thy virgin stole,
And near the whiteness of thy soul,
The mothers of the time to be.

An Alma Mater unto me
Thou seem'st to all who lovingly
Would live within thy love's control,
                    Sweet Mother-Maid.

By God endowed and reared, in thee
Is virtue's university ;
And while the Christian ages roll,
Through thee he grants, from pole to pole,
To ' sweet girl-graduates ' their degree,
                    Sweet Mother-Maid.

III. THE GRIEF OF GRIEFS.

You never knew the grief I know,
Mother of Sorrows, long ago ;
One sorrow never poured its stream,
E'en through the landscape of a dream,
To swell the ocean of your woe.

Throughout your sojourn here below
'Twas sin that made you suffer so,
But stain of sin, my sorrow's theme,
                    You never knew.

And since in many a mortal throe,
You wont such solace to bestow
As doth your motherhood beseem,
Nor fail me but in this, I deem
God wills the grief should ever flow
                    You never knew.

IV.   AS WOMEN WILL.

O MOTHER-MAID, and can it be
Thy mother's namesake did but see
With twilit eyes thy Baby's face,
Nor even for a moment's space
Share Simeon's felicity?

With her thou wast, it seems to me,
A Woman very womanly,
And lent'st thy Child to her embrace,
          O Mother-Maid.

And if thou didst, then well might she
Be eloquent of him and thee;
Of him, the Hope of all her race,
And thee, the Fountain full of grace,
The Source of all her holy glee,
          O Mother-Maid.

V.   NAME AND ADDRESS.

My mother taught my childish lips to say
Whose child I was, and where my dwelling-place,
To tell, she said, to the first friendly face,
If ever I should chance to go astray:
And once, when I had wandered far away
And could no more my truant steps retrace,
Back to my longing mother's warm embrace,
One led me by that clue at close of day.

We must be children once again, saith he
Whose Word is life's high law; so, when I roam
Out of the narrow way and stand in need,
Lest I be lost for ever, I will plead:
'My Mother's name is Mary, and my home
Is where she lives, in Heaven, and looks for me.'

VI. IN NESTING-TIME.

At St. Anne's, Rock Ferry, Birkenhead.

Lo, little Mary and her mother stand
In sculpture here : the Child, with downward look,
Is busied o'er the pages of a book
Saint Anne is holding ; on whose outstretched hand—
A final touch the sculptor never planned—
Are nesting birds that seemingly forsook,
For such a spot, full many a sheltered nook,
In swift obedience to some high command.

'Twas thus the Child bent o'er the sacred scroll
Prophetic of the Maid whose Virgin breast
God soon should tenant, while her destined soul
Dreamt not the graces of his great design
Within itself were gathering to a nest,
Beneath the shadow of the Dove Divine.

VII. A WHITE FLAG.

IMMACULATE ; O thou, in whom alone
Nor life nor death could find sin's slightest trace,
Thou sinless glory of the sinful race
Thy Son redeemed for children of thine own,
Mary ; in this thy purity is shown—
No shame distains that fearless face-to-face,
Thy face to God's, when for his pardoning grace
Thy white life sues before the Great White Throne.

Our trembling hope is still in thee, in thee ;
Plead for us with the King, for we have hurled
Our sins' despite against his sanctity :
Here we will wait for mercy in the world,
Nor fear the fate of rebels, while we see
The white flag of thine innocence unfurled.

VIII. REGINA CONCHARUM.

At Inchicore, Dublin.

HE did not write his meaning in the sand,
Who crowned and throned her in this rustic shrine
As ' Queen of Shells,' who is by right divine
O'er every ocean Queen, and every land.
I raise mine eyes, and lo, I see her stand
Beside the mystic sea that laves supine
The Feet of God with waters crystalline,
Listening to a sea-shell in her hand.

Upon that shore eterne the waves that break,
Advancing and retreating, are the waves
Of prayers preferred and granted.   Mother dear :
She sweetly smiles because her God-send saves,
For all the sound the many waters make,
The murmur of mine Ave for her ear.

IX. PROTOPLASM.

' The Lord God formed man of the slime of the earth.'

ADAM was fashioned of the slime,
But in the slime a Lily lay,
The Lily of the Stream of time ;
Adam was fashioned of the slime,
And fell ; then stirred a Seed sublime,
Saint Mary in his sinful clay :
Adam was fashioned of the slime,
But in the slime a Lily lay.

X. NAMESAKES.

THE image of his Mother came
To Jesus with the Magdalene,
Because she bore his Mother's name;
The image of his Mother came
Beside the sinner red with shame;
And well it was that, white and clean,
The image of his Mother came
To Jesus with the Magdalene.

XI. A SIGN.

A WIDOW'S only Son was he
Whom they were bearing to the tomb
Adown the slope of Calvary.
A Widow's only Son was he;
And some remembered hopefully
How once, in Naim's gathering gloom,
A widow's only son was he
Whom they were bearing to the tomb.

ENVOY.

'To paint the lily,' were in vain
That God has clothed in vesture white
And keeps so pure with dew and rain;
To paint the lily were in vain,
As knows the Virgin without stain
Who bore the mothers' lustral rite:
To paint the Lily were in vain
That God has clothed in vesture white.

L

De Assumptione.

WILLIAM FORREST (BORN C. 1505), CISTERTIAN MONK OF THAME, OXFORD.

The Beginning of a Poem from the 'Life of the B.V.M.' (finished in 1572) in the Harleian MSS. of the British Museum Library, first published in the 'History of the Church at Thame,' and edited by Frederick George Lee, LL.D., 1883. This extract has been slightly modernised.

OF her pure life double is there none,
For she of women was alone
In chyldinge, Child as erst before ;
She was a Maiden evermore,
She suckled Christ with her sweet breast,
    And now in heaven assumpta est.

Where with her Son she is indued
With joys of passing magnitude,
Above all Angels, next the Throne,
For her virtues that so high shone,
No Angel so with grace possest,
    And now in heaven assumpta est.

In flesh to live as she did here,
No fleshly lust in her t'appear ;
It was a life angelical,
Beyond the life of angels all,
For their number by her increased,
    And now in heaven assumpta est.

Though some doth hold the contrary,
She in the earth to putrify,
Her flesh and Christ's, sith both be one,
That were no good condition :
No doubt he did as seemèd best,
    Therefore in heaven assumpta est.

In things that reason cannot preve,
We ought Christ's Church for to believe,
Which holdeth she, soul and body,
To be assumpte most certainly,
Of long is holde from east to west,
    With whom I hold, assumpta est.

If saints in their bodies did rise,
When Christ arose, and did certise
His Resurrection to be true,
And did with him to heaven ensue,
Dying again their death-curst drest,
    Then she (as they) assumpta est.

Her reliques if in earth being
They should have had some mentioning,
As Saint John's head at Amyas ;
And other saints each in their place,
She passing all, with grace possest,
    No doubt in heaven assumpta est.

Her honour since that did excell,
Far passing all any can tell,
To God's own Son to be Mother,
To have then that hath none other,
Her soul in body now to rest,
    And in the same assumpta est.

In both or any of the twain,
Sith never sin did move or reign,
And sin of old compaction
Cause of all putrifaction,
They the most singularly blest
    In singular wise assumpta est.

That womb in which God's Son did lie,
Receiving Flesh, Blood and Body,
With pappes blest, as Luke doth say,
Although to have a dying day
To turn to dust had not been best,
    Therefore I say, assumpta est.

Whether or not to stand in doubt
Enough we have here bowlted out,
Let them that list on their peril,
Well am I sure God did fulfil
For his Mother that seemèd best,
    Therefore I say, assumpta est.

To thee, O God, Father of Might,
To Son and to the Holy Sprite,
That art One God in Trinity,
For her graces all praisings be,
Who grant to us at her request
    To come where she assumpta est.

NOTES.

St. IV. l. 3 : The original has " Chrystys," and no verb.
St. V. l. 1 : Preve ; a varient of prove.
    l. 4 : Assumpte, *i.e.*, assumpted, assumed.
    l. 5 : Holde, *i.e.*, holden, held.
St. VI. l. 5 : An obscure line. If the text be correct, drest may
    mean clay ; as dreste is found in Wyclif, &c., for
    drast, *i.e.*, dregs.
St. VIII. l. 4 : Then to have that (which) none other hath.
St. XI. l. 2 : Bowlted ; from "bolt," an Old French word,
    meaning to search, try, examine ; literally, to sift.

Tryste Noel, Lyric and Sonnets.

LOUISE IMOGEN GUINEY.

FROM 'A ROADSIDE HARP,' 1893, AND ' THE MARTYRS' IDYL,' 1899.

I. TRYSTE NOEL.

THE Ox he openeth wide the doore,
And from the snow he calls her inne;
And he hath seen her smile therefore,
   Our Ladye without sinne.
  Now soone from sleepe
  A starre shall leap,
And soone arrive both King and hinde;
   Amen; Amen:
But oh, the place co'd I but finde.

The Ox hath husht his voyce and bent
Trewe eyes of pitty ore the mow,
And on his lovelie neck, forespent,
   The Blessed lays her browe.
  Around her feet
  Full warme and sweete
His bowerie breath doth meeklie dwell;
   Amen; Amen:
But sore am I with vaine travel.

The Ox is host in Juda's stall,
And host of more than onely one;
For close she gathereth withal
   Our Lorde her littel Sonne.
  Glad hinde and King
  Their gyfte may bring;
But wo'd to-night my tears were there;
   Amen; Amen:
Between her bosom and his hayre.

II. MATER AMANTISSIMA.

VINES branching stilly
  Shade the open door
In the house of Sion's Lily,
  Cleanly and poor:
Oh, brighter than wild laurel
  The Babe bounds in her hand:
The King, who for apparel
  Hath but a swaddling-band,
Who sees her heavenlier smiling than stars in his
    command.

Soon, mystic changes
  Part him from her breast,
Yet there awhile he ranges
  Gardens of rest;
Yea, she the first to ponder
  Our ransom and recall,
Awhile may rock him under
  Her young curls' fall,
Against that only sinless, love-loyal heart of all.

What shall inure him
  Unto the deadly dream,
When the tetrarch shall abjure him,
  The thief blaspheme,
And scribe and soldier jostle
  About the shameful Tree?
When even an Apostle
  Demands to touch and see?
But she hath kissed her Flower where the Wounds
    are to be.

III. A MADONNA OF DOMENICO GHIRLANDAJO.

LET thoughts go hence as from a mountain spring,
Of the great dust of battle clean and whole,
And the wild birds that have no nest nor goal
Fold in a young man's breast their trancèd wing;
For thou art made of purest Light, a thing
Art gave, beyond her own devout controul;
And Light upon thy seeing, suffering soul
Hath wrought a sign for many journeying—
Our Sign.   As up a wayside after rain,
When the blown beeches purple all the height,
And clouds sink to the sea-marge, suddenly
The autumn sun (how soft, how solemn-bright)
Moves to the vacant dial, so is lain
God's meaning Hand, thou Chosen, upon thee.

IV. ON RAPHAEL'S MADONNA AT DRESDEN.

AFTER KARL THEODORA KÖRNER : WRITTEN IN 1811, AND
TRANSLATED IN THE AUTHOR'S METRE IN 1900.

BEFORE this picture I have held my place
Till life is touched and filled with victory,
And worlds of beauty open out, and me
No more for ever mortal gyves embrace.
Alas, for some who take amiss God's grace,
To whom no mystic Voice here speaketh free,
Who naught with thy foreboding eyes can see,
Mary, nor learn what love is, from thy face.

O Holy, Holy : floating seraphs sing
In throngs that aye upbear thee, wing on wing,
And thrill around thee, Bride of the Divine.
Man, too, soars from his dust ; and fair and well
With any, who by Faith ineffable,
Can meet thy look with heart as pure as thine.

Ibymn of the Templars.

JOHN HAY: COLONEL, U.S.A. ARMY.

FROM 'PIKE COUNTY BALLADS,' 1870, AND 'POEMS,' 1897.

'Guy of the Temple' speaks:

PITCH my pavilion here, where its high cross
May catch the last light lingering on the hill:
The savage shadows, struggling by the shore,
Have conquered in the valley; inch by inch
The vanquished light fights bravely to these crags,
To perish glorious in the sunset fire.

*   *   *

                 Heroes and Saints
To alien peoples shall they be, my brave
And patient warriors; for in their stout hearts
God's Spirit dwells for ever, and their hands
Are swift to do his service on his foes.
The swelling music of their vesper-hymn
Is rising fragrant from the shadowed vale
Familiar to the welcoming gates of heaven:

  Mother of God, as evening falls
    Upon the silent sea,
  And shadows veil the mountain walls,
    We lift our souls to thee:
  From lurking perils of the night,
    The desert's hidden harms,
  From plagues that waste, from blasts that smite,
    Defend thy men-at-arms.

Aye: Heaven keep them; and ye Angel-hosts
That wait with fluttering plumes around the great
White Throne of God, guard them from scath and
  harm.

*   *   *

But greatest are my warriors, as I deem,
In that their hearts, nearer than any else,
Keep true the pledge of perfect purity
They pledged upon their sword-hilts long ago:
For all is possible to the pure in heart:

   Mother of God, thy starry smile
     Still bless us from above;
   Keep pure our souls from passion's guile,
     Our hearts from earthly love:
   Still save each soul from guilt apart
     As stainless as each sword,
   And guard undimned in every heart
     The image of our Lord.

   In desert-march, or battle's flame,
     In fortress and in field,
   Our war-cry is thy holy name,
     Thy love our joy and shield;
   And if we falter, let thy power
     Thy stern avenger be,
   And God forget us in the hour
     We cease to think of thee.

        *   *   *

Night hangs above the valley; dies the day
In peace, casting his last glance on my cross,
And warns me to my prayers: Ave, Maria.

   Mother of God, the evening fades
     On wave and hill and lea,
   And in the twilight's deepening shades
     We lift our souls to thee:
   In passion's stress—the battle's strife,
     The desert's lurking harms—
   Maid-Mother of the Lord of Life,
     Protect thy men-at-arms.

Espousals of Our Lady: a Legend.

HUGH T. HENRY, PRIEST.

THEOLOGICAL SEMINARY, OVERBROOK, U.S.A.

FROM 'THE AMERICAN ECCLESIASTICAL REVIEW,' 1897.

WHO shall sing Our Lady's praise?
　Who shall tell her endless glory?
Surely childhood's sinless days,
　Or the head grown hoary
Like to Simeon's, serving still
In the Master's Temple till
God shall all his yearning fill:
　Let me—tell a story.

Once in Judah's poverished land—
　Land of old all fair and sunny,
When the Sceptre of Command
　Saw but milk and honey—
Dwelt a Princess wondrous fair,
Yet whose heart could only care
For a wealth of virtue rare,
　Not rich patrimony.

Poor she was in gifts of earth;
　Gold nor jewels ever telling
That the worth of royal birth
　In her heart was swelling:
But her virtues like a star
Whose calm beauty naught could mar,
Shone o'er Israel afar
　From her Temple-dwelling.

So from all the city wide,
  With the richest presents laden,
Suitors came to seek a bride
  In that lowly Maiden:
Came with pride of state and birth,
Came with all that Mother Earth
Hath of beauty or of worth
  Hearts of men to gladden.

See them in the Temple throng:
  Wealth shall proffer all its treasure,
Pride shall plead in accents strong,
  Love shall fill the measure.
Stands the Maiden modestly
While each suitor makes his plea:
Then the High Priest, 'Which shall be
  Choice of thy free pleasure'?

Which of them should be her choice?
  Now at last the hush is broken—
But her tender girlish voice
  Asks for surer token:
'Solve the riddle—what, think ye,
Should my fairest glory be?
He is dearest Spouse to me
  That shall best have spoken'.

Quoth the first with pensive pause,
  ''Tis thy silken veil concealing
Beauties rarer still because
  Shy of their revealing'.
Silence greets his flattering plea;
Then the Maiden modestly,
'Other must the token be
  To my heart appealing'.

Heli speaketh (Nadab's son,
  Richest treasure he possesses),
'Silks and satins she shall don
  Whom my heart caresses ;
Gold and silver she shall wear,
Emeralds and rubies rare,
Yea, what treasures yet more fair
  Earth or sea confesses '.

Blessed be the God above :
  Wealth or station cannot claim it :
Loftier than earthly love
  Still must seek to name it :
Purer yet must be the eye,
Holier heart must make reply :
Answer to her query high,
  Who shall know to frame it ?

One there was whose heart from youth
  Sought for aye as highest merit
Treasurings which simple Truth
  Can alone inherit :
So his clearer vision saw
In their speech a lurking flaw—
For he read the lettered Law
  But to learn its spirit.

Then said Agabus, ' To me,
  Fairest ornament of woman
Is her gentle modesty,
  More divine than human '.
Lesser good he cannot say
Who would best the Law obey,
Nor leave weightier things to pay
  Tithes of mint and cummin.

See the crowd with bated breath :
    'Sooth,' they whisper, 'he divineth
Well the riddle ; now what saith
    Mary ?'   Lo, she signeth
That the answer is not known :
Then must Heaven the secret own,
That high Heaven which alone
    Purest gold refineth.

Now at last the impatient crowd
    Sees her mock at their endeavour :
'Israel's shame,' they murmur loud,
    'Be to her who never
Hopes for blessed Seed to be
Israel's golden prophecy,
David's Son o'er Judah free
    Reigning high for ever'.

But she answered not a word
    Save the whisper, 'He abideth,
Who my dearest wish hath heard ;
    Yea, the Lord provideth'.
Suddenly, from out the throng,
'Sooth, ye do the Maiden wrong :
Wealth nor lands to me belong,
    But the Lord decideth'.

Spoke a Man whose royal mould
    Mocked his humble outer seeming :
Silver hiding midst the gold
    O'er his forehead streaming
Showed what strength and majesty
Can with added years agree :
Strength with wisdom—this should be
    Worth our best esteeming.

Joseph then, the Carpenter,
  Who in prayer with God hath striven,
Reads the riddle unto her
  Which the Maid hath given.
' Lo, I speak a mystery,
For the dearest thing to thee
Is thy blest Virginity,
  Chosen Child of Heaven '.

Blessed be the God above :
  Wealth or station hath not named it ;
Higher than an earthly love
  Now at last hath claimed it :
Gloried shame of Israel,
Blest the bosom where it fell ;
Blessèd word that broke the spell,
  Blessèd lips that framed it.

If we give with patient heart
  Unto God our poor endeavour,
Though earth's shame should be our part,
  God can fail us never :
Lo, within the Virgin's breast
Shall the Great Messiah rest,
In whom all the earth is blest
  For ever and for ever.

Our Lady's Easter and other Verse.

BENJAMIN D. HILL, C.P.

(FATHER EDMUND OF THE HEART OF MARY).

FROM THE 'CATHOLIC WORLD,' 'AVE MARIA,' AND 'MARIÆ
COROLLA,' 1869—1898.

I. OUR LADY'S EASTER.

SHE knelt expectant through the night—
    For he had promised. In her face
    The pure soul beaming, full of grace,
But sorrow-tranced—a frozen light.

But ere her eastward lattice caught
    The glimmer of the breaking day,
    No more in Joseph's garden lay
The buried picture of her thought.

The seal'd stone shut a void ; and lo,
    The Mother and the Son had met :
    For her a day should never set
Had burst upon the night of woe.

In sudden glory stood he there,
    And gently raised her to his breast :
    And on his heart, in perfect rest,
She poured her own—a voiceless prayer.

Enough for her that he has died,
    And lives, to die again no more :
    The foe despoiled, the combat o'er,
The Victor crowned and glorified.

II. INVIOLATA.

' WHO hast alone Inviolate remained,'
   Sings holy Church.   And I too, Lady sweet,
   Can find no word to murmur at thy feet
Melodious as this—which thou has deigned
To hear so often from a love unfeigned.
    Ah, could my heart the tender thought repeat—
    Inviolata—with its every beat,
And pour a ceaseless worship unrestrained.

Inviolate soul, inviolate body, thine :
   Sin could not touch thee, nor the tempter near :
    Pain no disease, and age no blemish gave.
More Virgin for thy Motherhood Divine :
   Serene, sublime, 'mid sorrows without peer ;
    Beauteous in death, untainted in the grave.

III. BEHOLD, THY MOTHER.

BEHOLD, thy Mother : words he might have said
   At Bethlehem, from the crib ; for she was then
   New Eve and Mother of our Life : or when
He rose, the deathless First-fruits of the dead :
Or forth to Bethany his loved ones led
    To watch the heavens receive him out of ken.
    But no : he chose this hour, and caused the pen
Of him who heard to write what we have read.

Yes, dearest Lord, our Mother was to be
   By thy gift doubly ours.   And thou didst wait
    Till she had shared thy passion—seen thee prove
Thy love for us, and proved her own for thee,
   To last excess ; then solemnly instate
    The Queen of Mercy, in her realm of love.

IV. REFUGE OF SINNERS.

How readest thou, my Queen, that wondrous Book
  Thou bendest o'er, the while with precious nard
  Thou closest rift and gash ? Dost thou regard
Our sins that scored the page ? Or rather look
At love's sweet argument—his love who took
  Their penance on himself, nor deemed it hard ?
  Let me not wrong thee. Nothing can retard
Thy pardoning pity. There is not a nook
In all thy bosom where a moment lurks
  Of aught but love for sinners. Thou didst share
  His passion for their sakes, and didst become
Their Mother by thy throes. 'Tis this that works
  Within thee—the new Mother's tender care
    That each child-soul shall find thy heart a home.

V. OUR LADY'S NATIVITY.

' Thou art the Casket where the Jewel lay.' George Herbert.

STAR of the Morning, how still was thy shining
  When its young splendour arose on the sea ;
Only the angels, the secret divining,
  Hailed the Long-promised, the Chosen, in thee.

Sad were the fallen, and vainly dissembled
  Fears of the Woman in Eden foretold :
Darkly they guessed, as believing they trembled,
  Who was the Gem for the Casket of Gold.

Though the deep heart of the nations forsaken
  Beat with a sense of deliverance nigh ;
True to a hope, through the ages unshaken,
  Looked for the Dayspring to break from on high ;
M

Thee they perceived not, the Pledge of Redemption—
  Hidden like thought, though no longer afar ;
Not though the light of a peerless exemption
  Beamed in thy rising, Immaculate Star.

All in the twilight so modestly shining,
  Dawned thy young beauty, sweet Star of the Sea :
Only the angels, the secret divining,
  Hailed the Elected, the Virgin, in thee.

Chaucer's 'Mother of God': an Orison.

The Orison may possibly have been composed for Anne of
Bohemia, Queen of Richard II., as Chaucer's A. B. C. was written
for the Duchess of Lancaster. This may explain an allusion in the
opening stanza. (Rob. Bell, 1856.)

THOMAS HOCCLEVE : 1370—1450.

MODERNISED (1890) BY WILLIAM JOHN BLEW, M.A.: 1808—1894.

MOTHER of God and Virgin Undefiled,
  O blissful Queen, our Queens' Imperatrice,
Pray thou for me, a sin-begotten child,
  To God thy Son, the Punisher of vice,
  That of his mercy high above all price—
Though reckless I and breaker of his law—
Unto himself my soul his mercy draw.

Mother of Mercy, Way of Gentleness,
  That of all virtue art superlatife,
Saviour of souls, through thy sweet will to bless—
  O humble Lady, Mother, Maid and Wife,
  Maker of Peace, that stiflest woe and strife,
My prayer unto thy Son do thou present,
Since of my guilt I wholly me repent.

Comfort benign of us poor wretches all—
    Be at mine ending when I come to die ;
Full of all sweetness, unto thee I call
    To help me weigh—O Well of Piety—
    Against the fiend, whose two clutched hands awry
Would pluck the scale and drag with all their might
To weigh us down : oh, keep us from his spite.

And for thou art the Palm of Chastity,
    And of all virtues worship and renown,
Above all women blessed must thou be ;
    Now speak, now pray our Saviour and thine own,
    That me he send such grace and favour down,
That all the hot lust burning me he slake
And quench, blest Maiden Mary, for thy sake.

Most Blessed Lady, clear Light of the day,
    The Temple of our Lord, Home of all good,
That by thy prayer wipest clean away
    The filth and scour of our soul's evilhood,
    Put forth thine hand ; help me in my sad mood :
And from temptation, Lady, rescue me
Of wicked thought—for thy benignity.

So be fulfilled the will of thy dear Son,
    And that the Holy Ghost upon me shine
Pray thou for us, as ever thou hast done ;
    All such emprize hath certainly been thine,
    For no such Advocate can man divine,
Lady, as thou—to give our griefs redress—
Our Refuge thou in all our sickliness.

Shaped by the ordinance of God thou art,
    To pray for us, Flower of Humility ;
Wherefore thine office lay unto thine heart,

Lest that the fiend (who ever in wait doth lie
By stealth to catch me through his subtlety)
Me with his treachery overcome: then give
Health to my Soul that, Lady, I may live.

Thyself of our redemption art the Way,
For Christ of thee disdainèd not to take
Both Flesh and Blood, full minded of the day
Of dying on the Cross for our poor sake:
His precious death made fiends and devils quake,
And Christian folk to joy thereat for ever;
Help, from his mercy that we nought dissever.

Remember—well thou dost—the sorrow and pain
That made the passion of his pangs thine own,
When water and blood from thy worn eyes like rain,
For sorrow of him, by thy wan cheeks ran down;
And well to thee the cause thereof was known,
That all his travail was to save mankind:
Mother of Mercy, have thou this in mind.

[Remember—thou dost well—of this same hour
The loving lesson Love alone could teach,
'Father, forgive them'; Love that, past the power
And pangs of death, on Mercy's wings could reach,
With the sweet words commending each to each,
The death charge of the dying Son and Brother,
'Mother, behold thy Son: good Son, behold thy Mother.'

Some connecting link between the ninth and the next Stanzas seems to be lacking, and one is here supplied.—Translator.]

Well then, to thee be praise and honour paid,
Palace of Christ, Flower of Virginity,
Seeing that upon thee the charge was laid
To bear the Lord of Heaven, of earth and sea
And of all things that ever formed might be,

Thus of Heaven's King wast thou predestinate
To heal our souls—of thine so high estate.

Thy Maiden's womb wherein our Saviour lay,
 Thy paps that gave him suck, gave forth the dew
For our salvation—blest be thou and they—
 The birth of Christ our bondage brake in two ;
 Bid then, Hosannas ring all ages through
To him and thee, from thrall that set us free
To life and light—aye, blest, right blest be ye.

Lady, by thee in peace were bonded close
 Angels and men (what man hath this to learn ?) ;
Blessed be God that such a Mother chose,
 Bounty supreme that passeth bound and bourne,
 Though that our hardened hearts be stout and stern ;
For thou to Christ such means of grace hast given,
That of all guilt we pardoned be and shriven.

Through thee the gates of Paradise stand open ;
 By thee are broken the grim gates of hell ;
Through thee the world restorèd is and holpen ;
 Thou of all virtue art the Spring and Well ;
 Through thee all goodness—as a word can tell—
In heaven and earth is ordinanced ; by thee
Our souls in health and wealth sustainèd be.

Now since thou art of such authority,
 Thou piteous Lady, Virgin without spot,
Pray thy dear Son my guilt to pardon me,
 And—for that he will grant it, well I wot—
 This my petition press thou and spare not
To pray for us, Mother of Christ so dear,
Spare not—for he as lovingly will hear.

 [Here, probably, ended the Prayer of Hoccleve to our Lady; and
here, probably, began his Prayer to Mary and John.—Translator.]

Friend and Apostle—bosom Friend of Christ,
    Virgin—of him the chosen, Holy John,
Shining Apostle and Evangelist,
    Beloved of Christ, than whom more loved were none,
    Be thou, I pray thee, with our Lady one :
That unto Christ for all of us ye pray ;
Darling of Christ, do this for us I say.

Mary and John, heaven's twofold gems of light ;
    Twain lights yourselves that shine before the face
Of our Lord God, now put forth all your might
    Far off our clouds, full charged with sin, to chase ;
    That we stand fast and not a foot give place
To the arch-fiend, and make him whine and wail
To see your prayers for us so much avail.

The twain ye be (that verily I ken)
    Whereon our Father, God the Lord most High,
Built for himself a temple among men,
    A House of God ; wherefore to you I cry,
    Be leeches of our sinful malady,
That ye to God, the Lord of Mercy, pray
Not to record, but wipe our sins away.

Ye be our help, our strong protection ye,
    For that in mercy of your tenderness
To comfort you, God, hanging on the Tree,
    Confirmed in you his privilege to bless,
    Breathing to one of you this fond address ;
Dear words—amiss I read not words so dear—
' Behold and see : Woman, thy Son is here.'

And to that Son said, ' Here, behold thy Mother' :
    You then, for this sweet love in prayer I press
(This holy love God gave you, one for other,

Wrought of his lips and his high holiness,
   That blessing you, commanded you to bless—
As Mother and Son) to help us at our need,
And for our sinnings make our hard hearts bleed.

Unto you twain I now my soul commend,
   Mary and John, for my salvation ;
Help ye me—that my froward life I mend ;
   Help ye me—that the Recreating One,
   The Holy Ghost, may rest my heart upon,
There make his dwelling now and evermore ;
And of my wounded soul wash off the sore.

Rosa Mystica, and Mary Compared to the Air we Breathe;
1878—1883.

GERARD HOPKINS, S.J.: 1844—1889.

I. ROSA MYSTICA.

FROM 'THE IRISH MONTHLY,' 1898.

'THE Rose in a mystery'—where is it found?
Is it anything true ? Does it grow upon ground ?
It was made of earth's mould, but it went from men's eyes,
And its place is a secret, and shut in the skies.
   In the Gardens of God, in the daylight divine
   Find me a place by thee, Mother of mine.

But where was it formerly ? Which is the spot
That was blest in it once, though now it is not?
It is Galilee's growth ; it grew at God's will
And broke into bloom upon Nazareth Hill.
   In the Gardens of God, in the daylight divine
   I shall look on thy loveliness, Mother of mine.

What was its season, then?   How long ago?
When was the summer that saw the Bud blow?
Two thousands of years are near upon past
Since its birth, and its bloom, and its breathing its last.
>   In the Gardens of God, in the daylight divine
>   I shall keep time with thee, Mother of mine.

Tell me the name now, tell me its name:
The heart guesses easily, is it the same?
Mary, the Virgin, well the heart knows,
She is the Mystery, she is that Rose.
>   In the Gardens of God, in the daylight divine
>   I shall come home to thee, Mother of mine.

Is Mary that Rose, then?   Mary, the Tree?
But the Blossom, the Blossom there, who can it be?
Who can her Rose be?   It could be but One:
Christ Jesus, our Lord—her God and her Son.
>   In the Gardens of God, in the daylight divine
>   Shew me thy Son, Mother, Mother of mine.

What was the colour of that Blossom bright?
White to begin with, immaculate white.
But what a wild flush on the flakes of it stood,
When the Rose ran in crimsonings down the Cross-wood.
>   In the Gardens of God, in the daylight divine
>   I shall worship the Wounds with thee, Mother of mine.

How many leaves had it?   Five they were then,
Five like the senses, and members of men;
Five is the number by nature, but now
They multiply, multiply, who can tell how.
>   In the Gardens of God, in the daylight divine
>   Make me a leaf in thee, Mother of mine.

Does it smell sweet, too, in that holy place ?
Sweet unto God, and the sweetness is grace ;
The breath of it bathes the great heaven above
In grace that is charity, grace that is love.
 To thy breast, to thy rest, to thy glory divine
 Draw me by charity, Mother of mine.

II. MARY, MOTHER OF DIVINE GRACE, COMPARED TO THE AIR WE BREATHE.

FROM 'A BOOK OF CHRISTMAS VERSE,' EDITED BY
H. C. BEECHING, M.A., 1895.

WILD Air, world-mothering Air,
Nestling me everywhere,
That each eyelash or hair
Girdles ; goes home betwixt
The fleeciest, frailest-flixed
Snowflake ; that's fairly mixed
With riddles, and is rife
In every least thing's life ;
This needful, never spent,
And nursing element ;
My more than meat and drink,
My meal at every wink ;
This Air which, by life's law
My lung must draw and draw,
Now, but to breathe its praise—
Minds me in many ways
Of her, who not only
Gave God's Infinity
Dwindled to Infancy
Welcome in womb and breast,
Birth, milk and all the rest,

But mothers' each new grace
That does now reach our race—
Mary Immaculate,
Merely a Woman, yet
Whose presence power is
Great as no goddess's
Was deemèd, dreamèd ; who
This one work has to do—
Let all God's glory through,
God's glory which would go
Through her and from her flow
Off and no way but so.

I say that we are wound
With mercy round and round
As if with air : the same
Is Mary, more by name.
She, wild Web, wondrous Robe,
Mantles the guilty globe,
Since God has let dispense
Her prayers his providence :
Nay, more than Almoner,
The sweet Alms' self is her,
And men are meant to share
Her life as life does air.

If I have understood,
She holds high Motherhood
Towards all our ghostly good,
And plays in grace her part
About man's beating heart,
Laying, like air's fine flood,
The death-dance in his blood ;

Yet no part but what will
Be Christ our Saviour still.
Of her flesh he took Flesh:
He does take, fresh and fresh,
Though much the mystery how,
Not flesh but spirit now
And makes, oh, marvellous,
New Nazareths in us,
Where she shall yet conceive
Him, morning, noon, and eve;
New Bethlems, and he born
There evening, noon, and morn—
Bethlem or Nazareth,
Men here may draw like breath
More Christ and baffle death;
Who born so, comes to be
New self and nobler me
In each one, and each one
More makes, when all is done,
Both God and Mary's Son.

Again, look overhead
How air is azurèd;
Oh, how; nay, do but stand
Where you can lift your hand
Skywards: rich, rich it laps
Round the four finger-gaps.
Yet such a sapphire-shot
Charged, steepèd sky will not
Stain light. Yea, mark you this:
It does no prejudice.
The glass-blue days are those
When every colour glows,
Each shape and shadow shows.

Blue be it: this blue heaven
The seven, or seven-times-seven
Hued sunbeam will transmit
Perfect, nor alter it.
Or if there does some soft,
On things aloof, aloft,
Bloom, breathe, that one breath more
Earth is the fairer for.
Whereas did air not make
This bath of blue and slake
This fire, the sun would shake,
A blear and blinding ball
With blackness bound, and all
The thick stars round him roll
Flashing like flecks of coal,
Quartz-fret, or sparks of salt
In grimy, vasty vault.

So God was God of old:
A Mother came to mould
These limbs like ours which are
What must make our Day-star
Much dearer to mankind;
Whose glory bare would blind,
Or less would win man's mind.
Through her we may see him
Made sweeter, not made dim;
And her hand leaves his light
Sifted, to suit our sight.

Be thou then, O thou dear
Mother, my Atmosphere;
My happier World, wherein
To wend and meet no sin;

Above me, round me lie
Fronting my froward eye
With sweet and scarless sky ;
Stir in mine ears, speak there ˙
Of God's love, O live Air,
Of patience, penance, prayer :
World-mothering Air, Air wild,
Wound with thee, in thee isled,
Fold home, fast fold thy child.

Poetry by Two Lords Houghton.

I.

RICHARD MONCKTON MILNES, FIRST LORD HOUGHTON: 1809—1885.

FROM 'POEMS OF MANY YEARS,' 1838—1840.

I. THE VIRGIN.

ON A PICTURE BY GIOVANNI BELLINI, IN THE CHURCH OF THE REDENTORE AT VENICE.

Our Lady speaks :

WHO am I, to be so far exalted
Over all the maidens of Judæa,
That here only in this lonely bosom
Is the Wonder-work of God revealèd ?
Oh, to think this little, Little Infant,
Whose warm limbs upon my knees are resting,
Helpless, silent, with his tender eyelids,
Like two pearl-shells, delicately closèd
Is informed with that Eternal Spirit
Who, between the Cherubim ˙enthronèd,
Dwells behind the Curtain of the Temple.
I can only gaze on him adoring,

Fearful lest the simple joy and passion
Which my Mother-love awakes within me,
Be not something bold and too familiar
For this Child of Miracle and Glory.

II. THE CHILD JESUS AND JOHN CON-
TENDING FOR THE CROSS.

ON A PICTURE BY SIMEONE DE PESARO, IN THE SEMINARY
AT VENICE.

The Virgin, with her hand upon the Cross, speaks:

My soul is weak with doubt—
What can I think or do?
To which of these dear Children shall I yield
The object of their earnest looks and words?
Ah me, I see within
That artless wooden Form,
A meaning of exceeding misery,
A dark, dark shadow of oncoming woe.
Oh, give it up, my Child:
I see your bright eyes close,
Your soft fair fingers spattered all with Blood,
Your cheeks dead pale: throw down the horrid toy.
He grasps it firmer still:
I dare not thwart his hand;
For what he does, he does not of himself,
But in the Will of him who sent him here.
And I, who labour blind
In this abysmal work,
Must bear the weight of dumb expectancy,
Of women first in honour and in woe.

II.

ROBERT MILNES, SECOND LORD HOUGHTON (EARL CREWE).

FROM 'STRAY VERSES,' 1891.

I. EASTER IN FLORENCE.

WE paced through frescoed Council-halls
　　Dim with the dust of buried ages ;
We lingered near the gorgeous walls
　　Where winds the train of Eastern Sages ;
And thoughtfully the cells we trod
　　Which held within their narrow border
The Prior who preached the wrath of God—
　　Stern Quixote of a Sacred Order.

The echoes of a bygone strife
　　Seemed surging round the dark Bargello ;
Marble and bronze sprang fresh to life
　　Beneath the wand of Donatello :
'Night' seemed to sleep, and ' Dawn' to wake
　　Behind the walls of old St. Lawrence—
There hung a spell we would not break
　　About our Eastertide in Florence.

　　　　*　　　*　　　*

From grave Mantegna's glowing reds,
　　To soft Correggio's milder graces ;
From Botticelli's down-cast heads,
　　To bright Andrea's smiling faces ;
And that good Friar, to whom alone
　　Of mortal men was spirit given
To pierce the veil that shrouds the Throne,
　　And paint the golden Courts of Heaven.

Silent we stood, in deepest awe,
    Where Raphael's hand has set for ever
The whirlwind Israel's prophet saw
    In vision by the captives' river:
Silent, where sits in loveliest guise
    The wistful Virgin Mother, leaning
To watch her wondrous Infant's eyes,
    Enkindled with divinest meaning.

NOTE.

Stanza 2. 'Night' and 'Dawn' are two statues by Michael Angelo, in the Medici Chapel of San Lorenzo, Florence.

II. MILLET'S L'ANGÉLUS.

AGAINST the sunset glow they stand,
Two humblest toilers of the land,
Rugged of speech and rough of hand,
        Bowed down by tillage ;

No grace of garb or circumstance
Invests them with a high romance,
Ten thousand such through fruitful France,
        In field and village.

The day's slow path from dawn to west,
Has left them, soil-bestained, distrest,
No thought beyond the nightly rest—
        New toil to-morrow.

Till solemnly the 'Ave-bell'
Rings out the sun's departing knell,
Borne by the breezes' rhythmic swell
        O'er swathe and furrow.

O lowly pair, you dream it not,
Yet on your hard, unlovely lot
That evening gleam of light has shot
      A glorious presage ;

For prophets oft have yearned, and kings
Have yearned in vain to know the things
Which to your simple spirits brings
      That curfew message.

Ancient Religious Song of Connaught.

TRANSLATED BY DOUGLAS HYDE, LL.D.

FROM 'THE NEW IRELAND REVIEW,' 1897.

MARY AND ST. JOSEPH.

The following poem was found in the County Mayo. The Translator wrote down the first part of it from the mouth of one native of the county, and afterwards got the last five verses from a second. The six-line verses, midway in the ballad, are, he says, alien to the spirit of the Irish language, and probably arise from the forgetfulness of the narrator of the omitted halves of each quatrain severally.

HOLY was good St. Joseph :
    When marrying Mary Mother,
Surely his lot was happy,
    Happy beyond all other.

Refusing red gold laid down,
    And the crown by David worn,
With Mary to be abiding
    And guiding her steps forlorn.

One day that the twain were talking,
    And walking through gardens early,
Where cherries were redly growing,
    And blossoms were blowing rarely,

N

Mary the fruit desired,
    For faint and tired she panted,
At the scent on the breezes' wing,
    Of the fruit that the King had planted.

Then spake to Joseph the Virgin,
    All weary and faint and low :
' O pull me yon smiling cherries
    That fair on the tree do grow.

' For feeble I am and weary,
    And my steps are but faint and slow,
And the works of the King of the Graces
    I feel within me grow.'

Then out spake the good St. Joseph,
    And stoutly indeed spake he :
' I shall not pluck thee one cherry,
    Who art unfaithful to me ;

' Let him come fetch you the cherries,
    Who is dearer than I to thee.'
Then Jesus hearing St. Joseph,
    Thus spake to the stately tree :

' Bend low in her gracious presence,
    Stoop down to herself, O Tree,
That my Mother herself may pluck thee,
    And take thy burden from thee.'

Then the great tree lowered her branches
    At hearing the high command,
And she plucked the fruit that it offered,
    Herself with her gentle hand.

Loud shouted the good St. Joseph,
    He cast himself on the ground :
'Go home and forgive me, Mary,
    To Jerusalem I am bound ;
I must go to the Holy City,
    And confess my sin profound.'

Then out spake the gentle Mary,
    She spake with a gentle voice :
'I shall not go home, O Joseph,
    But I bid thee at heart rejoice,
For the King of Heaven shall pardon
    The sin that was not of choice.'

        *   *   *

Three months from that self-same morning,
    The blessed Child was born ;
Three kings did journey to worship
    That Babe from the lands of the morn.

Three months from that very evening,
    He was born there in a manger,
With asses and kine and bullocks,
    In the strange, cold place of a stranger.

To her Child said the Virgin softly,
    Softly she spake and wisely :
'Dear Son of the King of Heaven,
    Say what may in life betide thee.'

THE BABE :

'I shall be upon Thursday, Mother,
    Betrayed and sold to the foeman,
And pierced like a sieve on Friday,
    With nails by the Jew and Roman.

'On the streets shall my Heart's Blood flow,
    And my Head on a spike be planted,
And a spear through my Side shall go,
    Till death at the last be granted.

'Then thunders shall roar with lightnings,
    And a storm over earth come sweeping,
The lights shall be quenched in the heavens
    And the sun and the moon be weeping.

'While angels shall stand around me,
    With music and joy and gladness,
As I open the road into Heaven
    That was lost by the first man's madness.'

       *   *   *

Christ built that road into Heaven,
    In spite of Death and the Devil,
Let us when we leave the world
    Be ready by it to travel.

Joan of Arc: 1412—1431.

I. ENDING OF THE SOLILOQUY OF JOAN OF ARC BEFORE HER DEATH.

MARY A. McMULLEN ('*UNA*'): 1844—1876.

FROM 'SNATCHES OF SONG,' 1874.

The writer was born in Antrim, Ireland; was married to Patrick Ford, Editor of the *Irish World*, New York; and died at Brooklyn, U.S.A. (M.R.)

    'AND, O my Mother, thou whose love
    Was valued next to heaven above,

Thy tender smile, thy fond caress
No more thy lonely child shall bless.
'Tis bitter agony to know
That I have blanched thy cheek with woe;
O Mother, Mother, that thy heart
For me is pierced by sorrow's dart.
Dear Queen of Sorrows, who didst feel
An earthly mother's anguish, heal
Her wounded soul; with tender care
Impart the strength her woes to bear.
My Father, let thy blessings fall
Like sunshine on my dear ones all,
And stretch thy strong, protecting hand
For ever o'er my native land:
To thee my spirit I commend,
Be with me, guide me to the end;
Oh, let my soul ne'er shrink nor flee
From death, since it but leads to thee.'

At length, by weariness oppressed,
The captive closed her eyes in rest,
And peaceful slumber deep and calm,
That brings a sweet though transient balm
For every ill, in pity stole
Its downy pinions o'er her soul:
She slept—the dreaded funeral pyre,
The yelling crowd, the blistering fire
Forgot, for God perhaps had given
To bless her dreams a glimpse of heaven,
While angels spread their wings to shade
The slumbers of the Martyr-Maid.

II. CONCLUSION OF A MONOLOGUE OF JOAN OF ARC.

KATHERINE TYNAN HINKSON.

FROM 'LOUISE DE LA VALLIÈRE,' 1885.

Scene : The Great Tower of Rouen Castle.   Time : Sunset,
29th May, 1431.

THE sun has gone an hour.   What light doth come
Gleaming a-sudden palely through the gloom?
Lord, whence is this to me.   Behold thy Cross :
Thy fair Face, pale with agony and loss,
Leaneth to my face.
                           Hold thine Arms still wide,
Nailed lest they tire and fall, O Crucified.
I come ; I come.   Thou hast waited long for me.
Lo, has the dungeon vanished utterly ?
I think this is the New Jerusalem.
Yonder I hear the seraph's raptured hymn
Before the Throne.   I see the pearly gate
And crystal walls.   My flying feet are set
On jacinth, gold and crusted porphyry.
Now, sweet Fire, come, take me, and burn from me
All earthly taints, and make me lily fair ;
Give me white Pentecostal robes to wear
Against the Bridegroom cometh.   With me be,
O sweet Saints, Katharine and Margery,
And guide me through the shadowed valley's ways
To where across a mystic shining haze
His arms await me.
                           Mary, take this hand,
And lead me by morass and shifting sand
Through yon white river of flames, that leap and roar,
To where Christ waiteth on the further shore.

Descant upon the Litany of Loreto, and an Ode.

LIONEL JOHNSON.

FROM 'POEMS,' 1897.

I. DESCANT UPON THE LITANY OF LORETO.

Written in 1885.

A FLOOD of chaunted love,
Love white and virginal,
Makes this rich temple gloom more musical
Than woodland glooms ; where slow winds nightly move
Soft leaves, that rise and fall .
Upon the branches of clear nightingales ;
Whose rapture, touched with lovelier sorrow, wails
And thrills and thrills
Until night fails ;
And in the sunrise on the eternal hills
The Angels of the Morning stand,
Blessing with lifted hand
The labouring land :
But here the glory of our holy song,
Sorrowless, flies along
Reaches of Heaven adoring and adored :
Where Angels worship ; whither men aspire,
Wielding their faith, a sword
Tempered and tried in fire.
Sorrowless song : for each predestined pang,
Of Calvary and Nazareth,
Changed to a passion of delight, when rang
An universal breath
Of salutation over death cast down :

When upon Mary's brow the crown,
For all her lowliness, proclaimed her Queen
Of Heaven and of our woes : she who had been
Woe once incarnate, as high God in her.
            Wherefore the pure concent
Of each fair voice, found fit to minister
            Its music to her ear,
Floods, with no underflow of doubt and fear,
This sacred house : while infinite content
            Urges forgetfulness
Of that which makes the Angels' rapture less ;
            The passionate countenance,
Wherewith the Prince of this World still blasphemes
            Against its God, and gleams
Angrily against Michael's lifted lance,
            Then falls beneath his glance.
            So be not quick to take
Your death of beauty on this trembling air.
            A little longer yet,
O voices piercing to the golden stair :
A little longer let the world look fair :
            A little longer make
Anguish of heart a light thing to forget :
            A little longer yet.
She will not weary of your harmonies,
The gentle Mother : for her memories
            Are full of ancient melodies,
Raised in the fashion of old Israel,
            Beside the cold rock well :
Under the glow of calm and splendid skies ;
            Jesus upon her breast,
Fronting the shadowy land, the solemn west.
Ah, Mother, whom with many names we name

By lore of love, which in our earthly tongue
Is all too poor, though rich love's heart of flame,
To sing thee as thou art, nor leave unsung
The greatest of the graces thou hast won,
      Thy chiefest excellence.
Ivory Tower; Star of the Morning; Rose
Mystical; Tower of David; our Defence;
      To thee our music flows,
Who makest music for us to thy Son.
      So when the shadows come,
Laden with all contrivances of fear,
      Ah, Mary, lead us home,
      Through fear, through fire,
To where with faithful companies we may hear
That perfect music, which the love of God,
      Who this dark way once trod,
Creates among the imperishable choir.

II. OUR LADY OF THE MAY.

Written in 1895.

O FLOWER of flowers, our Lady of the May,
    Thou gavest us the World's one Light of Light:
Under the stars, amid the snows he lay;
    While Angels through the Galilean night
      Sang glory and sang peace:
      Nor doth their singing cease,
For thou their Queen and he their King sit crowned
Above the stars, above the bitter snows;
They chaunt to thee the Lily, him the Rose,
      With white Saints kneeling round.
Gone is cold night: thine now are spring and day
O Flower of flowers, our Lady of the May.

O Flower of flowers, our Lady of the May,
 Thou gavest us the blessed Christmas mirth :
And now not snows, but blossoms light thy way ;
 We give thee the fresh flower-time of the earth.
  These early flowers we bring
  Are angels of the spring,
Spirits of gracious rain and light and dew.
Nothing so like to thee the whole earth yields
As these pure children of her vales and fields,
  Bright beneath skies of blue.
Hail, Holy Queen, their fragrant breathings say :
O Flower of flowers, our Lady of the May.

O Flower of flowers, our Lady of the May,
 Breathe from God's garden of eternal flowers
Blessing, when we thy little children pray :
 Let thy soul's grace steal gently over ours.
  Send on us dew and rain,
  That we may bloom again,
Nor wither in the dry and parching dust.
Lift up our hearts, till with adoring eyes,
O Morning Star, we hail thee in the skies,
  Star of our hope and trust.
Sweet Star, sweet Flower, there bid thy beauty stay :
O Flower of flowers, our Lady of the May.

O Flower of flowers, our Lady of the May,
 Thou leftest lilies rising from thy tomb :
They shone in stately and serene array,
 Immaculate amid death's house of gloom.
  Ah, let thy graces be
  Sown in our dark hearts. We

Would make our hearts gardens for thy dear care ;
Watered from wells of Paradise, and sweet
With balm winds flowing from the Mercy Seat,
  And full of heavenly air :
While music ever in thy praise should play,
O Flower of flowers, our Lady of the May.

O Flower of flowers, our Lady of the May
  Not only for ourselves we plead, God's Flower
Look on thy blinded children, who still stray
  Lost in this pleasant land, thy chosen Dower
   Send us a perfect spring :
   Let faith arise and sing,
And England from her long, cold winter wake.
Mother of Mercy, turn upon her need
Thine eyes of mercy : be there spring indeed ;
   So shall thine Angels make
A starrier music, than our hearts can say,
O Flower of flowers, our Lady of the May.

The Ghyrlond of the Blessed Virgin Marie.

BEN JONSON: 1573—1637.

FROM 'THE FEMALL GLORY,' BY ANTHONY STAFFORD, 1635,
EDITED BY ORBY SHIPLEY, M.A., 1860.

HERE are five letters in this Blessed Name
  Which, changed, a five-fold mysterie designe ;
The M. the Myrtle, A. the Almonds clame,
  R. Rose, 1. Ivy, E. sweet Eglantine.

These forme thy Ghyrlond : whereof Myrtle green
  The gladdest ground to all the numbered-five,
Is so implexed, and laid in between,
  As Love here studied to keep Grace alive.

The second string is the sweet Almond bloome
  Ymounted high upon Selinis' crest ;
As it alone, and onely it, had roome
  To knit thy crowne and glorifie the rest.

The third is from the garden called the Rose,
  The eye of flowers, worthy for his scent
To top the fairest lily, now, that growes
  With wonder on the thorny regiment.

The fourth is humble Ivy, intersert
  But lowlie laid, as on the earth asleep,
Preserved, in her àntique bed of vert,
  No faith's more firme, or flat, than where't doth creep.

But that which summes all is the Eglantine,
  Which of the field is clep'd the sweetest brier,
Inflamed with ardor to that mystick Shrine,
  In Moses' Bush, unwasted in the Fire.

Thus Love and Hope and burning Charitie,
  Divinest Graces, are so entermixt
With odorous sweets and soft Humilitie,
  As if they adored the Head whereon th' are fixt.

THE REVERSE ; ON THE OTHER SIDE.

These Mysteries do point to three more great
  On the reverse of this your circling crowne,
  All pouring their full showre of Graces downe,
The glorious Trinity in Union met.

Daughter and Mother and the Spouse of God,
   Alike of kin to that most Blessed Trine
   Of Persons, yet in Union, One, Divine,
How are thy gifts and graces blazed abro'd.

Most holy, and pure Virgin, Blessed Mayd,
   Sweet Tree of Life, King David's Strength and Tower,
   The House of Gold, the Gate of Heaven's power,
The Morning-Star whose light our fall hath stay'd.

Great Queen of Queens, most mild, most meek, most wise,
   Most venerable, Cause of all our joy,
   Whose chearfull look our sadnesse doth destroy,
And art the spotlesse Mirror to man's eyes.

The Seat of Sapience, the most lovely Mother,
   And most to be admirèd of thy sexe,
   Who mad'st us happy all, in thy reflexe,
By bringing forth God's Onely Son, no other.

Thou Throne of Glory, beauteous as the moone,
   The rosie morning, or the rising sun,
   Who like a giant hastes his course to run,
Till he hath reached his two-fold point of noone,

How are thy gifts and graces blazed abro'd,
   Through all the lines of this circumference,
   T' imprint in all purged hearts this Virgin sence
Of being Daughter, Mother, Spouse of God?

The Maiden Full of Grace.

ST. ROMANUS: V—VI CENTS.

A CHRISTMAS HYMN.

TRANSLATED (1897) FROM THE GREEK, BY
JOSEPH KEATING, S.J.

MOTHERLESS he of the Father born
Or ere the day-star's birth,
Assumeth Flesh from thee this morn
Without a sire on earth.
The Wise Men read in starlit space
The tidings glad while angels sing
To shepherds of thy stainless child-bearing,
O Maiden, Full of Grace.

The Vine a cluster putting forth, which owed
Nought to the care of man,
Embowered in bended arms the tender load
And thus in speech began :
' My Fruit art thou, yet of my life the cause,
For thou hast made me know
That I am still e'en as I ever was.
Thou art my God, to thee I owe
My seal of maidenhood unbroken so :
Hail to thee, changeless Word in garb of Flesh made low.
A field unsown
No soilure of the harvest have I known,
For pure am I who gave thee birth, and thou
Didst leave e'en now
With careful heed
Unchanged the womb from which thou didst proceed.

Wherefore with joy the whole created race
Acclaimeth me indeed
The Maiden Full of Grace.

Thus gifted, Lord, thy grace I make not void,
Nor have I aught destroyed
Of glory which in bearing thee I won.
Queen of the World am I, o'er all I reign,
Since in my womb hath lain
Thy Lordship, O my Son.
Thou hast made rich my state of penury,
And condescending so,
Thyself hast thou brought low,
But raised the human race on high.
Join in my mirth together, earth and sky:
Your Maker in my breast bore I.
Oh, lay aside your sadness,
Children of earthly race,
And gaze upon the gladness
Which brought I from my bosom undefiled—
I, who am styled,
The Maiden Full of Grace.

While to her Son, Mary, the Mother sang,
Fondling the Babe, her Only-born;
Eve, that well knew the child-birth pang,
Heard, and to Adam cried, no more forlorn:
'What voice is this hath echoed in mine ears,
Those words, my hope so long delayed,
Telling of One, a Mother yet a Maid,
Who ends the curse of years?
'Tis she, 'tis only she
Whose voice from woe my heart doth free;

And this her Child hath chained the foe
'That smote me long ago :
'Tis she, who was foretold
By Amos' son of old ;
The Rod of Jesse, that hath grown this hour
A Branch whereof my lips' embrace
Shall cause myself to flower ;
'Tis she, the Maiden-Mother, Full of Grace.'

Foot-prints of the Months.

WILLIAM D. KELLY, PRIEST: D. 1900.

FROM 'THE AVE MARIA,' 1889—1891.

I. DECEMBER :· THE CONCEPTION.

WHEN in white ermine wrapt December treads
  The paths her elder sister's feet forsake ;
  When in the woods the boreal bugles wake
Melodious echoes where, within their beds,
The flowers have buried deep their pretty heads ;
  And in the marshes every frozen lake,
  With beauty flashing like some moon-kissed brake,
Shines in the splendour that the sunlight sheds—
Come dreams, Madonna, of that city fair
  By the belovèd priest at Patmos seen,
Where golden streets divide the spacious square
  With crystal waters flowing clear between ;
Within whose jasper walls, of twelve-fold gate,
Thou sittest throned, the Queen Immaculate.

II. MAY : THE MONTH OF MARY.

MADONNA, in the orchard and the croft,
  All beautiful with blossoms and aglow
  With the warm kisses which the winds bestow
On their uplifted faces, white and soft ;

Lingering among them lovingly and oft
  Athwart the daisied meadows, to and fro
  Beneath the blue skies as they gaily go,
Their snowy shapes the fruit trees rear aloft:
For it is May, sweet Mother, when all things
    That in the gardens and the green fields grow,
    Because to thee the month is consecrate,
Assume their fairest forms and colourings,
    That we who see them thus arrayed may know
    The Queen they honour is Immaculate.

III. AUGUST : THE ASSUMPTION.

ACROSS an azure arch of star-lit skies,
  Full-orbed and fulgent, moves the harvest-moon
  Lulled by the lullabies the night-winds croon;
The flowers have folded fast their drowsy eyes,
The meadow land outstretched in slumber lies;
    And the soft splendour of the night's still noon,
    Which garish day will shadow all too soon,
Enwraps the dreaming world it beautifies:
On such another night long years ago,
    Methinks, Madonna, did the angels come,
Winging their downward way to earth below
    From yonder glorious, silver, starry dome,
And bear thee backward with them when they went
To be the Queen of that bright firmament.

IV. SEPTEMBER : THE NATIVITY.

How brightly must the morning stars have beamed,
  How soft have been the skies, how fair the earth,
  The harvests belting it with golden girth,
When all the prophecies whereof men dreamed
Were by thy birth, Madonna mine, redeemed :
  o

Alike the hour when grief gives way to mirth,
Alike the time when plenty follows dearth,
Must the first flushes of that dawn have seemed.
And year by year, as Summer slowly tenders
  To Autumn's hands the symbols of its sway,
Some semblance of its radiance and its splendours
  Returns a little while with us to stay,
And by its beauty all the lovelier renders
  Each glad on-coming of that blessed day.

V. NOVEMBER : THE PRESENTATION.

How blithely must her childish feet have crossed
  The Temple in their eagerness to win
  A refuge from the wicked world of sin,
Though all the tempter's wiles on her were lost :
Encircling her about, a white-winged host
  Of guardian angels hovered ; and her kin
  Was he, the priest, who bade her enter in—
Herself the Dwelling of the Holy Ghost.
And where can lips find language to pourtray
  The wondrous works of grace within her wrought,
  Or words to speak the happiness she felt
As gliding thus her maiden years away,
  Within the sanctuary she had sought,
    In blest communion with her God she dwelt.

Hymns from the Coptic 'Theotokia.'

TRANSLATED BY WILLIAM HENRY KENT, O.S.C.

FROM 'THE AVE MARIA,' 1898.

THEOTOKIA FOR THE FIRST DAY OF THE WEEK.

MYSTIC Altar, Seat of Mercy,
Covered by the guardian Cherubs ;
God the Word, who knows not changing,
Taketh Flesh in thee, the Stainless ;
And for sins becomes our Justice,
For the pardon of transgressions.
'Tis for this that all exalt thee :
Thou art God's, and God thou bearest ;
Thou for evermore art Holy.
   Lo, we pray that through thy pleading
   Unto him that loves his people,
   We may all obtain salvation.

Those two graven golden Cherubs
Covering the Seat of Mercy,
Every way their wings outspreading
Hovered o'er the Holy of Holies,
In the second tabernacle.
Thus it is with thee, O Mary,
Heavenly hosts in thousand thousands
Myriad myriads overshade thee,
Singing praise to their Creator
Who hath made thy womb his dwelling
And vouchsafed to take our likeness
Yet without all sin, or changing.

Rightly, then, do we exalt thee
With the praises of the prophets,
Who tell forth thy deeds of glory—
Thee the great King's Holy City.
 Now we pray thee and beseech thee,
 By thy prayer to him that loveth
 Men, may we attain to mercy.

Thou art the pure Golden Vessel,
Holding in its midst the Manna
Where the Bread of Life lay hidden
That for us came down from heaven,
Gave the world true life for ever.
'Tis for this that all exalt thee :
Thou art God's, and God thou bearest ;
Thou for evermore art Holy.
 Lo, we pray that through thy pleading
 Unto him that loves his people,
 We may all obtain salvation.

Truly meet the name we give thee,
Hailing thee the Golden Vessel,
Holding in its midst the Manna
Treasured by the sons of Israel
In the Covenant Tabernacle,
Mindful of the good God wrought them
On the holy Mount of Sinai.
Thus, O Mary, thou didst mother
In thy womb the Living Manna,
Which proceeded from the Father ;
And all stainless thou didst bear him,
Giving us his Blood all glorious,
And his Flesh for life for ever.
Rightly, then, do we exalt thee
With the praises of the prophets,

Who tell forth thy deeds of glory—
Thee the Great King's Holy City.
  Now we pray thee and beseech thee,
  By thy prayer to him that loveth
  Men, may we attain to mercy.

Pure gold Candlestick that bearest
That bright Lamp which ever burneth,
That which hath the world enlightened,
That whereto no one approacheth,
Out from which the Light proceedeth
Whereunto no one approacheth—
True God from True God proceeding,
Changeless taketh Flesh within thee,
By his bounteous presence bringing
Light to us that sat in darkness,
Dwelling in death's sombre shadow.
And our wayward feet, in mercy,
In the path of peace he setteth,
By the grace of the communion
Of his mystery all holy.
'Tis for this that all exalt thee :
Thou art God's, and God thou bearest ;
Thou for evermore art Holy.
  Lo, we pray that through thy pleading
  Unto him that loves his people,
  We may all obtain salvation.

There is naught among the highest
That to thee may well be likened,
Golden Candlestick that bearest
In thy midst the Light of Justice.
Hands of men that old lamp tended,
Wrought of gold all pure and chosen,

Set within the Tabernacle ;
Day and night with oil they fed it.
That within thy womb, O Mary,
Unto every man that cometh
To this world, true light hath given ;
For he is the Sun of Justice,
Thou hast borne for us—the Saviour,
Who hath pardoned our offences.
Rightly, then, do we exalt thee
With the praises of the prophets
Who tell forth thy deeds of glory—
Thee the Great King's Holy City.
   Now we pray thee and beseech thee,
   By thy prayer to him that loveth
   Men, may we attain to mercy.

Thou art the pure Golden Censer
Bearing the bright Coal of Blessing,
That was from the altar taken
For the purging of offences,
And the pardon of transgressions ;
It was God, the Word Eternal,
Who hath taken Flesh within thee,
And himself a Host hath offered
In sweet odour to the Father.
'Tis for this that all exalt thee :
Thou art God's, and God thou bearest ;
Thou for evermore art Holy.
   Lo, we pray that through thy pleading
   Unto him that loves his people,
   We may all obtain salvation.

Then, in sooth, I erred in nowise
Calling thee the Golden Censer ;

For therein sweet Incense, chosen,
Mounted upwards to the Holiest:
To the end that God might pardon
The offences of his people,
For the sake of that sweet savour
And the burning of the incense.
Thus didst thou conceive him, Mary—
Him on whom no creature looketh,
God the Father's Word Eternal,
Who a pleasing Victim offered
On the Cross for our salvation.
Rightly, then, do we exalt thee
With the praises of the prophets,
Who tell forth thy deeds of glory—
Thee the Great King's Holy City.
   Now we pray thee and beseech thee,
   By thy prayer to him that loveth
   Men, may we attain to mercy.

Hail, O Mary, Dove of Beauty,
God the Word, for us, conceiving:
Thou art that fair Plant of Sweetness
From the root of Jesse springing.
Aaron's Rod that bloomed, untended
And unwatered, was thy figure.
Christ True God, for us, a Virgin
Without seed of man thou bearest;
'Tis for this that all exalt thee:
Thou art God's, and God thou bearest;
Thou for evermore art Holy.
   Lo, we pray that through thy pleading
   Unto him that loves his people,
   We may all obtain salvation.

Holy Mary, well they hail thee
As the second Tabernacle,
As the dwelling of the Holiest,
Where was laid the Rod of Aaron,
With the fair Flower sweetly smelling.
O thou purest Tabernacle,
In and out all clad with brightness:
Lo, the armies of the Highest
And the choirs of saints proclaim thee,
Singing praises to thy glory.
Rightly, then, do we exalt thee
With the praises of the prophets,
Who tell forth thy deeds of glory—
Thee the Great King's Holy City.
  Now we pray thee and beseech thee,
  By thy prayer to him that loveth
  Men, may we attain to mercy.

*   *   *

Than all saints thou art more mighty:
Full of Grace, do thou pray for us.
Thou art higher than the fathers,
And more glorious than the prophets;
And thou speakest with more freedom
Than the Cherubim and Seraphs;
For thou art mankind's true Glory,
And of all our souls the Guardian.
For our sake beseech our Saviour
That in faith he may confirm us,
Grant us grace, our sins forgiving,
Show us mercy through thy pleading.

No one of the highest spirits,
Myriad angels and archangels,

To thy blessedness attaineth.
With the Lord of Hosts, thy glory,
Thou art clothed the sun outshining.
Thou art brighter than the Cherubs;
And the Seraphim before thee
Wave their wings in exultation.

The Spouse of Mary, &c.

FREDERICK C. KOLBE, D.D.,

PRIEST OF ST. MARY'S, CAPE TOWN.

I. THE SPOUSE OF MARY.

FROM 'ST. JOSEPH'S ANTHOLOGY,' EDITED BY MATTHEW RUSSELL, S.J., 1897.

I SOUGHT from far a peak whose summit proud
  Rose o'er its fellows like a giant's spear.
  In vain : the horizon, far across the mere,
Lay wrapt in an impenetrable shroud.
'You look too low,' they said.   Above the cloud
  I looked and saw, snow-white and crystal-clear
  High in the heavens, the mighty peak appear,
While the low hills lay hid, in homage bowed.

Thus towered, as o'er the hills in Holy Land,
  Saint Joseph; but I saw him not.   Forlorn
I entered Christ's true Church; then once more scanned
  The record of the days when Christ was born;
Lifting my new-purged eyes, I saw him stand
  Snow-white above the clouds that veiled the morn.

II. HOW SHALL THIS BE DONE?

FROM 'THE AVE MARIA,' 1898.

HEAVEN's balance was all trembling when it eyed
  Mary—unwonted trouble on her brow—
  Confronting God with an imperial 'How?'
For once, this once, Heaven hoped to be denied,
Nor hoped in vain.   To be no earthly bride
  Was always Mary's gift to Heaven; and now,
  Strong in the splendour of her Virgin-vow,
She waves the Motherhood of God aside.

O queenly Spirit, O Heart immaculate,
  This world contained no measure of thy worth,
    All other souls with inward strife are torn;
Thou wert so heavenly, thy royal state
  So towered supreme above the dross of earth,
    That even thy temptations were heaven-born.

III. THE HEART OF MARY.

FROM 'MARIANA,' 1898.

THE Heart of Mary looked above
And upward flew in flames of love;
In vain did earth around her call,
Her God to her was all in all.
Love, brought to earth by God her Son,
In Mary's Heart reflected shone.
        Heart of Mary, loving fire,
        My heart, too, with love inspire.

The Heart of Mary looks within,
And that abode all free from sin

Shows in a long line, far and wide,
Traces of sorrow glorified.
The life-long pain by Jesus borne,
Passed first through Mary's Heart forlorn.
  Heart of Mary, pierced with grief,
  Give my weeping heart relief.

The Heart of Mary looks around,
Heaven's mansions all with joy resound ;
Angels and Saints with rapture throng,
To join their music to her song.
The gladness Jesus ever gives,
Most in the Heart of Mary lives.
  Heart of Mary, throned in bliss,
  Free my heart from mournfulness.

The Heart of Mary looks below,
And waves of kindness overflow ;
Her children all for succour cry,
And she with help is ever nigh,
Recalling, as she stoops to them,
Her Baby's cry in Bethlehem.
  Lift your hearts to Heaven in prayer,
  Mary's Heart will keep them there.

NOTE.

No. I. The phenomenon described is a fact of experience. I had a repetition of it the last time I saw Teneriffe. But the mountain here referred to is one of the Apennines, and I stood on the Alban Mount when the phenomenon occurred—one of Nature's morals, expressed in a visible poem. I failed to see, because I looked too low (Author).

Assumption of Our Lady: an Ode.

'R. F. L.'

FROM 'THE CHURCH TIMES,' 1866.

SHE laid her down by Caÿster's spring,
  In the green Ionian sward,
The Maiden who bore the wondrous King,
  The Mother of Christ the Lord.
The message sped from her dying bed,
  Was carried by Angel hands ;
And to see her face, who is Full of Grace,
  Throng Apostles from distant lands.
There Peter hath come from his chair in Rome,
  And Paul with his kingly brow,
And he who stood by her at the Rood
  Is standing beside her now.

She in whose maiden features
Her Offspring we may trace,
The fairest of all God's creatures,
Goes to God's fairest place.
On earth there is low soft crying
Of women who shiver and wail ;
In Heaven is joy undying
Within the holiest veil.
On earth there is weeping and wringing
Of hands, in severest pain ;
In Heaven is gladsome singing
For the Queen who is coming to reign.

They laid her down, all womanhood's crown, with holy
    Mass and prayer,
And they carved the sign of the Cross divine above her
    with loving care ;
They deemed she would lie till the trumpet-cry should
    waken the dead from gloom ;
But he who in fight had quelled Death's might, hath
    opened his Mother's tomb.

      From the dwelling of Obed-edom,
        Midst those who serve below,
      Unto David's City of Freedom
        The Ark of God must go :
      Must go with shouting and gladness,
        With the King himself before,
      Till it pass from the land of sadness,
        Through the open heavenly door.

      Three days of longing and mournful cheer,
      Wait the Apostles who linger here ;
      Then they move the stone from her grave above,
      To look once more on the face they love.

The Body fair hath passed away from out that hallowed
    ground,
And roses bloom where Mary lay, and lilies spring
    around ;
The winding-sheet which wrapped her feet no longer
    holds the dead,
And useless lies the wimple white which bound the
    Virgin's head.

      She cometh from the wilderness
      By paths that cannot err,

The legions of Angels around her press,
And breathes from her hair the perfume rare
　　Of frankincense and myrrh.

　　　The Heavens are ringing
　　　　With musical tones
　　　Of Archangels singing,
　　　　Of Virtues and Thrones :

　　More intense grows the hymn
　　　Of the rapt Seraphim,
　　For she on whose bosom their Monarch lay
　　Is welcomed home by her Son to-day.

Unto the King she whom he sought
　　In his most low estate,
In golden vesture now is brought
　　Within his palace gate.
The Virgins upon her attending
　　Behind their Lady throng,
And their voices in praise are blending
　　With the clear angelic song.
She, pure from spot of earthly soil,
　　Pure from all human sin,
In raiment clad of curious toil,
　　Is glorious within.

Yet not for her a robe of gold with broidered art is
　　meet ;
Christ clothes her with the radiant sun, the moon is at
　　her feet ;
A crown of beamy stars is set upon her maiden
　　brow ;
Her soul doth magnify the Lord, high is the lowly
　　now.

He rises up to meet her,
He names her for his own ;
He bows, her Son, to greet her,
He sits upon his throne,
And he places her seat at his own Right Hand,
The Lady and Queen of that happy land.

Daughters of sorrow,
Mourners of earth,
Cometh the morrow,
Comes for you mirth :
After the sword hath pierced your soul,
After the Cross hath your dearest slain,
Ye shall go where the sick are whole,
Where the dead beloved are alive again.
Where, beside her Eternal Child,
Sitteth in glory his Mother mild,
Touching the top of his sceptre bright
When she prayeth for sinners her prayer of might.

Praise and bless him this festal day,
Whose is the kingdom and laud and sway,
Who abaseth the haughty and raiseth the meek,
Who breaketh the mighty and helpeth the weak.
And when to Jesus ye bow the knee,
Cry 'Ave, Maria, ora pro me.'

Lament of our Lady.

'M. A.'

FROM 'DOLMAN'S CATHOLIC MAGAZINE,' 1844.

This Lament is contributed from 'a Century of English Song in honour of the Blessed Virgin Mary,' a MS. volume compiled (1846) by Dom Alphonsus Morrall, O.S.B.

Our Lady speaks:

WEEP, Daughters of Jerusalem, weep your Saviour in
    sepulchre low ;
Steep, Daughters of Jerusalem, steep his sacred wounds
    in tears of woe.
       [There was Another, pale,
       Closely shrouded in her veil ;
       Not a murmur on her tongue,
       As she there in silence wept,
       Told how passion-deep and strong
       The tide of sorrow o'er her swept :
       Only once a quivering sigh
       In its long-drawn agony,
Told—attention towards her waking—how the Mother's
    heart was breaking.]
Jerusalem, what hath he done, that thou hast scorned
    him thus, my Son ?
       Ah, wilt thou yet disdain to mourn
       His sacred Body, bruised and torn ;
       And canst thou still refuse to weep
       Over his wounds, so sad and deep ?
Jerusalem, Jerusalem, see, how he was scorned and died
    for thee.

What hath he done? what hath he done, that thou hast
   used him thus, my Son?
       He brought thee from the land where thou
       In abject slavery bent thy brow;
       For thee he humbled Egypt's pride,
       Swept back the waters of the tide;
       For thee rained manna from the skies,
       Bade fountains from the rocks arise:
 Jerusalem, Jerusalem, see, how he was scorned and died
   for thee.

What hath he done? what hath he done, that thou hast
   used him thus, my Son?
       He bade thy foes before thee fly,
       The Gabionites in bondage sigh;
       For thee he humbled to the ground
       Proud Jericho, at trumpet sound;
       He gave to thee a chosen land
       That flowed with milk and honey bland:
Jerusalem, Jerusalem, see, how he was scorned and died
   for thee.

Jerusalem, what hath he done, that thou hast scorned
   him thus, my Son?
       Behold the thorns that bind his brow;
       Behold the wounds that bleed below;
       Behold the nails by hammers beat
       Into his sacred Hands and Feet;
       Behold the spear that torrents drew
       From the dear Heart, so pure and true;
       Behold the words of mocking scorn,
       By the gibbet-cross up-borne,
       Where the Victim hangs forlorn:
Jerusalem, Jerusalem, see, how he was scorned and died
   for thee.

P

What hath he done? what hath he done, that thou hast
   used him thus, my Son?
       He eased the bondage of thy care—
       A heavy cross thou hast made him bear;
       He saved thee from thy countless foes—
       Thou hast heaped on him unnumbered woes;
       He gave to thee a crown—and thou
       A crown of thorns hast given him now;
       A sceptre—and thou gavest instead
       Scourges and sceptre of a reed:
Jerusalem, Jerusalem, see, how he was scorned and died
   for thee.

What hath he done? what hath he done, that thou hast
   scorned him thus, my Son?
       He bore thee safely through the wild—
       Thou hast brought him hither Blood-defiled;
       He bade thee drink from springs rock-burst—
       Thou hast given him gall to quench his thirst;
       He gave the kingdom unto thee—
       Thou hast given to him the gibbet-tree;
       He took thee for his chosen bride,
       Exalted thee to power and pride—
       And thou hast lifted him on high,
       A spectacle and mockery:
Jerusalem, Jerusalem, see, how he was scorned and died
   for thee.

Weep, weep what thou hast done to him, thy Saviour and
   my Son;
       No longer fear with me to mourn
       His sacred Body, bruised and torn,
       No more disdain with me to weep
       Over his wounds, so sad and deep:

Repent, Jerusalem, and see—thou scornedst him who
died for thee.

[That mournful plaining ceased; and then she sat in
silent grief agen,

    Until they led her from that hill
    Where she would fondly linger still;
    But even in her secret bower
    Where 'neath her sweetly soothing power,
    Magdalen's sorrow grew less wild,
    'Till she wept gently as a child;
    And Peter, and the rest who drew
    Around her, felt that influence too,
    And wept, by softer feelings swayed,
    O'er him deserted and betrayed—
    E'en then the Loved-one drawing near
    Could still that soft lamenting hear,
' Jerusalem, Jerusalem, see, how he was scorned and died
for thee.']

Weep, Daughters of Jerusalem, weep your Saviour in
sepulchre low;
Steep, Daughters of Jerusalem, steep his sacred wounds
in tears of woe.

Verse

I. By FREDERICK GEORGE LEE,

AND

II. By ELVIRA LOUISA LEE: 1838—1890.

I.

I. THE MONTH OF MAY.

FROM 'THE AVE MARIA,' 1897.

ALL that before High God (rolled on dark Night)
In golden beauties of earth's prime out lay,

Bathed in rich silver dew or purple spray,
Or glowing green in heaven's supernal light—
Was his, and he declared it very good.
But where a stream divided into four,
A sword of flame and cry of loss on the wind,
Where darkness shut out sunshine—there full sore
Sank two poor souls, with Paradise behind ;
Yet with a pledge of grace and heavenly food,
And of a Friend all potent, in the years
To come and go for thorned and thistled earth.
One came in time—stainless, a Mother-Maid,
For all whose common instinct told of peace ;
Her Son, the Son of God, with grace and aid
For all who dreamt of a joyous day, when tears
Should be for aye and ever wiped away,
Yet passed from hence and never knew it break :
When power of life for noxious weeds should cease
And fresh life live in this bleared world—new birth,
With lilies opened in the glare and shine
Of diamond May, or rosy June ; and Earth
Own once again Creation's Lord, who was,
Is, evermore shall be.   Star, flower and grass,
The beauty of the trickling silver rill,
And the months passing, consecrate to him ;
The glory of the cloud-enveloped hill,
And strange Creation's strangely-blended hymn.
This now around, about—not face to face ;
We see by faith in this short, restless day,
(God grant us near the Throne some lowly place)
His hers, hers his—close knit to him by grace
And love divine : she claims the Month of May.

II. THE SHEPHERD BOY OF LOMBARDY ON SUNDAY.

FROM 'THE AVE MARIA,' 1880.

THIS day the Lord God-Man arose :
  On this wide moor I'm here alone ;
  Yon sancte-bell tells the hour hath flown ;
All still, as blinding sunshine glows.
     So wait I for God's promised rest :
     They walk in white and all are blest.

Prostrate I now low bend the knee ;
  Oh, sacréd awe ; Oh, transport high ;
  A host invisible glides nigh,
Adoring Christ with mine and me.
     So not alone I ask God's rest :
     They walk in white and all are blest.

Above, around God's sunny floor
  One dome of deep and cloudless blue,
  Where stoléd angels, listening through,
Worship sans words for evermore.
     I pray and work, yet long for rest :
     They walk in white and all are blest.

I love this quiet day of peace ;
  Prostrate I dwell with tearful eyes
  On Michael's blessed Paradise,
And Raphael's touch when all pains cease :
     So wait for God's eternal rest—
     Angels and men for ever blest.

And for the Lady Mary too,
  Who sits up near his Throne in white,
  Crowned with rose-coronal in light,
And over all a robe of blue.
      A narrow home on earth's lorn breast—
      Then calm and peace for ever blest.

II.

REGINA SANCTORUM OMNIUM.

THE light falls lustrous through the pictured pane,
  Mid incense clouds the tapers glare,
Swells or dies out the organ's solemn strain,
  Ascends the chanted prayer.

Hail, Mary; listen while we raise
  Our vesper hymn of love;
Bless us, thy children, and accept our praise
  And plead for us above.

Mother most Pure, of him who gives us peace,
  And calms life's stormy sea,
Pray that his gifts and grace in us increase,
  Our hearts more faithful be.

Low-kneeling with a trustful and adoring love,
  Before thy gleaming shrine,
We think of those bright throngs of saints above
  Which round thee glorious shine.

That peace which Jesus came on earth to bring
  Was their's through toilsome days;
But now they know it to the full, and sing
  Enduring songs of praise.

When in fierce conflict, Mother-Maid, they strove
  That heavenly rest to gain,
Thy prayers lit up their flame of ardent love
  And strengthened them in pain.

Thy love encircled them from morn till night
  When fiery trials came ;
In their last agony thou wert their light,
  Sweet comfort thy dear name.

They knew thy Son ne'er turned his face away
  From powerful prayer of thine ;
So in their Mother's arms they patient lay
  And gained their crown divine.

In peace they slept, and now in glory reign ;
  Then, Queen of Saints, look down,
Help us to bear like them our cross of pain
  And thus to win a crown.

To-night whilst kneeling here, the world shut out,
  May Christ thy pleadings hear,
And for his Mother's sake, hush every doubt
  And calm each anxious fear.

Pour down anew refreshing streams of grace
  From those dear hands of thine,
And lead us on at last to see thy face
  Where Saints in glory shine.

Legends and Ballads.

I. PILGRIMAGE TO KEVLAAR.

HEINRICH HEINE: 1799—1856.

TRANSLATED BY EDGAR ALFRED BOWRING.

FROM 'THE POEMS OF HEINE,' 1859.

I.

THE Mother stood by the window,
  The Son in bed lay he:
'Wilt thou not rise up, William,
  The fair procession to see?'
'I am so ill, my mother,
  I neither see, nor hear;
I think of my poor dead Gretchen,
  My heart is breaking near.'
'Arise, let's go to Kevlaar,
  Take book and rosary too;
The Mother of God will heal thee,
  And cure thy sick heart anew.'
In church-like tones they are singing,
  The banners flutter on high;
At Cologne on the Rhine this happens,
  The proud procession moves by.
The crowd the mother follows,
  Her son she leadeth now,
And both of them sing in chorus:
  'O Mary, Blessed be thou.'

II.

The Mother of God at Kevlaar
  Her best dress wears to-day ;
Full much hath she to accomplish,
  So great the sick folks' array.
The sick folk with them are bringing,
  As offerings fitting and meet,
Strange limbs of wax all fashioned,
  Yes, waxen hands and feet.
And he who a wax hand offers,
  Finds cured in his hand the wound ;
And he who a wax foot proffers,
  Straight finds his foot grow sound.
To Kevlaar went many on crutches
  Who now on the tight-rope skip,
And many a palsied finger
  O'er the viol doth merrily trip.
The mother took a waxlight,
  And out of it fashioned a heart :
'My son, take that to God's Mother,
  And she will cure thy smart.'
The son took sighing the wax-heart,
  Went with sighs to the shrine so blest,
The tears burst forth from his eyelids,
  The words burst forth from his breast :
'Thou highly-favoured Blest One,
  Thou pure and God-like maid,
Thou mighty Queen of Heaven,
  To thee my woes be displayed.
I with my mother was dwelling
  In yonder town of Cologne,
The town that many a hundred
  Fair churches and chapels doth own :

And near us there dwelt my Gretchen,
  Who, alas, is dead to-day;
O Mary, I bring thee a wax-heart,
  My heart's wounds cure, I pray.
My sick heart cure, Oh, cure thou,
  And early and late my vow
I'll pay and sing with devotion:
  O Mary, Blessed be thou.'

III.

The poor sick son and his mother
  In their little chamber slept,
The Mother of God to their chamber
  All lightly, lightly crept.
She bent herself over the sick one,
  Her hand with action light
Upon his heart placed softly,
  Smiled sweetly and vanished from sight.
The mother saw all in her vision,
  Saw this and saw much more;
From out of her slumber woke she
  The hounds were baying full sore.
Her son was lying before her,
  And dead her son he lay,
While over his pale cheeks gently
  The light of morning did play.
Her hands the mother folded,
  She felt she knew not how;
With meekness sang she and softly:
  ' O Mary, Blessed be thou.'

II.   A STATUE FROM THE SEA.

ELEANOR C. DONNELLY.

FROM 'THE AVE MARIA,' 1894.

A vessel from France, carrying statuary, was stranded off Sea
Isle, New Jersey, in 1861.   The sole relic of the wreck was a small
Statue of the Blessed Virgin.   It was washed ashore in 1891, and
came into the possession of the pastor on the Island, who presented
it to the writer.

THIRTY years since the good ship sank
On the stormy sands of the Sea Isle bank—
The good ship ' Mortimer Livingston '
(O'er the autumn seas from Havre bound
To the city of Penn), at set of sun,
On the shoals of Sea Isle ran aground.
Alas, for her fragile freight and fair,
Her wealth of sculpture rich and rare.
Parian image, vase and shrine,
Dashed in the foam of the boiling brine ;
Marvels from skilled Parisian hands,
Crushed like shells on the grinding sands.
Naught was spared of the cargo frail,
Save one small Statue of our Queen.
The billows sang as they kissed her veil,
And the sands grew soft where she sank unseen.
Sole Christian symbol, heaven-placed
On the lonely shores of the island waste.

Thirty years in the bed of the sea,
Through storm and sunshine slumbered she.
The tide ran up and the tide ran down,
The sea-wall groaned 'neath the surges' shock

Past sand and shingle, wet and brown,
The sea-gulls fluttered, a dreary flock.
But over beyond, the village shrined
A cross-crowned church, and the Master kind
There blessed his own.   The soft air through,
Sounded the Mass and Vesper bell.
Our Lady heard, and nearer drew
To the isle where her Jesus joyed to dwell.
Till lo, one golden autumn day
The billows, in their graceful play,
Lifted her little Image bright
And cast it, like a foam-wreath white,
Safe on the sands.
                    Just thirty years
Since the 'Livingston' sank on the sandy bar.
'Lady of Sea Isle, hail,' she hears :
'Welcome, Mary, our Ocean Star.'

III.   O MARIA, REGINA MISERICORDIÆ.

JAMES CLARENCE MANGAN
[*After KARL SIMROCK*]: 1803—1849.
FROM 'GERMAN ANTHOLOGY,' 1845.

THERE lived a Knight long years ago,
Proud, carnal, vain, devotionless ;
  Of God above, or hell below
    He took no thought, but undismayed,
Pursued his course of wickedness :
    His heart was rock ; he never prayed
    To be forgiven for all his treasons ;
    He only said, at certain seasons,
        'O Mary, Queen of Mercy.'

Years rolled and found him still the same,
Still draining Pleasure's poison-bowl ;
 Yet felt he now and then some shame ;
  The torment of the Undying Worm
At whiles woke in his trembling soul ;
  And then though powerless to reform,
 Would he, in hope to appease that sternest
Avenger, cry and more in earnest,
  ' O Mary, Queen of Mercy.'

At last Youth's riotous time was gone,
And loathing now came after Sin :
 With locks yet brown he felt as one
  Grown grey at heart ; and oft with tears
He tried, but all in vain, to win
  From the dark desert of his years
 One flower of hope ; yet morn and e'ening
He still cried, but with deeper meaning,
  ' O Mary, Queen of Mercy.'

A happier mind, a holier mood,
A purer spirit ruled him now :
 No more in thrall to flesh and blood,
  He took a pilgrim-staff in hand,
And under a religious vow
  Travailed his way to Pommerland ;
 There entered he an humble cloister,
Exclaiming while his eyes grew moister,
  ' O Mary, Queen of Mercy.'

Here shorn and cowled, he laid his cares
Aside, and wrought for God alone :
 Albeit he sang no choral prayers,
  Nor matin hymn, nor laud could learn,
He mortified his flesh to stone ;

For him no penance was too stern,
And often prayed he on his lonely
Cell-couch at night, but still said only,
    'O Mary, Queen of Mercy.'

And thus he lived long, long ; and when
God's angels called him, thus he died :
Confession made he none to men,
    Yet when they anointed him with oil,
He seemed already glorified :
    His penances, his tears, his toil
Were past ; and now with passionate sighing,
Praise thus broke from his lips while dying,
    'O Mary, Queen of Mercy.'

They buried him with mass and song
Aneath a little knoll so green ;
    But lo, a wonder-sight.   Ere long
    Rose, blooming from that verdant mound,
The fairest lily ever seen ;
    And on its petal-edges round,
Relieving their translucent whiteness,
Did shine these words in gold-hued brightness,
    'O Mary, Queen of Mercy.'

And would God's angels give thee power,
Thou, dearest reader, mightst behold
    The fibres of this holy flower
    Upspringing from the dead man's heart
In tremulous threads of light and gold ;
    Then wouldst thou choose the better part,
And thenceforth flee Sin's foul suggestions ;
Thy sole response to mocking questions,
    'O Mary, Queen of Mercy.'

IV. MARY STUART'S LAST PRAYER.

GEORGE SIDNEY SMYTHE,
LORD STRANGFORD: 1808—1857.

FROM 'THE BALLADS OF IRELAND,' EDITED BY EDWARD HAYES,
1855.

A LONELY mourner kneels in prayer before the Virgin's
fane,
With white hands crossed for Jesùs' sake, so her prayer
may not be vain ;
Wan is her cheek and very pale, her voice is low and
faint,
And tears are in her eyes, the while she makes her
humble plaint.
Oh, little could you deem from her, her sad and lowly
mien
That she was once the Bride of France, and still was
Scotland's Queen.

'O Mary Mother, Mary Mother, be my help and stay :
Be with me still, as thou hast been, and strengthen me
to-day :
For many a time, with heavy heart, all weary of its
grief,
I solace sought in thy blest thought, and ever found
relief :
For thou too wert a Queen on earth, and men were
harsh to thee,
And cruel things and rude they said, as they have said
of me.

O Gentlemen of Scotland, O Cavaliers of France,
How each and all had grasped his sword, and seized his
angry lance,

If ladie love, or sister dear, or nearer, dearer bride,
Had been like me your friendless Liege, insulted and
  belied :
But these are sinful thoughts and sad—I should not
  mind me now
Of faith forsworn, or broken pledge, or false, or fruitless
  vow.

But rather pray, sweet Mary, my sins may be forgiven ;
And less severe than on the earth, my Judges prove in
  heaven :
For stern and solemn men have said, God's vengeance
  will be shown,
And fearful will the penance be, on the sins which I
  have done :
And yet, albeit my sins be great, O Mary, Mary
  dear,
Nor to Knox, nor to false Moray, the Judge will then
  give ear.

Yes ; it was wrong and thoughtless, when first I came
  from France,
To lead courante, or minuet, or lighter, gayer dance :
Yes ; it was wrong and thoughtless, to while whole hours
  away,
In dark and gloomy Holyrood, with some Italian lay.
Dark men would scowl their hate at me, and I have
  heard them tell,
How the Just Lord God of Israel had stricken Jezebel.

But thou, dear Mary, Mary mine, hast ever looked
  the same
With pleasant mien and smile serene, on her who bore
  thy name :

Oh, grant that, when anon I go to death, I may not see
Nor axe, nor block, nor headsman, but thee and only
  thee.
Then 'twill be told, in coming times, how Mary gave her
  grace
To die as Stuart, Guise should die, of Charlemagne's
  fearless race.

Poems with Local Colouring.

I. ISLAND AND MOUNTAIN.

L. C. CASARTELLI, PRIEST.

I. OUR LADY OF THE ISLE.

FROM 'ST. BEDE'S MAGAZINE,' 1880.

The early Keltic and Norse inhabitants of the Isle of Man had
a remarkable devotion to the Blessed Virgin, and held her as the
Patron of the island. The Reformation swept away all traces of
the Faith, but in our times Catholicism has revived. In the new
Church at Douglas has been placed a statue of our Lady, with the
inscription, 'Our Lady, Patron of the Isle' (Author).

OUR Lady of the Isle, sweet Patron Queen,
  We come to sing thee a forgotten song,
  A hymn unheard for oh, so long, so long,
'Twixt days that are and days that erst have been.
We think thou lov'st, O Queen, the silver sheen
  That glances on the waters of our sea ;
  Thou lov'st the purple of the depths that be
Betwixt the main and our dear land's bright green.
Thou lov'st, O Queen, our fleet of white-sailed boats
  That sweep around our island-waters free ;
Thou lovest, Queen, our gallant fisher crew ;
  And oh, thou lov'st the wife and children wee
  That watch at home—e'en though they know not thee—
For sake of those of old that loved and knew.

Q

II. MARIA AD NIVES.

The little chapel of 'Maria zum Schnee,' standing by the shores of the 'Schwarzsee' (Black Lake), at the foot of the Matterhorn, two thousand feet above Zermatt, in one of the grandest parts of the Alps, is said to be the highest spot in Europe at which Holy Mass is said—and that only during the summer months. All the winter it is closed, and no human being then ascends the mountain. These lines were written on the spot in 1895 (Author).

MARIA, by thy dark and silent lake
　　All year thou guard'st thy lonely mountain shrine ;
　　Rustic its build and lowly, yet 'tis thine—
Its very lowness dear for thy dear sake.
All round the sentry Alps their station take,
Zealous to guard snow-helmed their Virgin Queen ;
Upon their breasts eternal glaciers lean—
Matterhorn's self commands their giant host.
So robed in ice and snow, sweet Mother, thou
　　Chastest of creatures, 'mid so chaste a scene,
Hearest the pilgrim's ' Ave,' as from far,
Nearing thy shrine with prayer and humble vow
　　Exulting, he beholds the sunlight sheen
Enlumine thy lone tarn, or evening's star.

II. ALPINE VERSE.

R. J. M'HUGH.

FROM ' THE AVE MARIA,' 1888.

I. OUR LADY OF THE PINES.

THE pass is narrow, wild, and steep,
　　Our footing treacherous through snow ;
But one false step—our grave yawns deep
　　Twelve hundred feet below.

Our limbs are stiff, our brains afire;
  Things swim before our aching sight;
Within us wakes the mad desire
  To slumber on the height.

But cheerily our guide: 'Fear not;
  Benignant Hope still o'er us shines;
For see, where guards this lonely spot
  Our Lady of the Pines.'

We look; and lo, within a cleft
  Of yonder pine—Hail, Full of Grace—
Some pious hand has kindly left
  Our Blessed Lady's face.

New courage thrills; all fear is past;
  Who e'er in vain to Mary prayed?
We grasp our Alpen-stocks—at last
  The pass is safely made.

O Lady, many a pass since then,
  By dangers deadlier far beset,
And fears that chill the hearts of men,
  My wandering feet have met;

And many a pass they still must brave
  Ere my brief day of life declines;
Then show thy power—thy servant save,
  Dear Lady of the Pines.

II. THE EDELWEISS AND ITS ANTI-TYPE.

To him who climbs alone some Alpine height
  Where all seems dead and drear, how sweetly blows
  In modest beauty 'mid eternal snows
The edelweiss—the star flower—pure and white.

In simple splendour on the aching sight,
  Soul-strengthening for further toil it glows,
  Bespeaking comfort, refuge and repose,
Ere Earth lies palled beneath the veil of Night.

Thus, Mother dear—Christ's Mother dear and ours—
  When rough becomes our lonely path and wild,
    We look to thee, all beaming from above;
O sweeter, fairer than all stars and flowers,
  Thou wilt not leave forlorn the wandering child
    But guide him safe to God's great home of love.

III. OUR LADY OF THE SNOW.

I. THE LIBERIAN BASILICA, 'AD NIVES,' ROME.

ANONYMOUS.

FROM 'THE AVE MARIA,' 1891.

THE dawn in misty gray stole o'er the sea,
And blushing at its image there enshrined,
With radiance flooded Rome; then swift untwined
The darksome bonds of night, and day was free.
Behold, the morn revealed a mystery;
For on a field of snow the summer wind
Was playing, where at dusk sweet flowers reclined;
And Rome, in holy wonder, bent her knee.

Ah, well, loved Mary, did the Pontiff know
Thy message in each spotless, heaven-sent flake:
Fulfilling thy behest, he bade fair Art
Immortalise that wondrous fall of snow,
From whose white depths thy accents seemed to break:
'Thrice blessed are the snowy-pure of heart.'

II.   SANTA MARIA MAGGIORE, ROME.

RICHARD HOWLEY, D.D.

FROM 'THE AVE MARIA,' 1894.

LIKE down, that from the swan's fair breast
Is shed to clothe her nurslings' nest,
From summer sky upon thy crest
    Old Esquiline,
Soft snow drops fell ; and virgin white
Remained upon thy burning height,
To make a bed and mark a site
    For Mary's shrine.

Bright Queen, refresh with heavenly snows
Our hearts, where guilty passion glows,
And o'er our ways false glamour throws
    And weaves a spell :
On our sad souls thy grace distil,
Our homes with light and beauty fill,
Like thine set on Rome's radiant hill,
    And with us dwell.

NOTE.

Allusion, both in the above Anonymous Sonnet and in the Lyric
of Dr. Howley, is made to a miraculous snow-storm which fell in
the month of August, A.D. 352, and marked the spot where the
Basilica was to be founded by Pope Liberius, and eventually was
built, the third in rank of the greater Roman Basilicas.

IV.   IN MID-ATLANTIC.

ARTHUR BARRY O'NEILL, C.S.C.

FROM 'THE AVE MARIA,' 1895.

'TIS midnight, and across the lowering sky
    Black cloud-battalions tempest-driven sweep,

The Storm-King wreaks his fury on the deep,
The huge waves toss their foamy crests on high,
Gigantic monsters that with hurtling cry
   Rush fiercely down the liquid cavern-steep,
   While swift the trembling ship with plunge and leap,
Evades the peril she may not defy.

Firm-braced I stand upon the reeling deck,
   By turns a prey to dread and strange delight;
Though raging billows threaten speedy wreck,
   The soul acclaims their grandeur, power, and might:
Yet thus acclaiming turns in prayer to thee,
Sweet Mary, Mother mine, Star of the Sea.

V. ITALIAN SHIPMAN'S CHANT.

THOMAS WILLIAM PARSONS: 1819—1892.

FROM 'VESPERS ON THE SHORE OF THE MEDITERRANEAN,' 1854.

At Savona, an ancient city on the coast of Genoa, there stands
by the light-house a statue of the Madonna under which are
inscribed two Sapphic verses, which are both good Latin and
choice Italian. They were made by Gabriello Chiabrera (1552—
1637), 'the prince of Italian lyric poets,' who was a native of
Savona, and form the refrain of the following chant; and are sung
to this day as the burden of a Litany, amongst the mariners of the
Riviera (Author).

   Tost rudderless around the deep
      By Apennine and Alpine blast,
   Which o'er the surge in fury sweep,
      And make a bulrush of our mast,
   We murmur in our half-hour's sleep
   To thee, Madonna, till the storm be past;
      In mare irato, in subita procella,
      Invoco te, nostra benigna Stella.

Whether for weeks our bark hath striven
   With death in wild Sardinia's waves,
Or downward far as Tunis driven,
   Threat us with life—the life of slaves ;
We know whose hand its help has given,
And locked the lightning in its thunder caves :
    In mare irato, in subita procella,
    Invoco te, nostra benigna Stella.

O Virgin, when the landsman's hymn,
   At vesper time, on bended knee,
In sunlit aisle, or chapel dim,
   Or cloistered cell, is paid to thee,
Hear us that ocean's pavement skim,
And join our anthem to the raging sea :
    In mare irato, in subita procella,
    Invoco te, nostra benigna Stella.

And when the tempest's wrath is o'er,
   And tired Libeccio sinks to rest,
And starlight falls upon the shore
   Where love sits watching, uncaressed,
Though hushed the tumult and the roar,
Again the prayer we'll chant which thou hast blest :
    In mare irato, in subita procella,
    Invoco te, nostra benigna Stella.

VI. AT OUR LADY'S WELL, AGHADA, COUNTY CORK, LADY'S DAY, 1885.

JOHN JAMES PIATT.

FROM 'AT THE HOLY WELL,' 1890.

ACROSS yon hill-top half a league away,
   Weird with its immemorial vine, on high

The Round Tower lifts its walls of dateless day—
 A solitary finger in the sky.

Near by, vague clumps of ruin ivy-grown
 With grave-mounds on the slope about them—look.
Patrick was preaching when they laid the stone,
 Gray priests who late their Druid rites forsook.

Here in this upland space of pasture-ground,
 Our Lady's Well pours forth its waters pure,
While groups of pious pilgrims kneel around,
 With ills of flesh or spirit, who seek their cure.

Beneath an ash-tree's boughs it flows to-day
 With flood perennial and crystal-clear ;
The Virgin close beside, in sculpture gray ;
 The Man of Sorrows on his Cross is here.

Among the restless leaves breeze-lifted, lo—
 Mute witnesses of many an August sun—
The abandoned staff, the votive garment show
 Their grateful signs of blessing sought and won.

Through the green fields, by many a dusty way,
 The rich, the poor, the sick, the blind, the dumb—
Ragged or bare, in silks or frieze, as they
 For fifteen hundred years have come—they come.

Aye, year by year as now on Lady's Day,
 Singly, in household groups—where'er they dwell—
To bathe in, drink its healing lymph and pray,
 These Irish pilgrims seek the Holy Well.

The blind one sees : the lame his crutch foregoes ;
 The bed-ridden walks : the pang of sense finds rest ;
To the wan cheek climbs back the unblighted rose ;
 The new heart throbs and warms the hollow breast.

O simple souls, whom Science has not taught
  Her earth-lore vain for Truth-Ineffable ;
For your belief such wonder-works are wrought,
  And common day grows quick with miracle.

VII. THE GROTTO OF LOURDES.

SISTER MARY RITA, OF THE HOLY CROSS, U.S.A.

FROM 'THE AVE MARIA,' 1896.

WHAT were the feet of centuries,
        O Pyrenees,
Unto thy rocky heart, so cold and still ?
The Gallic soldiers and the men of Rome,
The Vandal hordes that pillaged hearth and home,
        Left thee unmoved.

But 'neath the touch of Maiden Mary's feet,
        Triumph complete :
Thy heart knew glad creation's primal thrill,
And every vein that laced the mountain side,
In throbbing pulses of a living tide,
        Our Lady's presence proved.

O happy Grotto, happy Stream, the dower
        Of Mary's power :
With healing dost thou soul and body fill :
Would that our hearts were her sweet resting-place—
Our rock-bound hearts the shrine of peerless grace
        For Mary, our Beloved.

VIII. THE BATTLE OF LEPANTO,
7TH OCTOBER, 1571.

MAGDALEN ROCK.

FROM 'AVE MARIA,' 1892.

A THICKENING cloud of smoke the sun looked through,
And frenzied cries were heard and moan and prayer;
And standards old and royal ensigns flew
From all the lands of Southern Europe there;
Fluttering they flew, fanned by the noon-day breeze,
From galleys tall and stately argosies.

But though proud Austria's flag, blue as the sky,
Waved with the flags of Venice and of Spain,
Triumphantly the Crescent floated high,
And Christian blood was poured, and poured in vain
Upon Lepanto's waters; 'till at last
Colonna cried, 'The foes are gaining fast.'

But at that hour, the holy Pontiff prayed
In distant Rome beside our Lady's shrine,
And begged the Queen of Heaven's potent aid
For those who bravely fought beneath the Sign
Of man's redemption 'gainst the Infidel,
To save the Church her dear Son loved so well.

And lo, the Christian ranks fresh courage found
E'en as the holy Pontiff's prayer arose,
And brave Colonna's hopes with sudden bound
Revived again, and man to man the foes
Fought till the Crescent fell.   Since that blest day
To her, the Help of Christians, oft we pray.

NOTE.

Line 13. The holy Pontiff: St. Pius V. The Note on Father
Watson's sonnet, on the same theme, towards the end of the Volume,
may be consulted.

On the holy house of Loreto.

I. ON THE TRANSLATION OF THE HOUSE OF LORETO.

WALTER (SECOND LORD) ASTON, OF FORFAR, TIXALL: B. 1609.

FROM 'POEMS COLLECTED BY HERBERT ASTON, 1658' IN
'TIXALL POETRY,' EDITED BY ARTHUR CLIFFORD, 1813.

> Angels (they say) brought the famed Chapel there,
> And bore the sacred load in triumph through the air.
>> *Cowley.*

WHEN the mysterious Chamber first did move
From Jewry vales into the air above,
  A choir of angels held it down,
    Or to the highest heavens 't had flown.
      Gabriel led on before
      Towards the Hesperian shore,
    Whence west winds breathèd in their face,
    Not to resist, but to embrace.
O'er his own seas then, Dædalus might descry
A labyrinth itself of wonders fly;
Rhodes' great Colossus durst not ask a stay,
For here Immensity contracted lay;
    The Virgin Mother's Spouse's room
    At unchaste Paphos would not come;
      Truth's self disclaimed his seat
      Should dwell in lying Crete.
Delos in vain looked up with hope awhile;
The flying House past o'er the floating isle.
Unhappy eastern nations, daily thus
Suns rise with you, but always make to us.

The never-erring Chair is come
From your Antioch to our Rome ;
   Poor Nazareth's sole bliss
   Now too translated is :
On fair Loreto's hill, it stands,
Thither conveyed by angels' hands ;
Where the same roof that in our fathers' age
A pilgrim was, is now a pilgrimage.

II. THE HOLY HOUSE OF LORETO.

DOM BEDE CAMM, O.S.B.

SILENTLY, swiftly uplift your dear load,
Tenderly bear it, ye angels of God :
Over the mountains of sad Galilee,
Straight to its haven across the blue sea.

Great is the burden ye bear with such love,
None is more precious to Jesus above :
Dwelling of Mary, Immaculate-Maid,
Where the first Ave by Gabriel was said.

Raise it up and bear it swiftly
O'er the mountains and the sea,
Far from Islam's hate and outrage,
Far from wasted Galilee.

From the rage of the destroyer,
Save at least the Holy Place
Where the Word of God Eternal
Joined in marriage with our race.

Save the home where Mary Virgin
Bent her head in swift consent,
Where our God in humble labour
Many a year of silence spent.

Where our Jesù's Foster-father
When his humble path was trod,
Pillowed in the arms of Mary,
Gently gave his soul to God.

*   *   *

Alas, Dalmatia, thus to gain
This treasure, but to lose again:
Like the sweet dew that falls from heaven
One morn this House to thee was given,
But e'er thou scarce hadst known its fame,
It vanished, silent as it came.

*   *   *

Raise it up and bear it swiftly
O'er the mountains and the sea,
To a home more sure and sacred,
In our Lady's Italy.

*   *   *

Oh, rise and search in the laurel wood,
Seek for the treasure planted by God:
God hath worked wonders this blessed night,
Shout in your triumph, weep for delight:
Nazareth's shrine on Italy's soil
Given to her without trouble or toil.

Safely it resteth at last on this shore,
Sweetly reposing in peace evermore.
Mary and Joseph have found a sure home,
Close to the Vicar of Jesus at Rome.

*   *   *

Mother of Mercy, Queen most fair,
Bind our garlands in thy hair.

Mother of Jesus, Royal Maid,
Flowers of Nazareth quickly fade.

Garlands of laurels aye shall endure,
Queen of Loreto, Maiden most pure.

We enter then thy dwelling-place,
O Queen and Maiden fair,
And bind our perfumed laurel-wreaths
About thy golden hair :
We kiss the stones thy feet have pressed,
And tremble as we scan
The very Gate of Heaven below,
The House of God made Man.

Oh, give us grace
In this dread place,
To flee from sin
And mercy win,
To see at last with thee God's Face.

III. ON THE HOLY HOUSE OF NAZARÉTH AND LORETO,

ENRICHED BY POPE PAUL II.

BAPTISTA MANTUANUS: c. 1480.

TRANSLATED BY EMILY MARY SHAPCOTE.

FROM 'AMONGST THE LILIES,' 1881.

THE Building which on Picene shores you now far off
    behold,
Belongs to her who did God's Son in Virgin's womb
    enfold,
Which hither came from Syria, and by mighty Angels'
    aid
With passage strange above the sea, was through the air
    conveyed.

Loreto's Shrine, it hath been named, yet must it not be
thought

That this great Temple also was from foreign countries
brought;

These ornaments were added since, to grace the House
withal,

With charge and great devotion of the Prince of Prelates,
Paul.

IV.   THE HOUSE OF LORETO.

MARION AMES TAGGART.

FROM 'THE AVE MARIA', 1890.

Low nestled in the heart of Galilee
   Lay Nazareth, in days of old when came
   Archangel messenger, in God's own Name
Saluting her who would the Mother be
Of the Emmanuel: and unto thee,
   O blessed House—whose walls, the very same
   That now do make Loreto's holy fame—
Was borne that Ave, sweet and heavenly.
The Saviour's feet, his deeds and words divine,
   Have sanctified thee, humble place of rest.
     To Galilee the pilgrim goes no more,
For Mary's home is now Loreto's shrine;
   And lo, Hic Verbum Caro factum est,
     O'er portal writ, says, Kneel and here adore.

V.   FROM TASSO'S ODE:

' Behold amidst the storm-clouds and the winds.'

TRANSLATED (1901) *BY E. M. CLERKE.*

THE Sacred Dwelling here did Angels raise,
The Home of Mary and her Blessed Son,

And bore it through the storm-clouds o'er the brine.
O miracle, to which I lift in praise
A mind to earth by other objects won,
Oppressed by thoughts to which it doth incline.
The Mountain this, whereto thou didst consign
Of thy blest walls the freight,
O Maid Inviolate,
Abode of thee, and the great King of kings.

*   *   *

Which draws to view thy holy Image here
From furthest west, in crowds on crowds that roll
As pilgrims, 'neath the peaceful olive bough
Those that of Ebro drank and Tagus clear;
And from the signs that gird the frozen Pole
Past Danube, and where icier north winds sough.
And to the heavenly Lady many a vow,
Since she doth heal always,
Doth suffering mortals raise,
Whose prayers doth Heaven of its good grace allow;
And the great leaders, dearer in its sight,
Much silver bring and gold,
Rare gifts and fully told, unto thine altars bright.

VI. HYMN SUNG AT TERSATTO

BY CLERGY AND PEOPLE, AND INSCRIBED ON THE WALL OF
THE CHAPEL OF THE HOLY HOUSE.

Huc cum Domo advenisti.

TRANSLATED (1842) *BY ATHANASIUS DIEDRICH
WACKERBARTH.*

FROM 'LYRA ECCLESIASTICA,' 1843.

HERE thy sacred House thou broughtest,
Holy Mother, when thou soughtest
    To dispense thy heavenly grace:

Nazareth thy birth illumèd
But Ter-sanctum thee assumèd,
　　Seeking for a resting place.

Here thy House no more resideth,
But thy presence still abideth,
　　Queen of Heavenly Mercy fair :
Oh, may grateful love possess us,
That thou still dost deign to bless us
　　With thy fond maternal care.

From 'Love in Idleness,'

1883.

I. MADONNA INCOGNITA.

LADY, whose name I know not, but whose face
　　I know so well and knowing find so fair—
A pale young face crowned by pale drooping hair,
Like hers whose image Tuscan painters trace
Kneeling within some cloistered holy place
　　Where snowy lilies spring in sacred air,
　　Before whom e'en the Angel kneels to bear
Greeting of God, and hail her 'Full of Grace.'

Thy very look brings back lost Italy, ˙
　　And days more bright than these with sun and art ;
What shall be said of that same art and thee ?
　　Do Fra Filippo's Virgins lend thee part
Of that faint grace ; or rather, shall I see
　　More worth in them, remembering what thou art ?

R

II. ON A MADONNA AND CHILD OF BELLINI.

YEARS pass and change ; Mother and Child remain :
    Mother, so proudly sad, so sadly wise,
    With perfect face and wonderful calm eyes,
Full of a mute expectancy of pain :
Child, of whose love the Mother seems so fain,
    Looking far off, as if in other skies
    He saw the Hill of Crucifixion rise
And knew the horror and would not refrain.

Yet all that pain is o'er in very deed,
    And only love shines from those eyes alway ;
Love, to fulfil the world's enormous need ;
    Light, to illuminate the devious way,
Still brighter as the centuries recede,
    And more and more unto the perfect day.

III.   THE HANDMAID OF THE LORD.

LOOK down a moment ; let thy lips uncurl
    Into some word for us too ; droop thine eye
    Once from the heavenly city, distantly
Seen with its twelve gates, each a several pearl,
Whereunder undistinguishably whirl
    Influent and refluent eternally
    The silent-streaming worlds ; are these so nigh,
And we so far beyond thy seeing, Girl ?

Nay ; for the evidence of things not seen,
    The substance of things hoped for, this we know ;
    But what is that whereon thou gazest so ?
    What splendours of the morning from above,
What glory of God is in thee ?   ' I have been
    There, and seen him who is the Light thereof.'

IV. SONG OF THE THREE KINGS:
A LEGEND.

'And finding, by the sudden waning of the brightest star, that
the Blessed Virgin was sick, they made haste to take all manner of
healing herbs and depart to Nazareth.   But when they found her
already dead, they returned sorrowfully to their own country.'
'History of the Three Kings' (Author).

SHE is dead, ah, she is dead;
   Silent is that gentle breath,
Still and low that golden head,
   That sweet mouth is stopped in death:
Wherefore now we bring to her
Gold and frankincense and myrrh.

She is dead, yes, she is dead;
   Never may we see again
Purest, holiest Maidenhead,
   Mother without spot or stain:
Mid the sleeping lilies fold
Myrrh and frankincense and gold.

Lo, we come from very far
   With all simples that we have,
Caspar, Melchior, Balthasar—
   Ah, we came too late to save:
Scatter we ere we go hence
Gold and myrrh and frankincense.

Magnificat.

ODE IN HONOUR OF THE VIRGIN MOTHER OF
OUR LORD.

THOMAS B. ALLAN, PRIEST.

My Soul doth magnify the Lord :

FIRST of our kind, ethereal, mortal Maid,
Queen of Creation, Regent at God's Throne—
What equal praise to thee can e'er be said
By lips of flesh, though all to hymn are prone ?
Save her prophetic lips, none else are heard
To sing her worth in sweet becoming word—
And then, her modest soul but magnifies the Lord.

And my Spirit hath rejoiced in God my Saviour :

All born from Eve until the Doom of Day,
Who fall with Eve in that primeval sin,
All must to her the debt of homage pay,
Who sinless did our Ransom first begin
And crushed the fiery dragon's head by grace,
Enjoyed by her alone to Eve replace
And bear the True, the Saving Adam to our race.

*Because he hath regarded the humility of his handmaid : for
behold from henceforth all generations shall call me Blessed.*

The Alpha and the Omega is he
Whose shameful death won victory so great ;
At both his Crib and Cross alone was she,
The first, the last, the faithfullest to wait
Of all create or saved.   His high design
Thus sate her next his awful Throne divine ;
All tongues confess her Blessèd at that noblest shrine.

Because he that is mighty hath done great things to me:
and holy is his name.

To height of grace unwonted her he brought ;
For he not only is the Omnipotent,
But mightily his Might her splendour wrought
To be for God a comely Tenement :
Flesh innocent must clothe his Holy Name ;
Wherefore, and lo, the Holy Spirit came
To wondrous make a Mother, yet sweet Maid the same.

And his mercy is from generation to generation,
unto them that fear him.

No servile fear of him had she, but love ;
No pardon needed she who knew no fall :
Dear Mercy's Seat, in her the Ghostly Dove
Sat brooding Charity in Virgin-hall :
For needs must be, if Pity's self should come,
His majesty should die in lowly tomb,
The silent holy solitude, a Maiden-womb.

He hath showed might in his arm : he hath scattered the
proud in the conceit of their heart.

The Almighty Arm that struck the Moab crew—
Nor Ammon, nor the Philistine did spare—
Rested awhile its mailèd wrath and grew
Enamoured 'round Virginity all fair :
Which pure embrace begot the Warrior bright
Whose feigned defeat (what then whose war ?) could smite
Proud Satan's hosts and sin and hell to mornless night.

He hath put down the mighty from their seat ;

Her Son erst troubled Amalek and Saul ;
And Zeb and Oreb, all the Madian flower
He swept ; Sisera, Salmana, Gebal,
Baal and Astaroth and Dagon's power :

All thrones he levelled with the Persian's rod,
And in Augustus haughty kings he trod
To pave his path.   This Maiden bore that Mighty God.

And hath exalted the humble.

And therefore he exalted her to spheres,
Not only o'er the princelings of the earth—
Far o'er the heads of all the angelic peers
Who Avè her as 'kin their King by birth,
His solitary Kin—her shoes the moon,
Twelve starry worlds of light her radiant crown,
The blue of heaven her robe, the sun her meanest gown.

*He hath filled the hungry with good things ; and the rich
he hath sent empty away.*

She gave the hungry world its daily Bread ;
She made the Bread, the ruddy Wine did press
That make men gods : her Son, yea, Israel fed
With manna in the barren wilderness ;
The milk and honey-flowing land he gave,
And thence the swollen Chanaanites he drave—
They sank in famine's jaws to slow devouring grave.

He hath received Israel, his servant, being mindful of his mercy,

God wedded man—the Deity debased :
He deigned to dwell in flesh and bone and staid
With man, the son he loved and thus embraced,
And closed the gulf extreme 'twixt make and made :
Oft Israel, though prodigal, his hand
Led on, till all our woes his pity scanned,
And Maiden was the happy Bridge the Godhead spanned.

*(As he spake unto our fathers) to Abraham and to
his seed for ever.*

In her his promises fulfilled were known ;
This gentle One the old serpent's wile beguiled :

God's Son brought everlasting mercy down,
When she begot that Son, the great Man-Child :
More terrible to hell than war's array,
More beautiful to man than dawn of day,
This Light enlightens all who wend our weary way.

NOTES.

Stanza 7 ; l. 5 : the Persian's rod ; the rod of Cyrus ; l. 6 :
Augustus ; the Emperor Cæsar Augustus.

Chant Royal of the Conception.

CLÉMENT MAROT: 1495—1544.

TRANSLATED (1898) BY E. M. CLERKE.

WHEN the Great King, moved by intent benign,
Resolved his enemy to overthrow
And loose from prison darkling and condign
Those of his host consigned to torment slow,
He sent his heralds to Judea's land
To find a house well built and surely planned,
And bade them then erect in aspect fair
A bright Pavilion for his dwelling rare,
Wherein to order forth, he gave behest,
His own Camp-bed named in full Council there
The worthy Couch whereon the King took rest.

A painting in that Tent of rich outline,
Through whom our sins are pardoned, plain did show,
The Cloud was there, which held in its confine
The Wallèd Garden, promised long ago
To Man, the City by high Heaven scanned,
The Royal Lily, Olive tall and grand,
With David's Tower immovable, four-square,

Because the most skilled Craftsman anywhere
In site so noble sat, and did attest
That whereof spake the Sibyl unaware—
The worthy Couch whereon the King took rest.

Of work antique hath Nature wrought full fine
The carven frame, nor did one point forego,
But for the milk-white cushions did assign
That artist great a Dove as pure as snow,
Then Charity, so prized and in demand,
The Bed made smooth with Peace, her handmaid bländ,
Dame Innocence fine linen did prepare,
Divinity wove curtains three with care,
Then spread them round about the circuit blest,
To guard from chilling blast and mobile air
The worthy Couch whereon the King took rest.

Some did the Coverlet as black malign,
Most falsely—since from Heaven 'twas sent below
Undyed, in native lustre fair to shine,
By a great Shepherd's leave who willed it so,
Who formerly by grace of his command
His lambs' well-guarded fleece sent from his hand,
Did to the fold of subtle Nature spare
Who wove it to a tissue past compare,
The whitest e'er her hand had wrought and best
Wherewith she graced, with style unused elsewhere,
The worthy Couch whereon the King took rest.

No canopy it had of fringed design,
With damask, serge, or samite rich aglow,
For Heaven o'erarching all was for the shrine
Of such illustrious Couch fit roof, I trow:
A precious border had it to withstand
Attacks of vermin, thence for ever banned—

Hath not humanity a noble share
In work so great? since the asp may not dare
Here to intrude to slumber in this nest,
Servile to him is not, nor shall be e'er,
The worthy Couch whereon the King took rest.

ENVOY.

I, Prince, do in my narrow sense declare
The Tent Saint Anne, who did though sterile bear
Her who brought forth the King who Heaven possest;
And Mary is—I by the Gospel swear—
The worthy Couch whereon the King took rest.

Megalesia Sacra:

FESTIVAL IN HONOUR OF MAGNA MATER, ON THE FOURTH OF APRIL.

JOSEPH REEVE, S.J.—J. CUMBERLEGE.

This 'sacred Poem upon the Assumption of the great Mother of God was written originally in Latin by Mr. Reeve; was translated into English by J. Cumberlege;' and was copied (1893) from the Rawlinson MSS. in the Bodleian Library, Oxford, by Orby Shipley, M.A. The original has lately (1901) been identified, by Mr. Joseph Gillow, as the work of Father Reeve, of the Society of Jesus, who was born in 1733, and died in 1820, at Ugbrooke.

REUNION OF THE SOUL AND BODY OF THE BLESSED VIRGIN MARY.

THUS far immersed in this divine abyss
Of melting raptures and transporting bliss,
Purely dissolved into the heavenly line,
She was no more herself, but all divine

Yet could not banish from her tender mind
Her dear Co-partner sleeping still behind.
Their former strong alliance forced her love,
She sweetly mourned as does the turtle dove
With melting sighs the absence of her Love.
For this bright spotless pair were so secure
From any blemish, so divinely pure
That God himself did prove her Flesh might be
A rival to her Soul in purity :
And most deservedly—for if it's fit
T' examine titles, her Soul must submit.
For when his Incarnation did begin
He chose her Flesh to veil his Godhead in ;
Nor did her heavenly Soul all this deny   .
Though bathing in the stream of heavenly joy.
She loved her lonely Partner left behind,
And wished each moment they might be rejoined,
Seeing so many radiant bodies shine
Of glorious Saints with rays of Light divine :
More yet—the immortal members of her Son,
And well remembered when e'er they had begun :
And though she shone with Light divinely clear,
Yet to herself she naked did appear,
And wished and wished her friendly Flesh was there.

And now she speaks : ' Behold, I am (says she)
Both Spouse and Daughter to the Deity ;
A triple emblem my bright Soul does wear
Wherein my great Creator's Image does appear ;
Memory, knowledge and seraphic love,
The Father, Son and Sempiternal Dove.
But did I bear the Infant Deity,
Or help to clothe him with humanity,

Or ever lull the little God to rest,
Stealing into his mouth the welcome breast?
No, no: 'twas my dear Flesh performed that part,
And always bore a tender mother's heart;
And when he slept, she'd take a careful nod
And sweetly slumber o'er the Infant God.
Thrice happy Body slumb'ring in thy tomb
That bear'st Mankind's Salvation in thy womb.
My poor endowments, when I think on thee,
How undeserving they appear to me.
What's memory, or knowledge, or what's love—
Shall I alone be crowned a Queen above,
Whilst you, my dear Co-partner lie alone,
Shut in the horrors of the vaulted stone,
Who so much more than I deserve a throne?
But our Creator, though he's good to me
Will yet, without all doubt, be just to thee.'

Thus spoke her Soul; and like a turtle dove
She nothing whispered of her mate but love:
She now resolved to try her interest there
For a reunion with her sleeping dear.
'Behold, great God' (says she), 'my Spouse and King,
I hope you'll not deny me anything;
I have one request and 'tis the first I make,
That you would compassion on my Body take,
Which lies below within the shades of night,
Whilst I am Queen o'er all the realms of light,
And lost in the fruition of your sight.'

       *   *   *

Immediately the heavens began to shake,
Yet all were hush when their Creator spake.
He spoke: then all with one consent did bow

With all the glorious Spirits there, and now
The joyful orbs began again to roll,
And shouts of joy were heard from pole to pole.
The Eternal nods and all the signal take,
A glorious sight the glittering Seraphs make.
Legions of Angels fill the ambient air
And miriads of Cherubs to attend the Fair;
All in an instant into order stepped
Extending from the Throne to where she slept.
A radiant path behind, and on each side a line
Which like so many dazzling suns did shine.
All ready now she does the signal give,
And with a ling'ring embrace she takes her leave;
And now descends her Partner to release,
Attended by the harbingers of Love and Peace.
And now, behold, on wing the Heavenly Fair,
As swift as meditation cuts the yielding air:
Her hymning guards sang anthems all the way,
The spheres made music too as well as they
And all the elements were bright and gay;
The clattering orbs a clamorous joy exprest,
And universal nature now again was blest.
By soft dimission, lo, the Charmer's come
And like a dove alights upon the tomb:
Re-enters her dear Body, and the twain
Embrace, but never now to part again.
Immortal vows their juncture, which no time
Can e'er dissolve: to think it were a crime.

The Grotto of Lourdes; and Other Verse.

THEODORE A. METCALF, PRIEST.

FROM 'THE AVE MARIA' AND 'MESSENGER OF THE SACRED HEART, U.S.A.,' 1890—1897.

Grotto of Lourdes.

I. OUR LADY'S IMAGE.

Upon the hillside—looking o'er the stream
That kisses Mary's Grotto, as it flows
Beside the rocks where creeping ivy grows
And hanging blossoms cling to every seam—
I stood at night to watch the golden gleam
Of countless tapers, whose reflection throws
A blushing halo, like a budding rose,
Throughout that Grotto, making it a dream
Of blissful paradise; and spotless white
Our Lady's Image smiling in her shrine,
Seemed 'more immaculate' against the night
Which clothed in shadow each sweet eglantine;
E'en as her loveliness outshines the light
Of earthly beauty by its grace divine.

II. 'VOIS TES ENFANTS À GENOUX.'

And while entranced I gazed upon the view,
There came the melody of joyful song
That rose and fell in cadence sweet and strong
And sent its echoes all the valley through
Repeating, 'Vois tes enfants à genoux,'

The chanted anthem of a kneeling throng
Of Mary's children, on the banks along
The rushing Gave. Methought our Lady too
Leaned forward at that sound of music sweet—
   As once before when Bernadette was there
The ringing Angelus she bent to greet
   With all its memories of ' Aves ' fair—
And falling prostrate at our Mother's feet
   My heart went up to her in fervent prayer.

III. A SPOKEN ROSARY.

FROM out her Grotto Mary seems to bless
   The kneeling crowd assembled at her feet,
   Who come with canticles of joy to greet
The Queen Immaculate, and round her press
As though in eager longing to caress
   The blessèd footprints which our Lady sweet
   Has left within the depths of that retreat,
A heaven making of a wilderness.
And now her children pray : from out the night
   Ten thousand ' Aves ' float upon the air,
A spoken rosary ; while one of light
   From many coloured lamplets hanging there
In graceful garlands—music to the sight—
   Unites its litany of silent prayer.

IV. THE SILENT VOICES.

A THOUSAND banners float above thy aisles,
   O fair Basilica. Thy walls are set—
   Like jewels in a regal coronet—
With countless offerings and marble tiles
Whose sculptured records mark the tears and smiles
   Of grateful hearts ; and like a parapet,

The soldier's sword and golden epaulet
Are reared against thy sacred peristyles.
What would they say, those pledges mute and grave,
   If living words their forms should animate?
A mighty chorus through thy lofty nave
   Would rise and make its vaults reverberate
With joyous echoes of the tuneful wave,
   ' Hail Mother dear, our Queen Immaculate.'

V. 'LE PETIT GERS.'

How bleak it stands against the eastern sky,
   Yon mountain gray. See, on its rocky crown—
   Like sentinels of heaven looking down—
Three lofty crosses lift their arms on high
In benediction on the passers-by,
   And guard the entrance to that favoured town
   Whose holy Grotto rings with earth's renown
Since Mary came its shades to sanctify.
An image of our Lady hidden lies
   Beneath the crosses on that summit gray,
To mark a pilgrim's vow: with tearful eyes
   And telling rosaries along the way,
He mounted barefoot there with fear and sighs,
   In penance for a loved one gone astray.

Other Verse.

VI. THE FIRST CHRISTMAS.

O HAPPY Mother, if in heaven were known
   An envious thought, then angels envied thee
   That winter midnight when, in ecstacy,
They saw thee worship at the manger-throne
Of Bethlehem. They knew that thou alone,

By virtue of thy sweet maternity,
Couldst taste the fulness of the mystery
That made thy Babe, while God of Heaven, thine own
    And only Son.   When lovely Baby-eyes
    Looked up into thy face to sweetly smile
        Unspoken greetings, numbered with such charms,
Was full beatitude; and Paradise
    Came down to earth to dwell with thee, the while
        Thy neck was circled by those little arms.

VII. TO MARY MOTHER.

CELESTIAL choristers while carolling
    The joyful tidings that announced to earth
    The wondrous mercy of a Saviour's birth,
Were happy messengers of God, their King;
The lowly shepherds who were hastening
    To David's City knew not yet the worth
    Of that new ' Word' which spoke in songs of mirth
And made the mountains of Judæa ring;
But they were glad.   Thou, Mary, pure and fair,
    Whose virgin bosom throbbed with chaste delight
        At Jesus' touch, all joy to thee was given
As Mother's privilege.   We only share
    The promise of that happy Christmas-night;
        To thee it meant the very peace of heaven.

VIII. 'ALMA MATER.'

'TWAS dark, and hidden were the shadows grim
    Beneath the arches of the chapel, where
    The daughters of Saint Ursula at prayer
Were kneeling, and the golden cherubim
Beside the altar—for the lamp burned dim—
    Seemed genuflecting in the buoyant air;

When rich in harmony beyond compare,
Arose the music of our Lady's hymn
Behind the grated choir. So sweet and low,
  So full of tenderness, so like a tear
'That 'Alma Mater,' that it seemed as though
  The gates of Paradise were opened near.
Ah, Mother dear, it surely must be so
  'Tis sung in heaven: bring us there to hear.

NOTES.

No. II. l. 12: 'Aves' fair. Allusion to the legend of our Lady's
action at the sound of the Angelus bell: Bernadette, while praying,
saw the face of the Immaculate beam with joy, while at the same
time she leaned eagerly forward, as though to catch every note of
the Angelical Salutation.

No. V.: Le Petit Gers is a mountain east of the town of Lourdes.
From its quarries most of the stone used in the construction of the
religious houses was obtained. It is steep and difficult to climb
(Author's notes).

Hymn at Lourdes.

TRANSLATED BY ALICE MEYNELL.

FROM 'LOURDES: YESTERDAY, TO-DAY, AND TO-MORROW,'
BY DANIEL BARBÉ, 1893.

THE hour had come for evening prayer;
The Angelus chimed on the chilling air:
                    Ave, Maria.
A hidden Angel walked, and met
The unwitting steps of Bernadette:
                    Ave, Maria.
Across the mountain stream she hied;
A wind in the valley rose and died:
                    Ave, Maria.

S

Sudden it shook her, sudden it fell;
She saw the Virgin on Massabielle:
Ave, Maria.
She saw the tender and gentle face
Crowned with a light that filled the place:
Ave, Maria.
It was the Mother of God who smiled
Like her own mother on the child:
Ave, Maria.
Clad in white was the Lady chaste,
A ribbon of Heaven around her waist:
Ave, Maria.
Two open roses, yellow and sweet,
Lay upon her naked feet:
Ave, Maria.
Between her hands, and folded there,
The beads her people use for prayer:
Ave, Maria.
The child prayed fast; then from her eyes
The vision passed to Paradise:
Ave, Maria.
In her poor home the girl abode,
But daily pressed on the self-same road:
Ave, Maria.
'O Lady, Lady, what do you seek?'—
Then came the time for her to speak:
Ave, Maria.
'Come fifteen times to this mountain cave;.
Thou shalt be glad after the grave:'
Ave, Maria.
And day by day did the people press
After the feet of the shepherdess:
Ave, Maria.

And on her face they marked with awe
The brightness of the things she saw :
Ave, Maria.
She saw that bent was the Lady's head ,
' Madam, why are you sad ? ' she said :
Ave, Maria.
The Lady answered, ' Pray, my child ;
Entreat for the unreconciled :
Ave, Maria.
' I call upon the multitude
To walk, and pray, and bear the rood :
Ave, Maria.
' I will have here a holy shrine,
And the dedication shall be mine : '
Ave, Maria.
Then twice the morning dawned, but not
The light, the vision, in the grot :
Ave, Maria.
O Mother, and didst thou then not know
Thy little girl was troubled so ?
Ave, Maria.
Nought was the trouble when once more
The Lady stood by the torrent shore :
Ave, Maria.
' Madam, I am to ask a sign ;
There is no flower on the eglantine :
Ave, Maria.
' We pray you make a rose out-break
For our poor faith and your mercies' sake : '
Ave, Maria.
' Drink of the spring,' the Virgin said ;
The child went down to the river bed :
Ave, Maria.

' Nay, here is the spring of my command ; '
And a spring leapt under the little hand :
Ave, Maria.

' I am to ask you to tell your name,
That we may be certain whence you came : '
Ave, Maria.

Three times over this prayer was said ;
And the fourth time it was answered :
Ave, Maria.

'Twas the name that is sung at Heaven's gate ;
' I am called and conceived Immaculate : '
Ave, Maria.

See, Mother, thy people have done thy will ;
There is a church on the southern hill :
Ave, Maria.

These thirty years, and from age to age,
Thy children are coming on pilgrimage :
Ave, Maria.

The waters fail not, nor their feet ;
They drink, they are healed, they praise thee, Sweet :
Ave, Maria.

Hither the distant nation wins ;
France weeps here upon her sins :
Ave, Maria.

The sick, the mourner, the forgiven
Come to Lourdes on their way to Heaven :
Ave, Maria.

Part of 'the Protestant's Hymn to the Virgin.'

HENRY HART MILMAN: 1791—1868.

FROM 'ANNE BOLEYN, A DRAMATIC POEM,' 1826.

O VIRGIN Mother, . . .
To mortal name our jealous souls deny
The incommunicable meed of Deity.

* * *

Yet ne'er Incarnate Godhead might reside
Save where his conscious Presence glorified ;
 Thee, therefore, lovelier far we deem
 Than eye may see or soul may dream.
Unchanged—unwasted by the pains of earth,
Thou didst bring forth the fair Immortal Birth :
And Hope and Faith, and deep maternal Joy
 And Love, and not unholy Pride,
 With soft unevanescent glory dyed   .
Thy cheeks, while gazing on the Peerless Boy ;
And surer than prophetic consciousness,
That he was born all human-kind to bless.
The musical and peopled air was dim,
  Mary, where'er thy haunt,
  With angels visitant ;
Nor always did the viewless Seraphim
Stand with their plumed glories unconfest,
To see the Eternal Child while cradled on thy breast.

And what though in the winter, bleak and wild,
Thou didst bring forth the Unregarded Child,
 The summoned star made haste to shine
 Upon that new-born Face Divine,

And the low dwelling of the stabled beast
Shone with the homage of the gorgeous East.
Though driven far off to Nilus' reedy shore,
　As thou didst slake thy burning feet
　Where o'er the desert fount the arching palm-trees
　　meet :
Still its soft pillowed charge thy bosom bore ;
And thou didst watch in rapture his sweet sleep ;
Or gaze, while sportive he thy locks caresst,
Or drank the living fountain of thy breast.
　　　Yet, Mary, o'er thy soul
　　　A silent sadness stole,
Nor could thy swelling eyes refuse to weep
For Rachel, desolate, in agony,
And Bethlehem's mothers childless all but thee.

Nor failed thy watchful spirit to behold
The secret inborn Deity unfold :
　Nor e'er without a painless awe,
　The wond'rous Youth the Mother saw ;
For in the Baptist's playful love appeared
The homage of a heart that almost feared :
And though in meek subjection still he dwelt
　Beneath thy Husband's lowly home ;
　Oft from his lips would words mysterious come ;
The Soul untaught the present Saviour felt.
As more than prophet-raptures o'er him broke,
And fuller still the inspiration poured,
Half-bowed to earth unconscious knees adored :
　　　Mary, before thy sight
　　　The wonder-working might,
Prerogative of Highest Godhead woke ;
Unfearful yet—when instant at his sign
The water vessels blushed with generous wine.

Blest o'er all women : did thy heart repress,
Humble as chaste, each thought of loftiness,
  When wonder after wonder burst
  Around the Child thy bosom nurst—
The dumb began to sing, the lame to leap ;
His unwet footsteps trod the unyielding deep ;
Still at his word disease and anguish ceased,
  And healthful blood began to flow,
  Ruddy, beneath the leper's skin of snow ; .
And shuddering fiends the tortured soul released ;
And from the grave arose the summoned dead ?
Yet, ah, did ne'er thy Mother's heart repine,
When he set forth upon his dread design ?
     Mary, did ne'er thy love
     His piteous fate reprove,
When on the rock reposed his houseless head ?
Seemed it not strange to thy officious zeal—
All pains, all sorrows, save his own, to heal.

Yet, oh, how awful, Desolate, to thee,
Thus to have shrined the Living Deity,
  When underneath the loaded Rood
  Forlorn the Childless Mother stood :
Then when that Voice, whose first articulate breath
Thrilled her enraptured ear, had now in death
Bequeathed her to his care whom best he loved ;
  When the cold death-dew bathed his brow,
  And faint the drooping head began to bow,
Wert thou not, Saddest, too severely proved ?
As in thy sight each rigid limb grew cold,
And the lip whitened with the burning thirst,
And the last cry of o'erwrought anguish burst,
     Where then the Shiloh's crown,
     Mary, the Christ's renown,

By prophets and angelic harps foretold?
Was strength to thy undoubting spirit given?
Or did not human love o'erpower thy trust in Heaven?

But when Death's Conqueror from the tomb returned,
Was thine the heart that at his voice ne'er burned?
Followed him not thy constant sight,
Slow melting in heaven's purest white,
To take his ancient endless seat on high,
On the right hand of Parent Deity?
And when thine earthly pilgrimage was ended,
We deem not, but that circled round
With ringing harps of heaven's most glorious sound,
Thy spirit, redeemed through thy Son's Blood, ascended:
There evermore in lowliest loftiness,
Meek thou admirest, how that living God
That fills the heavens and earth in thee abode.
Mary, we yield to thee
All but idolatry;
We gaze, admire and wonder, love and bless;
Pure, blameless, holy, every praise be thine,
All honour save thy Son's, all glory but divine.

Mater Desolata.

HARRIET ELEANOR HAMILTON KING.

FROM 'THE DESOLATE SOUL,' 1897.

THIS is the end, O Mother Piteous:
This is the end of all those sanctitudes
Hid in thy heart and only known to thee;
And all is over, all is still as death,
Death which is here and face to face with thee,
Thou living One who wast the Gate of Heaven.

This is his hour; and he has bowed thee down,
And bruised thee to the earth: this hour is Death's.
This is the end which both have, hand in hand,
Ever foreseeing, journeyed to so long;
Yea, step by step and hour by hour, drawn near.
And thou, thou hast thy Son within thine arms;
As thou didst hold thy naked New-born Babe,
So on thy knees thy naked Newly-dead
Is laid, thy Child, his head is on thy arm;
Here hast thou him, O Mother, and even yet,
Sitting upon the ground and all the seas .
Of sorrow broken over thee, even yet
Art thou enthroned supreme in all this sphere,
The Queen of Sorrows upon Golgotha.

Mother, whose heart is deep as the deep sea:
What hast thou seen to-day, what hast thou done?
What is this place of slaughter and of skulls?
What day hath this been, since the first ray broke
And all the Temple precincts woke, and stirred
With bleatings of the lambs?   What hours were those
Till noon? when from the Temple steps there rang
The blast of trumpets, telling the Lamb was slain,
And over thee was reared and fixed the Cross?
What were those hours that passed—or were they
          years?
Here, and thou standing by?   Here didst thou stand;
Until a great cry rent the earth apart,
And in the Temple shook down right and left
The columns, and the Veil was rent in the midst.
In all the days was ever a day like this?
Or any Mother of mortal race like thee,
Whose feet have trod the long way dolorous?

Thou hast thy Dead, O Mother.   All is still :
The swords are in thy heart ; but in the air
Deepens the quiet of the Sabbath Eve ;
Trembles no more the earth to any moan,
Reverberates through the mountains no more cry :
The day is dying, silent as the dead.
Evening—there was one evening long ago,
When he had not yet come to Bethlehem,
And thou, and Joseph with thee, didst await
In an impenetrable ecstasy
The midnight under all the blissful stars.
He came, he came—and he is gone again,
In darkness deeper, more impenetrable.
Evening—and desolation uttermost,
A bleak and bitter waste of stony hills,
This, this remains, the fruit of all thy years ;
And before midnight thou must lose whate'er
Of treasure still thou holdest in thine arms.

What fire is this which burns behind the hills?
The hills in the South—a spreading, slow, white fire,
And now ascending, orbèd, great and pale?
O mighty Mother Moon, thou art all amazed ;
Thy face is changed even now from white to wan :
What dost thou gaze upon, thy heaven across?
And who are these left on the Hill with thee?
In all thy wanderings through the fields of heaven,
The happy fields of heaven where grow the stars
In clusters, and among the hollow clouds
Through silver centuries of centuries,
Mother of Months, thou hast not dreamt of this.

Still, still thou movest on, as in a trance—
That trance divine of ten enchanted moons

Which over earth and air and ocean shed
Such hush of heaven that still they sleep in it :
And thou awakest now in wonderment
And in a horror, and art turned to blood
Already in the darkness of the sky.
And what hast thou to do with Death, O Moon,
Who bringest all Earth's younglings to their birth?
For thou art musing still, how all that time
Each herb and moss and tree drew from thy beams
Benignant influence, and thou didst infuse
Undreamed of beauty into every form
That did unfold itself—while all the wings
Of butterflies waved glorious in the hues
Of other worlds ; and all the quickened earth
Heaved with the upward rush of lily stalks
Budding ; and every living thing rejoiced
In its own life, and all the harvesting
Was of the overladen corn and fruit.
The bees dropped rivulets of honey-gold
Through that unequalled year, and all the woods
Of the North were ravished with a music known
Never before among the nightingales ;
And the mystic flower of the Samoyedes
Blossomed at midnight starry from the snow ;
And from their fountains bubbling the swift streams
Sang to the stars a song of speechless joy,
Rushing along the rivers to the sea.
And all the brimming estuaries were filled
With many-coloured shoals ; and every beach
With the soft wash of each retreating wave
Was strewn with iridescent multitudes
Of shells ; and under the enrapturing skies
Auroral and nocturn, the halcyon earth
Lay brooding through the long white sacred dream,

While the White Rose of the World hid in her heart
The Life of the World, and it was one with hers.
And thou, O magical, mysterious Moon,
Knewest all through thy interwoven dance,
And incantations betwixt sphere and sphere,
The pulse responsive and the rise and fall
Of the Mother's bosom that kept time with thee.

For on thy breast he lay, O Mother—thy breast,
That could endure such sweetness, strengthened now
Through all thy days and nights of heavenly hope,
And marvelling desire, to bear at last
The consummation of beatitude.
The lovely limbs are thine, the downy head
That nestles on thy arm, the soft, small mouth,
The little hands are thine ; it is thy Babe
That smiles upon thee with celestial eyes ;
The Heaven of Heavens breathes low upon thy breast.
Yea, thou didst dare the dazzling deeps of joy
Whereof could none know, none endure but thee ;
And all these things are hidden in thy heart.
And deeper grows thy heart with every day,
A royal water-lily that expands
Crown within crown around its golden Sun,
Pale with the lustre of the heavens.　O Child,
How dost thou grow from day to day, and stand
Already in thy budded loveliness
The Darling of the World.　O Mother, the while
With what absorbed and passionate wistfulness
Thy guardian eyes above thy Nurseling move.
Thou didst prevent the dawn, because the day
Could not contain the measureless delight
That rose in thy unfathomable heart
A fountain ever-springing, which the wells

Of Marah had not over-flooded yet,
To speed the long day's hours from joy to joy
Within the Holy House of Nazareth.

He runs beside thee, and his eager eyes
Wait on thy wishes; thou hast watched him wake
From dreams of Heaven, and silent with excess
Of worship, thou, with many a delicate touch
Of delicate fingers, hast arrayed his limbs
And disentangled all the golden curls;
And out among the earliest twitterings
Already those two faces light the path
(The little grassy path of easy steps
With wild flowers opening, wet with early dew,
Stretching by unknown, steep, precipitous ways
Up to this awful rock of Calvary),
The Child and Mother, each so like to each,
And both so innocent and both so young,
The Child of Sunrise and the Morning Star.

This is the End, this is the Sun-setting:
Here is the Head once more upon thine arm,
O Mother, scarcely to thy bosom pressed
Because too bruised even to pillow there.
But one by one the piercing thorns are plucked
Out of the bleeding brows; the matted hair
Is parted tenderly; thy delicate hands
(Amidst the raining, raining of thy tears
Bathing the holy Face that looked on thee
Its first, its last, and was so like to thine)
Smooth into rest its agony once more.
Through every Wound of every virgin limb
Thy tender fingers feel and search and close;
The piercèd Hands drop lifeless in thine own,

And cold and stiff are growing even now ;
And no man sees thy face, because thy face
Is hidden in thy veil—and neither he
Beholds it now ; and thou hast closed his Eyes.

O Mother of Sorrows inconsolable,
Whose sufferings there could none compassionate
Save One, and he has left thee now alone.
The wrenched and ghastly Feet are the same feet,
The little warm feet fondled in thy hands,
O Mother-hands, that have not, many a day,
So held him on thy knees—and thou hast yet
His Body, made of thine, to dress once more.
Thou hast not faltered yet, thou hast not swerved
In all thy shuddering task ; thy quick soft hands,
Of face and form marred more than man's before,
Have made again the Image pitiful
Of a Divine, dead, marble Majesty.

This Babe whom thou didst wrap in swaddling-
    clothes—
Oh, that first kiss upon the dawning smile ;
Oh, this last kiss upon the livid brows :
The last, last touches on the Wounds that wring
Thy heartstrings, which God made too strong to break.
More priceless is this anguish than that bliss ;
For whatsoever light revealed, foreshown,
Pierces thy veilèd darkness with some dim
Presage of Resurrection, or of some
Crowned seat in Heaven far, far in other days,
Never will that Immortal Son again
Have need of mortal Mother—yet this once
A minute, and a minute more is thine.
This is thine own, to wash, to dress, to hold

Thy Son's own Body, fruit of thine own womb,
Yea, to anoint him for his burial,
And heap the herbs and spices round his limbs,
All things being past save this last agony,
And at the end to fold the winding-sheet.

But oh, this is the last time—be it joy
Or sorrow, Heaven or Hell, what matters it?
For these are minutes that are passing now;
The hours have passed, the last long hours of all,
Even as passed the days and years behind;
And never, never more through all the deeps
Of that Redemption which is finished now
Shall he be helpless, nursed within thine arms,
Nor shall thy hands do mother-service more.
Thou droopest lower and lower over him,
While even now the jealous winding-sheet
Beneath thy hands is stealing him away.
Is there no more to do?   Is there no more?

Prayer of Mary, Queen; and On Arras.

ROSA MULHOLLAND (LADY GILBERT).

I. PRAYER OF MARY, QUEEN.

FROM 'THE IRISH MONTHLY,' 1898.

I TRAVELLED on a windy cloud
    That sailed the midnight sky,
And saw, wrapped in a sable shroud,
    This world go whirling by.

Upon a circling wind I spun
    The moon and stars between;
Uprose from out a hidden sun
    The Holy Mary, Queen.

A golden flame her long hair was,
  Her eyes were wet with rain ;
As sweet a face no lady has—
  Two cherubs were her train.

Her gown was made of every flower,
  Her girdle gold entwist,
Her veil was all a rainbow shower,
  Her feet were silver mist.

She stood upon the world's dark rim,
  Her lifted hands implored,
Along with her sweet whisper, him,
  The Universe's Lord.

Most piercing sweet the voice : 'O mine
  Own Son, of Mortal born,
The robes are still incarnadine
  On Calvary were worn.

'Is earth grown barren to thy spade ?
  Yet grew it the rood tree ;
Of its sharp thorns thy crown was made ;
  It gave a grave to thee.

'Its daughter thou were wont to call
  Thy Mother ; Oh, be then
Still patient with her kindred, all
  The wayward sons of men.

'Thy purple robe is spread with stars,
  Thy head is crowned with suns,
The wheels of thy life-laden cars
  Turn while thine ordinance runs.

'A many gold ships navigate
  The seas of boundless space,
And carry their immortal freight
  To port of thy loved face.

'Their children follow their Sun, thee,
    To days without the light ;
Their souls sail for Eternity,
    And fearless, run the night.

'Yet hast thou Mother of their kin :
    My Babe upon my knee,
I link thee to a world of sin—
    Thou wilt not unmake me.

'My race shall yet put on the sun
    And darkness rule no more :
Now finish what thou hast begun,
    The law of light restore.

'O Child, who from my humble knee
    Unto the Temple strayed,
Thou didst come quickly home with me
    Because I wept and prayed.

'Remember, gracious Son of mine,
    The feast in Galilee ;
Thou gavest them the needful wine
    For but a word from me.

'O Heaven's Uncomprehended Lord,
    Thy Mother still am I :
Now hearken, hearken to my word—
    Let not the sinner die.

'But bid the rebel orb go by ;
    Sweet Son, Creator dread,
Be mercy only.   Saviour, die
    Again—to raise these dead.'

          ❉   ✳   ✳

T

The sun uprose, the heavens were rent
  And took her from my sight,
Rose-red grew the wide firmament,
  The morn was glad with light.

II. ON ARRAS.

FROM 'THE AVE MARIA,' 1898.

An old purple tapestry
  Swaying in an ancient chamber ;
There I saw the Virgin Mary
  Robed all in amber.
Her blue eyes adored her Child,
  Her pale mouth of roses sweet
Opened fair and faintly smiled.
  When she stirred her little feet
Under her gold drapery,
  Silver lilies round them curled—
  Feet that walked a thorny world.

That old purple tapestry,
  When the wind arose and shook it,
From its folds a many angels
  Hurried forward and forsook it.
Crowned with flame of heavenly fires,
Some had lutes and some had lyres,
Harps and cymbals, mandolinas,
Rose-encircled tambourinas.
Their gold plumage swept the stair,
Purple wings hung down the air ;
Faces shone like flush of flowers
Dropt from paradisic bowers,

And their hands that swept the strings
   Fluttered each like a small bird—
Hark, one of them sings:
   Blessèd Mary smiled and heard.

One sang: 'Mary, Maid divine,
   Worship thy sweet Son for me;
Kiss the Babe-lips close to thine,
   While I sing and bend the knee.'

Sang another: 'O good Mother,
Give to us our little Brother:
Sin's abroad, but he is God,
Lord of Love—there is no other.'

Then stepped forth and sang a third:
'Virgin Blest, let man and bird—
Everything that hath a voice,
Let it speak forth and rejoice.'

That old purple tapestry—
   Faded is the western glory,
Shrouded is the chamber high,
   Broken off the angelic story.
Mary hides away her Son
   In the folds of purple shadow
Till the long night's swoon is done,
   And gold lights dance in the meadow.
Through the dark doth Peter weep
   Listening for the cock's faint crowing,
While the songful angels sleep,
   Till the clear morn-trumpets blowing
Out of Paradise shall summon
Soul of man and soul of woman—
All that liveth in creation,
Unto morning adoration.

And as the wind-gusts rise and blow,
And as the sun-flares come and go,
The Virgin Mary in her amber
Sweetly haunts that ancient chamber,
Her Babe-Son upon her arm,
Her rose-face all love-light warm ;
Saints around her knees in hiding,
Angels from the shadows striding ;
Feet that stir 'mid lilies gleaming,
Mother-light from her eyes streaming.

Where I saw that ancient chamber,
   In a wood of sycamore,
Never can I quite remember
   With the sunlight on its floor.
This much I do know
It was centuries ago,
When the Baby Christ was young,
And his carol still was sung.
I can hear those cymbals ring,
Hear the angel-voices singing,
See gold plumage fan the curtain
   By our Mary's robe of amber,
Fluttering with a sheen uncertain
   As the sun filled all the chamber ;
See the blue within her eyes—
Blue that veileth mysteries ;
Lips that did to softness melt
As the minstrels prayed and knelt,
Where the folds hang dusk and high
Of that old purple tapestry.

Theotokos, Sine Labe Concepta.

MICHAEL MULLINS, PRIEST: 1833—1869.

FROM 'THE MESSENGER OF THE SACRED HEART,' 1868.

Father Mullins was born at Killimore, County Galway, and died in Chicago, U.S.A. The following poem was probably written in 1864.

HAIL, Mary, our Mother, Hail, Virgin the purest,
   Hail, Mary, the Mother of Mercy and Love,
Hail, Star of the Ocean, serenest and surest,
   That ever shone brightly in Heaven above ;
'Mid the shadows of death, stretching down o'er the
      nations,
   Thy children have always rejoiced in thy fame ;
Oh, proudly we witness, in our generations,
   The last crowning halo that circles thy name.

Tradition, which joined with its sister Evangel,
   God placed upon guard at the door of his Bride ;
Tradition, which beams like the sword of the Angel,
   As flame-like it 'turneth on every side' ;
Tradition shoots up o'er the ages victorious,
   Its summit in heaven, its base upon earth—
Like a pillar of fire, far-shining and glorious,
   And shows thee all sinless and pure in thy birth.

As fair as the rose 'mid Jerusalem's daughters,
   As bright as the lily by Jordan's blue wave,
As white as the dove, and as clear as the waters
   That flowed for the Prophet, and circled his grave ;
As tall as the cedar on Lebanon's mountain,
   As fruitful as vine-tree in Cades' domain ;

As straight as the palm by Jerusalem's fountain,
  As beauteous as rose-bush on Jericho's plain.

As sweet as the balm-tree diffusing its odour,
  As sweet as the gold harp of David the king;
As sweet as the honey-comb fresh from Mount Bodor,
  As sweet as the face veiled by Gabriel's wing;
The silver-lined sky o'er the garden of Flora,
  The rainbow that gilds the dark clouds within view;
The star that shines brightest, the dawning Aurora,
  As chaste as the moon and as beautiful too.

The Glass without stain and the Radiance immortal,
  The ever-sealed Fount in the City of God;
The Garden enclosed, on whose sanctified portal
  None e'er but the King of the Angels hath trod;
The Sign that appeared in mid-heaven, a Maiden,
  With the moon 'neath her feet and twelve stars on her
      head,
Sun-clothed, going up from the desert to Eden;
  Such was Mary, the Queen of the Living and Dead.

Oh, such are the words of the Saints now in glory,
  Whose voices are heard on the dark waste of time;
Like sentinels set through the centuries hoary,
  Proclaiming her free from original crime;
Of the Prophets and Pontiffs and Doctors and Sages
  Who once in this dark vale of misery trod,
Like lamps hanging out on the mist-covered ages,
  To light up the ways of the City of God.

We see by their light, with a swelling emotion,
  The barque of the Church as it onward doth ride,
Through tempest and gloom, where the Star of the Ocean
  Doth brightly illumine its path o'er the tide;

Where clouds become thicker, and hurricanes fleeter,
   And threaten to shut out its radiance from view,
We see through the darkness the figure of Peter,
   As he points it out still to the sailors and crew.

We hear the loud ring of the multitude's pæan,
   By the nations in triumph exultantly sung,
From the cliffs of the north to the distant Ægean,
   As Celestine silenced Nestorius' tongue :
In Ephesus' temple, the temple of Mary,
   The Fathers hold council by Peter's command ;
In Ephesus' streets, long expectant and weary,
   The crowd stand with joy-bells and torches in hand.

We see the grand figure of Cyril before us,
   Where John, her adopted, before him had trod ;
As pontiffs and people swell loud the glad chorus,
   That Mary, our Mother, is Mother of God :
And oh, that we've witnessed the last shining lustre,
   That Star of the stars in her diadem set,
The first in existence, last placed in the cluster,
   To shine through a long line of centuries yet.

There were journeys by land, there were ships on the
      ocean,
   That bore Judah's princes to Sion's bright walls ;
The peoples have heard with thrilling emotion
   The voice of the High Priest, as on them it calls :
Oh, bless them, dear Mother, we pray, with devotion,
   And bless this Green Island that looks up to thee ;
For this, dearest Mother, is Gem of the ocean,
   And thou art Immaculate, Star of the Sea.

Mystical Verse.

PREFATORY : The Preface may be consulted for an apology of the principle on which these and other Mystical Poems are introduced amongst the Carmina Mariana, the interpretation of which are left to the reader's critical judgment and imagination.

I. MADONNA AND THE OUTCAST.

ROBERT BUCHANAN : 1841—1901.

FROM 'THE OUTCAST,' 1891.

SUDDENLY, as he spake, the Barque
  With mist and cloud was wrapt around,
But as between the dawn and dark
  Soft lights of sunrise with no sound
Part the dim twilight and reveal
The morning-star as bright as steel,
E'en so the mist was blown apart
Like dark leaves round a lily's heart,
And in the core thereof were seen
Still brightning shafts of golden sheen
Dazzling his sight—yet dimly there
  He saw, or seemed to see, a Form
With saffron robe and golden hair,
Walking with rosy feet all bare
  The waters slumbering after storm

A Maiden Shape, her sad blue eyes
Soft with the peace of Paradise,
She walked the waves ; in her white hand
Pure lilies of the Heavenly Land
Hung alabaster white, and all
The billows 'neath her soft footfall
Heaved glassy still, and round her head

An aureole burnt of golden flame,
As nearer yet, with radiant tread,
  Fixing her eyes on his, she came.
Then as she paused upon the Sea,
Gazing upon him silently
With looks insufferably bright
  And gentle brows beatified,
He knew our Lady of the Light—
  Mary Madonna, heavenly-eyed.

How still it was.   The clouds above
Paused quietly and did not move;
The waves lay down like lambs; the air
Was hushed in sad suspense of prayer;
While coming closer with no sound
She hovered pale and golden crowned,
And named his name.   And e'en as one
  Who from dark dreams of night doth stir,
And fronts the shining of the sun
  With haggard eyes, he looked on her.
But as he gazed his sense grew clear,
His dazzled brain shook off its fear,
And all his spirit fever-fraught
From agonies of cruel thought
Rose up.

*   *   *

OUTCAST.   'I seem to know,' he said,
  'That face so fine, that form so fair—
They hung in childhood o'er my bed,
And from the village altar shed
  Soft influence over folk at prayer.'

*   *   *

How still it was—and could it be
A Voice that answered, or the sea
Just stirring softly in surcease
Of tempest into throbs of peace ?
Low as his own heart's beat, yet clear
And sweet, there stole upon his ear
An answer faint like Sabbath bells
Heard far away from leafy dells
Buried in leaves and page, so still
And soft it only seems the thrill
Of silence through the summer air—
A sigh of rapture and of prayer.

*   *   *

MADONNA.   By the charity
Of him who loveth even thee ;
By him whose feet, flashed down on dust,
Shall bruise the hydra heads of lust ;
By him, my Son, who cannot rest
E'en in the Gardens of the Blest,
But ever listening strains his ears
To catch the sound of human tears ;
From him who fain would kiss thy brow,
I offer thee redemption.

*   *   *

So saying, as a star grows bright,
Then flashes into sudden night,
She vanished.

II. THE POET'S IDEAL OF WOMAN.

PERCY BYSSHE SHELLEY: 1792—1822.

FROM 'EPIPSYCHIDION' (1821).

The Poet's mystical conception of Mary, as the 'Seraph of Heaven,' expressed mainly in the sacred language of the Canticle of Canticles, may be found in the First Series of the 'Carmina,' page 40. In the following lines—the headings of which have been added by the Editor, in conformity with the explanation given in the Preface—Shelley developes and enlarges upon his Ideal.

I. HIS IDEAL FULFILLED IN MARY.

SWEET Lamp, my moth-like muse has burnt its wings ;
Or like a dying swan who soars and sings
Young love should teach time, in his own grey style,
All that thou art.   Art thou not void of guile,
A lovely Soul formed to be blest and bless ?
A Well of sealed and secret Happiness,
Whose waters like blithe light and music are,
Vanquishing dissonance and gloom ?   A Star
Which moves not in the moving heavens, alone ?
A Smile amid dark frowns ? a gentle Tone
Amid rude voices ? a belovèd Light ?
A Solitude, a Refuge, a Delight ?
A Lute, which those whom love has taught to play
Make music on, to soothe the roughest day
And lull fond grief asleep ? a buried Treasure ?
A Cradle of young thoughts of wingless pleasure ?
A violet-shrouded Grave of Woe ?—I measure
The world of fancies, seeking one like thee,
And find, alas, mine own infirmity.

II. MARY, THE HARMONY OF TRUTH.

THERE was a Being whom my spirit oft
Met on its visioned wanderings far aloft

In the clear golden prime of my youth's dawn,
Upon the fairy isles of sunny lawn,
Amid the enchanted mountains, and the caves
Of divine sleep, and on the air-like waves
Of wonder-level dream, whose tremulous floor
Paved her light steps; on an imagined shore
Under the grey beak of some promontory
She met me, robed in such exceeding glory,
That I beheld her not.   In solitudes
Her voice came to me through the whispering woods
And from the fountains and the odours deep
Of flowers, which like lips murmuring in their sleep
Of the sweet kisses which had lulled them there,
Breathed but of her to the enamoured air;
And from the breezes, whether low or loud,
And from the rain of every passing cloud,
And from the singing of the summer-birds,
And from all sounds, all silence.   In the words
Of antique verse and high romance—in form,
Sound, colour—in whatever checks that storm
Which, with the shattered present, chokes the past
And in that best philosophy, whose taste
Makes this cold common hell, our life, a doom
As glorious as a fiery martyrdom:
Her Spirit was the Harmony of Truth.

III. MADONNA MIA.

ALGERNON CHARLES SWINBURNE.

FROM 'POEMS AND BALLADS,' 1866.

UNDER green apple-boughs
That never a storm will rouse,
My Lady hath her house
    Between two bowers:

In either of the twain
Red roses full of rain;
She hath for bondwomen
        All kind of flowers.

She hath no handmaid fair
To draw her curled gold hair
Through rings of gold that bear
        Her whole hair's weight:
She hath no maids to stand
Gold-clothed on either hand;
In all the great green land
        None is so great.

She hath no more to wear
But one white hood of vair
Drawn over eyes and hair,
        Wrought with strange gold,
Made for some great queen's head,
Some fair great queen since dead;
And one strait gown of red
        Against the cold.
        *   *   *
To her all dews that fall
And rains are musical;
Her flowers are fed from all,
        Her joy from these:
In the deep-feathered firs
Their gift of joy is hers,
In the least breath that stirs
        Across the trees.

She grows with greenest leaves,
Ripens with reddest sheaves,
Forgets, remembers, grieves,
        And is not sad:

The quiet lands and skies
Leave light upon her eyes
None knows her, weak or wise,
    Or tired or glad.

    *   *   *

Only this thing is said ;
That white and gold and red,
God's three chief words, man's bread
    And oil and wine,
Were given her for dowers,
And kingdom of all hours,
And grace of goodly flowers,
    And various vine.

This is my Lady's praise ;
God, after many days,
Wrought her in unknown ways
    In sunset lands :
This was my Lady's birth ;
God gave her might and mirth
And laid his whole sweet earth
    Between her hands.

IV. OUR LADY OF BEATITUDES.

JAMES THOMSON (BYSSHE VANOLIS),
1834—1882.

Written in 1861.

FROM 'THE CITY OF DREADFUL NIGHT,' 1888.

First thou, O Priestess, Prophetess and Queen,
    Our Lady of Beatitudes, first thou :
Of mighty stature, of seraphic mien,
    Upon the tablet of whose broad white brow

Unvanquishable Truth is written clear,
The Secret of the mystery of our sphere,
  The regnant world of the Eternal Now.

Thou standest garmented in purest white ;
  But from thy shoulders wings of power half-spread
Invest thy form with such miraculous light
  As dawn may clothe the earth with ; and instead
Of any jewelled-kindled golden crown,
The glory of thy long hair flowing down
  Is dazzling noon-day sunshine round thy head.

Upon a sword thy left hand resteth calm,
  A naked sword, two-edged and long and straight
A bunch of olive with a branch of palm
  Thy right hand proffereth to hostile Fate :
The shining plumes that clothe thy feet are bound
By knotted strings, as if to tread the ground
  With weary steps when thou wouldst soar elate.

Twin heavens uplifted to the Heavens, thine eyes
  Are solemn with unutterable thought
And love and aspiration ; yet there lies
  Within their light eternal sadness, wrought
By hope deferred and baffled tenderness :
Of all the souls whom thou dost love and bless
  How few revere and love thee as they ought.

Thou leadest heroes from their warfare here
  To nobler fields where grander crowns are won ;
Thou leadest sages from this twilight sphere
  To cloudless heavens and an unsetting sun ;
Thou leadest saints into that purer air
Whose breath is spiritual life and prayer :
  Yet lo, they seek thee not, but fear and shun.

Thou takest to thy most maternal breast
  Young children from the desert of this earth,
Ere sin hath stained their souls, or grief opprest,
  And bearest them unto an heavenly birth,
To be the Vestals of God's Fane above :
And yet their kindred moan against thy love,
  With wild and selfish moans in bitter dearth.

Most holy Spirit, first Self-conqueror ;
  Thou Victress over time and destiny
And evil, in the all-deciding war
  So fierce, so long, so dreadful.   Would that me
Thou hadst upgathered in my life's pure morn :
Unworthy then, less worthy now, forlorn,
  I dare not, gracious Mother, call on thee.

NOTE.

'Our Lady of Beatitudes,' or of Tears, is one of the 'Three Ladies,' suggested by the sublime sisterhood of Our Ladies of Sorrow, in De Quincey's 'Suspiria de Profundis' (Author)—or the Sequel to the Confessions of an Opium-eater, of which Professor D. Masson says that it is the most perfect specimen the author has left us of his peculiar art of English prose-poetry. 'The eldest of the Ladies is named our Lady of Tears. She stood in Rama where a voice was heard of lamentation. She it was who stood in Bethlehem, on the night when Herod's sword swept its nurseries of Innocents. Her eyes are sweet and subtle, oftentimes challenging the heavens : and I know by childish memories, that she could go abroad upon the winds when she hears the sobbing of litanies. She wears a diadem round her head. She carries keys more than papal at her girdle, which open every cottage and every palace. By the power of the keys it is that our Lady glides, like a ghostly intruder, into the chambers of sleepless men, women and children ; and because she is the first-born of her house, and has the widest empire, let us honour her with the title of Madonna ' (Works, vol. xiii. p. 365. Ed : Masson, 1890). Such, abbreviated, is the original which inspired James (B.V.) Thomson (Editor).

𝕸ay 𝕾ongs and others: 1849—1850.

JOHN HENRY (CARDINAL) NEWMAN,
OF THE ORATORY, D.D.: 1801—1890.
FROM 'VERSES ON RELIGIOUS SUBJECTS,' 1853.

I. CANDLEMAS.

THE angel-lights of Christmas morn
    Which shot across the sky,
Away they pass at Candlemas,
    They sparkle and they die.

Comfort of earth is brief at best,
    Although it be divine ;
Like funeral lights for Christmas gone,
    Old Simeon's tapers shine.

And then for eight long weeks and more
    We wait in twilight grey,
Till the high candle sheds a beam
    On Holy Saturday.

We wait along the penance-tide
    Of solemn fast and prayer,
While song is hushed and lights grow dim
    In the sin-laden air.

And while the sword in Mary's soul
    Is driven home, we hide
In our own hearts, and count the wounds
    Of passion and of pride.

And still, though Candlemas be spent
    And Alleluias o'er,
Mary is music in our need,
    And Jesus light in store.

                   (*Oratory*, 1849.)

U

II. THE PILGRIM-QUEEN.

THERE sat a Lady
    all on the ground,
Rays of the morning
    circled her round,
Save thee and hail to thee,
    Gracious and Fair,
In the chill twilight
    what wouldst thou there ?

' Here I sit desolate,'
    sweetly said she,
' Though I'm a Queen,
    and my name is Marie :
Robbers have rifled
    my garden and store,
Foes they have stolen
    my Heir from my bower.

They said they could keep him
    far better than I,
In a palace all his,
    planted deep and raised high :
'Twas a palace of ice,
    hard and cold as were they,
And when summer came,
    it all melted away.

Next would they barter him,
    him the Supreme,
For the spice of the desert
    and gold of the stream ;
And me they bid wander
    in weeds and alone,
In this green merry land
    which once was my own.'

I looked on that Lady,
   and out from her eyes
Came the deep glowing blue
   of Italy's skies ;
And she raised up her head
   and she smiled, as a Queen
On the day of her crowning,
    so bland and serene.

'A moment,' she said,
   'and the dead shall revive ;
The giants are failing,
   the saints are alive ;
I am coming to rescue
   my home and my reign,
And Peter and Philip
   are close in my train.'
       (Oratory, 1849.)

III. THE MONTH OF MARY.

GREEN are the leaves, and sweet the flowers,
 And rich the hues of May ;
We see them in the gardens round,
 And market-paniers gay :
And e'en among our streets and lanes
 And alleys we descry,
By fitful gleams, the fair sunshine,
 The blue transparent sky.

CHORUS. O Mother Maid, be thou our aid,
    Now in the opening year ;
    Lest sights of earth to sin give birth,
    And bring the tempter near.

Green is the grass, but wait awhile,
   'Twill grow, and then will wither ;
The flowrets, brightly as they smile,
   Shall perish altogether :
The merry sun, you sure would say,
   It ne'er could set in gloom ;
But earth's best joys have all an end,
   And sin, a heavy doom.

CHORUS.   But Mother Maid, thou dost not fade ;
         With stars above thy brow,
         And the pale moon beneath thy feet,
         For ever throned art thou.

The green green grass, the glittering grove,
   The heaven's majestic dome,
They image forth a tenderer bower,
   A more refulgent home ;
They tell us of that Paradise
   Of everlasting rest,
And that high Tree, all flowers and fruit,
   The sweetest, yet the best.

CHORUS.   O Mary, pure and beautiful,
         Thou art the Queen of May ;
         Our garlands wear about thy hair,
         And they will ne'er decay.

                    (*Oratory,* 1850.)

IV. MARY, QUEEN OF THE SEASONS.

(For an inclement May).

ALL is divine
         which the Highest has made,
Through the days that he wrought,
         till the day when he stayed,

Above and below,
            within and around,
From the centre of space
            to its uttermost bound.

In beauty surpassing
            the Universe smiled,
On the morn of its birth,
            like an innocent child,
Or like the rich bloom
            of some gorgeous flower ;
And the Father rejoiced
            in the work of his power.

Yet worlds brighter still,
            and a brighter than those,
And a brighter again
            he had made, had he chose ;
And you never could name
            that conceivable best,
To exhaust the resources
            the Maker possessed.

But I know of one Work
            of his Infinite Hand,
Which special and singular
            ever must stand ;
So perfect, so pure,
            and of gifts such a store,
That even Omnipotence
            ne'er shall do more.

The freshness of May,
            and the sweetness of June,
And the fire of July
            in its passionate noon,

Munificent August,
        September serene,
Are together no match
        for my glorious Queen.

O Mary, all months
        and all days are thine own,
In thee lasts their joyousness,
        when they are gone;
And we give to thee May,
        not because it is best,
But because it comes first,
        and is pledge of the rest.
                    (*Oratory*, 1850.)

The Vision of Joseph.

EDWARD W. B. NICHOLSON, M.A.

FROM 'THE CHRIST-CHILD AND OTHER POEMS,' 1877.

I, JOSEPH, son of Heli, of the tribe
Of Judah, Carpenter, at Nazareth
In Galilee abiding, being now
Well ripe with many years, and having hope
Before long time be past to be ingathered
Into the bosom of my father Abraham,
Have taken parchment, with mine own hand writ,
And with mine own seal signed, the memory
(Lest it should die with me) of that I saw
Upon the birth-night of my Step-son, Jesus—
Whom men do vulgarly repute my son,
Not being mine, but of the Spirit of God
Begotten, as an angel of the Lord
Forewarned me in a dream. Touching which Jesus

Did many strange things hap at Bethlehem,
Where he was born. Yea, and in afterwhile
Many strange things, whereof the certainty
Is known to faithful witnesses. Howbeit,
None dareth openly make speech thereof,
Lest men should thrust him from the synagogue
For liar and blasphemer, or perchance
Work him some greater evil. But one thing
I, Joseph, only know and none beside.
So, lest the knowledge of it pass away
When I pass, see, here I have written it
In goodly characters, to be revealed,
If God so pleaseth, when the hour shall come
That of this Jesus, Mary's Son, the Name
And presence shall be great in Israel.
For that it shall be so, that doubt I not,
Although mine eyes shall see it not, and though
Mine ears shall never hear it. The sun shall rise
Whose dawning dazzles me, and I shall go
Having beheld it not on earth, but hoping
It shall yet shine on me in Paradise.

Therefore be it known that, at the time ordained
Of Cæsar for enrolment, I went up
From Nazareth, my place of sojourning,
To Bethlehem-Judah, where my fathers sleep;
And with me Mary, my espoused Wife,
Being great with Child. And so it came to pass,
That as we drew anigh to Bethlehem,
She said, ' I am troubled : therefore, haste and fetch
Some woman.' And I took her from the ass
And laid her in a cave beside the way
And hastened me.

                    And suddenly, I, Joseph,
Was walking and not walking ; and I looked
Upon the heavens, and saw the heavens amazed :
The setting sun set not ; the rising moon
Rose not ; and all the flying things of air
Flew not, but rested hovering.   Then I looked
Upon the earth, and saw a company
Of labourers sitting round their evening meal ;
And lo, they eating ate not, and the hands
That gathered from the dish were stayed therein,
But all their eyes gazed upward.   And thereby
A shepherd drove his sheep into the pen,
And the sheep moved not ; and the shepherd's staff
Was raised to smite them, and the staff remained.
And hard beside me was a little brook,
And the brook ran not : and a flock of kids
Were come to drink, and drank not, but their mouths
Were resting on the stream.   And all the face
Of all the world was still.

                    But at the last
The world moved on : and straightway I beheld
A woman coming from the hill-country
Wearing a midwife's badge, and spake with her,
And brought her back with me.

                    But when we came,
Behold, we found this Jesus born.

                        The rest
I write not : Mary knows it, and can tell
When this Child Jesus stands revealed a Prophet
As one of Israel's prophets, yea, maybe
Elijah's self, or even—but my brain
Grows dull with many years, I dare not trust

The thing I think.   Only, I clearly know
That I have seen, and herein testified,
I, Joseph, son of Heli, of the tribe
Of Judah, Carpenter, of Nazareth
In Galilee, as my seal witnesseth.

NOTE.

This poem is founded on the story of Joseph's Vision, in the apocryphal ' Protevangelium of James.'   The rest of the work is ordinary narrative : but the Vision is told in the first person, as if it were taken from some statement by Joseph himself.   The third paragraph is a paraphrase of the original.   In the last paragraph, the reading of St. Mark vi. 15, 'a Prophet as one of the prophets,' is followed, as being presumably the true reading.   (Author.)

Mineteenth Century Poetry.

I.   CAROL OF THE KINGS.

THOMAS ASHE: 1836—1889.

FROM 'SONGS NOW AND THEN,' 1876.

THREE Wise Men kneel in a way-side inn
To a Little Child, his favour to win :
    The sheep lie still, and dawn's on the hill.

'O Mary Mother, we saw a star ;
It bade us bring these gifts from afar : '
    The sheep lie still, and dawn's on the hill.

'Ruddy gold we failed not to bring ;
But thorns may wreathe the brows of a King : '
    The sheep lie still, and dawn's on the hill.

'Incense have we here in the scrip ;
But heart's praise passeth praise of the lip : '
    The sheep lie still, and dawn's on the hill.

'Here is myrrh; but the women fair
Will seek in vain in the sepulchre:'
  The sheep lie still, and dawn's on the hill.

'Now lift him gently; flee for your life;
We on the dark see gleam of a knife:'
  The sheep lie still, and dawn's on the hill.

II. 'HIS MOTHER KEPT ALL THESE SAYINGS IN HER HEART.'

WILLIAM CULLEN BRYANT: 1794—1878.

A hymn not found in the English edition of the Author's
works: contributed by Louise I. Guiney.

As o'er the cradle of her Son
  The Blessed Mary hung,
And chanted to the Anointed One
  The psalms that David sung,

What joy her bosom must have known,
  As with a sweet surprise
She marked the boundless love that shone
  Within his infant eyes.

But deeper was her joy to hear,
  E'en in his ripening youth,
And treasure up from year to year,
  His words of grace and truth.

Oh, may we keep his words, like her,
  In all their life and power,
And to that law of love refer
  The acts of every hour.

III.   REPOSE IN EGYPT.

ARTHUR HUGH CLOUGH: 1819—1861.

FROM 'POEMS AND PROSE REMAINS,' 1869.

'Old things need not be therefore true,'
O brother Men, nor yet the new ;
Ah, still awhile the old retain,
And yet consider it again. (*Author.*)

O HAPPY Mother—while the Man wayworn
Sleeps by his ass and dreams of daily bread,
Wakeful and heedful for thy Infant care ;
O happy Mother—while thy Husband sleeps
Art privileged, O Blessed One, to see
Celestial strangers sharing in thy task,
And visible angels waiting on thy Child.

Take, O young Soul, O Infant heaven-desired,
Take and fear not the cates, although of earth,
Which to thy hands celestial hands extend ;
Take and fear not : such vulgar meats of life
Thy spirit lips no more must scorn to pass ;
The seeming ill, contaminating joys,
Thy sense divine no more be loth to allow ;
The pleasures as the pains of our strange life
Thou art engaged, self-compromised, to share.

Look up ; upon thy Mother's face there sits
No sad suspicion of a lurking ill,
No shamed confession of a needful sin ;
Mistrust her not, although of earth she too :
Look up ; the bright-eyed cherubs overhead
Strew from mid air fresh flowers to crown the just.
Look ; thy own Father's servants these, and thine,
Who at his bidding and at thine are here.

In thine own Word was it not said long since,
'Butter and honey shall he eat, and learn
The evil to refuse and choose the good'?
Fear not, O Babe Divine, fear not, accept.
· O happy Mother, privileged to see,
While the Man sleeps, the sacred mystery.

IV. 'AVE MARIA' IN ROME.

BY MATHILDE BLIND: 1847—1896.

FROM 'THE MAGAZINE OF ART,' 1894.

Far away dim violet mountains
    Fade away from sight ;
Flashing from fantastic fountains
    Jets the liquid light,
Where from Nymph or Triton's lip
Bubbling waters drip and drip,
    Bubbling day and night.

Pealed from tower to answering tower
    O'er the city swells,
Ringing in the hallowed hour
    Rhythm of bells on bells ;
And on wings of choral song
Confluent hearts to Mary throng
    From dim cloistered cells.

On the golden ground of even,
    Like a half-way home
On the pilgrim road to heaven,
    Floats St. Peter's dome :
High, high, in the air alone—
Man's dread thoughts transformed to stone,
    Pinnacled o'er Rome.

V. CHRISTMAS.

JOHN DENNIS.

FROM 'THE SPECTATOR,' 1874.

THE Christ is come, a God is born to-day :
A Woman's arms enfold the wondrous Child,
A Woman's breast sustains the Undefiled ;
And simple folk hear the first Christmas lay,
And hearing, haste to worship and to pray,
Trusting their flocks to angels on the wild—
While Mary looked upon her Babe and smiled,
Most Bless'd of Women on that morning grey.
So once again let the glad tale be told
Of love most human, yet of love divine :
Bring loyal gifts of frankincense and gold,
And lay thy heart's best treasures on his shrine ;
Bring Faith and Hope, but to these graces see
Thou add'st man's noblest virtue—Charity.

VI. MARY AT THE FOOT OF THE CROSS.

WILLIAM JOHNSON FOX : 1786—1864.

FROM 'HYMNS AND ANTHEMS,' 1845.

JEWS were wrought to cruel madness ;
Christians fled in fear and sadness ;
    Mary stood the Cross beside :

At its foot her foot she planted,
By the dreadful scene undaunted,
    'Till the gentle Sufferer died.

Poets oft have sung her story,
Painters decked her brow with glory,
    Priests her name have deified :

But no worship, song, or glory,
Touches like that simple story—
    Mary stood the Cross beside.

And when, under fierce oppression,
Goodness suffers like transgression,
    Christ again is crucified ;

But if love be there, true-hearted,
By no grief or terror parted,
    Mary stands the Cross beside.

VII. A MEDITATION.

DORA (DOROTHY) GREENWELL :
1821—1882.

FROM 'POEMS,' 1861.

'I believe in the Communion of Saints.'

O VIRGIN Lilies rayed
With light and loveliness that did declare
His perfect beauty here, that grew so fair
By gazing on him. From the shade
Where God hath planted me, I have essayed
To reach unto your sunshine. Though you keep
Your silence even from good words, I miss
No sign of greeting, nor have need of kiss
For sealing of our love ; for this is clear,
That ye are near me when I draw most near
To him in whom we meet. I see you shine
In Christ, as once I marked above a shrine
By midnight clear, yet moonless, pictured fair
A Virgin-Mother in a lowly place
Bend o'er a Sleeping Infant. Full of grace
His brow and lip ; with gifts and odours rare

Came kings adoring ; lowly shepherds there
Rejoicing knelt, and all the canvas dim
Was crowded up behind with seraphim
In goodly ranks.   Yet Mother-Maid serene,
Sage, seraph, lowly shepherd—all were seen
By Light that streamed from out the Babe Divine.

VIII.   TO TWO SISTERS.

ARTHUR HENRY HALLAM: 1811—1833.

FROM 'REMAINS IN VERSE AND PROSE,' 1863.

'Love thoughts be rich when canopied with flowers.' (*Shakespeare.*)

In Leigh Hunt's ' Indicator,' it is stated that the name of Mary
has its origin in a word signifying ' Exalted.' (Author.)

WELL do your names express ye, Sisters dear,
In small clear sounds awaking mournful thoughts,
Mournful, as with the refluence of a joy
Too pure for these sad coasts of human life.
Methinks, had not your happy vernal dawn
Ever arisen on my trancèd view,
Those flowing sounds would syllable yourselves
To my delighted soul ; or if not so,
Yet when I traced their deeper meaning out,
And fathomed his intent, who in some hour
Sweet from the world's young dawn, with breath of life
Endowed them, then your certain forms would come
Pale, but true visions of my musing eye.

For thee, O eldest Flower, whose precious name
Would to inspirèd ears by Chebar once,
Or the lone cavern hid from Jezabel,
Sound as ' Exalted '—fitliest therefore borne
By that mysterious Lady who reposed
In Egypt far, beyond the impious touch

Of fell Herodes, or the unquiet looks
Of men who knew not Peace to earth was born—
There happily reposed, waiting the time
When from that dark interminable day
Should by God's might emerge, and Love sit throned,
And Meekness kiss away the looks of Scorn.
O Mary, deem that Virgin looks on thee
With an especial care ; lean thou on her,
As the Ideal of thy woman's heart ;
Pray that thy heart be strengthened from above
To lasting hope and sovran kindliness ;
That conquering smiles and more than conquering tears
May be thy portion through the ways of life :
So walk thou on in thy simplicity,
Following the Virgin-Queen for evermore.

IX. BEGINNING OF THE 'EVE OF ST. AGNES.'

JOHN KEATS: 1796—1821.

FROM 'WORKS,' EDITED BY R. M. MILNES, 1856.

ST. AGNES' Eve—Ah, bitter chill it was :
The owl, for all his feathers, was a-cold ;
The hare limped trembling through the frozen grass,
And silent was the flock in woolly fold :
Numb were the Beadsman's fingers while he told
His rosary, and while his frosted breath,
Like pious incense from a censer old,
Seemed taking flight for heaven without a death,
Past the sweet Virgin's Picture, while his prayer he saith.

His prayer he saith, this patient, holy man ;
Then takes his lamp and riseth from his knees,
And back returneth, meagre, barefoot, wan,
Along the chapel aisle by slow degrees :

The sculptured dead on each side seemed to freeze,
　Emprisoned in black, purgatorial rails :
Knights, ladies, praying in dumb oratories,
　He passeth by ; and his weak spirit fails
To think how they may ache in icy hoods and mails.

Northward he turneth through a little door,
　And scarce three steps, ere Music's golden tongue
Flattered to tears this aged man and poor ;
　But no—already had his death-bell rung ;
　The joys of all his life were said and sung :
His was harsh penance on St. Agnes' Eve :
　Another way he went, and soon among
Rough ashes sat he for his soul's reprieve,
And all night kept awake, for sinners' sake to grieve.

X. 'MAGNIFICAT ANIMA MEA.'
FREDERIC W. H. MYERS: 1843—1901.
FROM 'ST. PAUL,' 1867.

YES, and to her, the Beautiful and Lowly,
　Mary, a Maiden, separate from men,
Camest thou nigh and didst possess her wholly,
　Close to thy Saints, but thou wast closer then.

Once and for ever didst thou show thy Chosen,
　Once and for ever magnify thy choice—
Scorched in love's fire, or with his freezing frozen,
　Lift up your hearts, ye humble, and rejoice.

Not to the rich he came and to the ruling—
　Men full of meat, whom wholly he abhors—
Not to the fools grown insolent in fooling
　Most, when the lost are dying at the doors.
V

Nay, but to her who with a sweet thanksgiving
  Took in tranquillity what God might bring,
Blessed him, and waited, and within her living
  Felt the arousal of a Holy Thing.

Aye, for her infinite and endless honour
  Found the Almighty in this flesh a tomb,
Pouring with power the Holy Ghost upon her,
  Nothing disdainful of the Virgin's womb.

XI. SAN ROCCO.

RODEN NOEL: 1834—1894.

FROM 'THE RED FLAG,' 1872.

THERE is a little chapel rude
  On a terraced hill,
With cypress round the solitude
  Of a platform still ;

Cypress flames of darkling green,
  Rich athwart the blue ;
Fair among them ocean-sheen
  Softly twinkles through.

Within one open end, in line,
  Vessels rudely made
Hang, with perils of the brine
  On either wall displayed.

Each unskilful picture shows,
  On the marge, a Form
Of her who, when the whirlwind blows
  Saveth men from storm.

There a lamp of silver gleams,
　　Like an evening star;
O'er a spangled altar beams,
　　In twilight cool afar.

Home-bound sailors from the deep,
　　When the belfry small
Of San Rocco on the steep
　　First appeareth, fall

At our Lady's feet of Grace:
　　When a woman old
Gaunt and homeliest of her race,
　　Falteringly told

The story of her son to me,
　　A bold young mariner,
How once he sailed, and from the sea
　　Came ne'er again to her;

And how he vowed before he sailed,
　　If ever he returned,
His votive vessel should be nailed
　　And in the lamp be burned

His votive amber oil above,
　　At yonder mountain shrine,
Where perilled sailors prove their love
　　To Mary the Divine;

Where every pious mariner
　　Leaves a lowly gift for her:
Fair the mother was with tears,
　　For all her homeliness and years.

Protecting Corselet of Mary:

ANCIENT IRISH HYMN OF THE XII. CENT.

TRANSLATED (1870) BY BRIAN O'LOONEY, CATHOLIC UNIVERSITY, DUBLIN.

FROM 'THE IRISH ECCLESIASTICAL RECORD,' 1870.

This Hymn was mentioned, in his last lecture in the University before his death, by Professor O'Curry, in 1862, as being well-known both to him from his childhood, and also to his father, who was wont to sing it nightly to a quaint air. The Professor translated twelve stanzas of the Hymn : but in later years Mr. O'Looney discovered a fuller MS. version, and made a new translation, the large portion of which is here quoted, as an interesting monument of the piety of our ancestors, and of their devotion to the Immaculate Mother of God. (From the Editor's introductory Note.)

DIRECT me how to praise thee,
Though I am not a master of poetry,
O thou of the Angelic Countenance, without fault ;
Thou hast given the milk of thy breast to save me.

I offer myself under thy protection,
O loving Mother of the Only Son ;
And under thy protecting shield I place my body,
My heart, my will and my understanding.

I am a sinner full of faults ;
I beseech of thee and pray thee do it ;
O Woman Physician of the miserable diseases,
Behold the many ulcers of my soul.

O Temple of the Three Persons,
Father, Son and Holy Spirit,
I invoke thee to come to visit me
At the hour of my judgment and of my death.

O Queen to whom it hath been granted by the King,
The Eternal Father, out of the abundance of his love,

As inheritance to be the Mother,
I implore thy assistance to save me.

O Vessel, who carried the Lamp
More luminous than the sun,
Draw me under thy shelter into the harbour,
Out of the transitory ship of the world.

O Flower of Beauty, O Mother of Christ,
O Lover of peace and mildness,
I pray thee hear me ; may it ne'er occur to me
In any trial to forsake thee.

O Queen, who refusest not any person
Who is pure in his deeds,
Beseech the Christ to put me
From the wily demons amidst the saints.

O Queen of the Saints, of the Virgins, of the Angels,
O Honeycomb of eternal life,
All-surpassing Power, presumptuous valour
Goes not far without thee.

I am under thy shelter amidst the brave,
O Protecting Shield, without being injured by their
    blows ;
O Holy Mary, if thou wilt hear thy suppliant,
I put myself under the shelter of thy shield.

When falling in the slippery path,
Thou art my smooth supporting Hand-staff ;
O Virgin from the southern clime,
May I go to heaven to visit thee.

There is no hound in fleetness or in chase,
North wind or rapid river,
As quick as the Mother of Christ to the bed of death,
To those who are entitled to her kindly protection.

O Heart without sin, O Bosom without guile,
O Virgin Woman who hast chosen sanctity,
In thee I place my hope of salvation
From the eternal torture of the pain.

O Mary, gentle, beautiful,
O Meekness, mild and modest,
I am not tired of invoking thee;
Thou art my guarding Staff in danger.

Turn thine eye, O Woman Friend,
Upon the distressed nobles of Erin;
To them restore the happiness of their lives,
And obtain for them from the Eternal Father,

Every sinner who has fallen into trouble
Of their number, and is in need of succour;
Redeem them, O Virgin Woman,
They are in misery until you do it.

To the true faith without dissimulation
May the kings of the world be obedient,
Through the invocation of Mary, which is not weak;
And may they renounce the false religion.

To those who are in the pit of pain in fire,
Whose portion is of evil,
Deign thy relief to them, O Mary,
And Amen, say, O Cleric.

*   *   *

Many are the countless virtues
Of the Protecting Shield-corselet of Mary,
If we be in the state of grace,
And pray to her at all times with devotion.

Sonnets and Lyrics.

ARTHUR BARRY O'NEILL, C.S.C.

FROM 'BETWEEN WHILES,' 1899.

I. 'AVE.'

> ' I have known one word hang starlike
> O'er a dreary waste of years,
> And it only shone the brighter
> Looked at through a mist of tears.'

ETERNAL 'Ave,' dwelling long unspoke
  For age on age within the Father's mind,
  Ere voice angelic, like caressing wind,
Low whispered thee to Mary; then there broke
O'er sin-dark earth a gladsome dawn, that woke
  Responsive thrills of joy in all mankind—
  Of joy in him who came earth's wounds to bind,
And save a race enthralled 'neath Satan's yoke.

O starlike Word, whose beauty pure, serene,
  Hath blessed the world for twice a thousand years,
Undimmed by time, thy fair celestial sheen
  Still glows o'er darkened minds and glowing cheers—
Eternal Word, thine echoes ne'er shall cease
To soothe the sad and bring the slave release.

II. SPES NOSTRA.

No day is ended till its sun hath set,
  Nor life completed till death's sombre gloom
  Steals o'er its twilight, and the yawning tomb
Engulphs its sin and sorrow, toil and fret.
Who most has cause to mourn with vain regret
  A guilty past, and dread eternal doom,
  May, if he will, his future course illume
And reap the Saints' rich, golden harvest yet.

For she, the Mother Blest whom Jesus gave,
  All-potent Advocate at Mercy's throne,
Lends willing ear when contrite sinners crave
  The sweet compassion she has ever shown
To bruisèd reeds. Ah, who would not be brave
  When Heaven's Queen doth make his cause her own?

III. SPIRITUAL MISERS.

THE miser joys to count his treasures o'er,
Nor deems that earth can purer bliss afford
Than still to gloat upon his hidden hoard,
And day by day increase his garnered store
Of sterile wealth. At length unto his door
The summons comes that may not be ignored.
What boots him now the gold through life adored?
His treasure's lost to him for evermore.

All otherwise we hoard who day by day
Tell o'er our blessèd beads, and still entreat
Our Mother's prayers both now and when Death's sway
O'er life shall rule supreme. 'Hail, Marys,' sweet
We garner up, each hour more and more,
And find our treasure on the eternal shore.

IV. THE ROSE-GARDEN.

IN olden days, as German legends tell,
Upon the castled banks of storied Rhine,
There bloomed a garden fair, a floral shrine
Wherein the Princess Criemhild loved to dwell :
All knights avowed her beauty's potent spell ;
And rapture thrilled his pulse like bodied wine,
The victor round whose brows her hands would twine
A rose-wreath—token that he jousted well.

A fairer garden blooms for us to-day,
A fairer Queen of Beauty dwelleth there ;
And oft as we our pleading ' Aves ' say,
Those mystic roses form a wreath of prayer—
A love-twined wreath we humbly offer thee,
Sweet Lady of the Holy Rosary.

V. GOD'S MASTER-PIECE OF BEAUTY.

WHENE'ER the poet's soul doth wander wide
  O'er all the boundless universe of dreams,
  Upon his vision clear at times there gleams
A peerless Form that, fleeting, will not bide ;
A beauteous Face, lost even as descried—
  A form and face would serve as fitting themes
  For pen inspired, or brush dipped in the beams
Of gold wherewith the summer clouds are dyed.

Yet can no poet sing, no artist paint
  The grace ideal of his vision bright,
Or show, save in a copy blurred and faint,
  The dreamland Queen who thus has blessed his
    sight :
'Tis she, God's Master-piece of Beauty rare,
The Spouse to whom he said, ' Thou art all Fair.'

V. 'TOTA PULCHRA ES.'

THOU art all Fair, O Mother Blest,
  In thee is found no stain—
Art purer far than whitest crest
  That decks the troubled main.

Thy soul no taint did ever bear
  Of imperfection's shade ;
And Satan never counted there
  The blots his wiles had made.

First creature formed since Adam's fall
　　Who shared not Adam's sin ;
Thy life was spent that mortals all
　　Celestial life might win.

Glad sight to Heaven's highest Court,
　　To view their peerless Queen ;
And feeble man's most firm support
　　In that fair Maid is seen.

O thou fond Mother, guard me well,
　　I trust my soul to thee ;
Defeat the serried ranks of hell,
　　Safe guide me o'er life's sea.

And when, all spent my mortal days,
　　I kiss Death's fatal rod,
Be ' Tota pulchra es ' the phrase
　　My soul shall hear from God.

VII.　MODERN CHIVALRY.

Victors in tourney for love and duty,
　　Chivalrous knights in their golden prime,
Knelt at the throne of the Queen of Beauty,
　　Ages agone in the olden time.
Kneeling they proffered and deemed it honour,
　　Guerdons of valour, the tourney's prize ;
More than repaid just to gaze upon her,
　　Reading their bliss in her love-lit eyes.

Lances no longer we tilt for glory,
　　Gone is the pomp of the tourney now ;
Still like the knights of the olden story,
　　Lovers the queens of their hearts avow.

Peerless is mine : with her grace none other
  E'er may compete here below or above—
Queen all unrivalled, O Mary Mother,
  Grant for my guerdon one smile of love.

VIII. TO THE IMMACULATE.

STAR of the Morning, whose splendour illumined
  Shadows that dark o'er the primal world lay,
Still doth thy glory redeem the sad story
  Angels record of mankind day by day ;
    Still art thou shining bright,
    Piercing the mists of night,
Steadfastly gleaming o'er life's troubled sea ;
    Gladly we hail thy ray,
    Hopeful the while we pray,
' Virgin Immaculate, guide us to thee.'

Lily of Israel, Nature's Ideal,
  Type the most perfect of woman most fair,
Poets have hymned thee and painters have limned thee,
  Art knows no beauty with thine to compare :
    Lily all free from stain
    Soul in whom Grace's reign
Ne'er was disturbed by the shadow of sin ;
    Virgin Immaculate,
    Teach ·us like thee to bate
Aught save the glory that lies all within.

IX. IN RANSOM.

WITH the plaintive tones of a mourner's moans
  Sigh the winds of bleak November,
And each ashen cloud is the trailing shroud
  Of some loved one we remember :

Through the mist of years, through a veil of tears,
  We recall friends tender-hearted,
And renew the woe felt long ago
  For the loss of our dear departed.

Though no sterile grief gives them blest relief,
  Though no tears from their pains can deliver
Those friends of yore on that farther shore
  Of Death's darkly-coursing river,
Rich treasures we may as their ransom pay,
  While life's sunlight still streams o'er us—
Tell our Lady's Beads for the urgent needs
  Of the loved ones gone before us.

Oratory Hymns.

FREDERICK WILLIAM FABER,
OF THE ORATORY, D.D.: 1814—1863.

FROM ' HYMNS', 1849—1861.

I. THE HAPPY GATE OF HEAVEN.

  FAIR are the portals of the day,
    The gateways of the morning,
  Whose pillared clouds the rising sun
    Is rosily adorning :
  Fair are the portals of the day,
    The gateways of the even,
  When through long halls of burning light
    Earth gazes into heaven.

REFRAIN. Of matchless light, of grace untold,
          All love be thine, fair House of Gold ;
            All praise to thee be given,
          Sweet Balm of all our sadness,
          Dear Cause of all our gladness,
            Thou Happy Gate of Heaven.

Fair are the passes in the hills,
　The gateways of the mountains,
Along whose sounding channels leap
　The many-gifted fountains :
Fair are the thresholds of blue sea
　The gateways of the ocean,
That guard the harbours of the earth,
　Swinging with placid motion.

But fairest of all gateways far
　Art thou, the sinless Mary ;
The Gate that opens, yet secures
　God's inmost sanctuary :
Gate of the one true Dawn art thou,
　Gate of the one sweet Even,
Gate of the angels into earth,
　The Gate of souls to heaven.

Thou art the Gate God entered by
　To visit his creation,
The Mountain-pass where leap and flow
　The wells of our salvation :
Thou art the Gate of azure sea
　With the lighthouse ever burning,
The exile's happy Landing-place
　To his Father's House returning.

Bright Gateway, through whose golden arch
　The Father's grace is flowing,
Whose steps the Son and Spirit wear
　With their incessant going ;
Porch of the Throne, what beauteous hosts
　Of angels cluster round thee ;
Oh, happy are the sleeping souls
　Whose faith and love have found thee.

REFRAIN.   Of matchless light, of grace untold,
All love be thine, fair House of Gold ;
All praise to thee be given,
Sweet Balm of all our sadness,
Dear Cause of all our gladness,
Thou Happy Gate of Heaven.

II. THE QUEEN OF PURGATORY.

· OH, turn to Jesus, Mother, turn,
And call him by his tenderest names
Pray for the Holy Souls that burn
This hour amid the cleansing flames.

Ah, they have fought a gallant fight ;
In death's cold arms they persevered
And after life's uncheery night,
The harbour of their rest is neared.

In pains beyond all earthly pains
Favourites of Jesus, there they lie,
Letting the fire wear out their stains
And worshipping God's purity.

Spouses of Christ they are, for he
Was wedded to them by his Blood ;
And angels o'er their destiny
In wondering adoration brood.

They are the children of thy tears ;
Then hasten, Mother, to their aid ;
In pity think each hour appears
An age while glory is delayed.

See, how they bound amid their fires,
While pain and love their spirits fill ;
Then with self-crucified desires
Utter sweet murmurs, and lie still.

Ah me, the love of Jesus yearns
  O'er that abyss of sacred pain,
And as he looks, his bosom burns
  With Calvary's dear thirst again.

O Mary, let thy Son no more
  His lingering Spouses thus expect ;
God's children to their God restore,
  And to the Spirit his elect.

Pray then, as thou hast ever prayed ;
  Angels and Souls all look to thee ;
God waits thy prayers, for he hath made
  Those prayers his law of charity.

III. MARY, OUR MOTHER, REIGNS ON HIGH.

O VISION bright ;
The Land of light
Beams goldenly beyond the sky ;
'Mid heavenly fires,
'Bove angel-choirs,
Mary, our Mother, reigns on high.

O Vision bright ;
The Father's might
All round his Daughter's throne doth lie ;
Where in the balm
Of endless calm
Mary, our Mother, reigns on high.

O Vision bright ;
The eternal light
Of the dear Son may we descry ;
Where brighter far
Than moon or star
Mary, our Mother, reigns on high.

O Vision bright ;
In softest flight
The Dove around his Spouse doth fly ;
Where in that height
Of matchless light
Mary, our Mother, reigns on high.

O Vision bright ;
Angels' delight,
The Mother sits with Jesus nigh ;
Her form he bears,
Her look he wears ;
Mary, our Mother, reigns on high.

O Vision bright ;
O dearest sight,
God, with his Mother's face and eye ;
Where by his side
All glorified
Mary, our Mother, reigns on high.

O Vision bright ;
Life's darkest night
Is fair as dawn when thou art nigh ;
Where 'mid the throng
Of psalm and song
Mary, our Mother, reigns on high.

O Vision bright ;
O Land of light,
Thou art our home beyond the sky ;
'Tis grand to see
How gloriously
Mary, our Mother, reigns on high.

Post hoc Exilium, &c.

FRANCES JANETTE (TURNER)
PARTRIDGE: 1828—1887;
AND S.N.D.

I. POST HOC EXILIUM.

FROM 'THE MONTH,' 1877.

AFTER this exile: not while groping here
In this low valley full of mists and chills,
Waiting and watching till the day breaks clear
Over the brow of the Eternal Hills—
 Mother, sweet Dawn of that Unsetting Sun,
 Show us thy Jesus, when the night is done.

After this exile: when our toils are o'er,
And we, poor labourers, homeward turn our feet;
When we shall ache and work and weep no more,
But know the rest the weary find so sweet—
 Mother of Mercy, pitiful and blest,
 Show us thy Jesus, in the Land of Rest.

After this exile: winter will be past,
And the rain over, and the flowers appear;
And we shall see in God's own light at last
All we have sought for in the darkness here—
 Then, Mother, turn on us thy loving eyes,
 And show us Jesus, our Eternal Prize.

II. NOTRE DAME DE L'EPINE: ST. BRIAC.

FROM 'THE MONTH,' 1875.

O MOTHER dear, our age is full of thee
 And the fair marvels of thy power and grace;
 From many a glorious shrine and famous place
Flows the full river of thy charity.

W

Nor thence alone—for there are spots obscure
  By angels honoured, to the world unknown,
  Where thou dost love to shed thy blessings down
Upon the meek, the simple and the poor.

Such is the chapel where I knelt one morn,
  Not knowing then it was a wondrous Shrine
  Where countless miracles of love divine
Are wrought by thee, our Lady of the Thorn.

Amid the fields and scattered trees it stands,
  Faint murmurs reach it from the hidden sea,
  It boasts no beauty—humbler cannot be—
A rustic chapel built by peasant hands.

Pictures of broken ships and stormy sea
  Hang on the walls ; each has its tale to tell
  Of perils past and saving miracle,
And loving meed of gratitude to thee.

No need of gold, or jewels to adorn
  That lowly chapel ; one quaint Image there
  Above the altar is its treasure rare ;
Hail, Full of Grace, our Lady of the Thorn.

Barefoot, bareheaded in the winter snow,
  Here thy poor loyal Breton children throng,
  Pilgrims of love ; hence, in fresh courage strong,
Back to the dangers of the sea they go.

With falling tears a sailor's bright-eyed wife
  Told me the story how the Shrine arose ;
  How their dear Mother showed them that she chose
To make that quiet place with wonders rife.

Oft and again, she said, when death was nigh,
  And human strength and skill were vain to save,
  Had Mary calmed the fury of the wave
The moment that she heard her children's cry.

And as I listened, every country sound
   Took a new meaning; angels led the strain,
   And earth's glad voices, mingling back again,
Told Mary's triumphs everywhere around.

The breezes rustling in the yellow corn,
   The lark's wild carol and the humming bee,
   The laughing children and the sighing sea,
All sang thy praise, our Lady of the Thorn.

S.N.D.
THE TENTS OF NOTRE DAME.

Founded on an American War-song, and applied to an English
Convent.

WE are tenting to-day on the old Camp-ground
   Where many have tented before,
Far from the range of shot and shell
   And beyond the cannon's roar:
Many are the souls that have come and gone
   And blessed the Camp on the Hill;
Many be the souls, O dear Notre Dame,
   That shall come and bless thee still.

We know that the time for rest is short
   For the strife is raging hard;
We must fight for the King who has fought for us,
   For we are his Mother's Guard:
But many is the time that our hearts shall turn
   To the dear old Camp on the Hill,
And its image shall nerve the wearied arm
   And shall brace the flagging will.

Oh, what of the years since it first was pitched
   On the Hill in the winter snow?
The Camp is the same, though its tents be more,
   As at Candlemas, long ago:

Still as of old, in the King's own tent,
　With its red lamp's waning light,
Still as of old, the regiments press
　Round his feet at the fall of night.

And what of the brave who have passed away
　Since that winter of years ago?
They fell as they fall that have tented here,
　With their faces towards the foe:
Many is the prayer which our comrades above
　In the city where the files are crowned,
Shall breathe for the troops that are fighting below,
　Or tenting on the old Camp-ground.

We will fight to the death in our Lady's ranks,
　And her medal shall be our shield;
We'll be true to the death to our hearts' dear Queen,
　We never will flinch, nor yield:
True to the training of bye-gone years
　And true to the home we found,
When we first bivouacked 'neath her banner blue
　On the Hill on the old Camp-ground.

Sponsa Dei et Regina Cœli.

COVENTRY PATMORE: 1823—1897.

FROM 'POEMS,' 1879.

I. SPONSA DEI.

WHAT is this Maiden Fair,
The laughing of whose eye
Is in man's heart renewed virginity;
Who yet sick longing breeds

For marriage which exceeds
The inventive guess of Love to satisfy
With hope of utter binding, and of loosing endless dear
    despair?
What gleams about her shine
More transient than delight and more divine.
If she does something but a little sweet,
As gaze towards the glass to set her hair,
See how his soul falls humbled at her feet.
Her gentle step, to go or come,
Gains her more merit than a martyrdom;
And if she dance, it doth such grace confer
As opes the heaven of heavens to more than her,
And makes a rival of her worshipper.
To die unknown for her were little cost.
So is she without guile,
Her mere refused smile
Makes up the sum of that which may be lost.

    Who is this Fair
Whom each hath seen,
The darkest once in this bewailed dell,
Be he not destined for the glooms of hell?
Whom each hath seen
And known, with sharp remorse and sweet, as Queen
And tear-glad Mistress of his hopes of bliss,
Too fair for man to kiss?
Who is this only happy She,
Whom, by a frantic flight of courtesy
Born of despair
Of better lodging for his Spirit fair,
He adores as Margaret, Maude, or Cecily?
And what this sigh,

That each one heaves for earth's last lowlihead
And the Heaven high
Ineffably locked in dateless bridal-bed?
Are all, then, mad; or is it prophecy?

'Sons now we are of God,' as we have heard,
'But what we shall be hath not yet appeared.'
O Heart, remember thee,
That man is none
Save One.
What if this Lady be thy soul; and he
Who claims to enjoy her sacred beauty be,
Not thou, but God; and thy sick fire
A female vanity,
Such as a bride, viewing her mirrored charms,
Feels when she sighs, 'All these are for his arms.'
A reflex heat
Flashed on thy cheek from his immense desire,
Which waits to crown, beyond thy brain's conceit,
Thy nameless, secret, hopeless longing sweet,
Not by-and-by, but now,
Unless deny him thou.

II. REGINA CŒLI.

SAY, did his Sisters wonder what could Joseph see
In a mild, silent little Maid like thee?
And was it awful, in that narrow house,
With God for Babe and Spouse?
Nay, like thy simple, female sort, each one
Apt to find him in husband and in son,
Nothing to thee came strange in this;
Thy wonder was but wondrous bliss:

Wondrous, for though
True Virgin lives not but does know
(Howbeit none ever yet confessed)
That God lies really in her breast,
Of thine he made his special nest.
And so,
All mothers worship little feet,
And kiss the very ground they've trod ;
But ah, thy Little Baby sweet
Who was indeed thy God.

Pearl :

AN ENGLISH POEM OF THE XIV. CENTURY.

AUTHOR OF 'CLEANNESS,' 'PATIENCE,' AND 'SIR GAWAIN';

EDITED, WITH AN UNRHYMED
MODERN RENDERING, BY ISRAEL GOLLANCZ, M.A.:
THE RHYMING STANZAS FREELY RENDERED
BY W. J. BLEW, M.A.: 1808—1894.

FROM 'PEARL,' 1891.

The theme of Pearl is a Lament and a Vision, developed in part by colloquy and in part by narrative, or mystical description. It tells of a Father's grief for the loss of a beloved Child, and how in his grief he was comforted and learnt the lesson of resignation by a vision of his Daughter transfigured as one of the Brides of the New Jerusalem. She describes her bliss in Paradise ; and is addressed by her father as following the Lamb in the train of the Heavenly Queen. The basis of the Vision may be found in the Gospel Parable of the Pearl, and the closing chapters of the Apocalypse : and its metre and arrangement of stanzas resemble, more than anything else yet discovered in English, the earliest form of the Sonnet-sequence. In this selection from ' Pearl,' stanzas 34, 35 and 66 are reprinted from the literal version of Mr. Gollancz : stanzas 36-38 and 63-65 are freely rendered, after Mr. Gollancz, in

rhyming verse (1893) by Mr. Blew.   The late Poet Laureate graced
Mr. Gollancz's volume (published by Mr. Nutt in 1891) with the
following tribute :

> 'We lost you—for how long a time—
> True Pearl of our poetic prime ;
> We found you, and you gleam re-set
> In Britain's Lyric coronet.' (*Tennyson.*)

I. QUEEN OF COURTESY.

STANZA 34.

'Now bliss betide thee, noble Sir ;'
Said that Maid so fair of form and face,
'Thou art welcome here to walk and to tarry,
For now thy speech is dear to me :
Masterful mood and mighty pride
I tell thee are hated full bitterly here ;
My Master loveth not to chide,
For meek are all that dwell him nigh :
> And when thou appearest in his place,
> Be deep and devout in all humbleness ;
> My Lord, the Lamb, aye loveth such cheer,
> He is the ground of all my bliss.

STANZA 35.

'A blissful life thou sayest I lead,
And thou wouldst know the state thereof ;
Thou knowest when thy Pearl fared forth,
I was so young and of tender age,
But through his Godhead, my Lord, the Lamb,
Took me in marriage unto himself,
Crowned me Queen to revel in bliss,
In length of days that ever shall last ;
> Yea, each Beloved holdeth in fee
> His heritage ; I am wholly his ;
> His praise, his price, his peerless rank
> Are root and ground of all my bliss.'

STANZA 36.

'Blissful,' quoth I, 'may this be true,
Displeased be not if wrong I speak,
Art thou the Queen of Heaven's blue
That all the world doth after seek?
We trust in Mary of whom grew Grace,
Who bare a Bairn of Virgin-flower;
The crown from her who might displace
But One that passèd her in power?
    So singularly soft and sweet
    Our Bird of Araby is she,
    This Phœnix noble winged and meet,
    To match the Queen of Courtesy.'

STANZA 37.

'Courtesy-Queen,' that Gay then said,
With knee to earth, with folded face,
'Dear matchless Mother, merriest Maid,
Blessed Beginner of all Grace.'
Then rose she and resumed her stay,
And spake toward me in that space:
'Sir, folk here chase and find their prey,
Supplanters none are in this place:
    That Empress, whom the Heavens embrace,
    While earth and hell her footstool be,
    None from her heritage can chase,
    For Queen she is of Courtesy.'

STANZA 38.

'Court of the King, the living God,
Hath in itself a power unseen,
That all who have its threshold trod
Of all the realm is king or queen;

And ne'er shall other them drive forth,
For fain that others have and hold,
If mending would increase their worth
Would, each, their crowns were five times told :
    My Lady, of whom Jesus sprang,
    Who empire holds o'er us full high,
    None it displeaseth of our gang,
    For she is Queen of Courtesy.'

II. SPOTLESS PEARL.

STANZA 63.

'O SPOTLESS Pearl, pure past compare,
Bearing,' quoth I, 'the Pearl of Price,
Who formed for thee thy figure fair?
Who wrought thy robe, he was full wise ;
Thy beauty ne'er stark Nature bore,
Pygmalion ne'er thy grace designed,
No Aristotle by his lore
Spake of thy properties and kind.
    Thy colour flouts the fleur-de-lys,
    So courteous is thine Angel-air,
    Tell me, Bright One, whate'er can be
    Kin of the Pearl, so spotless fair ? '

STANZA 64.

'My spotless Lamb, that blesseth all,'
Quoth she, 'my dear affianced One,
Chose me his mate, unmeet withal,
One day that sealed our union :
When from your world of toil and tear
I went, he called me to his bliss ;

"Come here to me, my Leman dear,
For mote nor spot in thee none is " :
    My weeds he washed in his own Blood,
    And gave me might and beauty gave;
    And crowned me in my maidenhood
    And decked with pearls spotless and brave.'

STANZA 65.

'Why spotless Bride, so starry bright,
These royalties so rich and rife?
And what this Lamb, all snowy-white,
That thee would wed unto his Wife?
Thou over all didst climb the high'st,
To lead with him a Queenly-life;
While many a comely maid for Christ
Hath lived in trouble and sore strife :
    Thou all those dear ones didst drive out,
    And from that marrying barred their lot ;
    All but thyself, so strong and stout,
    A Matchless Maid, without a spot.'

STANZA 66.

'Spotless,' quoth that blissful Queen,
'Unblemished I am, with ne'er a stain ;
This may I with grace avouch ;
But his Peerless Queen—that said I ne'er ;
We all are blissful Brides of the Lamb,
A hundred and forty thousand, iwis,
As in the Apocalypse it is seen ;
Saint John beheld them in a throng ;
    On the Hill of Zion, that beauteous spot,
    The Apostle beheld them in dream divine,
    Arrayed for the bridal on that high hill,
    The City of the New Jerusalem.'

The Perfect Woman:

A SELECTION FROM CL RHYTHMS IN HONOUR OF THE MYSTICAL LIFE OF OUR LADY.

EMILY MARY SHAPCOTE.

FROM AN UNPUBLISHED MS. WRITTEN IN 1894.

PREFATORY.

Perfection, in the order of nature, consists in the fitness of a thing to fulfil the object of its creation; and created Perfection, which presents itself conditioned to the senses, imagination and reasoning powers, exists absolutely in God, and manifests, as in a mirror, the infinite glory of the Uncreated. But the perfection of one created thing differs from that of another according to its purpose and place in creation; and human nature, being the most perfect of God's creatures contains capacity for reflecting most perfectly the Power, Wisdom and Goodness of God. If this be true of human nature generally, it is supremely true of our Blessed Lady. She is the sole and only perfect Mirror of Inorganic Perfection, because she alone, of all created things, was the most eminently fitted to perform perfectly the purpose for which she was created. And in the divine Wisdom and Fore-knowledge of God, the purpose of the creation of Mary was this—that she might become the Gate through which God would deign to pass from Heaven to earth, in order, first, to unite our passible, defectible nature with his own impassible and divine nature; and then, to enable each individual of the race to rise to that height of perfection for which he was individually created. This purpose in creation is the most magnificent that can be realised by the mind of man.

Our Lady, immaculately conceived and miraculously super-adorned with all God's gifts and graces, was thus raised necessarily and at once to the highest point of natural perfection. She became The Woman, the Woman Elect in the Eternal Counsels and Decrees of the Holy Trinity. She was literally 'the Immaculate Conception' of the Almighty design in forming the human nature in which God desired to clothe himself. She was, therefore, in every sense, spiritually, mentally and corporally, 'the Perfect Woman' because she was destined to give birth to the Perfect Man; and because as the Mother of God she was to become God's life-long, intimate and inseparable Companion upon earth. Moreover, by her ceaseless correspondence with grace, Mary was made worthy to take the place of that other Woman, our first Mother, Eve, who had unhappily failed in her almost equally magnificent purpose in creation. Mary was made worthy, by the side of the Second Adam, to work with him in undoing the mischief of the Fall; and in union with the incomprehensible, awful offering of the Eternal Father, to offer her only Son, the God-Man, for the world's ransom.

It is mainly in relation to us, however, as a Woman, that the writer has ventured to paint the beauty, strength and harmony of Mary's nature, and to attempt to keep before the reader what a woman in the natural order is capable of becoming, when freed from defectibility and inspired in a supernatural degree with devotion to her calling and with obedience to the purpose of her creation. The writer has endeavoured, further, to illustrate the truth that, in the case of our Blessed Lady, every act of her life, although on the one hand simple and natural, was also sublime and godlike through her divine relationships in the Triform Unity of Love—namely, as the Daughter of the Eternal Father by her Immaculate Conception, as the Mother of God by the Nativity of the Divine Word, and as the Spouse of the Spirit by the Over-shadowing of the Unitive Paraclete. Whilst in treating of Mary's intercourse with her Divine Son immediately, and of her intercourse with us, mediately, an effort has been made to show how our Blessed Lady acted and acts on the principle of the Dual-unity of human nature, that is, in conformity with the fact that the several perfections of human nature are distributed between the man and the woman, in such wise as to make together one undivided whole (Chiefly from the Author's Preface).

I. INVOCATION.

RHYTHM I.

DEAR Mother of my God, I come to thee;
Mother of my Creator, look on me;
In sorrow and in tears I turn to thee;
Oh, let thy sweet compassion reach to me,
And all my boldness do thou pardon me.

Mother of Fairest Love, unweariedly
Thy heart hath sought thy daughter, silently ;
And all through life that heart mysteriously
Hath drawn my untamed spirit unto thee,
Until the day dawn brake and rose on me.

At length thou camest, Mother, unto me,
When heresy had loosed its hold on me,
And with sweet force thy secret sympathy
My restless soul did draw so wondrously
That all my being, Mother, clung to thee.

And now my day is done, I come to thee ;
The remnant of my life I give to thee ;
All else hath vanished ; none remains but thee ;
All others weary.   Naught is there in me,
For I am nothing ; yet I hope in thee.

Oh yes, I hope that surely thou wilt be
My Advocate with him who calleth thee
The Mother of his Love : and utterly,
Sweet Mother, do I trust thy love for me
Who hast, for his dear sake, remembered me.

Then teach my failing voice to sing of thee ;
Let my last music ring in praise of thee ;
Let these last humble rhymes be full of thee
That, swan-like, this my latest song may be
A sweet and mystic melody to thee.

Then, while I sing this lowly hymn to thee,
Cleanse thou my thoughts, that they may worthily
Express the wonders of that Mystery,
By which our fallen Nature claims to be
United to the Eternal Word, through thee.

II. THE SECOND EVE.

RHYTHM II.

O WOMAN, greatly blessed, all praise to thee
Whom seers foretold, and saints in ecstasy
Have seen in light enthroned ; behold, on high
Thou sittest, Lady, in thy majesty ;
And I, in untaught accents, sing of thee.

Most valiant thou of women, made to be
The Mother of the new-born Race ; oh see,
To the sweet depths of thy humility
Hath God descended, and created thee
Mother and Queen of his Humanity.

It was the crown of this great grace that he,
God's Holy Spirit, overshadowed thee ;
More than the vows of thy Virginity,
Than the resignment of Maternity
Was the great strength of thy humility.

Oh, why art thou so fair? Why willeth he,
O Blessed Virgin, thus thy Spouse to be ?
Why ? but because he had forechosen thee
Before the worlds, his Own, such wise to be
That thou with him our Ransomer should'st be.

Rejoice, O Father Adam ; this is she
Who pleads with God, who chosen is to be
The Mother of the Saviour.   Joyously
Sing, Mother Eve, nor inconsolably
Weep for the wrong committed 'neath the tree.

Lo, she is come thy place to take, to be
A Second Mother to humanity :
Mary will satisfaction find for thee ;
For as by woman man hath fallen, he
By Woman shall be lifted, righteously.

Did Eve bring death ? by Mary life shall be ;
The baffled dragon shall, tormented, flee ;
By Man and Woman vanquished, lo, is he ;
Through Eve the curse was merited ; but see,
Mary.hath merited to set us free.

III.   THE CAUSE REVERSED.

RHYTHM CXLV.

Eve of the Fall was cause ; and yet, not she
But Adam wrought the death, and only he ;
Yet had she been obedient, verily,
Death had not struck the whole posterity—
For life had flourished in the parent tree.

Eve of our woe was cause ; yet verily,
It was not Eve, but Adam who would be
The worker of our grief, and none but he ;
He was the stock of our humanity,
Which stock was cursed when sin should grafted be.

Eve from the angel learned to love a lie ;
Yet Adam was it wrought delinquency :
Eve wrought the garment of his shame ; but he
Clothed him therewith, to hide impurity,
And life thus forfeited eternally.

This was of death the cause ; shall we not see
How by the strength of dual unity
That cause shall be reversed, so good may be
The conqueror of evil ?   Verily,
Wisdom condign thus wrought almightily.

The life arose ; and Mary, graced should be
Its cause to plead in our humanity :
She was obedient ; yet it was not she
Who wrought out Life for Man, but only he
Who Life hath purchased for the Parent-tree.

Mary of hope is cause ; yet verily,
It was not Mary ; it was only he,
Her Son and God's, who purchased hope : for he
The Father is of that Humanity
In which New Stock the curse hath ceased to be.

And Mary heard the Angel ; verily,
She heard the Truth and loved it ; yet was he
The Truth himself who spake—he verily,
For whom she wrought the garment in which he,
Clothed in her flesh, will live unendingly.

IV. THE CRYSTAL.

RHYTHM XI.

MOTHER of God, behold what majesty
That title crowns, what dread sublimity ;
What depths unfathomable lie in thee ;
Yea, saints have looked therein nor failed to see
A greatness bordering on infinity.

O sacred Virgin, whose humility
Proclaimed the distance between God and thee,
Since thou art God's own Mother, naught may be
Nearer to him.   Good Infinite is he,
And he his endless goodness shares with thee.

Mother of God, thou liest in a sea
Of boundless glory : who may a crystal see
Reflecting sun-rays, and not dazzled be ?
And though the crystal may be naught, yet we
Believe no less its fire-born purity.

Thou art the sun-born Crystal, and from thee
Proceeds the Ray that, Sun-born, dwelt in thee ;
The only perfect Crystal that could be
Unmolten by the Ray that entered thee—
The Ray, whose substance joined, yea, lived by thee.

  X   .

Thy Substance entered into Deity,
And Deity itself partook of thee:
Without confusion joined, he linked in thee
His Being with thy nature—mystery
Bordering on consubstantiality.

The Tree of Life thou wert: oh, verily
Blossomed the Flower of Life and grew in thee;
It took from thee thy substance, and to thee
Was rendered back, to grace the parent tree
The Fruit divine of Immortality.

Thou gavest God a Mother: it was he
Who gave to thee a Son—a Son to be
The type of sonship; so he honoured thee,
The type of motherhood, obediently—
This was the crown of thy Maternity.

V. THE DEWDROP.

RHYTHM XII.

CLOTHED with the sun, a Woman, lo, we see,
Receptacle of unborn Entity;
The Burning Bush, yet unconsumed is she;
The Vessel of God's awful Purity,
Mirror of Indestructibility.

High wert thou throned from all eternity,
Yet higher clombest through integrity;
The sunshine sought and rested still on thee
And drew thee heavenward to himself, to be
The Ray-begetting: glory be to thee.

Thou wert the Dewdrop resting lowlily
Upon the Flower of our Humanity;
The Sunshine found and penetrated thee
'Till all his hues refracted were in thee;
Then placed thee in the cloud, our Rain to be.

Rain down, O Fair One; let the Just One be
Thy gift in tears to our humanity;
Rain down the drops the Sunshine found in thee;
And of the countless graces poured on thee,
Oh, rain on us the dew of purity.

Open, O Earth; one spot of thine is free
From the dire curse of man's deformity:
Open and give; thy Maker calleth thee
To render back in its integrity
The faultless Creature that lies hid in thee.

Rise up, O Fair One, earth is not for thee;
For thee no law exists to hinder thee
From entering his Presence valiantly:
Thou art his Firstborn, and he loveth thee;
Thou art his Pure Conception; hail, to thee.

Mount up, mount up, time presses; thou must be
Ere long the partner of his Majesty;
Thou Giver of his sweet Humanity;
Thou Shadow of his sacred Infancy;
Thou Mother of his Sorrows—hail, to thee.

VI. THE RAINBOW.

RHYTHM XIII.

ARCH of the Heavenly spheres; the cloud shall be,
However dark, a resting place for thee;
Thus, where life's raindrops fall most heavily,
Art thou, O Mother, shining o'er the sea
Whilst we are toiling onwards wearily.

God shines on us through tears: we look to thee
And count his very rays which break in thee;
We dare not lift our eyes our Sun to see
Whose dazzling splendour needs some Veil, to be
Approached by us in our infirmity.

He veils his splendour in the cloud, that we
May gather up his promises in thee ;
And as on it we bend our gaze, we see
His graces all reflected beauteously
In sevenfold glory, as they rest on thee.

Thou Rainbow of our dark humanity,
Exemplar beauteous of the One in Three,
Whose sevenfold Gifts are found to be in thee,
Whose every grace doth blend harmoniously,
Each heightening one the other, endlessly.

Light, uniform, declares the Unity ;
Light, three in one, reveals the Trinity ;
And from this threefold oneness, lo, we see
The Love of God reflected gloriously
In seven bright rays, which find their home in thee.

Rainbow of our sad lives, we hope in thee,
For hope was given to them who look to thee :
Mother of Hope art thou ; for where we be
There looms the thunder-cloud, and yet we see
God's Love therein, so long as we have thee.

Promise of God, Who lives and shines in thee ;
Who may forget his wondrous Clemency ?
Who but adore such Love as points to thee,
That made thee what thou art, so thou should'st be
The Rainbow of his great Benignity ?

VII. ENVOY.

RHYTHM XCIII.

'In him shall be,
As Man, the force to conquer destiny ;
And Man the work to perfect needeth thee.' (*Author.*)

How can the Son of God be said to be
In need of aught ?   As Man alone can he

Fulfil all justice; and as Man can he
Alone the winepress tread of suffering.   He
The debt must pay: what need hath he of thee?

Lo, hath the Son of God most perfectly
The Law fulfilled, and the sad destiny
Of fallen man averted: wilfully
For every crime, his precious Blood would be,
Of broken Law, the boundless penalty.

Yet if, for every child of Adam be
A share reserved as his own penalty,
A share in union with those sufferings, see,
How deep and wide the awful mystery
Of God in Man—in dying Agony.

Man did not sin alone: and so will he
Not be alone in this great Mystery
Of retributive justice, though 'twas he
Whose pure obedience purchased victory,
Since perfect Man, and perfect God, was he.

The law condign of Justice sure must be
Shared by the Partner of man's destiny:
And she, the Perfect Woman, tenderly
Assumes her right and takes her share to be
Co-partner in his woes, ineffably.

Adam and Eve this wondrous unity
In human kind foreshadowed: for not he
Alone might live, nor yet alone might be
Ripe in perfection, since paternity
Created was—a Dual-unity.

Fallen was the race when that great unity
From its perfection drooped: nor would there be

A resurrection of the type, 'till he,
The Second Father of Mankind, should be,
With Perfect Woman joined, a Victim free.

NOTES.

No. I. St. v. l. 2 : My Advocate with him ; and

No. II. St. v. l. 2 : Who pleads with God ; the last is a thought
from St. Bernard ; but the title of Advocate was used of
Mary a thousand years earlier, by St. Irenæus. Compar-
ing the first Eve with the Second, he says : 'Though the
one had disobeyed God yet the other was drawn to obey
God—that, of the virgin Eve the Virgin Mary might
become the Advocate ; and as by a virgin the human race
had been bound to death, by a Virgin it is saved ; the
balance being preserved, a virgin's disobedience by a
Virgin's Obedience.' Adver. Hær. v. 19. St. Bernard's
words are quoted from the Breviary, on page vi.

St. vi. l. 5 : By Woman shall be lifted ; 'It is a great
sacrament that whereas through woman death became our
portion, so Life was born to us by Woman ; that in the
case of both sexes, male and female, the baffled devil
should be tormented when, on the overthrow of both
sexes, he was rejoicing : whose punishment had been small,
if both sexes had been liberated in us without our being
liberated through both.' St. Augustine, De Agone Christi,
cap. 24.

No. IV. St. i. l. 5 : Bordering on infinity ; St. Thomas Aquinas
says that three things in creation are as perfect as can be,
' 1. the Sacred Humanity, because of its union with God ;
2. created Beatitude, since it is the enjoyment of God ;
and 3. the Blessed Virgin, because she is the Mother of
God. All three have a certain infinite dignity from God,
who is the Infinite Good, and under this aspect no creature
could be made more perfect than they are, for nothing is
better than God.' Summa I. q. 25, a. 5 and 6.

St. v. l. 5 : Bordering on consubstantiality ; an unverified
expression attributed to St. Peter Damian, Serm. Nat.
Mariæ.

No. V. St. iv. l. 1 : Isaias xlv. 8.

St. vi. l. 2 : Esther xv. 13.

No. VI. St. vi. l. 3 : Ecclesiasticus xxiv. 24.

Poems on Pictures, from American Sources.

I. ON MURILLO'S 'IMMACULATE CONCEPTION.'

FROM 'THE AVE MARIA,' 1896.

O BLEST Murillo, what a task was thine,
  That Mother to portray whose beauty mild
Combined earth's comeliness with grace divine;
  To whom our God and Saviour as a Child
  Was subject; upon whom so oft he smiled:
Yet not less happy also in my part;
  For I, though in a world by sin defiled,
Though lacking genius and unskilled in art,
May paint that blessed Likeness in a contrite heart.

NOTE.

Written in pencil on the fly-leaf of an old catalogue of the Museum of the Louvre, and found on a sofa before Murillo's masterpiece.

II. ON FRANCIA'S PICTURE OF THE ANNUN-CIATION, IN THE BRERA AT MILAN.

FROM 'HARPER'S MONTHLY MAGAZINE,' 1891.

MINDST thou not—when June's heavy breath
Warmed the long days in Nazareth—
That eve thou didst go forth to give
The flowers some drink, that they might live
One faint night more amid the sands?
Far off the trees were as pale wands
Against the fervid sky; the sea
Sighed further off eternally,
As human sorrow sighs in sleep.

Then suddenly the awe grew deep,
As of a day to which all days
Were footsteps in God's secret ways;
Until a folding sense, like prayer
Which is, as God is, everywhere
Gathered about thee; and a voice
Spake to thee without any noise,
Being of the silence: ' Hail,' it said,
'Thou that art highly favourèd;
The Lord is with thee here and now;
Blessed among all women thou.'

III. TWO SONNETS FOR PICTURES OF OUR LADY.

RALPH ADAMS CRAM.

FROM ' THE KNIGHT ERRANT,' BOSTON, U.S.A., 1897.

I. FOR THE MADONNA OF THE MAGNIFICAT, BY SANDRO BOTTICELLI.

CIRCLED with solemn angels see her there,
  Mother of God, with the Incarnate Word
  Throned in her virgin bosom, and adored
Of earth and heaven; and she, all unaware
Of that bright crown the bending angels bear
  Above her weary head, with sweet accord
  Writing: ' My soul doth magnify the Lord,
And Holy shall his Name be everywhere.'

Behold how sad she is, and in her eyes
  Infinite sorrow, infinitely fair:
Not her own mother's grief it is that lies
  Upon her soul, a weary weight of care,
Not pity of self, but the blind, yearning cry
Of the world's hopeless, helpless misery.

II. FOR THE MADONNA OF THE STAR, BY FRA ANGELICO.

As when the night is deepest, and the far
    Forgotten day is very vague and vain,
    And no man knows if dawn may come again,
Until the day-star rise, oracular :
So in the night, God sent thee to unbar
    The doors of day and bring the glorious reign
    Of thy dear Son, O Mother without stain,
Thou star-crowned Queen of Heaven, thou Morning Star.

O Mary Mother, help my halting faith :
    The night is round me and I cannot see ;
The stars are hidden by the world's dead breath :
    Be thou my Star, and let me follow thee
Through this dim valley of the shadow of death,
    Into the sunlight of God's Majesty.

IV. MADONNA DI SAN SISTO.

T. WENTWORTH HIGGINSON: B. 1823.

FROM 'THE AFTERNOON LANDSCAPE,' 1871.

Look down into my heart,
    Thou holy Mother, with thy Holy Son ;
Read all my thoughts and bid the doubts depart,
    And all the fears be done.

I lay my spirit bare,
    O blessed Ones, beneath your wondrous eyes,
And not in vain ; ye hear my heartfelt prayer,
    And your twin-gaze replies.

What says it ?   All that life
Demands of those who live to be and do ;
Calmness in all its bitterest, deepest strife,
    Courage till all is through.

Thou Mother, in thy sight,
Can aught of passion or despair remain ?
Beneath those eyes' serene and holy light,
    The soul is bright again.

Thou Child, whose earnest gaze
Looks ever forward, fearless, steady, strong,
Beneath those eyes no doubt or weakness stays,
    No fear can linger long.

Thanks : that to my weak heart,
Your mingled powers, fair forms, such counsel give :
Till I have learned the lesson ye impart,
    I have not learned to live.

And oh, till life be done,
Of your deep gaze may ne'er the impression cease :
Still may the dark eyes whisper, 'Courage ; On' ;
    The mild eyes murmur, 'Peace.'

V. MADONNA OF DAGNAN-BOUVERET.

'*J.*'

FROM 'THE CENTURY MAGAZINE,' 1892.

Oh, brooding thought of dread ;
Oh, calm of coming grief ;
Oh, mist of tears unshed
Above that shining head
That for an hour too brief
Lies on thy nurturing knee :
How shall we pity thee,
Mother of Sorrows—sorrows yet to be.

That Babyhood unknown,
With all of bright or fair
That lingers in our own,
By every hearth has shone :

Each year that light we share
As Bethlehem saw it shine :
Be ours the comfort thine,
Mother of Consolations all divine.

VI. ON SEEING A COPY OF MILLET'S 'ANGELUS.'

MARY E. MANNIX.

FROM 'THE AVE MARIA,' 1890.

CHILDREN of toil, your simple life to live,
Its sweet abandonment and trust to know,
What would not the unhappy sceptic give ?
Scoff as he may, there is no task so low,
No lot so humble, no pursuit so rude,
But 'tis more grateful than the solitude
Of souls eclipsed by Faith's dark overthrow ;
For stripped of all that draws man near to God,
Nor love, nor wealth, nor power, nor songs of fame
Suffice for that which from the Eternal came.
Ah, closer to that Truth the patient clod
Than he who, treading self-appointed way
Bewildered, has forgotten how to pray.

VII. ON A PAINTING OF THE ASSUMPTION AT VERCELLI, BY GAUDENZIO FERRARI,

THEODORE A. METCALF, PRIEST.

FROM 'THE AVE MARIA,' 1894.

SWEET, golden-haired Madonna, toward thy throne
A charming host of angioletti spread
Their many-coloured wings : above thy head,

From flaming torches lifted, there is shown
An irridescent light of softest tone
　　Cast on thy snowy robe, whose every thread
　　Is brilliant through the opal, green and red
Of wondrous twinkling stars, with which 'tis sewn
From seam to seam.　Our senses realise
　　The rapture of those chanting heavenly choirs
　　That sing thy praises as they mount above
With thee ; and looking upward to those skies
　　Resplendent, we too feel the love that fires
　　Thy maiden bosom at such marks of love.

VIII. THE ANNUNCIATION :

A PAINTING BY PIERRE MIGNARD, IN THE POSSESSION
OF THE AUTHOR.

LLOYD MIFFLIN.

FROM 'THE CENTURY,' 1898.

THE radiant Angel stands within her room.
　　She kneels and listens ; on her heaving breast,
　　To still its flutt'rings, are her sweet hands pressed,
　　The while his lips foretell her joyful doom.
Tears—happy tears—are rising, and a bloom
　　Clothes her of maiden blushes that attest
　　The Rose she is.　The haloed, heavenly guest
　　Lingers upon his cloud of golden gloom.
He gives to her the lily which he brings.
　　Each cherub in the aureole above—
　　Where harps unseen are pealing peace and love—
Smiles with delight, and softly coos and sings ;
　　While over Mary's head, on whitest wings,
　　Hovers the Presence of the Holy Dove.

IX. OUR LADY OF PERPETUAL SUCCOUR.

SARA TRAINER SMITH.

FROM 'THE AVE MARIA,' 1891.

IT is a picture very odd and quaint,
  Not of to-day, nor of the art men teach ;
But of a higher lore, as though a saint
  Wrought its fair miracle of wordless speech.

Not beautiful, perhaps : I cannot say,
  So dear to me its every tint and line ;
Such meaning have those eyes, a living ray
  Of longed-for comfort always answers mine.

Such tenderness it has : her gentle face,
  Bent like a flower above the Holy Child,
Looks with sweet yearnings on our burdened race,
  And offers, pleading, all her pity mild.

Often I ponder, seeking still its charm ;
  And ever it charms me, though I know not why :
Fair is our Lord upon her folding arm ;
  And fair our Lady to my trusting eye.

O tender Virgin, with thy Babe Divine,
  Our hearts are bare before thee when we kneel ;
Thine is the secret of the lights that shine
  Through all our darkness. We can only feel.

Hymn of the Nuns, by Moonlight.

T. J. DE POWIS.

FROM 'URIEL,' 1857.

URIEL: SCENE XI.

A green space among large trees, near a Convent garden, in a valley sheltered by high mountains. Moonlight. (*Author.*)

WANDERING waters, ceaseless fountains,
Pending woods and lawny mountains,
Mystic whispers of the forest,
Midnight voices, echoed, choruss'd,
   Waters, woods and starry sheen—
   Choral Nature, chant our Queen.

Queen of all yon golden splendours,
Earth to thee her homage renders ;
From the crescent, where thou shinest
Starrier than the stars divinest,
   Flows thy blessing, beams thy light,
   Spreads thy glory, Lady bright.

Mary, O thou Name of Beauty,
Thine are we by love, by duty ;
From thy height of heaven behold us,
In thy heavenly love enfold us ;
   From thy holy heaven look down,
   Lady of the Starry Crown.

Moon of midnight, Star of ocean,
Sway our hearts to due devotion—
Hearts that swell to thee already,
As the waters to their Lady ;
   Lustrous Lady, beam benign
   Through our storms, and in us shine.

Thou that once on earth didst languish,
Pierced with more than mortal anguish,
When the world was darkened, shaken,
When himself seemed God-forsaken—
   Thou that watch'dst through all those hours,
   O thou Mother, thou art ours.

Thou that now hast thy fruition,
Throned beyond prophetic vision,
Robed in light of light God-given,
Crowned with lilies, growth of Heaven,
   Queen of Angels, Queen of Stars,
   Beam through this world's dungeon-bars.

All is beauty where thou bloomest;
All is fragrance where thou comest;
From the woodland, o'er the meadow,
Floats a sweetness, fleets the shadow;
   All is holy in thy sight;
   Thine the pure, pale, moonlit night.

In the brake the bird is dreaming
Songs of love while thou art beaming;
On the glade and in the bowers,
In the grass and on the flowers,
   All things rest, like lake and grove,
   Lulled in Mary's mother-love.

O our Lady, O our Mother,
Ours thou art, and ours no other;
How these poor lone hearts o'erladen
Steal to thee, Maternal Maiden;
   How they tremble at thy feet,
   Throbbing with their fancies sweet.

Take, oh, take each tender blossom,
O our Mother, to thy bosom;
O our dearest One and only,
Look, the world is cold and lonely;
  Wave us, with thy lily wand,
  To the groves and skies beyond.

There thou shinest, morn and even,
In the bliss of home and heaven;
Maiden-Mother, brightest, purest,
Hallowing all that thou allurest,
  Open thy sweet breast, and we
  There will die in dreams of thee.

Only thou these yearnings knowest;
Thou canst hear them murmured lowest;
In the midnight, in the forest,
Thou the haunted gloom explorest;
  When the world lies dark and dead,
  God and Mary guard the bed.

Down all depths wilt thou discern us;
To thy starry smile we turn us,
To thy golden heights upgazing,
Where the immortals meet in praising,
  Where thy weary child at last
  Nestles, on thy bosom cast.

Mary, O thou Name of splendour,
Mary, beauteous One and tender,
Take to thee the heart of maiden;
Take the flowers of earth to Eden;
  Take us now—our hour departs—
  Take our incense, take our hearts.

Take our midnight symphony ;
Take us from this night to thee ;
Star of Beauty, Star of Love,
Light us to the land above,
   Where the waning planets set,
   Where the immortal stars are met.

Legend, Carol and Ballade.

MAY PROBYN.

FROM 'PANSIES,' 1895.

I. IN HONOUR OF MARY: A LEGEND.

FROM 'THE MONTH,' 1886.

I.

THE setting sun an aureole made
About her hair.   With eyes that strayed
Not from the book : ' Lord God,' she prayed,

And ended not—for in the door
Her women beckoned : ' Lady, sore
In need, three pilgrims alms implore.'

And she fared forth those three to greet,
And set before them wine and meat,
And bathed and kissed their way-worn feet,

In honour of Three, that angel-told
Took their long journey—one growing old—
One weeping she could not warmer fold
Her Little Babe that wept for cold.

Y

II.

Dying was the sunset fire and flare
When at length she, climbing again the stair,
Returned untroubled to her prayer.

' Lord God,' began she—and from the hall
Came sudden shrilling clamour and call
Of her young children playing at ball,

With wrath of two and tears of one,
And in the door her eldest son,
Breathless and beckoning urged her : ' Run,

Sweet Mother of mine ; for sturdy blow
My brothers each on each bestow,
And stint not—.' Then, with no least show

Or of reluctance, or annoy,
In honour of One whose dear employ
Was to tend God, a Little Boy—
Whom God called Mother, and served with joy,

Descending she with gentlest word,
Sweetly through all the outcry heard,
Chid softly two and kissèd the third,

And hushed and healed their strife perplexed,
And up and down played with them next,
And to her prayer returned unvexed.

III.

Red glory of the West was gone ;
The first star white in the lattice shone ;
' Lord God,' she prayed—and on the stone

Rang steps ; and she was 'ware, before
The next word, of her husband in the door,
And blood that trickled to the floor.

'My half-tamed falcon,' said he, 'missed
The prey I tossed; and ere I wist,
'Twixt rage and sport, she rent my wrist:

Wilt balsam bring to cure the smart?
None virtue hath as thine, dear heart.'
Unfretted she set her book apart,

In honour of him whom Mary, Maid
And Mother and Queen, herself obeyed;
At bidding of whom she went or stayed,
Nor murmured once, nor once delayed.

Washed she and bound his hurt with care,
Nor time did count, nor labour spare,
And yet again turned back to her prayer.

Dusk was the lattice—and behold,
On the page the collect, still untold,
Stood written in letters of pure gold.

II. CHRISTMAS CAROL.

FROM 'MERRY ENGLAND,' 1890.

LACKING samite and sable,
  Lacking silver and gold,
The Prince Jesus in the poor stable
  Slept, and was three hours old.

As doves by the fair water,
  Mary, not touched of sin,
Sat by him—the King's Daughter,
  All glorious within.

A lily without one stain, a
  Star where no spot hath room—
Ave, Gratia Plena—
  Virgo virginum.

Clad not in pearl-sewn vesture,
　　Clad not in cramoisie,
She hath hushed, she hath cradled to rest, her
　　God the first time on her knee.

Where is one to adore him?
　　The ox hath dumbly confessed,
With the ass, meek kneeling before him,
　　'Et Homo factus est.'

Not throned on ivory or cedar,
　　Not crowned with a Queen's crown,
At her breast it is Mary shall feed her
　　Maker, from Heaven come down.

The trees in Paradise blossom
　　Sudden, and its bells chime—
She giveth him, held to her bosom,
　　Her immaculate milk the first time.

The night with wings of angels
　　Was alight, and its snow-packed ways
Sweet made (say the Evangels)
　　With the noise of their virelays.

Quem vidistis, Pastores?
　　Why go ye feet unshod?
Wot ye within yon door is
　　Mary, the Mother of God?

No smoke of spice is ascending
　　There—no roses are piled—
But choicer than all balms blending,
　　There Mary hath kissed her Child.

'Dilectus meus mihi
　　Et ego illi'—Cold
Small cheek against her cheek he
　　Sleepeth, three hours old.

III. MATER ADMIRABILIS: A BALLADE.

For a sewing party.

NEEDLES nimbly plying and thread,
  Wives and busy maids, behold
The Ladye Mary, about whose head
  Clung unseen the aureole's gold,
  Spinning fold on small fair fold,
Wherein, helpless Little One
  Sans all comfort save her kiss,
She should cherish her sweet Son.
(Pray ye) 'Bless our work begun,
  Mater Admirabilis.'

Maids and mothers, see her shed
  Tears, like pearls of price untold,
Over the white wool that red
  Should be, when the great drops rolled
  Shuddering to the garden mould.
Seamless garment—hast thou spun
  Length of it and breadth for this,
To stand by and watch it won
With rude dice, redeemed by none,
  Mater Admirabilis?

Ever 'neath her gentle tread—
  Sweetly she the while growing old—
Hums her loom, whence spring and spread
  Stores of raiment, amply doled
  To all poor folk in the cold.
From her loom what broideries run,
  For the altar woven, I wis,
Fair beyond comparison.
(Pray ye) 'Bless our work that's done,
  Mater Admirabilis.'

ENVOY.

'Queen, y-clad as with the sun,
     Thy meek toil our pattern is.
Give us grace all sloth to shun : '
(Pray ye) 'and thy benison,
     Mater Admirabilis.'

Present-Day Poetry.

I. HOLY MOTHERHOOD OF GOD.

A. WENTWORTH HAMILTON EATON.

FROM 'ARCADIAN LEGENDS AND LYRICS,' 1889.

> They bade me call thee Father, Lord—
> Sweet was the freedom deemed :
> And yet, more like a Mother's ways
> Thy quiet mercies seemed. (*F. W. Faber.*)

WHO kneels in silent rapture on the sod
     In open sky, or on the marble floor
     Of some dark church, his soul's true prayers says o'er,
Adores the holy Motherhood of God.

The Shrine of Mary is not reverenced less
     By men whose feet are swift, whose arms are strong,
     Than by sweet woman souls to whom belong
By right maternity and gentleness.

All lofty things in our conception meet
     In the Divine, all beautiful and good ;
     The sterner attributes of Fatherhood
Alone make not for man a God complete.

If we at Mary's altars best may feel
God's true Maternity, there should we kneel.

II. THE SILVER WEDDING.

ALFRED GURNEY, M.A.: 1843—1898.

FROM 'LOVE'S FRUITION,' 1897.

To my Lady I render thanks.

FAIR shines the harvest moon to-night
In silver pomp; but not so bright
As in your eyes love's beacon-light.
The day returns whose tender mood,
Ever remembered and renewed,
Enhances love's beatitude.
Your yielded hand I kneel and kiss—
Our Lady's grace be praised for this:
The love I bear your loveliness
No words can fittingly express;
Nor can I worthily proclaim
Your worth; yet will I try to frame
Some rhymes that shall embalm your name.

If loving words make music sweet
Whene'er we part, whene'er we meet,
I hear the words that Mary said
When she was Angel-visited;
If tender eyes return my gaze,
I picture Mary's smile, and praise
The Wisdom that was fain to make
All women gracious for her sake,
Whose was the Plenitude of Grace,
The Chosen of the Chosen Race:
I see her mirrored in your face.

Sweeter than sweetest roses far,
And lovelier than lilies are,

All, all, that is most pure, most good,
In God-created Womanhood
She was, and is—a Virgin-soul,
The stars compose her aureole,
The sunbeams clothe her, at her feet
The moonlight gathers soft and sweet ;
In all her excellencies meet.

Her daughter and handmaiden, you
Have done what love alone can do ;
Numbered with those who learn of her
To play the part of comforter,
Whose lips, conversant with her song,
Her lofty minstrelsy prolong ;
Numbered with those whose feet pursue
Her footsteps all life's journey through,
Her daughter and her sister too.

Beneath the love-light of your eyes
With homage, gratitude, surprise,
I kneel your yielded hand to kiss—
Our Lady's name be blessed for this :
My life to gladden, sweeten, bless,
To soothe its griefs, its ills redress,
You have revealed her loveliness :
Soft shines the silver moon to-night ;
A Lady robed in bridal white
Whose smile turns darkness into light.

III. GOD'S MOTHER.

LAURENCE HOUSMAN.

FROM 'SPIKENARD,' 1898.

A GARDEN, bower in bower,
Grew waiting for God's hour.

Where no man ever trod,
This was the Gate of God.

The first Bower was red—
Her lips which ' Welcome' said.

The second Bower was blue—
Her eyes that let God through.

The third Bower was white—
Her soul in God's sight.

These three Bowers of Love
Won Christ from Heaven above.

IV. LA MADONNETTA.

ESME HOWARD.

FROM 'THE SPECTATOR,' 1898.

A Statue of our Lady stands on a point of rock near the village
of Porto Fino, on the beautiful coast-line of the Genoese Riviera.

FROM the rocks where the pine-trees stand
At the meeting of sea and land
She looks out o'er the sea,
And the Child-God on her arm
Keeps the fisher from harm :
'My peace go with thee.'

Towards the East where he worked and died,
The land of the Crucified,

She gazes nor turns away ;
And God's light pauses a space
To rest on her dear face
At the spring of each day.

Though storms may beat on the strand,
Solemn and still and grand,
She heeds not their wrath ;
And the ships that pass to and fro
On the face of the waters below
She speeds on their path.

When at mid-day the sun, risen high,
Tunes water and air and sky
To one blue common chord,
Then myrtle and thyme at her feet
Wrap in incense pure and sweet
The Elect of the Lord.

And the winds and the pines and the waves
Sing in murmurous staves,
And repeat without cease
The words from her lips that fall :
' God's mercy rest on all,
And on all be peace.'

V. CANTICUM BEATÆ MARIÆ DEIPARÆ SEMPER VIRGINI.

SELWYN IMAGE.

FROM ' POEMS AND CAROLS,' 1894.

MOTHER of God on high,
We kneel at thy feet, dear Maid and Mother,
Who hast borne us God for our very Brother.

Mother and Maid, we lie
Here at thy feet, who cry to thee, love thee,
Praising none, but the Lord, above thee.

Mother of God's own Child,
We who are called by his name belong to thee,
We, thy children, chanting our song to thee.

Mother, the days are wild :
Oh, let those arms and that sweet smile round us
Cherish and guard, or our sins confound us.

Star of the Sea, we drive
Drenched and drowned 'mid the waves that deride us,
Lost on the rocks, if thou shine not and guide us.

How may we pass alive
Through the desert world, but with thee the Rose of it ?
By thy fragrance stayed, till the dim, parched close of it.

Vine and Lily and Rose,
In his garden, lo, thy Beloved sets us ;
Scorn not thou, though the earth forgets us.

Lady of Grief, unclose
Thy stricken soul to our souls that cry to thee,
Stricken of grief, that grief may fly to thee.

Lady of Joys, though seven
Times seven are the charms of sin to beguile us,
Lost in thy charm, what sin shall defile us ?

Lady and Queen of Heaven,
Here on earth we would serve before thee,
In thy very court at last to adore thee.

Mary, Mother and Queen,
Bring us at length, where the angels lean,
Choir on choir, beneath thy grace :
Bring us all to that hidden place,
Where face to face thyself thou art seen,
                    O Mary Queen.

VI. FOR AN ANNUNCIATION.
J. W. MACKAIL, M.A.
FROM 'LOVE'S LOOKING GLASS,' 1891.

Lo, this is she whom the Archangel saw
When, from the Inmost Presence earthward sped,
He sought in Nazareth God's Favourèd.
What strange fulfilment of the ancient law,
Uttered by angels, makes her eyes withdraw
Their gaze, and all her cheek forget its red,
While softly, round the pale gold of her head,
The shafted sunlight gathers into awe ?

Far off the daily bustle of the street
Murmurs unheard, when even now her feet
Among the village women lightly trod.
His voice has ceased ; and all around her there
Is drip of well-water, and in the air
A silver silence, and the peace of God.

VII. JESUS, MARY AND JOSEPH.
ARTHUR MIDDLEMORE MORGAN:
1834—1898.
FROM 'INTER FLUMINA,' 1885.

I.

FATHER and Mother and Young Child : how oft
In our own isle the gentle sight is seen,
When twilight falls upon the village-green,
When birds are silent in the bowery croft,
When cease to toil strong hands of sire, and soft
Yet docile fingers of light-hearted boy,
Ere cares of day with garb of day are doffed,
The little household at the hearth has joy.

Parted, or meeting, its dear souls are one.
While at the board they share the homely meal,
And talk the simple talk of toil and love,
My thoughts, the spirits which around them steal,
Forget the village green, the croft, the grove—
Remember Joseph, Mary, Mary's Son.

II.

HE sees a lovely river's lovelier well
Who flies in thought our age, our isle, and on
A House among the hills of Lebanon
Looks, as when o'er it other twilights fell.
Needs not to him the silent sky should tell
The wondrous past—the silent mountains wild—
To heavenly contemplation here they dwell,
The Mother-Maid, the Foster-Sire, the Child.
Here is the Home through which all homes have joy.
All pleasant fruits if Esdraelon bear,
If harvests fail not by that inland sea,
It is of him who stoops our bread to share,
Giver divine of rain and sunshine he—
He, gentle, loving, parent-subject Boy.

VIII. CAROL FROM THE LAND EAST OF THE SUN AND WEST OF THE MOON.

WILLIAM MORRIS : 1834—1896.

FROM 'THE EARTHLY PARADISE,' 1870.

CAROL.   Outlanders, whence come ye last?
Through what green seas and great have ye
past?
REFRAIN. The snow in the street and the wind on the
door:
Minstrels and Maids, stand forth on the floor.

From far away, O Masters mine,
We come to bear you goodly wine :
　　　　　The snow in the street, &c.
From far away we come to you,
To tell of great tidings, strange and true :
　　　　　The snow in the street, &c.
News, news of the Trinity,
And Mary and Joseph from over the sea :
　　　　　The snow in the street, &c.
For as we wandered far and wide,
What hap do ye deem there should us betide ?
　　　　　The snow in the street, &c.
Under a tent when the night was deep,
There lay three shepherds tending their sheep :
　　　　　The snow in the street, &c.
'O ye Shepherds, what have ye seen ?
To slay your sorrow and heal your teen ?'
　　　　　The snow in the street, &c.
In an ox-stall this night we saw
A Babe and a Maid without a flaw :
　　　　　The snow in the street, &c.
There was an old Man there beside,
His hair was white and his hood was wide :
　　　　　The snow in the street, &c.
And as we gazed this thing upon,
Those twain knelt down to the Little One :
　　　　　The snow in the street, &c.
And a marvellous song we straight did hear,
That slew our sorrow and healed our care :
　　　　　The snow in the street, &c.

CAROL.　News of a fair and a marvellous thing ;
　　　　Nowell, nowell, nowell, we sing :

REFRAIN. The snow in the street and the wind on the
    door :
    Minstrels and Maids, stand forth on the floor.

IX. TO OUR LADY.

FOR A PICTURE BY GIOVANNI BELLINI.

E. NESBIT.

FROM 'LEAVES OF LIFE,' 1888.

DEAR Mother, in whose eyes I see
All that I would and cannot be,
Let thy pure light for ever shine,
Though dimly, through this life of mine.
Though what I dream and what I do,
In prayer's despite are always two,
Light me through maze of deeds undone,
O thou, whose deeds and dreams are one.
And though through mists of strife and tears
A world away my star appears,
Yet let Death's sunrise shine on me
Still reaching arms and heart to thee.

X. TUSCAN MAY-DAY : A SONG.

A. MARY F. ROBINSON.

FROM 'AN ITALIAN GARDEN,' 1886.

THE village girls have gone away
    To sing at every shrine,
The whole day long they sing and pray
    To Mary, Maid Divine.

I know so well the way they go,
    The very turn they took,
And all the chants they sing I know,
    And every Virgin's look :

Yet should I sing with them, and stand
   Before the Poor in heart,
Would she not reach her holy hand
   To thrust me out apart?

Beside the glimmering sea I sit
   And watch the darkness fall;
The thirsty sand drinks up in it
   My tears, and hides them all.

The nearing voices swell and soar;
   'Ave, Mary'—hark—'Ave, Mary':
Before the shrine upon the shore
   The tirèd singers tarry.

I sang beside them at the spring,
   And in the weedy furrow;
But here I feel I dare not sing,
'Mary, Mary, Mary, Mother Mary,'
   My heart is mad with sorrow.

XI. THE SHADOW OF DEATH.

SUGGESTED BY HOLMAN HUNT'S PICTURE.

RICHARD WILTON, M.A.

FROM 'LYRICS,' 1878.

THE 'twelve hours' of thy 'day' of toil are fled,
  O glorious Workman; and the gorgeous West
And level shadows bid to evening rest:
Thy weary Arms to right and left are spread,
As heavenwards thou dost lift thy holy Head
  In praise. But lo, a sword has pierced the breast
  Of Mary. Orient gems no more arrest
Her eyes now fixed upon that omen dread.

She sees the shadow, but he fronts the sun ;
   Sufficient is the evil to the day ;
Not yet his silent years of work are done,
   Nor yields the toilsome to the 'dolorous way.'
O Sunlit Life, teach me thy lesson high ;
Then trusting in no shadow, let me die.

Queen of May: an Ode.

WILLIAM J. GOUGH.

FROM 'THE XAVIER,' NEW YORK, 1898.

BUT yesterday and all the earth was bare ;
   Bare were the plants, the groves, the trees,
No sign of verdure, barren everywhere,
   Naught that could the human vision please.
Through dreary forests did I wend,
   My sole companion was the mourning wind,
   Before whose sway in front, aside, behind,
In low submission did the branches bend.
   Bleakness, bleakness, bleakness :
How could such scenes the soul of man inspire,
   Sad as he was through grief and weakness,
Possessing all things save his one desire—
   To reach that calm Eternal Land
   Where free from feelings of distress,
   His soul might glide into unbounded bliss
Beneath the guidance of a parent hand.

To-day and all is brilliancy :
   The morning sun comes forth in rarest gold,
   Nor can the eye his dazzling gleams behold.
The earth is beautiful to see :

z

Waving blossoms in the meadows wide;
Laughing flowers on every side,
Tinted with the broken rays
Of a sun in ecstasy
That thus betrays its silent and unbounded praise.

* * *

Away, away, away:
Away to the forest high;
To dells sequestered from a peeping sky.
Happy sounds in every nook,
As chant the zephyrs soft their charming lay;
Happy sounds in every brook
As bounds the wavelet o'er the rocks in play:
It is the joyous chant of May.

The ocean hears it:
Far off with a mighty roar,
There is a washing,
A turbid lashing,
Of many breaking waves upon the shore.
The ocean hears it—
The wild triumphant lay.
From distant lands the waves in glee
Come bounding to receive a message great,
And then to others far across the sea
Return the joyous news to state.
See how with wings outspread
The sea-bird cleaves the misted air,
Or else with whirling dip
He doth the wave-crest sip,
With graceful motion of his glossy head,
Moved by the Spirit of the May.

Why bloom the plants with brighter hues
  Than man before has seen?
Why glisten now with diamond dews
  Too rare for spheres terrene?
The sparkling jewels of a dew-dropt glade,
The wonders of an ivy-bowered shade,
Those pretty buds by angel fingers made
    Are, it would seem, for One whom Heaven and
      Earth call ' Queen ' :
        The Queen of day and night,
          Of forests dark and meadows bright ;
        Of all things good the Queen.
There is a meaning in the swallow's song—
  The volume poured from out his silvery throat,
  Is naught save praise.   Each silvery note
Tells how all creatures long
  To vent their souls in one ecstatic song,
A mighty earnest song of gladness,
  The pent up feelings rising into spheres sublime,
Marred not by inharmonious tones of sadness,
  But rising sweetly into that celestial clime,
Where sits enthroned the Queen.

        *   *   *

      O Queen, Queen, Queen :
        Queen of a fallen race ;
The fairest Regent of the Universe,
Alone unsullied by the dark primeval curse.
Behold each subject, loyal, brave,
Willing to be thy champion or thy slave,
Bent low as is the weakest branch
Before the grand imperious wind,
But bent before a Regent kind ;

No angry blow was ever given
When man outraged thy name;
   But thou, great Queen of Heaven,
Like to a parent true became
   And chid the culprit, but with words of love,
And round his heart fine webs of mercy wove.

         O Queen, Queen, Queen:
      Monarch most humble and serene;
There is a boldness in the redbreast's hymn;
   A brain-confusing odour in the rose.
No sweeter lay e'er burst from Seraphim,
   No sweeter flower in heavenly garden grows.
'Tis not the May-time that inspires the scent;
   'Tis not the May that fills the songster's voice,
To breathe thy praises is the flower's intent;
   To sing thy virtues doth the bird rejoice.
Far, far away from folly's vain delusion,
   Far, far away in meadows strangely gay,
Poor Nature's gifts are scattered in profusion,
   Her lowly offering to the Queen of May.
One boon, O Lady, do I crave;
   The hymn melodious and the fragile flower,
The charming fancies of a fleeting hour,
   Accept them all I pray,
As though they came from me, thy prostrate slave;
   For nothing worthier can I give
Unto the Queen of May.

Ode and Lyric.

HENRY A. RAWES, O.S.C., D.D.: 1826—1885.

I. OUR LADY'S DEATH.

FROM 'THE WEEKLY REGISTER,' 1881.

Love is strong as Death. (*Canticle* viii. 6.)

THEY wait to welcome her in Heaven to-day :
The King who crowns for love,
Leaving his throne above,
From heights of Sion takes his earthward way,
Among his Holy Ones in white array :
This ever-gracious Lord,
Both God and Man, adored
By wondering worlds, doth come
To Mary's home,
Bringing new dowers
Of graces chosen for this Pearl of Hours.

She lifts her hands and turns to him in light
The longing of her eyes ;
His shadow on her lies ;
Her soul all joy, and on her cheek no tear ;
She prays to him, Beloved, her raiment white
Glittering through earth's dim night ;
She waits his voice to hear
Breaking the silence with a word of might.

In the great stillness of his Majesty,
Holding his Mother's hand,
Beside her he doth stand ;
No son so loving as her Son can be :
A conquering King,
He comes this day to bring

That Beatific Vision which she seeks ;
He looks and speaks,
Who bindeth as he will, or setteth free ;
Amidst the day-spring of the sinless land,
Death has for her no victory, no sting.

She stands adoring in the Holy Place,
No longer sorrowful and tired,
But in the Vision much-desired ;
His hand the weary reaper stays,
When harvest-songs resound in praise :
For her, ye Apostolic Princes cannot grieve,
But for yourselves now left
Of her sweet self bereft :
Yet going she doth leave
A heritage of love that makes you strong :
Through ages long
Her words and deeds of grace abide
A light of days,
Till all the Ransomed look upon her face,
The glory of the City of the Bride.

The rain is over and the winter gone,
The summer skies are clear,
The summer flowers appear,
The hills put on their robe of summer green,
A light upon the land of death has shone :
This Mother blest,
Heaven's Virgin-Queen,
Where death no more, nor pain can ever be,
Far past all storms and raging of the sea,
Above the echoes of a world of strife,
In God's own world of Life,
Upon the splendour of a throne

Kept for herself alone,
In calm fruition of tranquillity
Which cannot cease,
Reigns, wearing many diadems of peace.

II. NAME OF THE DESIRED.

FROM 'FOREGLEAMS OF THE DESIRED,' 1881.

In patient love and waiting, faithful Seers
    Watched silent and alone;
Upon their gaze, through veils, a glory shone;
They saw in vision, sometimes dimmed by tears,
  The harvest of the fruitful years.

The years went on: with footsteps long delayed,
    The World's Desired drew nigh;
At last in Flesh, the Wisdom from on High
Dwelt among men; in Mary's arms was laid
  The King who heaven and earth had made.

The earth was weary until Mary came,
    Bringing the Promised Child;
Weak hope again grew strong; the desert wild
Blossomed with rose and lily: then the Name
  Of Jesus glowed with heavenly flame.

Sceptred amidst the Apostolic band,
    Guarded by hearts of fire,
The Mother of our Lord in sweet desire
Passed through her sinless life: now round her stand
  The Princes of the King's own Land.

Our waiting souls look onward to the day
    When Mary shall be seen
Of Blessed Ones in light the Virgin-Queen,
Reigning with Jesus, in whose kingly sway
  Exulteth all that great array.

In restful gladness, with apparel white,
    Unceasingly they praise
Their crowned Redeemer; and adoring, gaze
On him who, dying, brought them to the height
    With his own glory ever bright.

Redeemed by Blood, where sorrow cannot be,
    The Saints of God are there;
High on the golden steps, elect, all-fair,
Where nought but holiness of love they see,
    In joy and peace, eternally.

Rhymers' Club Verses.

FROM 'THE BOOK OF THE RHYMERS' CLUB,' 1892.

I. CARMELITE NUNS OF THE PERPETUAL ADORATION.

ERNEST DOWSON: 1868—1900.

CALM, sad, secure; behind high convent walls
    These watch the Sacred Lamp, these watch and pray;
And it is one with them when evening falls,
    And one with them the cold return of day.

These heed not time; their nights and days they make
    Into a long, returning rosary,
Whereon their lives are threaded for Christ's sake—
    Meekness and vigilance and chastity.

A vowed patrol, in silent companies
    Life-long they keep before the Living Christ:
In the dim church, their prayers and penances
    Are fragrant incense to the Sacrificed.

Outside, the world is wild and passionate;
  Man's weary laughter and his sick despair
Entreat at their impenetrable gate:
  They heed no voices in their dream of prayer.

They saw the glory of the world displayed;
  They saw the bitter of it and the sweet;
They knew the roses of the world should fade
  And be trod under by the hurrying feet.

Therefore they rather put away desire,
  And crossed their hands and came to Sanctuary;
And veiled their heads and put on coarse attire—
  Because their comeliness was vanity.

And there they rest: they have serene insight
  Of the illuminating dawn to be:
Mary's sweet Star dispels for them the night,
  The proper darkness of humanity.

Calm, sad, secure; with faces worn and mild;
  Surely, their choice of vigil is the best?
Yea; for our roses fade, the world is wild;
  But there, beside the Altar, there is rest.

II. DISPUTE BETWEEN THE ROSE AND THE LILY.

EDWIN J. ELLIS.

THE Rose and Lily by the golden Gate
  Of Heaven's own garden, where the trailing dress
  Of the sweet Virgin, followed by a press
Of angels among angels fortunate,
Being the guard of her, Immaculate,
  Had now but passed and left a sacredness
  Like perfume in the air that God shall bless—

The Rose and Lily gently, without hate,
   Disputed which should be the Flower of choice.
' For being white as I,' the Lily cried,
   ' Mary was chosen.'   Then with tenderer voice,
' But loved for being like me,' the Rose replied.
   Returning, Mary laid upon her breast
   Both flowers, and none could answer which was best.

III.   IN A NORMAN CHURCH.

VICTOR PLARR.

As over incense-laden air
   Stole winter twilight, soft and dim,
The folk arose from their last prayer—
   When hark, the children's hymn.

Round yon great pillar, circlewise,
   The singers stand up two and two—
Small lint-haired girls, from whose young eyes
   The gray sea looks at you.

Now heavenward the pure music wins
   With cadence soft and silvery beat :
In flutes and subtle violins
   Are harmonies less sweet.

It is a chant with plaintive ring,
   And rhymes and refrains, old and quaint :
' O Monseigneur Saint Jacques,' they sing,
   And ' O Assisi's Saint.'

Through deepening dusk one just can see
   The little white-capped heads that move
In time to lines turned rhythmically,
   And starred with names of love.

Bred in no gentle silken ease,
   Trained to expect no splendid fate,
They are but peasant children these
   Of very mean estate.

Nay, is that true? To-night perhaps
   Unworldlier eyes had well discerned
Among those little gleaming caps
   An aureole that burned.

For once 'twas thought the Gates of Pearl
   Best opened to the poor that trod
The path of the meek Peasant Girl,
   Who bore the Son of God.

Irishwoman's Rosary, Sonnets and Rondeau.

MAGDALEN ROCK (E. BECK).

FROM AMERICAN, ENGLISH, AND IRISH MAGAZINES.

I. AN IRISHWOMAN'S ROSARY.

Och, Mary, 'asthore,' raise the window high,
   The air from the moorland is fresh and cool
And I fain would look once before I die
   On the spreading meadows and quivering pool;
And give me my Rosary in my hand—
   A decade or two I can, maybe, say
While the yellow sunlight floods all the land
   And tints the hills with his farewell ray.

Its forty years since I was a bride—
   Since your father brought me one day in June
To the Mission's close on a green hill-side
   In the mountain parish of Killnadroon;

And to-night I can hear the murmur loud
  That followed the words Father Dominic said ;
And the upturned gaze of the swaying crowd
  I see, and the hues of the candles red.

'Twas there that your father bought me these beads
  Of Irish oak, with their silver cross ;
And a friend they were in my direst needs :
  And in every season of grief or loss—
And sure, God knows best, but I've had my share
  Of trials, dear, since I saw him laid,
That wintry day when the earth was bare,
  With his kindred's clay 'neath the yew-tree's shade.

In that same sad winter poor Patrick died—
  God rest them all—and ere on his grave
The daisies bloomed, Kate slept by his side,
  And Michael and Norah went o'er the wave ;
I borrowed their passage from Ned Molloy—
  'Twas he had always the willing hand—
But many a time have my girl and boy
  Repaid the money from that New Land.

And when I am dead—now don't cry, 'aroon,'
  God knows I'm willing and glad to go
But for your sake—write to them soon
  And tell them all they would like to know,
And let me sleep where your father lies,
  And place my Rosary within my hand,
That his eyes may see it in Paradise
  And know me by it in that blessed land.

NOTES.

St. 1. line 1 : Asthore ; my darling.
St. 5. line 1 : Aroon ; my treasure.

II. EVER-BLESSED.

' All generations shall call me Blessed.'

THOU hast been praised in hut and monarch's hall,
In market-place and square, in street and lane,
In lonely cloister and in crowded fane ;
'Mid Arctic snows, and where the shadows tall
Of stately palms o'er tropic deserts fall ;
By smiling lips, by lips grown white with pain,
In humble prayer and in triumphant strain ;
In grief and joy, in troubles great and small—
By those that lived in vanished centuries,
Who now in heaven see thee face to face ;
By us yet striving for that glorious place ;
Aye, myriads still unborn shall bend their knees
And call thee Blessed, as thy tongue foretold,
O Mother of our God, in days of old.

III. CONSOLATRIX AFFLICTORUM.

FORGET not, Mother, though on ambient air
    From angel lips thy praises ever rise
    Around the Great White Throne in Paradise ;
Though countless saints pay homage to thee there,
Forget not all the woes that were thy share
    Once on this earth—thy bitter tears and sighs
    On dark Golgotha, under angry skies,
Nor thy long years of waiting and of prayer.

Forget not Simeon's prophecy, nor yet
    Thy flight to Egypt with thy Son and Lord
    Far from the reach of Herod's cruel sword ;
Not one of all thy many griefs forget
    When, Comforter of the Afflicted, we
    Kneel by thy shrine and beg thy clemency.

IV. BENEATH THE CROSS.

BENEATH the Cross on Calvary,
When Jesus died for you and me,
    With breaking heart and anguished eyes
    That saw not men, nor earth, nor skies,
His Mother stood in agony;
Her eyes nought save her Son could see,
And yet she bent to God's decree,
    And tried to still her moans and sighs
        Beneath the Cross.

And by that Mother's side was she
Who sinned yet loved so loyally;
    And her dear Master ne'er denies
    A prayer of hers in Paradise,
Who shared his Mother's misery
        Beneath the Cross.

Unknown 'Madonna' at Perugia, &c.

RENNELL RODD.

FROM 'THE UNKNOWN MADONNA,' 1888.

I. THE UNKNOWN 'MADONNA.'

I KNOW that Picture's meaning—the unknown,
Called 'School of Umbria'; it stands alone;
Those prayerful fingers never worked to fame—
A master's hand, though silence keep his name.
But for the meaning, gaze awhile and plain
The thought he worked inwarms to life again:

Love made those features living, such a face
Smiled once—on whom?   Say in a lofty place
He could not climb to—in those eyes' blue deeps
The reverence of unreached ideals keeps
The human memory, not a face of dreams,
And coldly beautiful, but one that seems
Caught in the likeness that a lover's eyes
Devoutly worshipped to idealise ;
And since creation is akin to prayer,
He made that face God's Mother, and set her there
Among the lilies by the hill-side town.

And then the Child, a flower-face to crown
The human love-dream, little hands entwined
Round one surrendered finger, to my mind
Just such close watching, tenderness expressed
As those who miss it learn to look for best.
Perugian, say we—look, the lilies lean
Against the mountain, dips the vale between ;
Yonder's Assisi on the nearer ridge ;
And that's the gorge that hides the giant bridge
Joining Spoleto ; and beyond, away
Hill-crests like waves in purple to mid day.
That was his thought, to make his art her shrine,
And lift her human up to the divine ;
So smiles Madonna, so evermore sits she
Against the Umbrian blue mountain sea.

Why do I think so?   Why, because if I
Could paint just one such picture ere I die,
Make one thought everlasting, I would choose
His theme, the Mother and the Child, and use
A face as sweet as this was ; in the Child
Reflect its beauty, only undefiled

Of pain and sorrow and knowledge, and would set
Both in a garden that is lilied yet
With beds her own hands tended, and enclose
All in a girdle of the hills she chose
Of earth's fair homes to dwell in, keeping so
The tender fragrance of dead years ago.

I would not change these few square feet for halls
Of Ghirlandajo, for the magic walls
Of this your Cambio—I would rather keep
My silent record of his nameless sleep,
Dream back his story through the long blank years—
Believe those lilies once were dewed with tears.

II. AVE, MARIA; AVE, MARIE.

Ave, Maria. Day declines,
　　Grows the peace of the evening star,
Shadows rise on the mountain lines—
　　Wide the heaven and God so far :
How should he stoop to the human sin :
Mother and human take me in ;
　　Thou hast suffered and thou canst see :
　　　Ave, Maria ; Ave, Marie.

Ave, Maria. At end of day
　　Rings thy peal on the evening air,
Calls the world to its homeward way,
　　Stays the heart in a pause of prayer ;
Ave, Maria, by storm or star,
The thought of the wanderer turns from far
　　To the shrine of his haven—Light of the Sea :
　　　Ave, Maria ; Ave, Marie.

Ave, Maria. Years roll by ;
　　Thy dominion shall endure ;

All who make for the hard and high,
  All the chivalrous, brave and pure,
Kneel in heart at an inward shrine
Built for a woman, and therefore thine—
  For we lift our love to the light of thee:
  Ave, Maria; Ave, Marie.

Madonna dell' Acqua.

JOHN RUSKIN: 1819—1900.

FROM 'POEMS,' 1891.

In the centre of the lagoon, between Venice and the mouths of
the Brenta, supported on a few mouldering piles, stands a small
shrine dedicated to the 'Madonna dell' Acqua,' which the gondo-
lier never passes without a prayer (Author). The poem was
written in the Author's twenty-fifth year.

AROUND her shrine no earthly blossoms blow,
No footsteps fret the pathway to and fro;
No sign, nor record of departed prayer,
Print of the stone, nor echo of the air;
Worn by the lip, nor wearied by the knee—
Only a deeper silence of the sea.
For there, in passing, pause the breezes bleak,
And the foam fades, and all the waves are weak.
The pulse-like oars in softer fall succeed,
The black prow falters through the wild seaweed—
Where, twilight borne, the minute thunders reach
Of deep-mouthed surf that bays by Lido's beach,
With intermittent motion traversed far
And shattered glancing of the western star,
Till the faint storm-bird on the heaving flow
Drops in white circles, silently like snow.
Nor here the ponderous gem, nor pealing note,
Dim to adorn—insentient to adore—

AA

But purple-dyed the mists of evening float,
In ceaseless incense from the burning floor
Of ocean, and the gathered gold of heaven
Laces its sapphire vault ; and early given,
The white rays of the rushing firmament
Pierce the blue quivering night, through wreath or rent
Of cloud inscrutable and motionless—
Hectic and wan and moon-companioned cloud.
O lone Madonna—Angel of the Deep—
When the night falls, and deadly winds are loud,
Will not thy love be with us while we keep
Our watch upon the waters, and the gaze
Of thy soft eyes that slumber not, nor sleep?
Deem not thou, Stranger, that such trust is vain ;
Faith walks not on these weary waves alone,
Though weakness dread, or apathy disdain
The spot which God has hallowed for his own.
They sin who pass it lightly—ill divining
The glory of this place of bitter prayer ;
And hoping against hope, and self-resigning,
And reach of faith, and wrestling with despair,
And resurrection of the last distress,
Into the sense of heaven when earth is bare,
And of God's voice when man's is comfortless.

NOTE.

After careful examination, neither as adversary nor as friend, of
the influences of Catholicism, I am persuaded that the worship of the
Madonna has been one of its noblest and most vital graces, and has
never been otherwise than productive of holiness of life and purity
of character. . . . There has, probably, not been an innocent home
throughout Europe during the period of Christianity, in which the
imagined presence of the Madonna has not given sanctity to the
duties and comfort to the trials of the lives of women ; and every
brightest and loftiest achievement of the art and strength of manhood
has been the fulfilment of the prophecy of the poor Israelite Maiden :
'He that is Mighty hath magnified me.' (Author; abridged from
'Fors Clavigera,' Letter 41.   1 April, 1874.)

Maria, Sine Labe Concepta.

MATTHEW RUSSELL, S.J.

FROM 'THE IRISH MONTHLY,' 1881.

> I think of thee and what thou art,
>   Thy majesty, thy state ;
> And I keep singing in my heart,
>   ' Immaculate, Immaculate.' (*F. W. Faber.*)

IMMACULATE ; Immaculate ;
  All sinless, spotless, pure and fair :
That Eden of the Tree of Life
  No Serpent's slime to stain could dare.
The human Adam erst was formed
  Of virgin earth unsoiled, uncursed ;
And shall the Heavenly Adam be
  Less blest, less favoured than the first ?

The life of the first Mother Eve
  In perfect purity began :
Shall she begin with lower grace—
  The Mother of the Perfect Man ?
Mother of all who truly live,
  Of earth redeemed the better Eve—
On her can sin's dark shadow fall,
  Her Father, Son, and Spouse to grieve ?

No, not for swiftest lightning-flash
  Of time or thought could faintest stain,
Though seen alone by God's pure eye,
  On this one chosen heart remain :
For this one heart that throbs with life—
  Life's earliest throb which God but hears—
Is the one heart for which that God
  Has waited through the sinful years.

And now it beats, that chosen heart
  To which a God shall cling as Child ;
The Mother of the All-holy God,
  Can she with sin be e'er defiled ?
No, not for briefest moment can
  The Creature, whom God loves so well
That he will soon her Son become,
  Be soiled with sin, a slave of hell.

Already heaven with gaze intent
  Is fixed on her, the Maiden blest,
Within whose womb, within whose arms,
  Within whose heart, God's Son will rest.
Destroyer of the serpent's brood,
  Foretold, prefigured from the first—
Shall God from her be forced to turn
  In horror as from thing accursed ?

What filial heart but fain would save
  Mother beloved from shame and harm ?
Would make her perfect, beautiful,
  With all that filial heart can charm ?
Would add fresh graces to her mind
  And every fault and flaw remove,
That so that dearest one might be
  More worthy of all filial love ?

Then, what unutterable store
  Of graces Mary's soul must fill ;
Her Son is God, and with a wish
  Can make her whatso'er he will.
Her Son is the Eternal Lord,
  To whom nought future is, nor past ;
He could not let her longed-for dawn
  By sin's eclipse be overcast.

As streams that foam adown the steep,
　If unrestrained, would upward mount,
In eager haste to reach again
　The level of their native fount:
The river of the Precious Blood
　Sends back its cleansing power divine,
Making its fountain, Mary's heart,
　For ever pure and bright to shine.

For say not that this privilege
　Doth Christ the Conqueror bereave
Of one high trophy—as if all
　The lost and outcast race of Eve
Were purchased by his Blood, while she,
　Exempt and unredeemed, apart,
Had need of no redeeming tide
　To purify her purest heart.

Hold—this were falsest blasphemy:
　Her, most and first, did Jesus save,
For his own Mother pouring out
　The Life-blood which that Mother gave;
Most glorious triumph of the Cross,
　Redeemed more plenteously than all—
From those outstretched and piercèd Hands
　Her countless gifts and graces fall.

　　　*　　*　　*

Immaculate; Immaculate;
　All sinless, spotless, pure and fair:
And yet these sinful hearts of ours
　To love that sinless heart must dare:
For God, who kept that heart all pure
　And filled it with each richest grace,
Has filled it, too, with mother's love
　For every child of Adam's race.

O Mother, canst thou love e'en me ?
 Thou canst.   From heaven thy smile doth fall
On all for whom thy Jesus died—
 And Jesus died for me, for all :
Sweet Mother, bless me through the days
 That I on earth must work and wait,
Until in heaven I greet Heaven's Queen,
 Immaculate, Immaculate.

NOTE.

Stanza 8 : Bossuet applies this idea to the Immaculate Conception.

from 'All's well that ends well.'
WILLIAM SHAKESPEARE : 1564—1616.

ACT III. : SCENE 4.

Rousillon.   The Count's Palace.
Enter Countess and Steward.

COUNTESS.

ALAS ; and would you take the letter of her ?
Might you not know she would do as she has done,
By sending me a letter ?   Read it again.

STEWARD READS :

' I am Saint Jaques' pilgrim, thither gone :
 Ambitious love hath so in me offended,
That barefoot plod I the cold ground upon,
 With sainted vow my faults to have amended.
Write, write, that from the bloody course of war
 My dearest Master, your dear Son, may hie :
Bless him at home in peace, whilst I from far
 His name with zealous fervour sanctify :

His taken labours bid him me forgive;
 I, his despiteful Juno, sent him forth
From courtly friends, with camping foes to live,
 Where death and danger dog the heels of worth:
He is too good and fair for death and me;
Whom I myself embrace, to set him free.'

COUNTESS.

Ah, what sharp stings are in her mildest words.
Rinaldo, you did never lack advice so much,
As letting her pass so: had I spoke with her,
I could have well diverted her intents
Which thus she hath prevented.

STEWARD.

     Pardon me, Madam:
If I had given you this at over-night,
She might have been o'erta'en; and yet she writes,
Pursuit would be but vain.

COUNTESS.

     What angel shall
Bless this unworthy husband?
     He cannot thrive
Unless her prayers, whom Heaven delights to hear
And loves to grant, reprieve him from the wrath
Of greatest justice.
     Write, write, Rinaldo,
To this unworthy husband of his wife;
Let every word weigh heavy of her worth
That he does weigh too light: my greatest grief,
Though little he do feel it, set down sharply.
Dispatch the most convenient messenger:
When haply he shall hear that she is gone,

He will return ; and hope I may that she,
Hearing so much, will speed her foot again
Led hither by pure love : which of them both
Is dearest to me, I have no skill in sense
To make distinction : provide this messenger :
My heart is heavy and mine age is weak :
Grief would have tears, and sorrow bids me speak.

NOTE.

Some persons have argued that Shakespeare, in writing certain expressions uttered by the Clown in this Play, 'meant to show that he was no Papist.' On the contrary, while he has put these scurrilities into the mouth of the unhappy Clown ('a wicked creature'), the words of the Countess are decisive the other way. When she first learns that her son has renounced his wife, she says, 'He cannot thrive unless her prayers reprieve him.' Whose prayers are these? Not those of Helen, his wife, but of One greater than any angel, whose prayers God 'delights to hear and loves to grant.' This is exactly the way in which Catholics speak of the Blessed Virgin, and the lines will not apply to any one but to her. The testimony is brief, but decisive. Shakespeare in these lines affirms distinctly, but not contentiously, one of the most characteristic doctrines that distinguishes the Catholic Church from the Protestant communion.' (From 'the Religion of Shakespeare.' by Henry Sebastian Bowden, of the Oratory, 1899.)

Prologue to the Magnificat.

P. A. SHEEHAN, P.P.

FROM 'THE CANTICLE OF THE MAGNIFICAT,' 1900.

O Lady Fair, a boon I ask of thee,
Ask it of thee in all humility,
  Ask it with beating heart, with pleading eye.
A leaf from thy red rose-crown?   Lady, no :
One waxen petal from this lily-blow?
  These would be dear ; but dearer still seek I.

Nay, do not frown : what claim have I to show?
What seal doth mark me as thy child below?
  Alas, no seal but seal of sin have I :
And yet, my soul, thou hast no stronger claim
On her who, Spotless from all sin and shame,
  Might yet redeem thy life's poor travesty.

As some sad knight, the scorn of chivalry,
Unspurred, dishonored by his peers, should flee
  To touch a lute to some fair dream that's passed;
Thus I, an outcast, weave a wavering rhyme
To thee, my Empress of that far-off time
  When with thy knights hope dreamed I might be
    classed.

For oft at night, when couched but slumberless,
Tossed by the burthen of some dire distress,
  I dreamed of thy sweet face, O Lady mine :
And when thy form did glimmer and grow pale,
Thine angel dropped his consecrated veil,
  And still in sleep thy face I did divine.

And often in the wild and windy dawn,
The sable skirts of night not yet withdrawn,
　　I saw thy form shine through my lattice-bars ;
I knew it from thy beauty, shy and sweet,
From the curv'd-scythéd crescent round thy feet ;
　　The sun, thy cincture, and thy crest, the stars.

Down through the ages, scattering as they go
Their mingled meeds of rapture and of woe,
　　One dream of beauty lingers to our ken ;
One song of power, enkindling sense and soul,
Vibrates on harp, and gleams on lettered scroll
　　Left by the kings of thought to weary men.

One crieth, ' I love the Weeping Mother best ; '
And one, ' The Babe upon the Virgin's breast ; '
　　And one, ' Immacolata ' shouts aloud :
For dusky painters, dark-eyed poets have limned
The beauty of my Mother, many-hymned,
　　'Mid songs and sorrows of the singing crowd.

No artist yet has struck the faultless grace,
The rapt inspirement of thy childlike face,
　　On that fair mount, on that fair summer eve ;
And I, the least of all the bardic train,
To consecrate my one poor gift would fain
　　Thy picture fair on this frail canvas leave.

' Salem alaïcom ; ' and the withered lips
Brushed the soft bloom, that erstwhile did eclipse
　　The Rose of Sharon in the pink-finger'd dawn;
And as at breath of spring the buds travail,
So her sweet Bud did leap to burst the veil
　　That by the Jordan's waters was withdrawn.

Waved the black palms, and clapped their glist'ning
    hands ;
Bubbled Nephtoa's fountain o'er the sands ;
    Smiled the broad reaches of the Syrian Sea ;
Down through the Hinnim valley, clear and bright,
Pierced the long, level lances of the light,
    As broke the whisper, ' Whence is this to me ? '

Hushed the black palms ; and heavenward as they
    bent,
Closed like the hands of children reverent ;
    Wavered the fountain's lily, and expired :
Sheathed, the lances of the level sun
Purpled the ocean dimples, one by one ;
    Hark, 'tis the anthem ages have desired.

O Child and Prophet, thy clear, liquid notes
Soar o'er the thunder that tumultuous floats
    From the starred choirs of farthest Paradise :
The Tri-une Godhead list'ning from afar,
Leans from his temple, meshed with many a star,
    To hear thy music trembling through his skies.

And I, a mortal, crouching at thy feet,
Here on this hill, where night and twilight meet,
    Have lost amid the future's echoings
The sweetness of the present ravishment,
As nightingale, with twilight dews besprent,
    Forgets, and dreams 'tis some far bird that sings.

Now I will listen, hushed in every sense ;
I will withdraw my soul from light intense,
    And wrap it round in sanctities of night :
And I will watch thy sacred syllables,
Tolled on the air like peals of fairy bells ;
    And I will think, and teach thy words aright.

Dumb as the white-haired priest that listeneth,
Reverent as the awed Elizabeth,
  Silent as stars or angels shall I be:
As when the white Host gleameth 'gainst the dawn,
Mine eyes are sealed, my very soul withdrawn—
  So shall I hearken to thy prophecy.

Psyche praises the Virgin Mother of her Bridegroom.

JOHANN SCHEFFLER (ANGELUS SILESIUS): 1624—1677.

TRANSLATED (1894) FROM THE GERMAN BY E. M. CLERKE.

I. IN PRAISE OF THE BLESSED VIRGIN.

THEE, God's Mother, do we praise,
Virgin, honour thee with lays;
Thee, the Holy Spirit's Bride,
All the earth hath glorified;
Heavenly hosts thy service share,
Its Thrones are as thy throne of state,
And of thy crown the splendour great
The Principalities declare.

On thee gaze the Cherubim,
Unto thee all Seraphs hymn,
Loud they chorus, ' Happy she,
God's Own Mother chosen to be;'
The court of heaven, the globe of earth,
Are filled with the dread Majesty
Of the Blest Fruit, which here through thee
Hath willed in time to take its birth.

Thee the Apostles' choir applaud,
Thee doth the host of Martyrs laud,
The Prophet's lips thy praises sing,
And Confessors their tribute bring,
Rejoicing Virgins hymn to thee,
Thou art the Joy of Saints on high,
All Christendom to thee doth cry
With boundless trust and jubilee.

The Eternal God's Pavilion thou,
And Ruler of the world e'en now ;
Thou Herald of immortal day,
And after God, man's Hope and Stay :
Of demons Terror and Affright,
The sick thou dost with healing aid,
And succour those who, sore dismayed,
See Death approach in awful might.

Thou Woman most supremely blest,
Who God conceivedst in thy breast,
That our poor human race might claim
The heavenly heritage and name,
Through thee is opened Heaven's door,
Thou next thine own dear Son dost stand,
Beside the Throne, at God's Right Hand,
Whence we his coming hope once more.

Wherefore we pray thee, Lady High,
Stoop to our aid from out the sky ;
Help us, whom thy Son's Blood outpoured
Hath bought in fee to him as Lord ;
Aid us to lasting life to soar,
Heal us through thy Child Christ, that we
May have some part in him through thee,
And him and thee praise evermore.

II. IN PRAISE OF THE VIRGIN MOTHER.

STAINLESS Maid, whose sanctities
Most the Eternal Father please,
And whose purity his Son
From his Throne in Heaven hath won,
Stainless Maid, thy praise unbounded
Be by my weak voice resounded.

Thee, O Mary, will I sing,
To thee, Maiden, service bring,
Thee, O fairest Morning Star,
I will trumpet wide and far;
For through thee to us is given,
Christ our Weal and Hope of Heaven.

Radiant as the noonday light
Are thy splendour and thy might;
Fairer than the moon's pale beam,
Or the stars with golden gleam;
Dreadful as a host victorious,
To protect from foe inglorious.

Mighty Fortress barred alway,
Fountain God hath sealed away,
Ivory Tower of fair device,
Casket filled with pearls of price,
Vernal Garden walled and spacious
Art thou, Maiden, sweet and gracious.

Maids and Daughters, come and see
Here a Queen in majesty,
Whom God to himself did plight,
Mother, Bride and Daughter hight;
See the Princess, loved of Heaven,
To whom he himself hath given.

See the Covenant's true Ark ;
Vessel full of graces, mark ;
The Almighty's House of Gold,
Where he enters, here behold ;
Noah's Ark, see flood-invested
Where the Dove Divine hath rested.

See the lovely Hind appear,
How she shines in radiance clear ;
How the sun from Heaven to earth,
She hath drawn and brought to birth ;
See, how Life to us she giveth,
And the Light to all that liveth.

O thou heavenly Car of Gold,
Which unto us Christ hath rolled,
Solomon's true Throne of Peace,
And Gideon's Mystic Fleece,
Vessel filled with God, o'erwelling
With his grace his roof and dwelling.

Queen of the bright Seraphim,
Regent of the Cherubim,
Leader of the Martyr band,
Who dost Confessors command,
Chief of Saints and Virgins holy,
To the Lamb troth-plighted solely.

Mary, Full of Grace, I pray,
Help to drive the Fiend away,
That I may, when time is o'er,
Steeped in bliss for evermore,
See thee, Crown of Virgins, ever
With thy Son, to lose thee never.

Stabat Mater Speciosa.

BLESSED JACOPONE DA TODI:
XIII CENTURY.

TRANSLATED BY EDWARD CASWALL, OF THE ORATORY, M.A.: 1814—1878.

This rendering was made, at the request of a friend, during Father Caswall's last illness, and it is, probably, his final contribution to the religious verse of the day which he had so greatly enriched. The Sequence was published in 'the Messenger of the Sacred Heart,' in 1879, and is not included in the Author's volume of collected 'Hymns and Poems.'

O'ER the holy Manger bending,
 Where, upon his bed of hay,
Her Celestial Babe was lying
 In the dawning Christmas Day,
Stood the Mother fair to see,
Lost in joy and jubilee.

Oh, what glowing exultation
 Through her sinless bosom thrilled:
What felicity unbounded
 All her soul and being filled,
Gazing on her glorious Son,
Perfect God and Man in One.

Could your mortal eyes have witnessed
 That dear Maiden-Mother's bliss,
Fondling now, and now adoring,
 Now returning kiss for kiss,
How transported had you been
In the pure and lovely scene.

Oh, the wonder: Angels singing;
   Shepherds kneeling round in prayer;
Beasts of burden o'er their Maker
   Breathing through the frosty air;
At the stable of an inn
Ransom pledged for human sin.

All the while our great St. Joseph,
   Guardian of the Heavenly Bride,
Standing with a heart astonied
   At his holy Spouse's side,
Silent rapt in speechless awe
At the mysteries he saw.

Lovely Mother, Love's own Fountain,
   Mother of my Lord and mine,
Intercede for me, I pray thee,
   With this lovely Child of thine;
Gain me grace to please him well
All the days that here I dwell.

Let me share in those compassions
   Which your tender bosom fill,
For your little gentle Jesus
   Born of his own sweetest will;
Born for us in winter sore,
Eden's summer to restore.

Here I live in painful exile,
   Banished from my native home;
Here I have my only comfort
   In the hope of life to come;
Where below is joy for me,
Save in thy dear Christ and thee?

BB

Let me in your loving worship
  Of your Jesus bear a part,
Let me kiss the Life Incarnate,
  Let me hold him to my heart,
Who in taking human breath,
Dying comes to conquer death.

Of his mighty Spirit's fulness,
  Let me drink with thee my fill ;
Let me all his life and being
  Into all my veins instil ;
Every sense obscured and dim
In the very thought of him.

Now and ever may communion
  With the Father's Son and thine
Be my joy and jubilation,
  Be my energy divine,
Be my spirit's dance and song
Through my life-time all along.

In the secret of his presence
  May I find my earthly rest,
In his grace my perseverance ;
  And, oh, be his Vision blest
In another world my bliss,
When I leave the light of this.

Songs from Over-seas:

TRANSLATED (1897) FROM THE GERMAN, WITH A
DEDICATION TO OUR BLESSED LADY.

ELINOR MARY SWEETMAN.

DEDICATION.

THOU loveliest Thought of God's most lovely Mind;
O thou, the Light and Melody of Heaven,
From all eternity designed
To be the Centre-sun of tuneful spheres,
To keep celestial harmonies at even
Balance of sound and sweetness in God's ears ;
While earth was still a ring of whirling fire
And stars of morning sang together, thou,
Thou in the Father's bosom didst inspire
The full angelic choir.
The angels sang thee yet unborn, and now
Thy prophets rise, one voice
To bid thee weep and bid the world rejoice.
And who are these?
Yea, Lady, who are these
That flash from out the East unto the West,
Through all the clouds of all the centuries?
These are the nations that have called thee Blest—
Thy poets.   O ye tongues of fire,
Sweet singing mouths, how do ye star the deep
With Mary's name : how do your hymnals keep
Their holy ardours quick throughout all time.
Come, ye who hold the lyre,
Ye later-born of song who fain would climb
The starry path sublime ;

Come, tell me what within these fields ye hear ?
Sphere answering unto sphere,
Voice in voice striking, chime that echoes chime ;
The spirit blowing where it listeth, swells
Songs of lost peoples, like a peal of bells,
Out of the vast ;
Systems overcast
That once did Mary rhyme,
To systems uncreated still bequeath her ;
And still the stars of morning sing together.

Ye singers past, ye poets long since dead,
On earth your harp is hushed, your mortal light
Put out ; yourselves are fled
To where, in bosom of the Infinite,
Unceasing cadences fulfil your ears ;
But for her sake of whom ye uttered praise,
I, the least minstrel of these latter days,
Would lift the dusty curtain of the years,
Untomb ye, make your names
Once more a glory, and your flames
Revive and shine for all men's eyes to see.
Ye antique lyrists of an alien tongue,
Come, radiate through me and let me be
A crystal medium for your burning song,
Your latter day expression and your speech.
O sunken fires, thus shall your influence reach
Beyond the grave to newer centuries,
As light that travelling from a star in ashes,
Through limpid ether, falters on and flashes,
After a hundred years upon our eyes.

Hail, Full of Grace, who sittest now in Heaven ;
Hail, Full of Grace :

Would that to me, unworthiest, were given
To hymn to thee like bards of ancient race ;
But doubtful of mine own poor fashionings,
Yet longing ardently thine ears to please,
I sound this borrowed lyre of seven strings—
Seven sweet Songs from Over-seas,
Seven sweet melodies
Once framed by elder lips in other keys.
Now let us pray,
All we that sing, the quick, the dead, and they
Who shall take up this present poet's rhyme ;
And thou, Compassionate, bow down thine ears ;
Thou art the Centre-sun of tuneful spheres ;
Let none fall off from thee in after time.
Thou, in whose praise the ancient heavens leaped,
Keep thou the heights, the deeps ; be thou the bond
That linketh star with star to where beyond
Are golden fields of knowledge still unreaped.
O Centre-sun,
Gather all voices in thy realms of light ;
Let us be one,
And in one glorious canticle unite.
And if that mystic seer of northern land
Spake truly when he said
That the first angel by the Father made,
Was ever youngest of the heavenly band ;
First made, first blest, and ever further drawn
Into the freshness of eternal dawn,
Into the source of light, the birth of things
With dews of morning ever on his wings—
Then, Lady, in the coming afterwards,
When melodists unknown
Shall be in fresher orbits newly-strown ;

Draw them to heaven, hold them, let all bards,
Seers, prophets, quiring cherubim,
All spirits of sweet song, all systems, whether
Youngest of heaven or earth, for ever fill
All spaces with thy praise—for ever hymn
Thee, Blessed over all.

                  Thus, Lady, still,
Still shall the stars of morning sing together.

I. TO MARY.

MEISTER GOTTFRIED VON STRASBURG: XII—XIII CENTS.

Thou Lily-leaf, thou Roseal-bud,
Thou Queen in City of our God,
      Wherein ne'er trod
Maid like to thee, most high.
Thou Balm that every pain allays,
Thou Joy in harsh and bitter ways,
      Honour and praise
      Be thine eternally.
When that thy purest breast became
The living Godhead's Shrine,
As rays of sun through glass will flame
Thou, in thy virginal chaste frame,
Most sweetly didst proclaim
Christ's indwelling divine.

Thou Violet-field, thou Valley-rose,
Thou Bloom of budded hedge-rows,
      Thou Heart's repose,
Who makest heaven glad ;
Thou bright and orient-beaming Morn,
Thou truest Friend in lives forlorn—

Of thee is born
Jesus, the Living Bread,
That many darkened hearts and cold,
Consumed and kindled be
In love's enchantments manifold,
And through love's potency consoled ;
Thence be there told
Forever praise of thee.

Thou Blossom-gleam on clover-lea,
Thou burgeoned Spray of aloe-tree,
Thou bounteous Sea,
Whereon we gladly float ;
Thou sheltering Roof of all delight,
Inviolated by the night ;
Thou Chamber bright,
Whose splendour endeth not ;
Thou helpful and thou mighty Tower,
Before the face of hell—
When Satan comes in storm and power
With princes of the evil hour,
When passions rage and tempests lower,
Thou dost all terrors quell.

II. THE BIRTH OF MARY.

PROCOPIUS, THE MONK : 1608—1680.

LIKE the little woodbirds sweet,
That with myriad pipings greet
The dawning of the day ;
While the ruddy morning shrines
And the sky encarnadines,
Making roundelay ;

Men and women, rise and sing,
  Break into melody and ring
Joyful salutation.
  Lo, a Babe is born to earth,
Blessed Anne hath brought it forth
  For your consolation.
Towards the cooling dawn and wet,
  Grass and leaf and blossomlet
Lovingly bow down ;
  She with tenderness no less
Swift revives their weariness,
  Meekly made her known.
Like the dew o'er parchèd grass
  Doth our Heavenly Lady pass,
Comforting each soul ;
  Mild, she greeteth every one,
And in sorrow, she alone
  Makes our bruises whole.
Mary, help, we pray to thee
  From our hearts most earnestly ;
Hear us, Heaven's Flower.
When our earthly day is done,
  Oh, be thou our Evening Sun ;
Grant a golden hour.
  Make us, when in Heaven we rest
With the angels and the blest,
  Sing thy praises then ;
To this end thou cam'st on earth,
  And to Jesus gavest birth,
Who is our Help.   Amen.

III. FOR MARY'S NATIVITY.

SONG-BOOK OF MICHAEL VEHE, 1537.

To thee, O Heavenly Lady, now
I cry in this my direful need ;
God's debtor am I, but do thou
That I may serve thee, intercede.
    Oh, turn away,
    The dreadful day
    Of Jesùs' wrath ;
In thee my soul its refuge hath.

O thou in whom I put my faith,
Thou tender Maid and Mother of God,
When I consider coming death
What trouble doth my mind forebode ;
    How fearfully,
    I quake to see
That I must think upon my soul ;
Free-will hath led me from my goal.

Therefore, O Virgin undefiled,
Do thou ask pardon for my sin,
Since all thy prayers can reach thy Child,
And I must die I know not when.
    Sin's yoke I bear ;
    Yet through thy prayer,
Repentance true I now invite ;
Help that my Soul the flesh may fight.

IV. THE ANNUNCIATION.

HOLSCHER: XV—XVI CENTS.

A HUNTSMAN left the fields of God,
    To hunt in heath and wild ;
Mary, the Virgin Undefiled,
    Met him upon the road.

The huntsman strange of whom I tell
    Unto us all is known ;
He stands before the heavenly throne,
    His name is Gabriel.

The huntsman blew his horn apace,
    The echoes answered free :
' All hail, O Mary, hail to thee,
    For thou art Full of Grace.

' Hail, Mary, noble Maid and Blest,
    Virgin without a peer,
A Little Infant shall thou bear
    And nurse upon thy breast.

' A Virgin shalt thou bring him forth,
    And nurse upon thy knee,
And he that shall be born of thee
    Is King of Heaven and earth.'

Mary, the pure and spotless One,
    Knelt to the Lord in heaven ;
Thus was her humble answer given :
    ' Thy holy will be done :

' Thy holy will, it shall be done
    By her whom thou hast graced.'
Thus her heart virginal embraced
    Lord Jesus Christ, her Son.

V. ON THE FEAST OF THE ASSUMPTION.

SONG-BOOK OF MICHAEL VEHE, 1537.

Who prayeth, when his prayer he saith,
Let him give joyful thanks on high ;
To-day hath Mary vanquished death,
And liveth never more to die ;
    Yea, this we know, that here below
    Her heart was prest,
    With longing for eternal rest ;
Now dwelleth she among the Blest.

Oh, what divine felicity
Flows on to thee, thou Virgin bright :
All thy sorrows ceased to be,
With thy holy heavenly flight.
    Next Christ our God, in blest abode
    High over all,
    On thee the fairest splendours fall,
Who art the saints' best coronal.

Therefore, O pure angelic Queen,
And Virgin Mother of God on earth,
Remember thou what anguish keen
Awaits us at our going forth ;
    Help us to flee with speed to thee,
    Make us obtain,
    Through Christ, the Father's grace again—
Without thy Son all hope were vain.

VI. OUR DEAR LADY'S EASTER JOY.

FROM THE COLOGNE HYMN-BOOK: XVI CENT.

MOTHER of the Risen, weep no more,
   Neither shall your children more lament ;
   Lo, at dawn beside the monument
Saw you him whom once in womb you bore.

PEOPLE :   The Lord is risen :
         Mother, weep no more ; Alleluia.

Mother, faithful to the Cross that held him,
   Mother whom we pierced and wounded sore,
   Jesus is delivered—weep no more ;
Empty lies the place wherein they sealed him.

Come, O Rich in joy ; yea, come O Sweet ;
   Jesus hath regained our liberty :
   Jesus lives and Death alone must die ;
Come, oh, come this day of gladness greet.

Blest are they who heard what Jesus spake ;
   Blest who gazed upon our Saviour Risen ;
   To our fathers also in their prison
Drew he nigh, and Limbo's portals brake.

Lo, the sleeping saints, the captive dead
   Lingered there : he sought them to deliver ;
   You, who shared their longing, may for ever
Share their joy that they are comforted.

Hence, we all exalt you now, and all
   Lay our happy hearts upon your breast ;
   Remembering, while on Easter-lamb we feast,
Your diviner joy celestial.

Alleluia : let your praises rise ;
  Give her thanks, each newly-risen sinner ;
  Joy o'erbrims the Mother's heart within her,
And on us she thinks in Paradise.

PEOPLE :   The Lord is risen :
               Mother, weep no more ; Alleluia.

VII.   UPON THE BLESSED VIRGIN MARY.

UNKNOWN : c. 1500.

MAID Mary mild, Rose undefiled,
  Blowing our thorns among,
Thou hast rebuilt what Adam's guilt
  Lost to the world so long.
God's holy choice, St. Gabriel's voice
    First uttered unto thee ;
    Help thou, that heaven on me
Wreak not my sin ; forgiveness win ;
All hope is vain, till thou obtain
  Compassion from on high ;
Therefore I pray, turn not away,
  Lady, when I shall die.

Maid Mary mild, thou hast fulfilled
  Our forefathers' desire,
Who day by day in Limbo lay
  With tears and moanings dire.
And evermore they burned for war,
    That heaven's portals wide
    Might ope on every side ;
And One come thence whose countenance
Should them deliver ; but this for ever,
  Through thine unstainèd bringing-forth,

Is ended now ; therefore art thou
    Honoured and crowned o'er all on earth.

Maid Mary chaste, thou alone hast
    Comfort for souls in fault ;
Hence the Most Wise in Paradise
    Doth thee as Mother exalt
Of him our Healing, who cometh sealing
        Sentence on us at last.
        O Lady, hold me fast ;
In thee, sweet Fruit, my trust I put ;
To me like John, thy dying Son
    Gave thee upon his Cross,
That thou in love a Mother should'st prove
    Howe'er life might me toss.

Maid Mary pure, thou didst endure
    Intact from sin or spot,
No tongue on earth can utter forth
    The glories of thy lot.
Thy praises high eternally
    Ascend from earth and heaven ;
Nor shall this world be given
    Thy peer again.   O Pure of Stain,
When speech on these my lips shall freeze,
    My soul from body flee,
Remember then that with this pen
    I sought to honour thee.

NOTE.

Dedication, last line but 17 : That mystic seer of northern land ;
Swedenborg, as quoted by Carlyle.

Sacro Monte, Varallo, &c.

JOHN ADDINGTON SYMONDS:
1840—1893.

I. ON THE SACRO MONTE, VARALLO.

FROM 'ANIMI FIGURA,' 1882.

I.

STAIR over stair we scaled the gradual way,
 Through chestnut woods and smooth deep-sheltered
  lawns
 Unshaven, where the starry wind-flower dawns ;
 And as we rose, outspread beneath us lay
The Lombard champaign—lake and castle gray
 And liquid lapse of river, and the line
 Of dim aërial snow-touched Apennine,
 With Milan like an island far away.
And still at every turning, as we trod,
 A chapel rose before us, built for prayer,
 With dome and pinnacle and statue white
Sculptured upon that azure depth of air ;
 Till on the mountain's brow the house of God
 Flung wide huge portals to the orient light.

II.

'TWAS Easter morning. We too knelt and prayed
 Among the country folk who sought that shrine,
 And felt with them a something more divine
 Breathe in the gloom of arch and colonnade ;
As though some god, high o'er this hill, had made
 A meeting-place where heaven on earth might shine,
 Between gross plain and pure skies crystalline,
 With more of lustre and with softer shade.

How many a century of pilgrim feet
  Have worn those flinty ways whereby we came ;
  How many a deity from yonder seat
Hath gazed across the incense and the flame
  To mountains where yon vapours roll and meet,
  And nature reigns, changeful, unchanged, the same.

III.

WHO knows the names of all the powers who held
  This holy mountain and this seat of prayer ?
  With what blood-sacrifice and horrid blare
The first rude wood-god's bestial rage was quelled.
Then reigned a queen of heaven, whose smile compelled
  The wandering stars and soothed tempestuous air ;
  Hers were the cubs of wild beasts, hers the fair
Virgins who clashed their timbrels silvery-belled.
She passed ; and in her stead great Alpine Jove
  Dwelt on this summit, with fraternal nod
  Hurling his thunders southward to the grove
Iguvian, where his brother ruled, a god :
  And when he failed, came Mary and her Son,
  And all those elder creeds were blurred in one.

II. PART OF THE PRELUDE TO 'TEMA CON VARIAZIONE.'

FROM 'MANY MOODS,' 1878.

I WENT a roaming through the woods alone,
And heard the nightingale that made her moan.

The voice, methought, was neither man's, nor boy's,
  Nor bird's, nor woman's, but all these in one :
In Paradise, perchance, such perfect noise
  Resounds from angel choirs in unison,
  Chanting with cherubim their antiphon
To Christ and Mary on the sapphire throne.

I went a roaming through the woods alone,
And heard the nightingale that made her moan.

III. FOR ONE OF GIAN BELLINI'S LITTLE ANGELS.

FROM 'MANY MOODS,' 1878.

My task is to stand beneath the throne,
  To stand and wait whilst those grave presences,
Prophet and priest and saint and seraph, zone
  Our Lady with the Child upon her knees ;
  They from mild lips receive the messages
Of peace and love, which thence to men below
They shower soft-falling like pure flakes of snow.

I meanwhile wait ; and very mute must be
  My music, lest I break the golden trance
Of bliss celestial, or with childish glee
  Trouble the fount of divine utterance ;
  Yet when those lips are tired of speech, perchance
It may be that the Royal Babe will lie
And slumber to my whispered lullaby.

Then all those mighty brows will rest, and peace
  Descend like dew on that high company ;
Therefore I stand and wait, but do not cease
  To clasp my lute, that silver melody,
  When our dear Lady bends her smile on me,
Forth from my throat and from these thrilling strings
Dove-like may soar and spread ethereal wings.

NOTE.

The figures of winged boys, sitting or standing beneath the throne on which Madonna is seated with her Court of Saints, holding instruments of music and playing on them, or seeming to wait for her permission to begin, will be familiar to all who know the pictures of Bellini, Carpaccio, and other early Venetian masters. (Author.)

CC

Octave of Quatrains, Sonnet and Lyrics.

JOHN B. TABB, PRIEST.

FROM THE 'INDEPENDENT' (1887), AN 'OCTAVE TO MARY' (1893), 'POEMS' (1894), 'LYRICS' (1897), AND 'MESSENGER OF THE SACRED HEART' (1898), U.S.A.

I. OCTAVE OF QUATRAINS.

I. IMMACULATE CONCEPTION.

A DEW-DROP of the darkness born, wherein no shadow lies ;
The Blossom of a barren thorn, whereof no petal dies ;
  A Rainbow-beauty passion-free,
  Wherewith was veilèd Deity.

II. INCARNATION.

SAVE through the Flesh thou wouldst not come to me ;
  The Flesh, wherein thy strength my weakness found
  A weight to bow thy Godhead to the ground
And lift to heaven a lost humanity.

III. CHRISTMAS.

THE womb of silence bears the Eternal Word,
  And yet no sound is heard :
The womb of Mary, Virgin Undefiled,
  Mothers the Heaven-born Child.

IV. SON OF MARY.

  SHE the Mother was of One—
  Christ, her Saviour and her Son ;
  And another had she none ?
  Yea ; her Love's beloved—John.

V.   THE LAMB-CHILD.

WHEN Christ the Babe was born, full many a little
  lamb
Upon the wintry hills forlorn was nestled near its dam ;
And waking or asleep, upon his Mother's breast
For love of her, each mother-sheep and baby-lamb he
  blessed.

VI.   THE DEBTOR CHRIST.

WHAT, Woman, is my debt to thee,
  That I should not deny
The boon thou dost demand of me ?
  ' I gave thee power to die.'

VII.   STABAT MATER.

THE Star that in his splendour hid her own
  At Christ's nativity,
Abides—a widowed Satellite—alone
  On tearful Calvary.

VIII.   THE ASSUMPTION.

NOR Bethlehem, nor Nazareth
  Apart from Mary's care,
Nor heaven itself a home for him
  Were not his Mother there.

II.   MARY.

MAID-MOTHER of Humanity Divine,
  Alone thou art in thy supremacy,
  Since God himself did reverence to thee
And built of flesh a temple one with thine,
Wherein, through all eternity, to shrine
  His inexpressive glory.   Blessed be
  The miracle of thy maternity,

Of grace the sole immaculate design.
  Lo, earth and heaven—the footstool and the throne
Of him who bowed obedient to thy sway,
  What time in lowly Nazareth, unknown,
He led of life the long-secluded way—
  Pause, till their tongues are tutored of thine own
' Magnificat ' in wondering love to say.

III.   THE SONG OF THE MAN.

' THE woman gave, and I did eat.'
  Whereof gave she ?
' 'Twas of the garden fruitage sweet—
  A portion fair to see ;
She plucked and ate, and I did eat,
  And lost alike are we ; '
      God saith,
    ' Ye die the death.'

' The Woman gave, and I did eat.'
  Whereof gave she ?
' 'Twas of her womb a Burden sweet—
  But sad, alas, to see ;
She took and ate, and I did eat,
  And saved alike are we ; '
      God saith,
    ' So dieth death.'

IV.   ' FIAT.'

' FIAT ' : the flaming word
Flashed, as the brooding Bird
Uttered the doom far heard
    Of death and night.

' Fiat ' : a cloistered Womb,
A sealed, untainted tomb,
Wakes to the birth and bloom
  Of life and light.

V.   MOTHER-BIRD AND FLEDGLING.

Behold, the Mother-bird
The Fledgling's voice hath heard ;
  He calls anew,
  It was thy breast
  That warmed the nest
  From whence I flew.
Upon a loftier tree
Of life I wait for thee ;
Rise Mother-dove and come,
Thy Fledgling calls thee home.

The Palace of Art.

ALFRED, LORD TENNYSON: 1809—1892.

FROM 'POEMS,' PUBLISHED IN 1832.

. ' I send you here a sort of Allegory.' (*Author.*)

I.

I BUILT my Soul a lordly Pleasure-house,
  Wherein at ease for aye to dwell :
I said, ' O Soul, make merry and carouse,
  Dear Soul, for all is well.'

*   *   *

To which my Soul made answer readily :
  ' Trust me ; in bliss I shall abide
In this great Mansion, that is built for me,
  So royal-rich and wide.'

II.

FULL of great rooms and small the Palace stood,
    All various, each a perfect whole
From living Nature, fit for every mood
    And change of my still Soul.

For some were hung with arras green and blue,
    Showing a gaudy summer-morn,
Where with puffed cheek the belted hunter blew
    His wreathed bugle-horn.

      *   *   *

And one, an English home—gray twilight poured
    On dewy pastures, dewy trees,
Softer than sleep—all things in order stored,
    A haunt of ancient Peace.

Nor these alone ; but every landscape fair,
    As fit for every mood of mind,
Or gay, or grave, or sweet, or stern was there,
    Not less than Truth designed.

      *   *   *

Or the Maid-Mother by a Crucifix,
    In tracts of pasture sunny-warm,
Beneath branch-work of costly sardonyx
    Sat smiling, Babe in arm.

III.

SINGING and murmuring in her feastful mirth,
    Joying to feel herself alive,
Lord over Nature, Lord of the visible Earth,
    Lord of the Senses five ;

Communing with herself : 'All these are mine,
    And let the world have peace or wars,
'Tis one to me.'

IV.

FULL oft the riddle of the painful earth
    Flashed through her as she sat alone,
Yet not the less held she her solemn mirth,
    And intellectual throne.

And so she throve and prospered ; so three years
    She prospered : on the fourth she fell—
Like Herod, when the shout was in his ears,
    Struck through with pangs of hell.

*   *   *

So when four years were wholly finished,
    She threw her royal robes away.
' Make me a cottage in the vale,' she said,
    ' Where I may mourn and pray :

' Yet pull not down my Palace-towers, that are
    So lightly, beautifully built :
Perchance I may return with others there
    When I have purged my guilt.'

Assumpta Maria.

FRANCIS THOMPSON.

FROM ' NEW POEMS,' 1897.

' Thou need'st not sing new songs, but say the old.' (*Cowley.*)

' MORTALS, that behold a Woman
    Rising 'twixt the moon and sun ;
Who am I the heavens assume ? an
    All am I, and I am One.'

Multitudinous ascend I,
    Dreadful as a battle arrayed,
For I bear you whither tend I ;
    Ye are I : be undismayed :

I, the Ark that for the graven
  Tables of the Law was made ;
Man's own heart was one, one heaven,
  Both within my womb were laid
      For there Anteros with Eros
        Heaven with man conjoinèd was,
        Twin-stone of the Law, Ischyros,
          Agios Athanatos.

I, the flesh-girt Paradises
  Gardenered by the Adam New,
Daintied o'er with sweet devices
  Which he loveth, for he grew :
I, the boundless strict Savannah
  Which God's leaping feet go through ;
I, the Heaven whence the Manna,
  Weary Israel, slid on you.
      He the Anteros and Eros,
        I the Body, he the Cross ;
      He upbeareth me, Ischyros,
          Agios Athanatos.

I am Daniel's mystic Mountain,
  Whence the mighty Stone was rolled ;
I am the four Rivers' Fountain,
  Watering Paradise of old ;
Cloud down-raining the Just One am,
  Danae of the Shower of Gold ;
I the Hostel of the Sun am ;
  He the Lamb and I the Fold.
      He the Anteros and Eros,
        I the Body, he the Cross ;
      He is fast to me, Ischyros,
          Agios Athanatos.

I, the Presence-hall where angels
  Do enwheel their placèd King—
Even my thoughts which, without change else,
  Cyclic burn and cyclic sing :
To the hollow of heaven transplanted,
  I a breathing Eden spring
Where the venom all outpanted
  Lies the slimed Curse shrivelling.
      For the brazen Serpent clear on
        That old-fangèd knowledge shone ;
      I to Wisdom rise, Ischyron,
        Agion Athanaton.

See in highest heaven pavilioned
  Now the Maiden Heaven rest,
The many-breasted sky out-millioned
  By the splendours of her vest :
Lo, the Ark this holy tide is
  The un-handmade Temple's guest,
And the dark Egyptian Bride is
  Whitely to the Spouse-heart prest.
      He, the Anteros and Eros,
        Nail me to thee, sweetest Cross :
      He is fast to me, Ischyros,
        Agios Athanatos.

'Tell me, tell me, O Belovèd,
  Where thou dost in mid-day feed :
For my wanderings are reprovèd,
  And my heart is salt with need.'
'Thine own self not spellest God in,
  Nor the lisping papyrus reed?
Follow where the flocks have trodden,
  Follow where the shepherds lead.'

He, the Anteros and Eros,
　　Mounts me in Egyptic car,
'Twin-yoked ; leading me, Ischyros,
　　Trembling to the untempted far.

' Make me chainlets, silvern, golden,
　　I that sow shall surely reap ;
While as yet my Spouse is holden
　　Like a lion in mountained sleep.'
' Make her chainlets, silvern, golden,
　　She hath sown and she shall reap ;
Look up to the mountains olden,
　　Whence help comes with lioned leap.'
　　　　By what gushed the bitter Spear on,
　　　　　　Pain, which sundered, maketh one ;
　　　　Crucified to him, Ischyron,
　　　　　　Agion Athanaton.

Then commanded and spake to me
　　He who framed all things that be ;
And my Maker entered through me,
　　In my tent his rest took he :
Lo, he standeth, Spouse and Brother,
　　I to him, and he to me,
Who upraised me where my Mother
　　Fell, beneath the apple-tree.
　　　　Risen 'twixt Anteros and Eros,
　　　　　　Blood and Water, moon and sun,
　　　　He upbears me, he Ischyros,
　　　　　　I bear him, the Athanaton.

Where is laid the Lord arisen ?
　　In the light we walk in gloom ;
Though the Sun has burst his prison,
　　We know not his biding-room :

Tell us where the Lord sojourneth,
　For we find an empty tomb?
'Whence he sprung, there he returneth,
　Mystic Sun—the Virgin's Womb.'
　　　　Hidden Sun, his beams so near us,
　　　　Cloud enpillared as he was
　　　　From of old, there he, Ischyros,
　　　　Waits our search, Athanatos.

Who will give him me for Brother,
　Counted of my family,
Sucking the sweet breasts of my Mother?
　I his Flesh, and mine is he;
To my Bread myself the bread is,
　And my Wine doth drink me; see,
His left hand beneath my head is,
　His right hand embraceth me.
　　　　Sweetest Anteros and Eros,
　　　　　Lo, her arms he leans across;
　　　　Dead that we die not, stooped to rear us,
　　　　Thanatos Athanatos.

Who is she, in candid vesture,
　Rushing up from out the brine?
Treading with resilient gesture
　Air, and with that Cup divine?
She in us and we in her are,
　Beating Godward; all that pine
Lo, a wonder and a terror;
　The Sun hath blushed the Sea to Wine.
　　　　He, the Anteros and Eros,
　　　　　She the Bride and Spirit; for
　　　　Now the days of promise near us,
　　　　And the sea shall be no more.

Open wide thy gates, O Virgin,
  That the King may enter thee :
At all gates the clangours gurge in,
  God's paludament lightens, see :
Camp of Angels ; well we even
  Of this thing may doubtful be—
If thou art assumed to heaven ;
  Or is heaven assumed to thee ?
      Consummatum : Christ, the Promised,
        Thy maiden·realm is won, O Strong ;
      Since to such sweet kingdom comest,
        Remember me, poor Thief of Song.

Cadent fails the stars along :
  ' Mortals, that behold a Woman
    Rising 'twixt the moon and sun ;
Who am I the heavens assume ? an
    All am I, and I am One.'

ſive 'ꟁew ꟁaꬸonnas.'

WILLIAM HENRY THORNE.

FROM THE 'GLOBE REVIEW,' NEW YORK, 1898.

I. AFTERGLOW OF LOVING GLORY.

THROUGH many weary centuries thy race
  Did battle bravely for the Truth divine
  Which did, at length, through thy rare beauty shine ;
And with ineffable and perfect grace,
More radiant grows, as thy most radiant face
  Of perfect love—we never may define—
  Inspires to Motherhood like unto thine,
Yet unlike thine, in all created space

For through the centuries' ever-onward flow,
  Not once again, in all the tides of time,
Shall God's own perfect, golden Afterglow
  Of loving glory, from its source sublime,
Find such a heart of chastened, whitest snow,
  Through which to breathe its God-like overflow.

II. WEDDED UNTO THEE.

CHOICE Motherhood of all the human race,
  What dreams were thine unto that vital morn
  When Love itself, upon its bugle-horn
Far heralded the sweet majestic grace
That since hath shone in thy rich, glowing face,
  And still shall shine until the race forlorn
  Hath learned the Sweetness that through thee was born
That day, whence all earth and heaven shall trace

The very stars with glory—till the sea,
  The sun-wreathed world, and all the arts of song
Unite in everlasting harmony,
  And lift earth's millions into one vast throng
Of choral singers, wedded unto thee,
  In love's own music of eternity.

III. LOVE'S FULLEST TIDE.

IF ever Love was beautiful, in thee
  It found Love's fullest tide of beauty--far
  Beyond all earthly taint or human scar :
As is the faultless rose, the crested sea,
The silver dawn, the day's own destiny
  Of fadeless glory, and the one brave star
  That heeds nor storm, nor wreck, nor bloody war,
But holds its way unto eternity.

So shines thy stainless love, O Love, for me ;
  And when life's stormy billows o'er me roll,
And human madness seems as fierce and free
  As demon-wreckers of the stranded soul,
I call from out the depths to thee, mine own,
  And know that thy dear love will aye atone.

IV. THE LIFE INEFFABLE.

DEAR Heavenly Maiden, in thy heart, aglow
  With all the dreams of past and future time,
  There dwelt the Life ineffable, sublime,
That marks God's own supremest overflow
Of life and love—the rarest we may know.
  Of all his vintage—the celestial wine
  Of love's immortal sacrifice divine,
The joy of joys whence all our glories grow.

Sweet Motherhood, thy lustre o'er the stars
  Hath shed a radiance that is not their own ;
And over all our bloody, human wars
  Of greed and hate and passion there hath grown
A charity far deeper than their scars,
  And still shall grow till war is overthrown.

V. GOD'S OWN LOVINGNESS.

IT seems to me that even with God's light
  Omniscient, and with his power sublime,
  There was not, in eternity or time,
Another way, so sweet, so pure, so bright,
So sure to win the utmost love and might
  Of constancy in human souls, would climb
  The heights celestial, set the stars to chime
Love's melodies of joy, attain the right

In each highest ideal human dream
And crowd the skies with loving souls redeemed—
As that the central Sweetness of the gleam
Of God's own lovingness, by all beteemed
Ineffable—our Loveliest should find,
And through her grace the countless ages bind.

ffrom the Towneley Mysteries
XIV CENTURY.

MODERNISED BY F. M. CAPES.

DIVINE COLLOQUY BETWEEN JESUS, MARY AND JOHN.

FROM 'THE NINETEENTH CENTURY,' 1883.

The following extracts are taken from 'Crucifixio,' a Miracle Play, published by the Surtees Society, 1836.

JESUS FROM THE CROSS.

I PRAY you, People, that pass by,
That lead your life so thoughtlessly,
　　Heave up your hearts on high ;
Behold, if ever ye saw body
Suffer and beat thus bloody,
　　Or yet thus doleful dight ?

　　　　＊　　.　＊　　　　＊

All creatures on this earth that roam,
Birds, beasts, all kinds, they have their home
　　When they are woe-begone ;
But God's own Son, that should be best,
Hath not whereon his Head to rest
　　But on his shoulder-bone.

　　　　＊　　　　＊　　　　＊

My Brother, that I came to buy,
Hath hanged me here thus hideously,
 And friends are foes become ;
They have thus dight me drearily,
And all bespit me spitefully,
 An helpless Man, all lone.

  * * *

MARY.

Alas, the dole I dree, I droop, I quake with dread.
All blemished is thy hue ; I see thy Body bleed.
Why hang thou, Son, so high ? My grief begins to
 flow.
Never, Son, in this world had we such madd'ning
 woe.
  My Offspring that I've fed,
  Through life along have led,
  Full straitly thou'rt bestead
   Among thy foemen fell.
  Such sorrows for to see,
  My dearest Bairn, in thee
  Is mourning more to me
   Than any tongue may tell.
  Alas, thy holy Head
  Has no upholding bed ;
  Thy Face with Blood is red,
   Was fair as flower in field.
  How can I stand indeed,
  To see my Bairn thus bleed,
  Beat as blue as lead,
   And have no limb to wield ?

  * * *

JOHN.

Comely Lady, good and kind, fain would I comfort
    thee :
Me minds, my Master with his mouth told to his
    company,
That he should thole full mickle pain and die upon
    a Tree,
And to the life rise up again—the third day should
    it be.
        Therefore, my Lady sweet,
        Forbear awhile to greet :
        Our pain he will relieve,
        As he did promise give.

MARY.

My sorrow is so sad, no solace may me save,
Mourning makes me mad, no hope of help I have ;
Nought may make me glad, till I be in my grave.
        To death my Dear is driven,
        His robe is all-to riven
        That of me was him given,
        And shaped by mine own sides.
Alas, my comely Child, why wilt thou from me go ?
        Maidens, make your moan,
        And weep, ye Wives, each one,
        With wretched me all lone.
        My Child, of all the first,
My heart is stiff as stone, that for no grief will burst.

       *   *   *

JESUS.

My Mother mild, now change thy cheer,
Cease of thy sorrow and sighing sere ;
    It sits upon my heart full sore.

DD

The sorrow 's sharp I suffer here ;
But dole thou drees, my Mother dear,
   Martyrs me mickle more.
Take there John unto thy Child—
   Mankind must needs be bought—
And thou her kin now be in thought,
John ; lo, there thy Mother mild.

       *   *   *

Such life forsooth I led, that scarcely may I more,
   This thole I for thy need,
   To give thee, Man, thy meed—
Now thirst I wondrous sore.

NOTES.

Lines 6 and 16 : Dight ; treated.
   19 and 64 : Dole ; sorrow : Dree ; suffer.
   25 : Bestead ; placed.
   41 and 71 : Thole ; endure.

Mater Dei and other Lyrics.

KATHERINE TYNAN HINKSON.

FROM 'THE AVE MARIA,' 1895.

I. MATER DEI.

SHE looked to East, she looked to West,
   Her eyes unfathomable, mild,
That saw both worlds, came home to rest—
   Home to her own sweet Child :
God's golden Head was at her breast.

What need to look o'er land and sea?
   What could the winged ships bring to her?
What gold or gems of price might be,
   Ivory or miniver,
Since God himself lay on her knee?

What could th' intense blue heaven keep
  To draw her eyes and thoughts so high?
All heaven was where her Boy did leap,
  Where her foot quietly
Went rocking the dear God asleep.

The angel-folk fared up and down;
  A Jacob's Ladder hung between
Her quiet chamber and God's town:
  She saw unawed, serene;
Her God himself played by her gown.

II. THE KING'S ALMONER.

Who is she cometh forth
  Twelve stars crowning her,
In her hands gifts of worth,
  Moonlight gowning her?
She is the King's Almoner,
  The King's purse hers to hold,
  Broidered with gems and gold—
Wonder past compare.

Why so young, why so fair?
  King's almoners are grave
Old men in miniver,
  Lutestring and ermine brave,
Velvet hoods on their hair;
  Old wise heads, still and gray;
  All unlike her are they—
Whence this King's Almoner?

Know you not whence and where
  Comes the King's Almoner,—
Mary, beyond compare?
  All hearts shall turn to her.

Queen, who in stable bare
  Kissed thy New-born Son,
  Hear me, Most Holy One,
Bounteous King's Almoner.

Mother of Heaven's King,
  Bounteous King's Almoner,
Ope to my needy prayer
  Thy purse, O Purse-bearer:
Give me what I entreat
  From thy Son's gems and gold,
  That I my babe behold
Safe out of darkness, Sweet.

III. ON A FEAST OF OUR LADY.

THE Lady of Good Counsel, she
  Leaneth her ear untiringly.
Sweet is the counsel of her mouth—
Sweeter than odours of the South
In some untravelled, purple sea.

About her knees she gathereth
Her folk perplext with life and death ;
  Stauncheth the tears that flow like rain,
  Maketh the light and darkness plain,
Bloweth off trouble with her breath.

In every one her Son she sees,
Therefore the world her baby is,
  That like a hurt and frightened child,
  Sobs on her breast the Undefiled,
Or hides its face upon her knees.

And none shall fear to hear her say :
'You would not hear another day,
  But went your way, and so are sad.'
  Seeing you come, she will be glad—
That is our sweet-heart Lady's way.

Harbinger of the Day-Star's rise,
Star of our rainy April skies,
  Shine through the mists and light our way,
  And chiefly those whose footsteps stray
Far from thy counsel and thine eyes.

IV. THE DREAM OF MARY.

From an Ancient Welsh traditional Poem.

'MARY, Mother, art thou asleep?'
  'Nay, dear Son, but waking and dreaming.'
'Mary, Mother, why dost thou weep?'
  'I saw thy dear Blood flowing and streaming.'

'Mary, Mother, tell me thy dream.'
  'Blessed Son, thou wert trapped and taken,
Scourged with stripes in a hall didst seem,
  Mocked with laughter, despised, forsaken.'

'Blessed Mother, thy dream tell all.'
  'Blessed Son, on a Cross wert lying,
While a black, blind knave from the hall
  Pierced thy Heart that was warm from dying.'

'Mary, Mother, thy dream is true;
  True thy dreaming, sad Mother Mary;
Whether the years be many or few,
  Still the hunters gain on the quarry.'

Over a hill, and a cold, cold hill,
  I saw Mary dreaming and weeping,
Making a space betwixt souls and ill,
  Snatching men from hell and its keeping.

Ode on the Annunciation.

AUBREY DE VERE.

FROM 'POEMS,' 1855.

SUBSIDING from those heavenly wings the air
Lies motionless : yet on that forehead fair
Still hangs a pearly gloom, as if the shade
Of those departing pinions
On her brow were stayed.
Still sits she on that virgin bed
From which so late she reared her head ;
Forward she bends in prayer.
Her hands upon her heart are crossed ;
Her heart in heavenly vision lost ;
Her silver lids are closing—mark
A tear is trembling on their lashes dark.
It falls : to earth that tear is given ;
That sigh an echo finds in heaven.

O Joyful Virgin, henceforth blessed ever
Among all nations, cause for joy thou hast ;
Not vain henceforth shall prove man's great endeavour ;
Henceforth no more his Future
Shall be but as the Past :
Henceforward wise, good men
Shall toil no more in vain
The seeds of Hope and Love and Peace to sow
Among their kind below.
Faith, mover of the mountains,
From earth's o'er-burdened heart
The Sinai mount at last shall raise :
The Law hath done its part ;

Henceforth men shall not gaze
On the stars with blank amaze,
And vainly pine for wings to bear them
From the tumult of Life's mart.
No more self-caused afflictions;
No more self-willed transgressions;
But Gladness, Benedictions,
And humbly-toned Confessions;
And anthem and loud hymn
Sent up from earth responsive to the harping Cherubim.

Are such the thoughts whose radiant trains are passing,
Thrice-hallowed Virgin, through that pure, calm breast
Which swells to meet them, as the ocean glassing
In its tide-wave those splendours
That woke it from its rest?
Knowledge with men is stored
By many a slow degree;
But all thy shining lore is poured
In a gentle stream on thee.
'Tis Hope thy brow doth gird
With that second, heavenlier bow:
'Tis Love that, breathing hymns unheard,
Warms sweetly with faint crimson
Thy lips through which they flow.
Thou tastest first the joy of all thy kind:
Grace first in thee fulfils her earthly mission;
Thy tearful eyes, to outward objects blind,
Of God and Heaven have deep and full fruition.
O Second Eve: but she
Said not, ' Even as thy Word, so be it unto me.'

Mournful till now to the o'er-experienced ear,
Mournful were all the harmonies of earth,
As Autumn's dirge over the dying Year:

Yea, more than sadness blended
With melodies of mirth.
The ocean, murmuring on the shore,
Breathed inland far a sad 'no more':
The winds but left their midnight cells
To fill the day with lorn 'farewells.'
'Tis o'er. The reign of force is o'er:
The arm of flesh is Lord no longer:
More dear henceforth is peace than war:
The weak henceforward is the stronger.
Earth's fountains, touched by breath Divine,
Gush up, henceforth, in bridal wine:
Now children (creatures lowly)
Point upward to the sky:
Honour henceforth is holy,
And Virgin Purity.
In star-pierced thickets the night-bird
Translates henceforth each rapturous word
That she all day in Heaven hath heard—
Peace, peace; misdoubting Earth, be dumb:
Her Christ his power shall take: his kingdom it shall
    come.

Lo, round her feet celestial flowers are lying:
The breath pathetic of those mild perfumes,
Comes it from them, or from her blessed sighing?
Lo, silver gleams alternate
With diviner glooms.
The air, at every pore alive,
Sings like the golden murmur of the hive:
All round a paradisal light is glowing:
Down, down the Virgin sinks by slow degrees:
Her tender hands unfold; her tresses flowing
O'er that declining brow, upon her knees.

Daughter of God, Mother-Elect, low-bent
She kneels ; and adoration is consent.
Two beams of Light, down-shining from above,
Fall, on her bosom one, one on her head ;
Between those two great beams on plumes outspread,
Hovers and gleams the Everlasting Dove.

Verses with Personal Associations.

I. A MEMORY OF ONE WHO WAS NOT A CATHOLIC.

ANONYMOUS.

FROM ' THE CATHOLIC WORLD,' 1872.

'TWAS only a prayer I heard
  In that vast Cathedral grim,
Where the incense filled the air
  And vesper lights burnt dim.
'Twas only a woman's form,
  Kneeling with upturned face
That looked through the pictured altar
  Up to the Throne of grace.
Clasped in her small white hands
  An amber rosary telling,
While from her glorious eyes
  Tear-drops fast were welling.
No thought for the world without,
  No thought for the stranger near,
As pausing and sobbing she murmured,
  ' O Mother of Sorrows, hear.'
And I, in a land of strangers,
  Joined in the pleader's prayer ;
Praying for her that I knew not,
  To her who I felt was there.

II. THE PAINTER.

C. W. BARRAUD, S.J.

FROM 'THE MESSENGER OF THE SACRED HEART,' U.S.A., 1898.

A FORM of heavenly loveliness, a face
That stirred the still depths of the unfathomed heart—
Words may not utter what the painter's art,
To lend thine Image in God's holy place,
Had borrowed of his love, O Full of Grace.
Long had he knelt within the minster gray
Ere venturing those features to essay.
But now 'tis done, and back he strides a pace
Along the dizzy plank, and yet another,
Eyeing his work.   Great God ; he slips—he falls ;
And falling shrieks, as young birds in the nest,
When the tree totters, clamour to their mother.
So he to thee ; and from those living walls
Thine arms stretch forth and clasp him to thy breast.

III. BRIJINDOPE—THE DELUGE:

BEGINNING AND ENDING OF A GIPSY POEM.

TRANSLATED BY GEORGE BORROW:

1803—1881.

FROM 'ZINCALI, THE GIPSIES OF SPAIN,' 1841.

I WITH fear and terror quake,
Whilst the pen to write I take ;
I will utter many a prayer
To the Heaven's Regent fair,
That she deign to succour me,
And I'll humbly bend my knee ;

For but poorly do I know
With my subject on to go ;
Therefore is my wisest plan
Not to trust in strength of man.
I my heavy sins bewail,
Whilst I view the woe and wail
Handed down so solemnly
In the book of times gone by.
Onward, onward, now I'll move
In the Name of Christ above,
And his Mother true and dear,
She who loves the wretch to cheer,
All I know and all I've heard
I will state—how God appeared,
And to Noah thus did cry :
'Weary with the world am I ;
Let an Ark by thee be built
For the world is lost in guilt ;
And when thou hast built it well,
Loud proclaim what now I tell :
Straight repent ye, for your Lord
In his hand doth hold a sword.'

*   *   *

In this manner wend they all,
And the seeds of nations lay.
I beseech ye'll credence pay,
For our Father, high and sage,
Wrote the tale in sacred page,
As a record to the world,
Record sad of vengeance hurled.
I, a low and humble wight,
Beg permission now to write

Unto all that in our land
Tongue Egyptian understand.
May our Virgin Mother mild
Grant to me, her erring child,
Plenteous grace in every way,
And success.   Amen, I say.

NOTE.

PRAYER TO THE VIRGIN, IN THE GITANO LANGUAGE.

O most Holy Virgin, Mother of all Christians, in whom I
believe, for the agony which thou didst endure at the foot of the
Cross of thy most Blessed Son, I entreat thee, Virgin, that thou wilt
obtain for me, from thy Son, the remission of all the crimes and
sins which I may have committed in this world.   Amen, Jesus.
(Author.)

IV.   ST. LUKE.

ARTHUR CORNWALLIS.

FROM 'ST. LUKE'S MAGAZINE,' 1895.

ARTIST, Physician and Evangelist,
   Who didst in precious parables express
   The Saviour's mercy, and his tenderness ;
We seek thy patronage, sweet Hellenist :
Whose radiant pen illumed the life of Christ,
   Who bore our sins and made our sorrows less,
   And did, through thee, endow his Church and bless
With peace and light to penetrate the mist.

Thy pencil on the canvas did pourtray
   The saintly features of the Virgin-Queen ;
   To balm her name and keep her memory green,
Thou sung her glories in a triple lay :
   No sweeter canticles have ever been
Than thine, whose praise shall never pass away.

V. FIRST PERFORMANCE OF PERGOLESE'S 'STABAT MATER.'

EMMANUEL GEIBEL : 1815—1884.

TRANSLATED BY CHARLOTTE O'CONOR ECCLES.

FROM 'THE IRISH MONTHLY,' 1889.

THE pious work at last completed,
The Master, at the organ seated,
   Pours his thanks to God's high Throne :
Solemn swell, like spirit marches
Through the vast Cathedral's arches,
    Sweetest song and organ tone—
    Stabat Mater dolorosa.

Of the Virgin Mary's sorrow
Human hearts a knowledge borrow,
   With the organ's louder swell :
At the deep-toned angel-voices
E'en the weariest soul rejoices,
    Eyes long dry the soft tears fill—
    Quis est homo qui non fleret.

Pious trembling, terror holy
Wrap the Master's soul, and slowly
   Death's forebodings, grave and mild :
While with faith and deep devotion,
Turn his eyes with upward motion
    To the pictured Maid and Child—
    Virgo virginum præclara.

Hark, those sounds, the Seraphs' singing,
Soft and sweet in chorus ringing,
   As to earth they slow descend :
Now they rise to heaven faster,
Bearing in their flight their Master,

And the song peals without end—
Christe, cum sit hinc exire,
Da per Matrem me venire
Ad palmam victoriæ.

NOTE.

'Stabat Mater,' the last and best work of Pergolese, was written for soprano and alto voices, with strings and organ. The Master died from pulmonary consumption, aged 26 years, a few days after its completion, at Pozzuoli, near Naples, 17 April, 1736.

VI. GOETHE'S DEATH.

FROM 'THE LAMP,' 1877.

FAINTER and fainter grew his breath;
His hour had come—the hour of death.
'Oh, see,' the dying poet said,
'The Woman with the lovely head.'
Sweet Virgin Mother, ever dear,
Oh, tell me, didst thou linger near?

Death's shadows close and closer crept;
And ere his last the poet slept
He faintly uttered, 'Light; more light':
Then silence fell and all was night.
Had Light come down and kissed him there?
Or were his dying words a prayer?

VII. THE FOUNTAIN OF LIFE:

THOUGHTS ON THE IMMACULATE CONCEPTION.

LAURENCE HOUSMAN.

FROM 'SPIKENARD,' 1898.

The Soul speaks:

THINE Earth, O Lord, is full of grief;
Thy Heaven is full of Love:
Tell me what power it was in chief
Which drew thee from above?

Where Love stands ever, all in all,
    No entrance is for grief :
Say then, how came to thee the call
    That won the world's relief?
Since nothing mortal grief may move
    Wholly to cast out fear ;
How came the marvel, that pure Love
    Could ever enter here ?

Love answers :

Love said : One Law ordains relief
    All other laws above,
That earth cannot contain its grief,
    Nor Heaven contain its Love :
So from the grief which has to mount,
    The Love which has to run,
There fills and flows a Living Fount
    Till Earth and Heaven be one.

Envoy :

O SINLESS Love that cast out dread ;
    O Grace that let God in ;
Heaven formed of thee its Fountain-head
    To wash the world of sin.

VIII. DEATH OF ST. JOSEPH.
A. M. M.: 1834—1898.

FROM AN UNFINISHED, PARTIALLY PRINTED, AND UNPUBLISHED
POEM, 'THE PRINCE OF LIFE,' 1898.

The last work of the Author, sent by him in MS. to the Editor.

In Memoriam.

Now thrice ten summers from the silent hills
Departed, lo, the Three were Twain.   How fell
The stroke, what sickness to the threshold came,
And when the hour of passing, none may read,

But all may deem whose eyelids have known tears.
As through the valley of the shadow of death
Abel had passed, and Abraham, God's Friend,
And righteous Joseph, one in name and soul,
And David, Minstrel-King, to whom in blood
The Prince of Princes traced far ancestry—
So, from his place, the Foster-father went,
Through the same valley of the shadow, home.
As there were tears for Israel's ancient dead,
So by the Corse the Son and Mother mourned.
Thoughts of the love that was the Childhood's guard,
Nurtured the Boyhood, and beheld with awe
The Wisdom growing with the stature's growth,
Kindled to words. Blest Mary praised the life,
Virgin with Virgin, lived so long, so well,
For the Maid-Mother and the Foster-Child
To work and wait, in silence, all its joy;
Twin Guardian-angel of the Word-made-Flesh,
Spirit with spirit, through the shadowy vale
She fared, scarce conscious that the staff and rod,
The parted Soul's one comfort, were of him
Who, in a lowly workman's toil-stained garb,
Beside her listened, weeping wordless tears.

IX. IN A COUNTRY CHURCHYARD ON
'MEMORIAL DAY,' U.S.A.

MARY E. MANNIX.

FROM 'THE AVE MARIA,' 1889.

AVE, Maria, low they lie
Under the blue and smiling sky;
Roses blossom and grasses wave
Over each faithful soldier's grave:
    While we scatter the flowers of May,
    Sancta Maria, for them pray.

Ave, Maria, guard their rest :
Whether shriven, or unconfessed,
They died the death that martyrs die ;
Mercy never has passed them by :
 While we scatter the flowers of May,
 Sancta Maria, for them pray.

X. RAPHAEL'S DEATH-BED: A FRAGMENT.

GEORGE H. MILES : 1824—1871.

FROM 'CHRISTINE,' 1866.

Raphael speaks :

   WHAT ; Leo's self has sent
To ask of Raphael ? Kindly done ; and yet
The Iron Pontiff, whom I painted thrice,
Had come. No matter : these are gracious words,
' Rome were not Rome without me.' My best thanks
Back to his Holiness ; and dare I add
A message, 'twere that Rome can never be
Without me. I shall live as long as Rome.
Bramante's temple there, bequeathed to me
To hide her cross-crowned bosom in the clouds—
San Pietro, travertine and marble-massed
To more than mountain majesty—shall scarce
Outlast that bit of canvas. Let the light in.
There's the Ritonda waiting patiently
My coming. Angelo has built his chape
In Santa Croce, that his eyes may ope
On Ser Filippo's Duomo. I would see—
What think you ?—neither Dome, nor Giotto's shaft,
Nor yon stern Pantheon's solemn sullen grace,
But her, whose colours I have worn, since first
EE

I dreamed of beauty in the chestnut shades
Of Umbria—her, for whom my best of life
Has been one labour—her, the Nazareth-Maid,
Who gave to Heaven a Queen, to man a God,
To God a Mother.   I have hope of it :
And I would see her—not as when she props
The Babe slow tottering to the Cross amid
The flowering field ; nor yet when Sibyl-eyed,
Backward she sweeps her Son from Tobit's Fish ;
Nor e'en as when above the footstool-angels,
She stands with trembling mouth, dilated eyes,
Abashed before the uncurtained Father's throne—
But see her wearing the wrapt smile of love
Half human, half divine, as fast she strains
Her Infant in the Chair.

NOTE.

Line 15 : Chape ; a Shakesperian word, the catch of anything
by which it is held ; a sheath, cope, or covering ; hence, a place of
burial.

XI. PRAYER OF A PRISONER,
WRONGLY CONDEMNED, THE SON OF
A PIOUS MOTHER.

MARY McMULLEN ('*UNA*'): 1844—1876.

FROM 'SNATCHES OF SONG,' 1874.

O QUEEN of Mercy, who didst stand
    Beside the Sacred Rood
When earth in giddy horror reeled,
    Drunk with her Maker's Blood ;
When darkness veiled the noontide sun,
    And through the inky pall

Above the shrunken stars seemed tears
    That wished, but feared to fall.
O Pitiful, Compassionate,
    Behold my anguish wild :
My Mother loved thee—for her sake
    Protect her erring child.

O tender Soul, that bore a woe
    Whose weight might crush the world,
Behold me in the blackest depths
    Of direst ruin hurled ;
My sinful lips dare not pronounce
    The awful Name of him
Whose death-sigh shook the universe :
    So through the shadows dim
Of wrong and sorrow, hopefully
    I raise mine eyes to thee,
Whose aid was never sought in vain ;
    Oh, pray to him for me.

Pray ; and although upon his Blood,
    His Love, his Law I trod,
He will forgive if thou but plead—
    He is thy Son, though God :
Save for my honoured father's sake
    My name from felon brand ;
Though many are my sins, thou know'st
    No blood is on my hand.
O riven Heart, that 'neath the Cross
    Couldst pray for sinners, thou,
Though all the world may jeer and scoff,
    Wilt not forsake me now.

XII. A SORROW OF MARY'S.

OLIVE KATHARINE PARR.

MOTHER of God, I long to hear the story,
Of that sad day when thy dear Son left home
To enter on his public life of sorrow
    And meet the woe to come.

Oh, bitter day : the last day of that home-life,
So long, so sweet, so free from grief and pain ;
The dear home-life which earth or even heaven
    Can ne'er bring back again.

The last meal ended and the last word spoken,
Crossed, the last time, the threshold of the door,
The last sound of his feet along the road-way—
    His home knew him no more.

No sound, no touch : ears, lips and hands had lost him ;
'Thine eyes alone their sad task had not done;
Didst thou not strain to catch, O tender Mother,
    The last glimpse of thy Son ?

I wonder, was the heartless sunlight flooding
'That path which led the way to pain and death ?
And were the careless olive branches dancing,
    Stirred by the west wind's breath ?

Or haply, were the pitying heavens weeping ?
Did silv'ry mist veil from that path all light ?
Were not the gray-green olives hushed and trembling,
    As he passed out of sight ?

And then, didst thou seek out the silent chamber,
To look with tears upon the empty bed,
Knowing the Son of Man would have henceforward
    No place to lay his Head ?

Mother of God, I long to learn the story
Of that sad day when thy dear Son left home :
Pray that at last, from thine own lips to hear it,
    The time for me may come.

XIII. SONNET TO OUR LADY.
EMILE PÉHAUT.
TRANSLATED BY E. M. CLERKE.

Written when the Author was dying of hunger in Paris, in 1876.

BLEST Virgin, Mary, Morning Star benign,
From mine own mother comes my love for thee ;
To thee did her fond care my fate consign ;
Prove that her trust was no false fantasy.
Of unbelief long have I drunk the wine,
But bitter doth its cup now seem to me ;
Would that a place at God's high Feast were mine,
But I, late-comer, from his wrath must flee.
My pardon, Mother of our Saviour, gain,
Repentant hearts ne'er sue to thee in vain,
Our Refuge in despair art thou in sooth.
Since when for penitents thy prayers are won,
God the stern Judge forgets to be in ruth,
Remembering only that he is thy Son.

XIV. A WIDOW'S PRAYER: DONEGAL.
GEORGE NOBLE PLUNKETT.
FROM 'HIBERNIA,' 1883.

O MOTHER of pure Sorrows
    That make the young heart old,
Amid the Summer's promise,
    The hunger and the cold

From life all hope are draining,
    I would not fear to die—
But for my sinless baby
    Bid Heaven hear my cry.

Remember, Blessed Mother,
    How your own heart has bled
When your dear Jesus found not
    A refuge for his head :
When, on your bosom lying,
    He stretched a puny hand—
Ah, you will take my baby's,
    And his moan will understand.

His moan is my soul's prayer ;
    But take him to your breast,
But speak of him to Jesus,
    To whom I leave the rest :
And if he claims the blessing
    He gave, we shall not part ;
For my lone life's only flower
    Is rooted in my heart.

XV. MARGARET'S HYMN BEFORE THE IMAGE OF MARY.

JOHN EDMUND READE: 1800—1870.

FROM 'MEMNON AND OTHER POEMS,' 1868.

AVE, Maria, lowly kneeling,
    Hear my prayer before thy shrine ;
To thy Martyred Son appealing,
    Holy Virgin, aid be thine.

Thou hast suffered mortal sorrow ;
  Thou hast seen thy Son depart ;
Thou didst feel, when rose the morrow,
  All the Mother's breaking heart.

By those sorrows in complaining ;
  By the tears poured forth by thee ;
By the hope, thy soul sustaining—
  Give, oh, give thy grace to me.

Ave, Maria, lowly bending,
  Hear my prayer before thy shrine ;
By thy vows to heaven ascending,
  Holy Virgin, bend to mine.

XVI. THE MAN AND THE WOMAN :
TWO PICTURES.

EMILY MARY SHAPCOTE.
Written at Arenberg, 1890.

I. DEATH.

MID aromatic flowers reclines the man,
With all his wealth of intellect and grace
And converse sweet with God ; with all the power
To choose, or to refuse.
                    The woman given
To be his counterpart, his other self,
Conscious of guilt, asks him to share her sin.
' She shall not die alone' : her pleading eye
Half wistful, half afraid, tempts not—and yet, he falls.

II. LIFE.

BEHOLD, again, the Man, sin's Victim, lies
Stretched on the hard bed of the dreadful Cross.
No blandishments of woman here ; but meek,

Steadfast, courageous and resigned, the Woman stands.
'He must not die alone': but she, transfixed,
Will die with him; and dying, through his death,
Rise up the Co-redemptrix of her race.

NOTES.

I. l. 8. : Tempts not; 'Adam was not seduced; but the woman
being seduced, was in the transgression.' 1 Tim. ii. 14.

II. l. 6. : Will die with him; Our Lady, by 'compassion,' suffered
in all that her Son suffered. She had to suffer as the
New Mother of the Race. As Adam had elected to
come under the curse for Eve's sake, so Mary stood
beneath the Cross to share death with Jesus.

XVII. THE BLESSED VIRGIN'S EXPOSTULATION

WHEN OUR SAVIOUR, AT TWELVE YEARS OF AGE, HAD
WITHDRAWN HIMSELF.

NAHUM TATE: 1652—1715.

COPIED (1901) FROM 'A COLLECTION OF SONGS SET BY HENRY
PURCELL,' MS. K. 4, 9, IN CHRIST CHURCH LIBRARY, OXFORD.

The Author was born in Dublin, obtained the Laureateship in
1692, and died at Southwark. The Poem was eventually published
in 'Miscellanea Sacra,' edited by Nahum Tate, in 1698.

TELL me, some pitying Angel; quickly say
Where does my Soul's sweet Darling stray?
In tigers,' or more cruel Herod's way?
Ah, rather let his little footsteps press
Unregarded through the wilderness,
Where milder savages resort:
The desert's safer than a tyrant's court.
Why, fairest Object of my love,
Why dost thou from my longing eyes remove?

Was it a waking dream that did foretell
Thy wondrous birth? no vision from above?
Where's Gabriel now, that visited my cell?
Gabriel, I call; Gabriel, Gabriel . . .
He comes not: flattering hopes, farewell.
Me Judah's daughters once caressed,
Called me of mothers the most blest;
Now (fatal change) of mothers most distressed.
How shall my soul its motions guide?
How shall I stem the various tide
While faith and doubt my labouring soul divide?
For while of thy dear sight beguiled,
I trust the God; but oh, I fear the Child.

XVIII. TWO SONNETS FROM AMERICA.
UNKNOWN WRITERS.

I. TO F. W. FABER; A POET OF OUR BLESSED LADY.

FROM 'THE CATHOLIC WORLD,' 1878.

WITH thee, my Poet, lie our souls at rest
  In the soft glory of our Mother's smile—
  The Maid Immaculate, who could beguile
Her God to be a Child on her pure breast:
With thee we labour, that our little life
  Shall learn to lose itself, that it be found
  In that far, other life eternal crowned
'Mid Hero-saints, whose prayers were ours in strife;
Humbly with thee our dearest Lord before,
  Veiled in the little, pale and helpless round
  Wherein on earth he chooseth to be crowned,
We bend with love that yearneth to love more:
  Fond children at the Father's feet we kneel,
  Finding the love his Spirit doth reveal.

II.   AD MARIAM PRO MARIA.

FROM 'THE AVE MARIA,' 1888.

MOTHER of Sorrows we still call thee, though
    In Paradise thou reignest, tasting nought
    But perfect joy.   More comfort to our thought
Thy mortal sympathy with pain and woe.
Mother of Sorrows, it is mine to know
    One named from thee, of life so trial-fraught,
    Full sure am I of gracious purpose wrought,
For some rare fruit the destined hour will show.
But ah, she needs thy tender help—the might
    Of thy true heart to lean upon.   I trust
    My sister to thy keeping.   If she share
Thy desolation when the shades of night
    Came down on silent Calvary, 'tis just
    She find thy bosom her own refuge there.

from Verstegan's Odes: 1601.

EXTRACTS FROM THE SIBYLLIAN
PROPHECIES OF CHRIST.

RICHARD VERSTEGAN: XVI—XVII
CENTS.

Copied (1893) from one of three extant copies only which are
known to the Editor, in the Bodleian Library, Oxford, by Orby
Shipley, M.A.

SIBYLLA PERSICA.

THOU Serpent fraught with craft and cruelty
    Shalt by a mightier Strength be trodden low,
And on base earth, the High God born shall be
    And from a Maid the Branch of Bliss shall grow :
And that True Word, unseen before of all,
Shall now be seen, and shall be felt withal.

SIBYLLA LIBYCA.

In obscure darkness Light shall glistering shine ;
  The Synagogue's straight bands unbound shall be :
The King of Life be seen of mortal eyen
  And in a Maiden's Lap shall nourished be ;
And high above the Gentiles he shall reign,
And shall in mercy his estate maintain.

SIBYLLA DELPHICA.

Attend, O Earth, thy Sovereign Lord to see,
  And know thy God, which is God's only Son ;
Child of the Highest, and Most High is he,
  Whose being by no earthly wight begun ;
He shall the great expected Prophet be
Of worthy greatness, and great dignity.

SIBYLLA CUMÆA.

A Maid excelling all in sanctity,
  And whose clear beauty shall the stars exceed,
Of Child, in future time, conceived shall be,
  And of the rarest sacred Blood and Seed ;
And from the heavens the sweet dew down shall fall
Into her breasts to nourish him withal.

SIBYLLA ERITHREA.

In later age, High God will him abase,
  And unto low estate himself incline,
Mixing his Nature with our human race,
  His Godhead to our manhood to combine ;
And lo, the little Lamb, in strawy bed,
Shall of a Maid be nourishèd and fed.

SIBYLLA SAMIA.

O fond Judea, why dost thou neglect
  The certain knowledge of thy Very God ?

Thy happy days why dost thou so reject?
  Oh, why dost thou prepare for him a rod?
With thorny crown his head why dost thou press?
And for his taste a bitter potion dress?

SIBYLLA CUMANA.

WHAT time the third day's sleep had taken end,
  The time prescribèd also end shall take
Of death, whose rule to that space did extend,
  And then, as from his sleep, shall wax awake;
He whose now bringing life's revived joy,
Shall show how men from death may life enjoy.

SIBYLLA HELLESPONTIACA.

E'EN from the heavens' most high and stately throne
  The eyes of God the earth shall over-view,
And of all creatures take regard of One,
  Of modest meekness, and most gracious hue;
And as a Man-God shall be borne on earth,
And of a Hebrew Virgin have his birth.

SIBYLLA PHRYGIA.

THE earth shall rend at fearful trumpet sound,
  And kings as vassals at God's seat appear;
In Justice all his judgments shall abound,
  Yielding to men as men deserved here;
Unto the good, still-during heavenly joy,
And to the ill, long-lasting hell's annoy.

SIBYLLA TIBURTINA.

THOU, Bethlehem, art the birth-place of thy Lord,
  That doth from Nazareth assume his name;
O Blessed Mother, bliss doth thee afford
  His love, that leaves himself pledge of the same;
Oh, blessed be that sweet milk-yielding breast,
To nourish God, right happily addressed.

Villon's Ballad: 1431—1463:

THAT HE (FRANÇOIS DE MONTCORBIER) MADE AT THE REQUEST OF HIS MOTHER, WHEREWITHAL TO DO HOMAGE TO OUR LADY.

TRANSLATED (1874) *BY JOHN PAYNE*
FOR THE VILLON SOCIETY.

FROM 'THE POEMS OF MASTER FRANÇOIS VILLON OF PARIS,' 1892.

THE GREATER TESTAMENT OF THE POET.

I GIVE the Ballad following
   To my good Mother—who of me
(God knows) hath had much sorrowing—
   That she may worship our Ladie :
   I have no other sanctuary
Whereunto, when overcome with dole,
   I may for help and comfort flee ;
Nor hath my Mother, poor good soul.

BALLAD.

LADY of Heaven, Regent of the Earth,
   Empress of all the infernal marshes fell,
Receive me, thy poor Christian, 'spite my dearth,
   In the fair midst of thine elect to dwell :
   Albeit my lack of grace I know full well ;
For that thy grace, my Lady and my Queen,
Aboundeth more than all my misdemean,
   Withouten which no soul of all that sigh
May merit heaven. 'Tis sooth I say, for e'en
   In this belief I will to live and die.

Say to thy Son, I am his—that by his birth
  And death my sins be all redeemable—
As Mary of Egypts' dole he changed to mirth,
  And eke Theophilus', to whom befell
  Quittance of thee, albeit (so men tell)
To the foul fiend he had contracted been.
Assoilzie me, that I may have no teen,
  Maid, that without breach of virginity
Didst bear our Lord that in the Host is seen :
  In this belief I will to live and die.

A poor old wife I am, and little worth :
  Nothing I know, nor letter aye could spell :
Where in the church to worship I fare forth,
  I see heaven limned with harps and lutes, and hell
  Where damnèd folk seethe in fire unquenchable :
One doth me fear, the other joy serene ;
Grant I may have the joy, O Virgin clean,
  To whom all sinners lift their hands on high,
Made whole in faith through thee their go-between :
  In this belief I will to live and die.

ENVOY.

THOU didst conceive, Princess most bright of sheen,
Jesus the Lord, that hath no end, nor mean,
Almighty that, departing heaven's demesne
  To succour us, put on our frailty,
Offering to death his sweet of youth and green :
Such as he is, our Lord he is, I ween :
  In this belief I will to live and die.

Love's Greatest Pain.

CLARENCE A. WALWORTH: D. 1900.

RECTOR OF ST. MARY CHURCH, ALBANY, U.S.A.

FROM 'ANDIATOROCTE' NEW YORK, 1888.

'Love's Greatest Pain,' from 'Revelations of Divine Love,' is versified from the original treatise of Mother Juliana, an English Recluse of the fourteenth century.

Oh, 'twas a heavy passion ;
Oh, 'twas a weary pain ;
And though I saw it not
Except in thought,
Except in such a form and fashion
As things are painted in the brain,
I would not dare,
For all the world I could not bear
To see it so again.
Said I, in my soul's bitterness :
' Is hell pain more than this ? '
Quick and sharp came the reply,
To my reason it was answered : ' Aye ;
For there, and only there
Grief is bottomed in despair.'
Yet of all the pains that lead to bliss,
The pains to hearts in hope which offer,
No keener woe is found than this—
To love, and see Love suffer.
Alas ; I saw him on the rood
Down-bowing ;
Alas ; I saw the purple flood
Down-flowing ;

I saw in his fair face the colour
Coming and going,
And alternating with deep pallor.
Oh, it was heart-rending :
Life and death I saw contending—
As wrestlers put forth their full power,
From burning noon to the ninth hour.
Christ knows if that keen grief of mine
Were earth-born, or divine ;
Christ knows if sacred charity
Gave me such pain ;
But methought no sorrow could come to me
Ever again
Like the sorrow I felt then.
Cometh a day that shall disclose,
Christ knows
I would that day were now begun—
Yea, done.

Now, when the sorrow of my own sad heart
Had passed in part,
I thought of that dear innocent Dove,
Our Lady Mary, who stood by his side
When he was crucified ;
All through that burning mid-day clove
So fondly to his side—
All through the bitter dying, till he died.
And then, I saw more plain
How the greatness of her love
Was the greatness of her pain.
For in kind, her love was a mother's ;
But it passed all mothers' in degree.
Ah then, how could it be
Her grief should not surpass all others ?

Dear Lady, I in sorrow
Do pity thy Love's great agony ;
Yea, fain would my poor bosom borrow,
If so it might, more love from thee.

Lyric, Rondeau, and Four Sonnets.

MICHAEL WATSON, S.J.

FROM 'IN MADONNA'S PRAISE,' 1898.

. I. MATER ADMIRABILIS.

How fair art thou,
 O Mater Admirabilis,
Fair as the blushing dawn in silver dight ;
 Fair as the violets blue,
 Or crystal dew
Transpierced with arrows of the sun's first light ;
Fair as the queen-moon, throned in starry realms above ;
Fair as the radiant eyes of hope, or heavenly love.

 How pure art thou,
  O Mater Admirabilis,
Pure as the mantling snow on Alpine crest ;
 Pure as mid-ocean spray,
 The star's mild ray,
Or lily's cup with pearls by morning drest ;
Pure as the milk-white dove that bathes in woodland
   spring ;
Pure as the Seraph's thought before the Almighty King.

 How sweet art thou,
  O Mater Admirabilis,
Sweet as the perfume of the perfect rose
 FF

That lifts her stately head
Of royal red,
And freights with fragrance every wind that blows ;
Sweet as the amber honey hived by summer bee ;
Sweet as thy guileless heart ; sweet as thy purity.

How wondrous thou,
O Mater Admirabilis,
Thou art Heaven's Boast, O Sweet and Pure and Fair.
Robed with the dazzling sun,
Thou glorious One,
Naught else created can with thee compare ;
A marvel and a joy to me thou ever art,
O peerless Mother-Maid, sole sovereign of mine heart.

II. ANGELS' SONG ON OUR LADY'S ASSUMPTION.

Oh, who is she from desert dark and lone,
That cometh up with song and jubilee,
That cometh up to sit upon a throne?
        Oh, who is she?

Fair as the moon, and shining gloriously
As sun that flameth in earth's central zone ;
And round her Seraphs throng with holiest glee.

Ascending, crowned with gold and flashing stone,
She comes, majestic as an Empress—see ;
Heaven's Lord upbears her as his very own :
        Oh, who is she?

III. THE VIRGIN MOTHER PRAISING GOD.

As from deep ocean's bed sweet waters spring
And rise, untainted, through the salt sea brine,
So mounts all spotless to the Throne Divine,
From this sad earth, the praise she gives her King.

And as an eagle sweeps on lusty wing
Toward golden clouds o'er wooded Apennine,
Her spirit soars to realms where sunlike shine
Angelic Choirs, and joins in strains they sing.

' My soul,' she says, ' doth magnify the Lord,
Whose strong Arm shatters pride's ambitious crest,
And lifts the humble (Holy is his Name)
To thrones of honour as a meet reward :
He hath regarded me who nought can claim,
And men in every age shall call me Bless'd.'

IV. MARY'S INTERCESSION : BATTLE OF LEPANTO, 7 OCTOBER, 1571.

By order of the Pope, St. Pius V., the Rosary was recited in the churches of Rome for the success of the Christian fleet at the time when the battle was fought ; and St. Pius himself, fixing his eyes for a while on the sky, said to the Cardinals at the moment of victory : ' Let us give thanks to God for the triumph which he has just granted to the Christian arms ' (Author, from Alban Butler's ' Lives of the Saints,' May 5th).

CHRIST's Holy Church sends up a cry for aid :
That cry from hearts that bow them to the dust,
Upsoaring to the Virgin's seat august,
There weeps and pleads, by sore affliction swayed :
' Hear, Queen of Heaven : or, hear, pure Mother-Maid.
Thy children rescue from the scorn and lust
Of Moslem hordes : appease God's vengeance just,
That he may dower with might the Christian blade.'

Sweet Mary turns her towards her Son's great Throne
In suppliant guise; then girt with Seraph bands,
Earthward she speeds to succour and to save.
Serene above two warring fleets, she stands—
Lo, shattered lies the Moslem power, and prone;
And Christian warrior-swords triumphant wave.

V. OUR LADY'S GIRLHOOD: IN THE SPRINGTIME.

WITH gold the sun has crowned the young Girl's hair:
Now Nature wakes and smiling greets the Spring;
Cool winds breathe balm; the tuneful brooklets ring;
And flowers, earth's modest stars, shine pure and fair.
The world with joy is throbbing everywhere:
The new-born buds ope eyes a-wondering;
Lambs skip; and birds, at rest or on the wing,
With songs of gladness thrill mead, wood and air.

Joy's fount is God. In Mary's perfect soul
This fount's pellucid tide serenely wells
And forms a mirror where—all bright and whole—
Earth's quiet loveliness, reflected, dwells:
Hark, hark, she sings: oh, sweet as silver bells,
The notes like rising incense heavenward roll.

VI. STELLA MATUTINA.

PURE Star of Morning, whose propitious ray
Brought to the nations hope in cheerless hour,
Oh, shine within mine heart with gladdening power;
Bright Herald of the Sun, drive gloom away.
When over earth and sky the night holds sway,
Fierce beasts can wreck at will the fairest bower—
So demons ruin souls when sorrows lower:
Shine, then, white Star, and be my Joy and Stay.

Shield, shield me, Mother, from the deadly foe:
Thy Son, who honours thee with boundless love,
Will mark thy pleading voice and save from woe.
Be pitiful and hear; I crave for light—
Lo, darkness flees; the Day-star gleams above—
Flame on, sweet Splendour, ever pure and bright.

NOTE.

No. I. St. iv. line 3 : Heaven's Boast ; after ' our tainted nature's
solitary boast,' of Wordsworth's Sonnet.

Translations from the Latin:

I. (1897) ST. ANSELM, BISHOP OF LUCCA : XI CENTURY ;
II. (1897) M. CASIMIR SARBIEWSKI, S.J. : 1595—1660 ;
III. (1885) RICHARD CRASHAW : 1613—1650.

RICHARD WILTON, M.A.

I. THE VIRGIN'S LAMENTATION.

VIRGIN of Virgins, by the Cross of Jesus
Stands she transfixed with sword of inmost sorrow ;
Her Son's suff'rings and streams of Blood beholding
She bears in spirit what he endures in body.

Stands by her Only Son his Mother dear bewailing :
Whither to turn for very grief she knows not :
Now beats her bosom, now with sighs adores him—
Her virgin graces by her grief untarnished.

With anguished face his Mother sees him hanging—
From his wounds pouring precious Blood in torrents :
His face she watches pale with mortal shadows ;
Truly her sorrow tears her soul in pieces.

Nature's stern edict now its debt demandeth,
Which passed her over when about to embrace him ;
Now claims with interest all the pains and sorrows
Due from human mothers since the fall of Adam.

Now at length, in travail, thou art surely feeling
How 'tis meet a Mother with her Son should languish :
Bitter are the groanings from thy heart extorted
As thy Son thou seest drooping in his passion.

Truly art thou piercèd with the sword of sorrow,
Seeing his fair arms upon the Cross extended,
While his royal Body hangs as on a balance
And his spotless members with his Blood are crimsoned.

II. COLLOQUY BETWEEN CHRIST ABOUT TO DIE AND BLESSED MARY.

CHRIST : 'TIS come—the destined moment, Mother Blest,
　　　　Which bears me from thee, at the high behest
　　　　　　Of God my Father, to the Tree
　　　　　　Dreaded by men, desired by me.

MARY :　My Son, dost leave thy Mother thus forlorn?
　　　　Alas, me wretched : my poor heart is torn
　　　　　　With the sharp spear-point of thy tongue
　　　　　　On which, my Light of life, I hung.

CHRIST : 'Now Death its earliest strokes begins to send ;
　　　　My Heart the spear itself shall not so rend,
　　　　　　As this dire grief of thine
　　　　　　Consumes this soul of mine.

MARY :　If once thine infant lips from out my breast
　　　　Their comfort drew, oh, leave me not opprest
　　　　　　My Son, by such a pang to-day ;
　　　　　　Ah, let me die for thee, I pray,

CHRIST : Lo, at my dying, through thy heart must steal
    The pang which, bearing me, thou didst not feel:
      Life was not purchased by my birth,
      My death shall bring it to the earth.

MARY :   Then let me, miserable, before thee die.
CHRIST : That thou shouldst live the Father rules on high ;
    That I should die, his changeless will.
MARY :   To die with thee, oh, grant me still.

CHRIST : Thou mayst embrace me : nought else doth
    remain :
    Why do thy folding arms so long detain ?
    Mother, I must abandon thee :
    The kiss of Judas summons me.

III. EPIGRAMS

CONCERNING THE ANGELIC SALUTATION.

ITS ' Hail,' Cæsarean Eagle need not bring ;
'Thy ' Hail ' comes wafted on a whiter wing.

But, let the ' All-hail ' Angel e'en be still ;
My ' Hail ' comes flitting on a whiter quill.

To say my ' Hail ' what whiter being can be,
Than that white Being who utters thine to thee ?

Virgin, dost ask what whiter than that white
Might be ? The Virgin, who is asking, might.

That white One, Virgin, may give ' Hail ' to thee ;
But thou, more white, dost give my ' Hail ' to me.

My ' Hail ' o'er thy ' Hail '—wouldst thou know its worth ?
He utters thine, but mine thou bringest forth.

Verse from the Greek, Early English, Old German and later;

TRANSLATED OR IMITATED.

GEORGE RATCLIFFE WOODWARD, M.A.

I. THEOTOKION.

LADY Mary, Blissful Dame,
What shall be thy proper name?
Heaven? Forasmuch as he,
Sun of Justice, dawned in thee.
Paradise? Because thy bower
Grew the Everlasting Flower.
Maid? Because, withouten stain,
Virgin aye thou dost remain.
Is it, Mother Undefiled?
Seeing that the Holy Child,
Whom thy spotless arms did bear,
God and Lord, is everywhere.
Him, upon him, prithee, call,
For to save us one and all.

II. TWO INVOCATIONS FROM A BALLADE:

'COMMENDATION OF OUR LADY.'

JOHN LYDGATE OF BURY, XV CENT.

FROM 'CHAUCERIAN, AND OTHER POEMS,' EDITED BY
W. W. SKEAT, 1894.

O STAR of starrès, with thy streamès clear,
Star of the Sea, to shipman Light or Guide,
O lusty Living, most pleasànt t' appear,
Whose brightè beams the cloudès may not hide:

O Way of Life to them that go or ride,
Haven from tempest, surest up t' arrive,
On me have mercy for thy Joyès five.

*   *   *

O goodly Gladded, when that Gabriel
With joy thee gret that may not be numb'rèd,
Or half the bliss who couldè write or tell,
When th' Holy Ghost to thee was obumbrèd,
Wherethrough the fiendès were utterly encombrèd?
O wemless Maid, embellished in his birth,
That man and angel thereof hadden mirth.

NOTE.

Line 3 : O lusty Living : O pleasant living One : or perhaps the phrase should be read according to the Sloane MS., 'O lusty lemand ' (= leming), O pleasant shining One.

III. MARIA, MUTTER JESU CHRIST.

FROM THE 'KÖLN GESANG-BUCH :' XVI CENTURY.

Lo, Jesùs' Mother, Mary, May : Alleluia ;
Is taken up to heaven to-day.   Alle—Alleluia.

Erst shadowed by the Spirit blest,
By grace secure she findeth rest.

The Ark, that bore the Holy One,
Is prey to no corruptïon.

Her Son, of hell that hath the key,
Would not that she should graven be.

Mother and Child shall part no more ;
On Angel-wings, up, Lady, soar.

Down came a troop of Angels, fain
To bear their Queen to heaven again.

What joy and glee to man doth come :
Sing, all good folk through Christendom.

From henceforth, in the heavenly hall,
A Mother have we, one and all.

Above, she sitteth Queen, i-wis ;
Below, she is our Guard and Bliss.

Then praise to God, the One, Two, Three : Alleluia ;
And Three, Two, One, for ever be.   Alle—Alleluia.

IV. OUR LADY'S VISITATION.

FROM THE 'KÖLN GESANG-BUCH:' XVI CENTURY.

Our Lady took the road
To Zachary's abode ;
O'er mountain, vale and lea,
Full many a league sped she
Toward Hebron's holy hill,
By God's command and will.

Full light did Mary make
Of trouble for his sake.
God's Very Son of yore
Within her breast she bore ;
And Angels bright and fair,
Unseen, her fellows were.

She, ere she took her way,
An orison would say,
That God her steps might tend
Safe to their journey's end ;
And there, in manner meet,
Her cousin she 'gan greet.

Elizabeth full fain
Eft bowed her head again ;
She wist 'twas God's own Bride,
As, worshipful, she cried :
'O Lady, Full of Grace,
Whence do I see thy face ?'

O House and Home of bliss,
O earthly Paradis—
Nay, Heaven itself on ground
Wherein the Lord is found,
The Lord of Glory bright,
In goodness great and might—

Clean Maiden thou that art,
Come, visit this my heart ;
And bring me chief my Good,
God's Son in Flesh and Blood ;
Bless body, soul ; and bide
For ever by my side.

V. CANDLEMAS.

FROM THE 'KÖLN GESANG-BUCH :' XVI CENTURY.

MARY, that Mother mild,
Sped with her Heavenly Child ;
From Bethlehem to-day
To Salem-ward her way ;
Needs to the Temple there
Babe Jesus would she bear ;

Would at the Law's behest
Present her First-born blest ;
And to the priest full fain

Then offer turtles twain,
And thus redeem thereby
The World's Redeemer high.

Hard by, by God's command,
Good Simèon did stand;
That old man fondly pressed
The Youngling to his breast—
The Christ expected long,
The burthen of his song:

'Lord, suffer now thy thrall
To fare in peace withal,
Because mine eyes have seen
My Saviour Christ, I ween;
To Gentiles candle-bright,
And Israel's delight.

'Set is the Child Divine
A stumbling-block and sign
For fall and rise again
Of many a Jew certain.
Thy soul, too, Mother dear,
Shall hurt be by a spear.'

A prophetess then came,
Saint Anna was her name;
Of Mary's gentle Boy
She spake with holy joy—
E'en so, Christ-Child, draw near,
Our souls in such wise cheer.

VI. SONG SUGGESTED BY 'ICH WEISS EIN RÖSLEIN.'

JOHANN SCHÜTZ OF STRANBING, XVI CENTURY.

I KNOW a Rose, full fair to see,
　　Within a Lady's bower :
It is the joy and pride of me,
This Rose-Marie,
　　And like none other flower.

May, June, July may boast to be
　　The time for lovely roses,
When maids and men, through Christentie,
From bush and tree
　　Cull buds to make them posies.

But mine doth follow other rule ;
　　For well I can remember,
My Rose-Marie, at time of Yule,
When winds blow cool,
　　Bare Fruit in mid-December.

VII. TWO NIGHTINGALES.

FROM ' PROCOPII MARIALE FESTIVALE,' XVII CENTURY.

Two nightingales we often hear
　　Down in some valley singing :
Tis wonder-sweet when far and near
　　They set the place a-ringing :
Their carols charm the passer-by
　　As vie they one with other,
Yet either would far liefer die
　　Than give way to his brother.

Two nightingales, I hear them yet :
　　An Angel sent from glory,
Yet not by chance, to Nazaret,
　　Into one upper-storey.
How sweetly sung that Virgin bright,
　　The blissful Maid, Maria ;
No mortal tongue can sing aright
　　Her dulcet harmonïa.

'Twas no mere echo of thin air—
　　Her voice with his united ;
Would God I had been standing there—
　　My heart had been ignited.
No sweeter song in heavenly hall
　　Than this is sung ; no, never ;
When Hallows chant in chorus all
　　'Thy will be done' for ever.

A Greek Madonna and other Verse.

SIR THOMAS WYSE: 1791—1862.

FROM A MS. 'BOOK OF SONNETS' (1851—1852) IN THE POSSESSION
OF THE AUTHOR'S NIECE, W. M. WYSE.

I. A GREEK MADONNA.

OH, look not on me with thy Gorgon eyes,
　　Thy beautiful Gorgon eyes of sullen light,
　　Filled up with silent soul, Medusa-bright,
Star burdened as thy blackest midnight skies ;
No tear ere crossed them for our human sighs,
　　Nor maiden pity bent to sinners prayer ;
　　But queen-like glory, and holiness severe
Bowed down the slave, so that he dare not rise.

Oh, not for me thy sceptre and thy Throne
  Apocalyptic, nor mere regal seat,
Nor gem-like mysteries of thy Eastern crown—
  O Virgin-Mother, to thy gentle feet
Other the charms that bring thy children down—
  The weeping sense of earthly feelings sweet,
Thy heavenly Womanhood and half-angel birth,
Sitting by God's right-hand, yet not forgetting earth.

II. PURIFICATION.

O VIRGIN Mother, Purest of the pure,
  Well it beseemed, before a stubborn race
  That thou, the God-selected, Full of Grace,
Shouldst lowly bow thy head and calm endure
Rites meant to cleanse the uncleanly, and to cure
  The soul-diseased. Before the Temple stood
  A gentle Mother in her mother's mood
Of overflowing love, yet insecure
Of the great future, with her Child ; when rose
  A Prophet with his song : ' A Light hath come
To those who dwell in darkness, from her woes
  Rescue to Israel : now unto my tomb
Dismiss thy Servant, Lord ; for I have seen
  Thy full Salvation.' And the Mother mild,
As if she late on Calvary had been,
  And now stood by the Sepulchre, to her Child
Turned inward-worshipping. And so to-day
We hail with lights and songs, this just night's
      morning ray.

III. ASSUMPTION.

SLEEP on, until in Heaven thou next shalt wake
   Pure Maiden-Mother, through this slimy plain,
   Heading thy crystal waters, without stain—
On holy mount the still unmelted flake
Cast from God's skies. Oh, pass away and make
   Joy 'mongst the angel choirs that come to gaze
   With beautiful love upon thy Woman's face
Pleading, not needing words for our poor sake ;
Yet ere assumed unto thy rest, behind
   Leave to those Sister-watchers round thy bed
And those who after come Love child-like, kind
   Care, motherly and virgin Truth, and dread
Of nought save evil.   Guides leave to the blind ;
   Staffs to the lame ; to women, Womanhead.
The prayer was heard. Whene'er there's want or woe,
There are thy sisters still : thou watchest still below.

3 Zingari.

VARIOUS AUTHORS.

NOTE : The following Verses, on various grounds and for different reasons, could not be placed in their several and normal positions, and are therefore printed together in a miscellaneous section.

Songs.

I. MONTH OF MARY.

THOMAS (CANON) HOLLAND.

FROM 'THE LAMP,' 1851.

THE sunbeams are tinging
The beautiful fringing
Of the vestments with gold,
Whilst palsied and old,

With silverwhite hair
And a heart free from care,
The priest is beginning the Mass of to-day
In honour of Mary, the Queen of the May.

And Nature is throwing
The flowers that are blowing
O'er meadow and hill
By river and rill,
And children their baskets
Are decking like caskets
With the beautiful blossoms they pick on their way,
To offer their Mother, the Queen of the May.

The altars are blazing
And angels are gazing
Whilst the Mighty and Holy,
Moved solemnly slowly,
Appears through the wreathing
Of the thurible's breathing,
And bells are announcing from altar and steeple
The presence of God in the midst of his people.

Where the sunbeam reposes
I'll gather primroses,
And pale daffodillies
And snowy white lilies
And violets sweet
To lay at thy feet,
And kneeling I'll breathe on the flower-scented air,
In simple devotion, a whispering prayer.

Mary, when thou didst rise
To thy home in the skies,
With trumpet and sound
There gathered around

GG

The angels to greet thee
And Jesus to meet thee,
The Mother who shared in his sorrow and love,
And crowned thee the Queen of the regions above.

II. MAY CAROL.

MARY ANTONIA, SISTER OF MERCY
(' *MERCEDES* '), *U.S.A.*

SEE the robins swinging
  'Mid the orchards' snow ;
Feel the perfumed breezes
  Wafted to and fro ;
Listen to the music
  Heard from bird and spray ;
Lift your hearts, ye sad ones,
  'Tis the lovely May.

Ah, our hearts were weary
  Waiting for the light,
For the frosts to vanish
  With their bitter blight :
See, the earth's brown bosom
  Heaves, where zephyrs play ;
See, she thrills and answers
  To the touch of May.

May, all fresh and smiling,
  Sweet—from heaven above ;
May, our souls beguiling
  With her dreams of love :
Violet-eyed and fragrant—
  How our pulses play
'Neath the virgin beauty
  Of the radiant May.

Lift your hearts up : floating
　　Through the gold and blue
Where the liquid sunlight
　　Streams and filters through,
There a Lady, smiling,
　　Stands 'mid cloudless day—
Snow-white Virgin-Mother,
　　Dazzling Queen of May.

Early English hymns.

I.　A LITTLE SONG; c. 1325.

CENTO FROM WILLIAM DE SHOREHAM'S TRANSLATION
FROM THE LATIN, OR FRENCH, OF ROBERT GROSSETESTE.

MODERNISED BY F. M. CAPES.

FROM 'THE PUBLICATIONS OF THE PERCY SOCIETY,' EDITED
BY T. WRIGHT, 1849.

MARY, Maiden, mild and free,
Chamber of the Trinity,
A little while now list to me,
　　As greeting I thee give ;
What though my heart unclean may be,
　　My offering yet receive.

Thou art the Queen of Paradise,
Of heaven, of earth, of all that is ;
Thou bore in thee the King of Bliss
　　Without or spot or stain ;
Thou didst put right what was amiss,
　　What man had lost, re-gain.

The gentle Dove of Noe thou art
The Branch of Olive-tree that brought,
In token that a peace was wrought,
    And man to God was dear :
Sweet Ladye, be my Fort
    When the last fight draws near.

Thou art the Sling, thy Son the Stone
That David at Goliah flung ;
Eke Aaron's rod, whence blossom sprung
    Though bare it was, and dry :
'Tis known to all, who've looked upon
    Thy childbirth wondrous high.

In thee has God become a Child,
The wretched foe in thee is foiled ;
That Unicorn that was so wild
    Is thrown by Woman chaste ;
Him hast thou tamed, and forced to yield,
    With milk from Virgin breast.

Like as the sun full clear doth pass,
Without a break, through shining glass,
Thy Maidenhood unblemished was
    For bearing of thy Lord :
Now, sweetest Comfort of our race,
    To sinners be thou good.

Take, Ladye dear, this little Song
That out of sinful heart has come ;
Against the fiend now make me strong,
    Guide well my wandering soul :
And though I once have done thee wrong,
    Forgive, and make me whole.

II. A GOODLY ORISON; C. 1210.

BEGINNING AND ENDING.

MODERNISED (1895) *BY WALTER WILSON GREG, M.A.*

FROM 'OLD ENGLISH HOMILIES,' EDITED BY RICHARD MORRIS,
1867—1873.

CHRIST's Gentle Mother, Saint Marie,
   Light of my life, beloved Ladie,
To thee I humbly bow the knee
   And vow my dearest blood to thee.
Thou art as Light unto my soul,
   Thou art my Hope and my heart's bliss,
Thy touch hath power to make me whole,
   My life is in thy hands, i-wiss.
Thee must I praise with all my heart,
   Thee must I serve with all my might,
And ever sing with highest art
   Love-songs to thee by day and night.

     *   *   *

May God me grant, of his mercie,
   That I may see thee throned above:
In mede of this my song to thee
   In favour look on those I love.
Lead thou thy monk into thy bliss,
   Thou Holy One, I pray of thee,
That sang to thee this song of his,
   Christ's gentle Mother, Saint Marie.

3n time of and against the plague.

I.   HYMN TO B.V.M.

JOHN DRYDEN (POET LAUREATE):
1631—1700.

FROM 'THE PRIMER,' 1706.

HEAVEN's brightest Star, thy influence shed,
　Who with thy virgin breast
Thy Son, heaven's Sovereign Maker fed,
　That healed our nature's pest.

O thou auspicious Star, restrain
　The stars' contagious ill ;
Whose baleful frown portends our bane,
　To scourge our ulcered will.

Star of the Sea, receive our vows,
　From plague thy suppliants free ;
Thy Son will not thy prayers refuse,
　So much he honours thee.

A Virgin Mother and a fruitful Maid
For sinners pleads : O Lord, vouchsafe thy aid.

II.   PRAYER TO THE SACRED VIRGIN-MOTHER, CALLED THE 'MIRACULOUS.'

FROM 'JESUS, MARIA, JOSEPH,' AMSTERDAM, 1663.

THE Star of Heaven (whose snowy breast
Did suckle our sweet Lord), supprest
The Plague of Death, whose origen
Was from the very first of men ;
May that clear Star at present daign
Those constellations to restrain ;

Whose wars deprive men of their breath
By the destructive wound of Death.

[Repeat thrice these ensuing verses.]

Bright Star o' th' Sea, 'gainst Plague your help
    afford :
Nought is denyed you by your Son, our Lord,
Who honours you, Blest Maid : us, Jesu, save,
Which for us, at your hands, she daigns to crave.

Centos.

I. PART OF A PROCESSIONAL HYMN.

WILLIAM T. BROOKE.

Let Cherubim and Seraphim upraise
Their highest songs in Holy Mary's praise,
    The Ever-Virgin Mary.
Thrones, Dominations, Virtues, Princedoms, Powers,
In hymns exalt your Holy Queen and ours,
    The glorious Virgin Mary.
Let Angels and Archangels all unite
To sing her praise who bore the Light of Light,
    The Blessed Virgin Mary.
Let Patriarchs the growing chorus swell
In praise of her whose Son slew death and hell,
    The spotless Virgin Mary.
Holy Apostles, spread her praise abroad,
The Daughter, Mother, and the Spouse of God,
    The holy Virgin Mary.
O goodly fellowship of Prophets, sing
The Virgin Mother of the Virgin King,
    The stainless Virgin Mary.

Martyrs, who for your Master shed your blood,
Hymn her who weeping stood beneath the Rood,
    Mother of Sorrows, Mary.
The Holy Church through all the world shall be,
In humble fashion, followers of thee,
    O lowly Virgin Mary.

II. HAIL, MARY: A FRAGMENT.

WILLIAM RODDY.

FROM 'THE FRANCISCAN TERTIARY,' 1891.

HAIL, Mary, Full of Grace—

Greeting angel-borne sublime,
Sounding sweetly far as distant music,
    In the long-drawn aisles of time.

Oh, wondrous, yea, stupendous thought ;
Lo, Christian, pause in awe and ponder here—
    The Majesty of mystery's wrought.

A carillon of prayer and praise ;
A rosary of radiant words to wreathe,
    Star-lit, thy Virgin brow always.

Jesus, the Saviour of mankind—
In reverence here, O God, to faith we yield
    The deep stirred heart, the finite mind.

Hope thou of souls sin-desolate—
Now—at the hour of death, God's Mother pray ;
    Blest Passport ours at Heaven's gate—

Holy Mary, pray for us.

Mediæval Prayer.

TO OUR BLESSED LADY, ADVOCATE
OF SINNERS.

DAME GERTRUDE MORE, O.S.B.:
OB. 1633.

ALL Hail, O Virgin crowned with stars
    and moon under thy feet,
Obtain us pardon of our sins
    of Christ, our Saviour sweet ;
For though thou art Mother of my God,
    yet thy humility
Disdaineth not this simple wretch
    that flies for help to thee.
Thou knowest thou art more dear to me
    than any can express,
And that I do congratulate
    with joy thy happiness.
Thou who art the Queen of Heaven and Earth
    thy helping hand me lend,
That I may love and praise my God
    and have a happy end.
And though my sins me terrify,
    yet hoping still in thee,
I find my soul refreshèd much
    when to thee I do flee ;
For thou most willingly to God
    petitions dost present,
And dost obtain much grace for us
    in this our banishment.
The honour and the glorious praise
    by all be given to thee,

Which Jesus thy beloved Son
  ordained eternally;
For thee whom he exalts in heaven
  above the angels all,
And whom we find a Patroness
  when unto thee we call.

O Mater Dei, memento mei.   Amen.

NOTE.

This Prayer was written by the grand-daughter of Blessed Sir
Thomas More, a Nun in the Convent of Our Lady of Consolation,
at Cambray, and was printed in a Book of Spiritual Exercises of
St. Gertrude, Paris, 1658, whence it was copied by Dom Morrall,
O.S.B.   The above, collated with the printed copy, was taken from
the beginning of 'Confessiones Amantis; Fifty Meditations,' by a
Nun, on the 'Love of God and Religious Life,' an early xvii
century (Rawlinson) MS., in the Bodleian Library, Oxford, where
it was copied (1893) by the Editor.

Three Modern Hymns.

I.   FISHERMAN'S HYMN.

CECILIA M. CADDELL: 1813—1877.

FROM A MS. BOOK, WRITTEN C. 1863.

STAR of the Sea,
All hail to thee,
O Maiden Mother, chaste and mild;
  Dry all our tears,
  Chase all our fears,
Light us o'er the ocean wild.

  White are the waves,
  The tempest raves
Around our sad and drooping band;

Yet could we see
One ray from thee,
We would be firm both heart and hand.

Shine, gentle Star,
Shine from afar
And say that Mary for us pleads
Then without dread
Our sails we'll spread,
While the strong wind our vessel speeds.

Fishers are we
Of the deep sea,
Like the Twelve Men to Jesus dear ;
Then for his love
Shine from above
And our frail barque to harbour steer.

II. TO THE BLESSED VIRGIN.

DUGALD MACFADYEN.

Written in 1889.

O MARY, Virgin-Mother,
O Queen of vernal May,
To thee, we weary pilgrims
With trustful bosoms pray ;
Thy light of grace shed over us
Through life's uncertain way.

When shadows dark of sin and care
With gloom obscure our sky,
To thee, our Refuge and our Strength,
. For peace and light we fly ;
Our trials all are sweet to bear
When, Mary, thou art nigh.

Oh, may our souls in purity
   And love of thee still grow,
And pray that we may frame our lives
   By thine on earth below,
That serving here with faithful hearts
   Thy Jesus we may know.

Then from this world's delusive snares
   And earthly bondage free,
Our souls may reap the rich reward
   Of dwelling nigh to thee,
And with thee singing praise to God
   Through all eternity.

III.   RESPICE STELLAM, VOCA MARIAM
(ST. BERNARD).

FRANCIS STANFIELD, PRIEST.

FROM 'CATHOLIC HYMNS,' 1858—1860.

DREAR is the night-fall,
   Lonely we roam,
Wandering exiles,
   Far from our home ;
Borne on the billows
   Of life's stormy sea,
Bright Star of Heaven,
   Our trust is in thee :
When night falls drearily, when life flows wearily,
Respice Stellam, voca Mariam.

Winds of affliction   ·
   Raise their rude blast,
Ruffling the ocean
   Whereon we're cast ;

Waves of temptation
   Mountain-like roll,
'Neath their dark billows
   Sinking the soul:
Fear not, but gaze afar on the soft shining Star;
Respice Stellam, voca Mariam.

When shall lone spirits
   Sorrow no more?
When shall our aching eyes
   Gaze on the shore?
Oh, for the twilight
   To break through the gloom;
Oh, for the rest
   Of our only true home:
Stay, mourner, stay thy fears; joy shall dry up thy tears;
Respice Stellam, voca Mariam.

Gentle and beautiful,
   Beaming above,
Shines out all brightly
   The fair Star of Love;
Rest of the weary,
   Hope 'mid the night,
Guiding the lonely
   In its soft light.
Yes, 'mid the darkest night, that Star still shineth bright;
Respice Stellam, voca Mariam.

Ancient Irish Prayers.

I. TO THE HOLY TRINITY.

MUIREADACH ALBANACH (THE ALBANIAN) O'DALY: c. 1215.

DONE INTO ENGLISH, AFTER THE METRE OF THE GALL, BY GEORGE SIGERSON, M.D.

FROM 'BARDS OF THE GAEL AND GALL,' 1897.

TEACH thou me, O Trinity,
O Lord, whose speech is sweet ;
Teach my tongue, O Trinity,
Bless it with blessing meet.

*   *   *

Thee, O Trinity, from thee,
Ah, Lord, grant healing balm,
Like a fair and fine oak tree,
With cankered core I am.

Yet of blood I bear no stain,
No stain of spoil I bear ;
Then, for Mary's love, oh, deign
Give answer to my prayer.

II. TO HOLY MARY.

DONAGHA MORE O'DALY: OB. 1244.

TRANSLATED FROM A POEM WRITTEN IN A METRE WITH SEVEN SYLLABLES IN EACH LINE AND EACH LINE ENDING IN A MONOSYLLABLE, BY DOUGLAS HYDE, LL.D.

FROM 'RELIGIOUS SONGS OF CONNACHT' IN THE 'NEW IRELAND REVIEW,' 1895.

MARY, Mother dear of God,
    Hear this clod that prayeth—I,
Now and at the hour of death
    When the breath spreads wings to fly.

Pray unto thy Son, that he
  Like to thee be minded still ;
Thy will is to succour me,
  Pray that he be of thy will.

Pray unto the Father most,
  With the Holy Ghost for me,
They together with thy Son
  Three in One are, One in Three.

Lyrics.

I. TOTA PULCHRA ES, MARIA.

DOM MICHAEL BARRETT, O.S.B.

FROM 'THE CATHOLIC WORLD,' 1887.

HARK, an earth-born song of gladness
  Floating through the Golden Gate
Floods with joy the seraphs bending
  Low at Mary's throne of state :
Hark, to dulcet harp and cymbal
  Angel voices swell the lay :
'Tota pulchra es, Maria ;
  Macula non est in te.'

Long ago, when evening breezes
  Leafy shades of Eden fanned,
Pure of soul and fair of feature,
  Fresh from his Creator's hand
Man met God—as friend rejoicing
  Greeteth friend. Oh, wondrous grace ;
God conversed in sweetest union
  With his creature, face to face.

All too soon, like sleep-born vision,
   Fade those radiant hours away ;
Tempted—longing, tasting, sinning—
   On an ever-rueful day
Man—a rebel and an outcast,
   Doomed with toil his bread to win—
Brandeth e'en his unborn children
   With the shame and taint of sin.

But a light breaks mid the darkness :
   Many a thousand years have rolled,
When to earth the angels welcome
   One whom prophets had foretold :
Eva's Daughter, Pure and Spotless,
   Wholly free from every stain,
Brings to humankind long fallen,
   Grace and dignity again.

As of old when Jordan's torrent
   Parted, and the priestly throng
O'er the river-bed rejoicing
   Bore the golden Ark along ;
So, from Mary's soul receding
   Sin's dark waters swiftly glide,
Leaving that New Ark untainted
   By their pestilential tide.

Mary, Mother, in the fountain
   Of my Lord's redeeming Blood,
Cleansed was I from all defilement
   Of that overwhelming flood ;
Angels stooping down from Heaven,
   With a holy rapture glad,
Saw my soul from sin delivered
   And in shining raiment clad.

Spake the priest in that blest moment :
   ' Keep thy robe from blemish free,
Till thy God, when life is ended,
   Claim a dread account of thee ;
Till the angel's clarion pealing
   Call thee to the great White Throne ;
Till thine everlasting portion
   To the listening world be known.'

Ah, my Mother, drear and toilsome
   Seemed the road I had to tread,
Rough the stones and sharp the brambles,
   Lowering dark the skies o'erhead :
Red, red roses, sunny meadows,
   Lured my careless feet astray ;
Mire of sin and thorns of passion
   Rent and stained that white array.

But the well-spring still is flowing—
   Never will its streams abate—
Whose forestalling virtue clothed thee
   In thy robe immaculate :
Lead me to that Fount, O Mother,
   Scarlet-red my sins may glow,
Yet my soul washed in its waters
   Needs must glisten white as snow.

Cleansed in Sacramental laver,
   Keep me free from deadly stain ;
When the tempter seeks to win me
   May he ever plead in vain ;
Then before thy feet in Heaven
   I may hope to sing, one day :
' Tota pulchra es, Maria ;
   Macula non est in te.'

HH

II. WHEN THE QUEEN COMETH:

EVE WAITETH FOR MARY.

EMILY M. P. HICKEY.

MOTHER of Men, uplifted
　　　　Through love and grace,
Out of the watching and waiting,
　　　　To that fair place
Where the light of light is shining
　　　　From Jesus' Face :

Thee hath his dying quickened,
　　　　His hunger fed,
White thou art washed where floweth
　　　　The Royal Red
That gushed from his blessed Body
　　　　To death wounded.

Bruised is the head of the serpent
　　　　That bruised his heel ;
Floweth the Balm of Gilead
　　　　For help and weal ;
Life to thy sons and daughters
　　　　Thy Son doth deal.

Thou, who didst follow him gladly
　　　　The way he trod
When he harrowed the dusk of Hades,
　　　　And made a road
Of purple glory and splendour
　　　　From God to God—

Wherefore lookest thou, Mother,
     So yearning-eyed?
Seekest thou yet some finding,
     O glorified?
'I wait for the Lady of ladies,
     The Spirit's Bride.

'She hath known her soft departing
     From earth away,
Whose will was alway and ever
     Set to obey
That Will which now doth call her
     To Heaven this day.

'She heard the welcome summons
     That Michael bare;
Her spirit hath waited happy
     In God's sweet where,
Till now doth it glad re-enter
     Her body fair.

'Oh, I am waiting, waiting,
     With joy to greet
This One who cometh with lovely
     And blessed feet:
Fain would I kneel to kiss them,
     In welcome sweet.

'The sun will be her clothing,
     And she will tread
Upon the moon's white radiance,
     And on her head
Will shine a twelve-starred glory
     Of love and dread.

' He who hath gone to bring her
                His truth will prove,
Setting her over all creatures ;
                Enthroned above
The cherubim, first in knowledge,
                The seraphs, in love.

' 'Thrills of her blessed coming
                Have past through me :
Mother of God's forgiveness
                Upon the Tree,
Mother of Love embodied
                Eternally.

' Child of my strain, my sinless,
                My perfect One,
Come in thy peerless honour,
                And take thy throne ;
Sit, as the Great King's Mother,
                Beside thy Son.

' And because he will give his Darling,
                Who willeth as he,
Whate'er she may choose to ask for,
                I ask of thee,
Pray, pray for his erring children
                Fordone by me.'

Index of First Lines.

Estimates and Criticisms

EXTRACTS FROM SOME REVIEWS OF

THE FIRST SERIES OF

CARMINA MARIANA

MAY—NOVEMBER, 1893

SPECTATOR.

'In the present volume Mr. Orby Shipley chooses a theme
interwoven with the highest mystery, and the initial dogma
of the Christian's creed. It is a theme, moreover, that can
only be interpreted fitly by the eagles of song, the high
priests of art, or by simple and childlike souls who have
claim to our sympathy with their faith, rather than with the
expression of it. . . . We do not examine this volume as we
should a literary monument. It has other and greater
interest, as it expresses the sentiment of many centuries. It
is important as a witness to the marvellous agreement,
through vast periods full of change, in recognition of the
Mother of Christ. Readers of Catholic prayer-books are
sometimes startled by the varied epithets applied to her.
This book is witness that, in none of them sanctioned in
Catholic practice, is there novelty of respect. It seems
certain that the Christian Church of East and West accepted,
rather than imposed, the cult which the common reverence of
Catholics spontaneously and logically offered. As we have
said, much of the poetry in these lauds of Mary has the lisp
of infantine utterance, and the simplicity of intuitive certainty
proper to the unlearned. It was felt by souls eager to
believe, that the Virgin of Nazareth is the guardian for all
time of the doctrine of the Divine Incarnation. She is the
visible sign of that union between the creature and the
Creator which is the "desire of all nations," and the fountain
of all mysticism of all nations. Seeing this with his half-
inspired eyes, Dante has made St. Bernard—and Mr. Shipley
has chosen a singularly good translator of St. Bernard's
hymn in Father Russell, S.J.—the chief votary of Mary,
and put on the Saint's lips the sublime invocation with
which Dante's final vision of God is prefaced.'

A

MONTH.

'The compiler having proposed to himself the two-fold aim of raising a pious monument to the honour of Mary, and at the same time of attending to its artistic beauty, much judgment was required to secure at all times merit and edification. Yet, we are bound to acknowledge that whilst the latter is uniformly attained, the general level of merit is remarkably high. It was not to be expected that the tribute of love and praise paid by non-Catholic poets should be as bold, unfaltering and rich in volume as the strains of her Catholic clients ; yet, it is both pleasing and edifying to observe how tenderly loving is the sentiment even of those whom we might least have expected to be in sympathy with Marian devotion. Amongst such writers, however, it may not be impertinent to remark that fulness of sympathy is invariably proportionate to appreciation of the great central Christian dogma of the Incarnation. The title "Mother of God" is at once the best vindication against heresy of the Divinity of her Son, and the main source of all inspiration, poetic and devout, in her honour. . . . We do not wish to underrate any testimonies to the sweet attraction of Mary's influence upon unbelieving, or misbelieving, or as yet imperfectly believing souls. It would have been a great pity if Mr. Orby Shipley had omitted them from his collection. We only want to accentuate the intimacy of the nexus between devotion to our Lady and belief in and devotion to Jesus Christ, as God Incarnate. . . . The reality of perception based on steadfast belief, appears in the beautiful hymn, "Virgini Deiparæ," extracted from Francis T. Palgrave's recent poem, "Amenophis" ; and to no other source, we think, may be traced the fervour which, chastened in utterance, cannot be suppressed in the sonnets on the "Childhood of Immanuel," by Arthur M. Morgan. There are eight of them reproduced in this book. Our readers must have recourse to them there. But, the key to their depth is contained in the following lines (from the second of them)—

Through thee are one the twain whom sin would sever ;
Through thee comes back the gift whence Eva fell.'

AVE MARIA: NOTRE DAME, U.S.A.

'In this noble volume is to be found by far the largest anthology of poems in Mary's praise that the world has yet seen. The remarkable thing is that it has not been done earlier—that it has been left to an English convert of the latter half of the nineteenth century to make us an exclusive hymn-book of her who is the Mother and Queen of all mankind. . . . Crashaw's contributions are as burning as one would expect from the most ardent of all English poets. His symbol might be indeed a heart on fire. Fire and snow, ardour and purity, blended with a great simplicity, were in this burning bush amongst the forest trees of Elizabethan poetry. . . . Coventry Patmore's ode is full of a great and stately magnificence, which, in its grandeur of imagery, sets him in a line of succession to Crashaw, though the passion of his verse be less. Poetry like this belongs by royal right to the great age of Elizabethan poetry. He prays her aid in his song :

> . . . Grant me the steady heat
> Of thought, wise, splendid, sweet . . .

In such a thunderous ode as this, with its long roll and reverberation, Patmore is the "organ voice" of the nineteenth century in England. What diversity—that the man who could have written the exquisite and rounded subtleties of the " Angel in the House " could be also wielder of this tremendous measure. Some of the old poems translated from foreign tongues into English are also full of innocent beauty. Of these are the " Colloquy between Christ, Our Lady and the Angel " of Jacopone, translated by E. M. Clerke ; John Kenyon's Provençal " Ballad of the Gipsies " who tell the Infant Christ's fortune from his palm ; the Dialogue between the Child Christ and his Mother of Sarbiewski, translated by Richard Wilton, notably. But, there are many others. " Our Ladie's Lullaby," of Richard Verstegan, a Catholic of Elizabethan days, the friend of Chideock Tichbourne and other martyrs for the faith, is very tender. . . . I cannot conclude better than with this very exquisite snatch of song to a dead astronomer, Father Perry, S.J., by one of the youngest of our English poets, Francis Thompson :

> Starry Amorist, starward gone,
> Thou art—what thou didst gaze upon.'

Manchester Guardian.

' Whether the whole arrangement could with advantage have been a chronological sequence is a question on which we are unwilling to express a decided opinion, more especially as we could not pretend to have formed it on the basis of a careful consideration such as the subject has evidently received from Mr. Shipley. On the one hand, we are unable to shut our eyes to the various phases, inevitably affected by the contemporary history of the Church, through which the veneration of the Virgin has passed, from the days of the

Nestorian Controversy to those of the Vatican decrees. . . .
On the other hand, the freer method of arrangement which
Mr. Shipley has preferred, and which whilst loosely alphabetical has left it in his power to introduce many a concerted
harmony, undoubtedly furnishes opportunities both more
facile and more frequent for artistic enjoyment. And inas-
much as this anthology consists wholly of modern English
verse, the historical method of arrangement could hardly
have been adopted without becoming misleading in its own
way. We are therefore, on the whole, well contented with the
succession of " Beads, white, green and red " . . . which have
been strung together for us by Mr. Shipley ; and if by the
side of such pearls as Henry Constable's Sonnets, or such
genuinely modern, yet not less worthy, companions as Aubrey
de Vere's " Mother of Orphans," a more or less dubious item
may have here and there found acceptance, no serious
damage has been done to the total effect. This effect is that
of a very beautiful monument of art, consecrated to one of
the most characteristic conceptions of the Church of Rome,
which, though not peculiar to herself, has repeatedly revived
with her revivals, and seems enduringly associated with her
endurance.

CATHOLIC NEWS.

' It will be remarked with what sympathy non-Catholic
writers are moved when touching on Our Lady ; in some
cases amounting to compassion. There is, perhaps, less of
sympathy than of surprise in Shelley's lines from " Epipsychidion "—we are happy to have Mr. Shipley with those who
hold them to be an invocation to Mary—but the former is
very amply shown in Egerton-Warburton's Sonnet on the
Marien Capelle, Carlsbad. . . . But, it is in Rossetti the
highest appraisement of our Lady, by a non-Catholic, will be
found ; united to a fuller insight and suggestion whereby
many of his poems about her bear a strange perception, a
singular cognisance of the significance attaching to the
Mother of God, of the imports crowding the Madonna's life.
We know nothing by a non-Catholic, of finer feeling, of more
subtle intention than his "Ave" . . . How sensitively the
girlhood of Mary is touched in ; with what delicacy he
suggests the waiting years when she was widowed of her
Son, closing with the prayer of faith, of love, of hope. How
came Rossetti so close to the understanding of her ? Was it
because he drank so deeply of the Paradiso ? If the book
shows Rossetti as the high-water mark of non-Catholic thought
of Our Lady, the Catholic appreciation is highest touched by
Faber and De Vere. The quantitatively inadequate results

Faber left of his deep poetic gifts make precious almost every line that he wrote ; and the excerpts Mr. Shipley gives in no way assuage our sense of loss that he allowed those gifts to slumber, that other energies might be. With De Vere it is otherwise. Energy is in essence in his poetic thought ; no tinsel, no mere prettiness : the language sane and full ; the movement large and equal ; the thought spiritual and un-hesitatingly direct. When he moves, there is no dragging of the robes about his feet : he is clear girt ; and in the spacious meade wherein he passes, the where he took is marked and unmistakeable. His lines on Murillo's picture bear the sense of amplitude in imagination and thought, which are his distinction. The faith of " Ancilla Domini " has no mist in it : from his Paradiso there are no " eloping angels," and there is no " happiness" in his hell.'

NEWCASTLE DAILY CHRONICLE.

' It is only on its purely literary side that we have to do with this volume ; and its purely literary merits are great enough to appeal to all English readers who have a genuine power of appreciating real poetry. Whatever may be said ; this must be admitted, that nothing in Christianity has brought such perfect and spontaneous expression into Christian art as the Catholic ideal of the Maiden-Mother of God, looking down with eyes of pity, womanly-divine, upon the earth, and raising tender intercession for the wretched and the lowly. And just as the artists of the middle-ages loved to brood over a vision no less full of graciousness and splendour than of solace and humanity, so religious poetry —so full in general of frigidities, slovenliness and conceits— has also found in the Catholic vision of the Madonna some-thing so exalted, affecting and definite as to inspire real feeling and beautiful imagination. Whether owing or not to the magnetic influence which Italy exerts upon the highest type of human minds, most of our poets have felt and ex-pressed at least an æsthetic sympathy, with this ideal of the old faith. Some of the noblest verse in this book—perhaps the noblest of all—is not by Catholic poets. . . . However, the bulk of the book is by Catholic writers, and the outcome for the most part of direct devotional impulse. . . . For the rest, " Carmina Mariana " is an anthology which includes so many beautiful things, and is of so unique a character, that it ought to find a place on many other than Catholic shelves. It is not only in the households of Mr. Shipley's co-religionists that an engraving after Raphael or Murillo may hang upon the wall.'

WEEKLY REGISTER.

' In this department—pieces marked, more or less, by a poetic quality—Mr. Orby Shipley's anthology proves English literature to be richer than most of us knew, or expected. Amongst the foremost things in any conceivable " Carmina Mariana," the literary Catholic looks for the two beautiful poems which we owe to one who was not a Catholic, though of Catholic descent—Rossetti. The " Ave " and the lovely sonnet on the " Girlhood of Mary Virgin " are certainly among the few things which one feels completely worthy of their high theme. Mr. Shipley has included the " Ave " . . . but the " Girlhood " finds no place among them. This we cannot but think a regrettable omission. . . Mr. Alfred Austin, who can at least write polished verses, has one specimen here—a touching ballad on a Breton legend, of an idiot whose one utterance was the evening hymn " Ave Maria." One morning he was found frozen in the snow, and carried to a house, only to die. Let the sequel be told in Mr. Austin's lines. . . Miss Katharine Tynan is represented by several poems touched with her characteristic wealth of colour. . . From the little-known poet, Robert S. Hawker, are quoted four poems. Three are unnotable ; but the first is fine to a surprising degree. It is called " Aishah Shechinah." From another poet, of whom we confess we know but little—Dora Greenwell—comes a snatch of truest poetry, "The Blade of Grass". . . We must note the noble stanzas of Francis Thompson, and two other poems contributed to " Merry England," by Albert Fleming and Father Fitzpatrick, O.M.I. . . Here is a song of the time of Henry VI.—it is a veritable wild hill-flower—as monotonous as a cuckoo, and as fresh. But, the gem of all its kind, is the lovely sixteenth-century Carol. The hand of the moderniser, William J. Blew, has touched it ; but touched it with a skill and reverence worthy of all praise. " This other night I saw a sight." What modern poet can write anything of such irresistible unconscious " naïveté " as this ? '

TABLET.

' Mr. Orby Shipley describes the intention he had in view in the beautiful collection which fills this goodly volume. The sources from which he has culled the flowers of the Anthology are enumerated in his Preface. . . . To this we can only add, as our own appreciation of the work, that, both in design and execution, it is worthy of the highest praise ; and that not the least of its excellencies is in the wide range of authors from which the poems have been chosen. We cannot resist the temptation of quoting from a few. One we like very much is headed "A Sinner to the Blessed Virgin," a French poem of the fifteenth century, Translated by John O'Hagan : " Queen, by God supremely blest." . . . Of saddest interest is " The Wreck of Walsing-ham," contributed by Dom Hunter Blair, from the Rawlinson MSS. in the Bodleian Library, Oxford. The late R. S. Hawker's " Lady's Well," so exquisitely beautiful, yet well known to our readers, finds its place, as was fitting ; and is followed by the "Song of the Sailors at Havre," by (his daughter) Morwenna Hawker. But we prefer to quote from Wordsworth, "The Nun's Well, Brigham." Our last extract must be " The Bells of St. Hugh's, Parkminster," from " Merry England," 1890 (by Frederick George Lee). . . . When we say that 350, or thereabout, poetical pieces inserted in this volume have been selected from nearly 200 different authors, it will give our readers some idea of the extent of the selection, though not of the judgment and taste that has guided the compiler, nor of the labour it has involved. We are writing these lines on the eve of the solemn re-consecra-tion of England to the Mother of God and the Prince of the Apostles ; and of the many beautiful literary tributes to Mary's honour, laid at her feet by her devout clients, there are few that equal in worth Mr. Orby Shipley's " Carmina Mariana." '

IRISH MONTHLY.

' This is the richest tribute that English literature has ever paid to the Queen of May, for it contains the best of all, and some of nearly all, that has been written about the Blessed Virgin in England, Ireland, and the United States. Even those who have a right to consider themselves fairly well acquainted with the subject will be surprised at the unknown treasures discovered by Mr. Shipley's diligence, from Richard Verstegan of Queen Elizabeth's time, to Richard Wilton of Queen Victoria's . . . The book opens auspiciously with an excellent translation by "A" from Adam of St. Victor, in the metre of the original. This, we think, appears here for the first time, and is worthy of such perfect transla-tors as Wackerbarth and John O'Hagan. Few who read the translation by the latter, at page 241, will guess how literally he keeps to the old French original of the fifteenth century. One who reads Rossetti's exquisite "Ave," at page 334, will not wonder at his death-bed cry, reported even by the unsympathetic W. D. Scott, "Send me a priest; I want to be absolved from my sins." Among the Laureates of the Madonna to which the Anthology introduces us is the Rev.

Arthur Morgan, who describes the "Childhood" of Jesus in
sonnets very devout in feeling, poetical in expression and
skilful and accurate in construction. Another discovery is
Clarence Walworth, an American convert priest. The first
of three excellent samples given here resembles Mr.
Coventry Patmore's "Unknown Eros" in form, and is
almost equally elevated, though borne up by a less ethereal inspiration. But, we cannot linger any further over this rich, and
—strange to say of a compilation—most original collection.'

DAILY CHRONICLE.

'"Our tainted nature's solitary boast," Wordsworth said
of Our Lady ; and this supreme position of the Madonna has
been praised and glorified throughout Christendom in proportion as men have recognised the greatness of that human
instrument through whom God became Man. So, at least,
it appears to a Roman Catholic reviewer. If Catholics hold
Mary great, it is because Christ, so unspeakably greater,
was her Son. Here is the logical justification, put not con-
troversially, but historically, of this devotion . . . In the
earliest ages, East and West, in Saxon England, all over the
Christian world, this devotion was expressed in language of
rapture and enthusiasm. There is not a phrase used in
modern Tridentine, or "Ultramontane," times by the most
eloquent Jesuit or Redemptorist, which cannot be paral-
leled in the writings of the primitive Fathers, or of those
of old England. England, indeed, as we have been lately
reminded, was called "Our Lady's Dowry," so great was the
devotion to her of the English . . . Catholicism knows well
that human aspect of the "Mother and Child" ; but, in the
mingling of divinity with humanity lies the inexhaustible
beauty of the theme. The "Holy Family," so venerated to-
day in the Catholic Church, typifies the perfect social life of
men as the general veneration of Saints reminds Catholics
of the solidarity of mankind. "What a sanction," writes Mr.
Pater of the Antonine age, "what a provocative to natural
duty lay in that image of the new Madonna, just then rising
upon the world like the dawn." Readers, then, who examine
Mr. Orby Shipley's great Anthology of poems in praise of the
Virgin Mother, whatever be their own beliefs and habits,
need not be distressed, or shocked. They will see that as
the primitive Christians of the Roman Catacombs honoured
the Mother of God, so do the Catholic Christians of to-day ;
and that every fresh form and feature of that devotion does
but bring out some old truth in a new and living light.'

BRADFORD OBSERVER.

'It has evidently been a labour of love on Mr. Shipley's part to cull the fairest flowers of poesy which bloom around the name of the Woman to whom the highest function of her sex has been ascribed. It matters little whether the reader shares the peculiar reverence with which the story of the Mother-Maid of the Godhead is enshrined in devout Catholic hearts. Whether this be so or not, every cultivated lover of pure, melodious, imaginative verse will cherish this exquisitely chosen collection of lyrics, odes, hymns and ballads which have been inspired by this most mystic of all legends. He includes Tennyson's " Mariana in the South" because the lovesick maiden found her strength in orisons night and morn to the Madonna ; he makes an extract from George Eliot's " Agatha" because of the lovely refrain of Hans, the Tailor's, Song to the " Heart of Mary, mystic Rose" ; and he includes Byron's matchless lines beginning

> Ave, Maria, o'er the earth and sea
> That heavenliest hour of heaven is worthiest of thee.

And so on, through the whole range of English poetry. . . . It needs a collection like this to make one realise how completely the story of the Virgin Mary has grown to be a part of the warp and woof of our imaginative life. The Irish chaplet of verse is, naturally, one of the brightest in the volume, for the Irish songs are, without exception, not only the outcome of a highly sensitive artistic sense, but of profound and true religious devotion.'

UNIVERSE.

'Cardinal Newman rarely gave expression to a more impressive sentiment when he declared, that " is the boast of the Catholic Religion that it has the gift of making the young heart chaste ; and why is this, but that it gives us Jesus for our food, and Mary for our nursing Mother." These are striking words which every Catholic would do well to commit to memory. Mr. Orby Shipley, whose charming Anthology in honour of the Immaculate Mother of the God-Man lies before us, quotes these words of the great Oratorian Cardinal (in a Note to the Sonnet " The world shines bright for inexperienced eyes," from the pen of Father Matth. Russell, S.J.) . . . We rejoice to see that Irish poets are so numerously represented. This is as it should be. In no country in the world has the devotion to Mary Immaculate been so pronounced in the past, just as in the present, as in Ireland :

And in no country has that devotion produced more splendid results in true nobility of manhood and absolute purity
of womanhood. . . . One of the sweetest poems in the book
is a Breton legend by Alfred Austin, entitled " Ave, Maria."
. . . There is a charming translation of the Latin verse of the
present Holy Father. . . . We will make one more extract
—a poem of two verses, entitled " Pilgrim's hymn," by that
noble high-souled Protestant Irish patriot, Thomas Davis,
" Fading, still fading, the last beam is shining."'

Liverpool Daily Post.

' It will be easily seen, that the remarks we are about to
make are written by a Protestant, and Roman Catholic
readers will doubtless understand the point of view. They
are penned, however, with more sympathy and emotion than
is general with Protestants in regarding the Marian cult.
The late M. Renan, in one of his wisest sayings, pronounced that Humanity would be poorer if one of the
elements that compose it were wanting. One or more of
these elements is represented in the honour paid to the
Blessed Virgin, and in the poetry which has been written in
her praise. Some of this is modern in spirit and senti-
mental in key. Much of it is mediæval and quaint. Some
of it is gravely, if not profoundly theological. Some of it is
simple with an archaic and infantile simplicity. Some of it
is subtle and full of those figures of very various merit which
are called conceits. Some of it is purely spiritual ; and
some expatiates in distasteful physical detail. Mr. Orby
Shipley has made his selection impartially, and without
erecting a standard of taste, or even of theological propriety.
The cult of Mary takes as many forms as the worship of
God ; and it is never for those who cannot sympathise, to
dogmatically reject or condemn . . . Among the traditions
incidentally treated may be cited—Father Prout's very
pretty version of the " Zingarella," a story of the Holy Family
in Egypt ; a touch of unbelieving Thomas, after the death
of Mary, given in the verse of Sir J. C. Barrow : Mrs.
Browning's exquisite " Mary to the Child Jesus " . . .
Matthew Bridges is drawn upon for a poem in which the
Oriental idea of Mary as an Ivory Tower is prettily
worked out : the origin of the expression " Gossamer-threads "
is illustrated in some exquisite lines of Emily Bowles . . .
And the feeling of simple Catholics could not be better given
than in this earnest appeal from the pen of Matthew Russell,
S. J., " Look down on us thy children, O Mother dear." From
Mr. Lewis Morris comes an equally beautiful recognition

. . . and "Ave, Maria," is more decidedly infused with dogma, but still beautiful and winsome. It is by Rosa Mulholland.'

IRISH DAILY INDEPENDENT.

'A collection of poems about the Mother of God could scarcely fail to be a beautiful book, seeing that poets of all nations and all creeds, taking her for the highest standard of womanhood, have sung her praises. It is a little remarkable that in a time when anthologies and collections are so universal, it should be left so late in the day to make a gathering of Mary-songs. Her lilies are in many gardens, and her love in many hearts ; and this is a book which will be dear as literature and doubly dear as love-songs. It has not been left to the Catholic Church to praise her. The most unlikely names meet one. Here are some at random —Byron, Shelley, Goethe, Coleridge, Wordsworth, Charles Lamb, Schiller and Southey. Sometimes one cannot help thinking that the compiler of this very beautiful volume has strained a point, to bring certain authors within his scope —as where Tennyson is represented by his "Mariana in the South." Ordinarily, however, authors are here legitimately ; Rossetti, of course, with "Ave," but also Longfellow, Moore, the Brownings, Dora Greenwell, Scott and Edgar Allan Poe . . . I will select here and there from Mr. Shipley's gleanings. Here, for example, is that "Lament for Walsingham" which is at once so simple and so piercing . . . Another lovely simplicity is the "Colloquy between Christ, our Lady and the Angel," from thirteenth-century Italian (translated by E. M. Clerke). "The Romaunt of Blessed Johann," by T. P. Bullivant, and the sixteenth-century Carol "This other night I saw a sight" are also lovely : but, here is a stave, most airy and delicate, gathered by Mr. A. H. Bullen, prince of collectors, from the thick dusts of the Wars of the Roses, "I sing of a Maiden" . . . Ireland, needless to say, is largely represented in this Anthology. I wonder if the lines ascribed to Thomas Davis are genuinely his ? . . . Other Irish Marian poets are, D'Arcy McGee, Father Prout, Gerald Griffin, A. de Vere, D. F. MacCarthy, Professor Dowden, Count Plunkett, Father Russell, Rosa Mulholland, Katharine Tynan, E. H. Hickey, Dr. Madden and R. D'Alton Williams. Of course, there are a host of others ; and besides, the Irish-Americans figure largely.'

ACADEMY.

'Probably the gem of this book is Crashaw's pathetical descant upon the devout plain-song of "Stabat Mater dolorosa." Like most variations by virtuosos on classical themes, it is no doubt overdone ; and the ingenuity of Crashaw's generation was singularly unchastened. But, with all his extravagance, he is sincere and passionate and moving. . . . Another English hymn of the seventeenth century, by Richard Verstegan, a Catholic printer and publisher, is full of loving *naïveté* : it is not unlike " Jerusalem, my happy home." Of the nineteenth-century poems none deserve popularity better than the "Shrines of Mary" by Adelaide Procter. Father Bridgett's expansions of St. Bernardine's paradox, "All things obey the commands of God, even the Virgin ; and all things obey the commands of the Virgin, even God," is very subtle and strong. The excerpts from Father Caswall's "Drama Angelicum" and "Tale of Tintern" are not without attractions for the sympathetic ; and the "irony" of Mary's Song from the former is both elegant and edifying. Many readers will prefer the verses by Father Prout and an old Provençal poet (translated by John Kenyon) founded on the fancy that the Holy Family had their fortune told by gipsies in the course of the flight into Egypt. Of course, the older poet is the naiver and more serious. A sonnet on Father Passaglia (by W. D. Kelly from across the Atlantic) makes the obvious points both neatly and kindly.'

CATHOLIC FIRESIDE.

' The poem that has been selected from the " Father of English poetry" is the series of stanzas each beginning with a different letter of the alphabet, known as " Chaucer's A. B. C." and said to have been written by him at the request of Blanche, Duchess of Lancaster. Old Geoffrey's verses are given in a modernised form (from the pen of William John Blew) . . . In a later page we meet with Chaucer again, in this case associated with a laureate of our own century, the passage being Chaucer's invocation at the beginning of the " Prioress' Tale," as modernised by William Wordsworth.' ' From the poets of our own time, Mr. Orby Shipley has gathered a rich wealth of verse ; but, it is curious to note that some of the most strikingly beautiful poems are those written by Protestants, or at least non-Catholic pens. It has been well said that the poet is something of a prophet, and true poetic insight reveals to him much of the reality of things ; and so it is that the beauty of Catholic devotion to our Lady has drawn sweet strains from singers who were not themselves aware how well their verse expressed the underlying truths of Catholic devotion. Thus, among the gems of the later period covered by the " Carmina" must be numbered E. B. Browning's verses "Sleep, sleep, mine Holy One." In Longfellow, we find, in the words put into Prince Henry's mouth in one of the Italian scenes of the "Golden Legend," a wonderfully true picture of Catholic devotion to our Lady.'

St. James's Gazette.

'Primarily intended for Roman Catholics, the book will carry weight with them by reason of the legend "Nihil Obstat : Imprimatur" : and its dedication "to the revered memory" of Cardinal Manning will not detract from its interest to those who profess the doctrines of the Church of Rome. But, the general reader will find much that is beautiful in Mr. Orby Shipley's Anthology. Thus, we may quote a few lines from a section of the book entitled "Old Catholic Verse" (collected in 1840 by Father Morrall, O.S.B), and reprinted from a MS. volume. "The sun was sinking in the west, Ave, Maria." . . . Some of the best poems printed in this volume are inspired by old Italian paintings of the Madonna and Child, such as those by Murillo (by Trench and De Vere), by Lorenzo de Credi (by Michael Field), or by Raphael. Raphael's Sistine Madonna is the subject of three separate poems by Alfred Gurney, Charles Kent, and G. H. Miles, of New York. The great poets of England of the last three centuries were not, as a rule, Roman Catholics. But, we find nothing more beautiful in Mr. Orby Shipley's volume than Byron's " Ave, Maria," or than Shelley's lines from " Epipsychidion," somewhat doubtfully assigned to the same object of adoration. Nothing will surprise the reader more than that this Anthology should consist so largely of songs addressed to the Virgin Mary by writers who were not Catholics. A very singular poem of Keble's is included in the " Carmina Mariana" which is described as having been withheld from publication with Keble's consent, but against his wish. As a whole, the work has been done with great taste and judgment ; and it is a book which may find favour with Protestants as surely as it will with Roman Catholics.'

Dublin Review.

'Among the shorter tributes to our Lady are many fugitive pieces—English, Irish and American—which would otherwise have been lost in the pages of old periodicals, sometimes of great beauty, and which it is an especial merit of Mr. Orby Shipley to have preserved. It is particularly interesting to observe how large a part of the volume is made up of poems by non-Catholic writers, and how beautifully even those express themselves who have no belief in the divinity of Mary's Son : a striking example of the *testimonium animæ naturaliter Christianæ*. The volume is headed with a very graceful and touching dedication to the revered memory of Cardinal Manning, "who encouraged the idea of our Blessed Lady's Anthology, and counselled its development." '

GLASGOW OBSERVER.

' There is no scarcity of anthologies . . . In the forties the genius of Clarence Mangan gave us even a German Anthology, enshrining those matchless renderings of his from the most favoured lyrists of the Fatherland . . . But, not until now has Our Lady had an anthology—at all events in the English tongue. [A Jesuit Father, Antonio de Balinghem, published a Latin Anthology, *Parnassus Marianus*, in 1624.—Editor.] Here, however, it is at last—a stately octavo of more than four hundred pages. The appearance of such a work is a notable event in our Catholic literary history. But, more remarkable than the publication of the work are its contents . . . Two names have to be mentioned that we should expect to come across in such a volume. One is the illustrious Petrarca ; the other, the reigning Supreme Pontiff. One inevitably looks for Petrarch's immortal ode : and there it is—a very successful English version indeed, by the late C. B. Cayley. But, what rendering could reproduce the music, the majesty, the sublimity—albeit, the glorious simplicity of the original? Could human language be simpler, or more sublime than that in which is clothed the apostrophe to Mary—*Vergine Santa, d'ogni grazia piena*? His Holiness has also a place in this work. A Latin poem of his faces the first page and serves, in a sense, as a text for the volume. This is how Leo's muse addresses the Blessed Virgin Mary, *Ardet pugna ferox* . . . Suffice it to say that a very good and at the same time faithful English version of the poem is found in the body of the work :

Now that the war is raging, fierce and fell.

Scotland is represented in this book—Protestant Scotland, by Sir Walter Scott and W. Edmonstoune Aytoun (Goethe's Holy Family) ; and Catholic Scotland by Robert Campbell, of Skerrington (de Santeuil's Hymns from the Paris Breviary), and Father Oswald Hunter Blair, O.S.B., and W. Dunbar, modernised by E. M. Clerke . . . I cannot say the book is absolutely unique—in English Catholic literature it certainly is. The compiler has merited the gratitude of English-speaking Catholics ; and very few have rendered a more notable service to Mary than this English convert. He has laid at Our Lady's feet a precious gift ; and beyond all doubt her recompense and her reward to him will be exceeding great.'

Historisch-Politische Blätter : Munich.

'There is a double object in the volume—to combine art and piety. All the poems tend to edification ; but, the reviewer would fulfil his office in but a onesided manner if he overlooked the fact that they are not all equally so. Orby Shipley is not to be blamed for having admitted into his collection the hymns in praise of Mary by non-Catholic poets. Far from it. Some of these are of unusual beauty. But, as all art, in the widest sense of the word, so, in a special manner religious art and religious poetry rest on the faith of Christianity and the Church, it is impossible that poets should extol worthily the dignity of Mary, who do not believe in her Son as the Incarnate God. With this un-changeable principle in our minds, we judge of the works of the well-known George Eliot, and others . . . Looked at from another point of view, the collection of verse in praise of Our Lady has earned our deepest gratitude. It embraces all periods of English literature. Even old Catholic Scotland brings its tribute, and an important tribute, viz., two ballads of the poet Dunbar, modernised by E. M. Clerke . . . Amongst the Catholic poets of our own day, perhaps the most conspicuous is Frederick W. Faber. It is well known that the distinguished poet Wordsworth placed the then Protestant Faber in the foremost rank of modern poets as regards a subtle comprehension of Nature.'

Katholik : Mayence.

'This English Anthology in honour of the Mother of God ought to be welcome, by reason of its copiousness and its happy selection, to all friends of religious poetry. The com-piler of this splendid work has, in truth, presented us with what is not only an edifying book of poetry, but a work of art of the highest class. The greatest poets from the thir-teenth century to our own time are represented in its pages by verse . . . distinguished by depth of thought, glow of feeling and true poetic form. The name not only of Catholic Marian poets, but also of prominent Protestants . . . figure in the collection. There is a touching ring about an "Ave"

of the Protestant Keble, which at the pressing solicitation of
his friends, but against his own wish, was first published
after his death . . . The poetic productions of the Marian
literature of England, Ireland, and America form, as is only
natural, the principal contents of the Anthology ; translations
from the works of poets of the Romance languages, notably
the Spanish and Italian, deserve likewise the place of honour
assigned to them.   But, why the soulful melodies which our
German Catholic poets have sung in praise of the Queen
of Heaven have been altogether overlooked is incomprehensible to us ; for we cannot assume that the ancient
Minnesingers, and the names of our modern Marian poets—
Görres, Hahn-Hahn, von Droste, Dreves, Weber, &c.—are
unknown to the Editor of the work before us.   This work,
the most important one ever issued in the department of
Marian poetry, is dedicated to the memory of the late
Cardinal Manning, who has specially recommended and
furthered its publication.'

NOTES AND QUERIES.

'With the theological point of view of this interesting
volume, we need hardly say, we are in no way concerned.
There are, however, both literary and historical reasons why
a collection of this nature should have its uses for our
readers.   The Blessed Virgin holds a place in the devotional
literature, not only of Roman Catholic countries, but also of
those Eastern forms of Christianity which are in antagonism
to the Papal claims.   In England there have always been
poets who realised the significance, as regards the art, of
her who was called in the Middle Ages "the dear Dove of
Paradise" . . . Until we read his pages we had no idea
that so much had been written on this subject by our leading
poets, more especially by those who can have had no sympathy with the views which have led Mr. Shipley to bring
out this beautiful book.   One important service of the "Carmina Mariana" is, that it draws attention to Richard Verstegan, and others of our old minor poets, whose verses are
worthy of being rescued from the oblivion of our great libra-
ries.   Verstegan's poem entitled "Our Blessed Ladie's Lullaby" (1601), though it contains here and there a harsh line,
is well worthy of reproduction.   The specimens of our modern
minor poets might have been added to with advantage.'

AMERICAN CATHOLIC QUARTERLY REVIEW :
PHILADELPHIA.

'Frederick Stokes, in his brilliant introduction to Mait-

land's " Dark Ages," states rather strongly a fact whose
general truth has been the subject of animadversion by the
intelligent and cultivated Catholic body. He says : "It is
hardly too much to say that modern literature as a whole
is Protestant." . . . Nevertheless, it must be a matter of
congratulation that the intellectual power erst given to
polemic battles, now exerts itself to great effect in the
quieter emulation of religious "belles lettres." . . . While this
is true, still must the Catholic heart confess to remissness
in one large field of modern literary research—that of
Hymnody. . . . Whatever the cause may have been, it is
true that converts from Protestantism are almost the only
eminent expounders, translators and editors of our great
hymnologic treasures, of whom the Catholic body can
boast. . . . And so it happens that, in this age of collections,
we have waited long for a worthy tribute of song to Our
Lady ; but happily, our long waiting has been answered at
last. . . . In conclusion, the present reviewer ventures to
intrude a personal predilection suggested by his theme. In
the midst of so many names of Celtic bards who have sung
the praises of Mary, he desiderates that of the tender,
devout but ill-starred Mangan ; a few stanzas from his fine
translation from the German, "Mary, Queen of Mercy,"
would serve art no less than piety, and would enshrine in
many a heart the "dream-encircled" mystic whom cultured
Irishmen, by a consensus of opinion, place on the very
pinnacle of Ireland's "House of (poetic) Fame."'

CATHOLIC TIMES.

'The first poem in the book is the "Hail, Mary," standing
alone upon its page ; then come Latin verses by Pope
Leo XIII. The whole four hundred pages are a practical
commentary on the words, "From henceforth all generations
shall call me Blessed." . . . Very interesting are the lines
by Heber, R. S. Hawker and Keble. . . . There are a few
lines composed by Agnes Strickland, on hearing Persiani
singing in the Church of St. Mary's, Moorfields, in 1840.
They are testimony from a Protestant to the power of music
in the service of religion. . . . Among the examples of Faber
is the poem of the " Expectation," verses flowing with his
own fervour. There are some characteristic lines by Lady
Georgiana Fullerton, beginning, " Mother of Him who never
strove, nor cried." Of course, the Anthology leaves many
flowers ungathered ; but it was to be a volume, not a shelf
of volumes.'

B

SCOTTISH REVIEW.

'Some years ago Mr. Shipley did excellent service by compiling one of the best anthologies we have for the Ecclesiastical Year. His present work, though of a similar nature, is somewhat different from his "Annus Sanctus." . . . The poems selected are gathered from a wide field, including such writers as Chaucer, Dunbar, Crashaw, Donne, Beattie, Coleridge, Scott, Wordsworth and Tennyson. The collection is Catholic in almost every sense of the word. . . . The poems are of all kinds and in all measures, and represent the poetry of many languages, Greek, Latin, Italian, Spanish and Portuguese, as also Syriac and Armenian. As for the English poems, some are gathered from many out of the way corners, and have been written in all parts of the world, wherever, indeed, the English language is spoken.'

AMERICAN ECCLESIASTICAL REVIEW : OVERBROOK, U.S.A.

'A rich treasury of fairest gems whose beauty appeals not only to the devout lover of the Virgin Mother of Christ, but to the admirer of poetic genius and to the singers of sweet song. . . . It contains not only echoes of, and answers to, the affectionate speech of a Mother whom every Christian cherishes in his heart, but the expressions of attraction to which the genius of the stranger, accustomed only to the harmony of nature's voice, confesses in regard to our Blessed Lady. . . . We possess nothing like it in our language, either as to choice of material or wide range of subjects, illustrating that central figure of Christian art which, though lovely in every feature of her unblemished humanity, derives her ideal beauty from the divine light of the Infant's face at her bosom.'

SATURDAY REVIEW : FEBRUARY, 1894.

' By some accident, the first edition of Mr. Orby Shipley's "Carmina Mariana," which was published last year, failed to reach our hands ; and we are all the more glad to have an opportunity of doing justice to the second. For the book is one of real interest and value. It would be childish and would savour of that most foolish of all conduct, which induces men to say, " Peace, where there is no peace," to affect to ignore the fact that there is a certain danger—a certain burning character—about the subject. Unwise extremists in various branches of the Catholic Church have brought it about, that the name which of all names in Christian hagiology ought to be that exciting the least hostile feelings, has been one of the chief apples of religious discord.

But we, at least, see nothing in this volume which an English Churchman, though here and there he may bar a phrase or question a doctrine, need exclude from his library. Mr. Shipley has drawn impartially on Anglican and Roman sources. And it is the peculiar happiness of the English Church that she has never varied one jot or tittle, in any authoritative utterance, from the Catholic doctrine of the θεοτόκος. We have added nothing, and we have detracted nothing . . . and every English Churchman, who knows what Churchmanship means, speaks of her by the simplest and most gracious appellation accorded to any being, human or divine, that of " Our Lady." . . . It is natural, and it is by no means due to any corruption of nature, that the religious sentiment should blend freely and eagerly with the sentiment of devotion to the Eternal Feminine ; and with such encouragements as have been offered by the whole Catholic Church to the honouring of the Virgin, a plentiful outpouring of poetic expression of the feeling was certain. Excellent and characteristic as Mr. Shipley's Anthology is, he would, we suspect, be the last to hold it up as complete, even in respect of English. Thus (to point out only one thing that he has not given) there is one of not the least exquisite stanza-pictures of Tennyson's " Palace of Art," that which begins

> Or the Maid-Mother by a Crucifix,
> In tracts of pasture sunny-warm,

a stanza only, but worth a long poem. The maker of Anthologies is not a maker of a *corpus poetarum* ; and we should not be surprised if Mr. Shipley were able to find another and even yet another volume as full, though not as good, as he has given. . . . But, we have not to do with what we have not, but with what we have ; and very good it is. In more than four hundred pages, Mr. Shipley has collected an Anthology neither unreadably full, nor conspicuously select.'

NOTE.

The following estimates were published, or reached the Editor, after the above extracts had been made.

GUARDIAN : 1895.

' The first edition of this Anthology of poems in honour of the Blessed Virgin was published two years ago, and met with so favourable a reception that a re-issue has been called for. This contains an index of authors and other slight improvements on the first edition, but the book is in all essentials unaltered. The plan on which the Editor has worked,

and which has resulted in a selection which may be praised
almost without reservation, is sufficiently indicated by the
appearance of the *imprimatur* of Cardinal Vaughan, and in
the list of authors of the names of many writers outside the
Roman Catholic communion, not merely of such typical
English Churchmen as Keble and Trench, but of avowed
Agnostics such as Shelley and George Eliot. Thus, while
working under a due sense of responsibility, the Editor has
freely included whatever beautiful expressions of love or
praise of the Blessed Virgin were to be found in English
poetry, without imposing on their authors any test save that
of the literary merit of the passage quoted and its religious
inoffensiveness from the standpoint of a Roman Catholic.
The result is a very beautiful and interesting Anthology,
which maintains a far higher poetic level than is usual in
collections of religious verse. It is always pleasant for a
reviewer to clear away any points on which he differs from
the author of a good book, and we will therefore state two
details in which we think Mr. Orby Shipley has erred. The
first relates to a so-called modernised version of Chaucer's
" A.B.C.," which is so gross an insult to a great poet that we
cannot pass it over. . . . To call this (extract) Chaucer
"modernised" is absurd, for the "A.B.C.," as should have
been stated, was not an original poem, but a translation
from the French of Deguilleville, so that the matter was
never Chaucer's, and of the form which he gave it no vestige
is left. Our second, and much milder, difference is as to the
order of the poems. . . . We should ourselves have preferred a chronological arrangement, and the present system
is little better than haphazard. The great thing, however,
is that the poems are all here. We have searched for one
favourite after another in Mr. Orby Shipley's pages, and—by
the help of the index—have found them all, not one missing.
The result is a wonderful tribute of love and honour. At the
head of it we may place the translations from the Sequences
of the Church, the Little Offices, and the Paris Breviary.
The flow of English verse begins with some thirteenth-
century lyrics imitated by Augusta Drane ; then we have
Chaucer and his followers, Dunbar and Barclay. The
prosaic period of our literature which followed yields but a
scanty contribution, nor could the recently published " Poems
from the Vernon MS.," full as they are of the praise of the
Blessed Virgin, have added any tribute of importance. Towards the end of the sixteenth century, with the great out-
burst of Elizabethan verse, we have lyrics and sonnets from
Constable and Byrd, Southwell and Sir John Beaumont.
Of the Jacobeans, Crashaw and Donne are the only repre-

sentatives. The eighteenth century, as we should expect, is again a blank ; but with the revival of poetry we have a chorus of praise to which Scott and Byron, Wordsworth and Coleridge, Shelley and Charles Lamb all contributed. Since then it may fairly be said that there is hardly any English poet of note who has failed to write on this theme. . . . With these, as is natural, come the little band of Roman Catholic poets, whose verse is one of the notes of the day. . . . Ireland and America have both contributed largely ; Italy is represented by translations from Dante, Petrarch, Jacopone da Todi and Savonarola, many of them from the versatile but always skilful pen of E. M. Clerke ; Germany by renderings from Goethe and Schiller ; Portugal by some sonnets from Camoens. . . . Mr. Orby Shipley's Antho- logy makes it clear that whenever tenderness and passion have been the predominant notes of a school of poetry, beautiful verse in honour of the Blessed Virgin forms one note in the chorus of song, and it is to this fact that his book owes its abiding charm.'

LYCEUM : 1896.

' He is a poor tyro in art who knows not how the great masters devoted their genius to the glorification of Our Lady ; there is not a gallery of note but has its walls sancti- fied with countless Madonnas. Yet poetry is not a whit behind her sister art in this devotion, though even the approved *connoisseur* in poetry may not realise the fact. For the hundreds familiar with that miracle of painting, the Madonna "di San Sisto," or the Virgin "de la Maison d'Albe," is there one who has heard, say, of Dante's portrai- ture of her "whose visage most resembles Christ," and reflects that it forms the noblest passage in the " Paradiso "? The lover of painting has no difficulty in recalling to mind Leonardo da Vinci's "Our Lady of the Rocks," and has probably dwelt with delight upon the exquisite "Annuncia- tion," by Rossetti—it is one of the treasures that the collec- tion in Trafalgar Square may boast of; but the chances are slight, indeed, that he should be equally acquainted with this painter-poet's lines on that work of the earlier artist :

> Mother, is this the darkness of the end,
> The shadow of death ?   And is that outer sea
> Infinite, imminent eternity ?

No more fruitful source of inspiration exists for the artist, whether the conditions under which he expresses his crea-

tions be those of the chisel, of the brush, or of the pen, no
more suggestive subject could exist, than the life of God's
Virgin Mother with all its agonies and triumph ; and hence
it is not to be wondered at that such a vast body of poetry
has taken birth from the contemplation of it. To gather
together into one Anthology what has been written in English
alone should be a labour of no limited love, in order not to
be a labour upon which the compiler would grow faint and
weary. Had the task not been successfully performed, one
might boldly have ventured the prophecy that years and
years must elapse before such an Anthology could ever be
attempted. Hence Mr. Shipley " in our wonder and astonishment, has built himself a livelong monument " ; by unflagging
zeal and persistent energy he has managed to produce a
goodly volume, " Carmina Mariana," drawing its materials.
from the whole array of poets between Chaucer and Tennyson.
Within the compass of a single volume lie side by side the
sacred poetry of St. Alphonsus ; excerpts from Byron and
Shelley ; lines from St. Victor and lines from Coleridge,
from Aubrey de Vere and from Alfred Austin and Lewis
Morris. . . . The work professes to be a work of piety ;
and edification rather than merit was its criterion. With
materials so selected and derived from every quarter, naturally the volume is somewhat bizarre ; but this eccentricity
once surmounted, it proves in many respects pleasant
enough. Of course, opinions will differ as to what yields
edification and what does not ; but this at least will be con-
ceded, that a religious poem cannot be edifying if it be not
artistic ; its failure in point of poetical considerations will
mar its effectiveness as an agent in piety. And on this view
it is matter for regret that Mr. Shipley should have been
so free in granting admittance where literary discrimination
must have made for exclusion.

'It is a curious circumstance that so much has been
contributed to this volume by non-Catholic writers. . . .
Mr. Shipley culls some beautiful verses in praise of "the
sweet Maid-Mother," by Lewis Morris, and one in particular
is worth quoting.

> Thou art the universal praise
> Of every human heart, the secret shrine
> Where seer and savage keep a dream divine
> Through growing and declining days.

Perhaps what will best indicate how little that touches in
any manner upon the subject of our author's worship has
escaped his eye is the fact, that he has drawn even from

Browning the tribute contained in Act II. of "Colombe's Birthday":

> There is a Vision in the heart of each
> Of justice, mercy, wisdom, tenderness
> To wrong and pain, and knowledge of its cure;
> And these, embodied in a Woman's Form
> That best transmits them, pure as first received,
> From God above her to mankind below.'

ATHENÆUM : 1894.

' Mr. Orby Shipley has had no little difficulty in forming his Anthology of poetry inspired by the memory of the B.V.M. Within the limits he has assigned to the task, he has been remarkably successful, and the compilation before us is one of singular interest and beauty. It is easy to question his reasons for permitting various of the fragments to appear. He himself seems to have doubts as to the applicability of twenty lines from Shelley's "Epipsychidion," beginning,

> Seraph of Heaven, too gentle to be human,

in which the supposed object of adoration is variously addressed as "thou living Form among the dead," "thou Terror," "thou Mirror in whom, as in the splendour of the sun, all shapes look glorious which thou gazest on." Mr. Shipley includes Chaucer's "A.B.C.," a curious acrostical prayer "like Psalm cxviii."; and a fine posthumous poem of Keble's, which is stated (on Bishop Moberly's authority) to have been withheld from publication with Keble's consent, but against Keble's wish. . . . Of course, the book is better suited to Catholic readers than to Protestants, but both Catholic and Protestant will agree in regarding Mr. Shipley's work as evidencing a wide and well-instructed appreciation of poetry.'

DOWNSIDE REVIEW : 1894.

' Mr. Orby Shipley is to be congratulated on the success which has attended his volume of collected poetry in honour of our Blessed Lady. It is not a year since it appeared, and a second edition is already published. The arrangement and printing of this edition correspond with those of the first, while the volume is all the more handy for daily use by the paper not being so thick and unbending. The few oversights in correcting the press which had crept into the former edition have been corrected in the present one; the table of contents has been improved in utility by employing varieties of type to distinguish the leading sources or subjects of the verses, and to emphasise the names of the authors. It has also been improved by the insertion of an alphabetical

index. It was a happy thought on the part of Mr. Orby
Shipley to collect these fugitive pieces in honour of our
Blessed Lady. They have been gathered from many countries and languages, and we can only realise the time and
trouble that must have been expended in collecting and
arranging them when an attempt is made to tabulate some
of them. Without professing to give an exhaustive list, we
find translations from Latin, Greek, Italian, French, Portuguese, German, Polish, Armenian, and Icelandic. We cannot
liken the volume to a *bouquet* of wild or uncultivated flowers,
for the authors and translators include many of the greatest
scholars and poets of the times in which they lived. This
will not cause any surprise in those who call to mind the
place which the Virgin Mother of God necessarily occupies
in the teaching of the Catholic Church and in the devotion
of all her children. We are somewhat astonished to find so
few excerpts from the French and Spanish. Few, we think,
will be prepared to find such a galaxy of great English poets,
who when under the influence of the divine *afflatus* of poetic
inspiration have broken forth into praise of her holiness,
purity and greatness, while their private lives were often the
contradictory of hers. From Chaucer in 1400 to Tennyson
in 1892, through Wordsworth, Shelley, Byron, Scott, Coleridge,
Southey, Moore, the Brownings, and Longfellow, we have
schismatics, heretics, deists, and atheists, all uniting to show
that the lowly Virgin of Nazareth was a true prophetess
when she declared that all generations should call her
Blessed.—J. A. M.'

GLASGOW HERALD : 1893.

'Although Mr. Shipley had not informed us, it would
have been easy to guess that "Carmina Mariana" is the
result of some years' labour. It is altogether a wonderful
book, not only for the mass, but also for the quality, of its
contents. These are no doubt accounted for by the singular
historical position and tender personality of Mary, which
have made her the theme of poets, painters, and romancers,
and the subject of a species of worship in the Catholic
Church. Into the interesting subject of Mariolatry, however, we are not called upon to enter. It is enough to say
here that the poems which constitute this Anthology, and
which Mr. Shipley had gathered from the pages of British
and foreign authors, from Chaucer to Tennyson, serves to
show forth the spirit in which the Virgin Mother has been
regarded from the earliest times. Mr. Shipley informs us
that he has not, as in some collections, based his selection
solely on poetical merit, which is only one factor. . . .

The result amply justifies the claim. We miss certain pieces, especially Milton's " Hymn to the Nativity" ; but doubtless that remarkable poem has been excluded in accordance with the scheme of the book. Dunbar and Sir Walter Scott are, so far as we can make out, the only Scotch authors quoted. That is, of course, not surprising, considering the intensely Protestant spirit of the Scottish people. We may anticipate for such a work a wide circulation among the English-speaking Catholics of Christendom.'

ST. MARY'S CHIMES : NOTRE DAME, U.S.A., 1894.

'The Anthology compiled by Mr. Orby Shipley gives the reader a feeling somewhat akin to that experienced in walking through a gallery of pictures on whose canvases the brush of genius has flashed various types of the Maiden-Mother's face. Mr. Shipley's collection of pictures, however, are word-mosaics, put together with varying degrees of skill, some showing the hand of "little employment," others reflecting the inner light of the true artist in words. The Catholic poets, as becomes loyal children of Mary, are represented by much of their noblest verse ; but the general reader will be surprised to find so many non-Catholic singers among those whose highest inspiration has been obtained at the shrine of our Lady. Wordsworth is here, with his sonnet beginning,

> Mother, whose virgin bosom was uncrost
> With the least shade of thought to sin allied,

and we read again with pleasure the hymn which Scott puts upon the lips of Ellen Douglas ; while the ranks of the singing train are recruited from such poets as Shelley, Byron, Coleridge, Lamb, Browning, Edwin Arnold, and our own Longfellow. The last is represented by lines so reverent that it is hard to believe they were not written by a Catholic. E. B. Browning's fine ode, " The Virgin Mary to the Child Jesus," is the voice of adoring mother-love, the entire poem being seemingly underlaid with tears. As the divine Babe lies asleep, his Mother says :

> No other babe doth wear
> An aspect very sorrowful as thou ;
> No small babe-smiles my watching heart has seen
> To float like speech the speechless lips between.

But of all the tributes from non-Catholic sources, Rossetti's " Ave" is the warmest expression of love and devotion to our Blessed Mother.

'The poems of the early English writers have a quaintness

of phrase, a simplicity of expression hard to describe, as if in those days people drew nearer in thought to our Lord and His Mother, and simply, but fearlessly addressed them. Of this character is the Carol of the sixteenth century—modernised by William J. Blew—beginning, "This other night I saw a sight," also the Provençal Ballad of the Three Gipsies. "The Lady of the Well," a poem of several stanzas by R. S. Hawker, is sweetly simple. Chief among the modern Catholic poets here represented are De Vere and Patmore. The first-named contributes, besides his fine "Ancilla Domini," two sonnets of classic versification, very lovely and tender, while Patmore's stately ode is worthy its high theme. To the new English poet, Francis Thompson, according to the critics a disciple of Crashaw, are credited three short poems, "The Passion of Mary," "Our Lady of Night," and "A Dead Astronomer." On this side the Atlantic, that magazine of our Lady, the "Ave Maria," has been largely drawn upon for contributions to these songs of Mary, the poems chosen being conspicuous for sweetness and beauty. American Catholic poesy is well represented in "Carmina Mariana" by J. B. O'Reilly, M. F. Egan, C. W. Stoddard and Eleanor C. Donnelly.'

AUSTRAL LIGHT: MELBOURNE, AUSTRALIA, 1896.

' A book which the British press has received so favourably deserves to be known in Australia. " Carmina Mariana" is an Anthology of singular interest in both its manner and its form, and while it is full of true poetry, it has this further merit that it rescues from oblivion gems contained in rare volumes of early English verse, and many modern lyrics of great beauty which had lain buried in old periodicals. The direct effect of this collection is, doubtless, to give pleasure to the lover of melodious verse ; but " Carmina Mariana" subserves indirectly a far higher cause, that of truth. The non-Catholic mind seems to have a peculiar difficulty in grasping the practical teaching of the Catholic Church with respect to our Blessed Lady, and the position which Mary holds in the mind and heart of every Catholic. Simple as the matter seems to a member of the Church, this difficulty is a real one. Even Cardinal Newman tells us that before he became a Catholic he found it one of the greatest obstacles in his path. " Only this, I know full well now," he says in his "History of My Religious Opinions," "and did not know then, that the Catholic Church allows no image of any sort, material or immaterial, no dogmatic symbol, no sacrament, no saint, not even the Blessed Virgin herself, to come between the soul and its Creator. It is face to face, *solus cum solo,* in all matters between man and his God. . . . The devotions, then, to Angels and Saints as little interfered with the incommunicable glory of the Eternal, as the love which we bear our friends and relations, our tender human sympathies, are inconsistent with that supreme homage of the heart to the Unseen, which really does but sanctify and exalt, not jealously destroy, what is of earth."

'To a Catholic, every dogma formerly taught by the Church, or practically believed by the general body of the faithful, is of vital importance. He cannot deny what the Church holds to be revealed truth : if he does not confess Christ's teaching before men, Christ will not confess him hereafter before the Father. It seems ludicrous to him who has imbibed Catholic teaching, so to speak, with his mother's milk, and who has had countless proofs of the practical working of such teaching in the daily lives of his fellow Catholics, to be told by an outsider, "You Catholics do not hold what you say ; you set the Blessed Virgin on a level with God, and practically you give her the worship and adoration due to Him !" There is not a Catholic who, either in theory or in practice, gives to Mary the adoration due to God, or who does anything more than honour her for the sanctity with which the Lord has enriched her soul, and ask the help of her intercession with the Almighty. All hymns, praises and petitions offered to her or in her honour, must be interpreted in the light of this teaching, and are animated by the implicit intention of denying to her any honour which is due to the Deity, and of giving to her only such reverence as may be fittingly accorded to the Virgin, " Blessed among women,"

> Our tainted nature's solitary boast,

who has been chosen to be the Mother of the Man-God, the Saviour of the human race. The Catholic Church is sensitive with respect to the "deposit of faith," and she represses, with promptitude and sternness, every attempt made to impair or corrupt the body of revealed truth, which has been committed to her guardianship. If one of her children obstinately maintained, either in theory or practice, that Mary is in any way equal to God, or is to be adored and prayed to as we adore and pray to the Creator, she would at once condemn him as guilty of heretical blasphemy and cut him off from the household of the faith. The true Catholic doctrine is abundantly manifest from the poems in " Carmina Mariana," and thus the book has an important theological bearing, which may be of service to non-Catholics whose minds are not warped by misrepresentation or prejudice.—M.W.'

CATHOLIC WORLD : NEW YORK, 1894.

'Sometimes one is inclined to think that we are enteiing or have already entered a Renaissance of Religion. That name is historically connected with the older reawakening into life which attained its growth nearly four hundred years ago. Call that outbreak of the human spirit what you will—the exclusive worship of things physically beautiful, or the substitution of the natural for the supernatural in the ideals of art and literature, it was, nevertheless, a new birth of the human intellect. So distinctly different from the Middle Ages which preceded it was the Renaissance, that it shocked the best men of the time ; and yet in its types of beauty, and even its pagan spirit, it still maintains the first place it so suddenly assumed at the end of the fifteenth century. . . . But, after all, that older awakening into birth was nothing more than the worship of the natural. Whatever was beautiful in nature, whatever was beautiful in man and his works—this was proposed as the end and object of man's aims and aspirations. Protestantism was powerless to lift men out of this humanism. How could it do so, being purely human itself? . . . The English-speaking world especially gradually fell into a state in which man's grosser qualities of excellence are made the instruments of endeavour. This modern condition is the Renaissance indeed, only shorn of its passionate love of the beautiful, its general culture, its cultivation of the fine arts. We are in a rapid naturalism of industry and thrift and money-getting, which leaves but little room for things beautiful in music and poetry and art, and no room for things spiritual.

'But, in protest against this, we greet with joy the evident signs of a new birth both intellectual and religious. The Oxford Movement, which stands for men and times and intellectual activity, was the beginning of what I would wish to call a Renaissance of Religion. Surely one may say that the Oxford Movement, which for so many thousands of choice spirits was the beginning of eternal salvation, leading them sometimes slowly, sometimes by rapid stages, within the fold of God's Church, was a veritable dawn of an age of spiritual awakening. It is more than probable that we have yet only seen the beginning. . . . Individuals count for little in general movements unless by virtue of their super-eminent qualities of heart and mind, but they are all in greater or less degree types of their class. Among the many who came into the Church, either on the tidal wave of the Oxford Movement or on the natural flow of the tide which that movement created, is Mr. Orby Shipley. Here

are his own words concerning his conversion, (written) in
November, 1878, to the London "Times." . . . These
extracts from Mr. Shipley's letter illustrate the reality of that
new birth of God's truth, in both the inner and outer life of
Englishmen, to which reference has been made : not simply
the fruits of controversy or even of God's ordinary care for
honest souls in error, but the persistent impulse of divine
grace in a whole nation. But it is the fact that Mr. Shipley
has lately put forth a volume of delightful poetry that has
connected him in our mind with this Christian Renaissance,
for the cultivation of religious verse is one of its works.
Keble's "Christian Year" is one exemplification of its excellence, and Faber's poetry and poetical prose another. Mr.
Shipley's "Carmina Mariana" shows how general and
various it has been on the fruitful subject of the Mother of
God. And though the selections range from Chaucer to
Tennyson in this book of compilation, yet much of it is
modern and not a little of quite recent date, and indicates
the extent of Catholic influence on the poetical natures of our
day.

'It is impossible within the scope of this paper to give
any extended review of the literary value of this volume.
Nor is this necessary, for a list of the authors from whom
the poems are taken goes far towards fixing the general
standard of excellence. English poetical writing in all its
great and varied extent, both original and in translation,
has been made to pay tribute to the work. . . . He has
reached across the Atlantic, and amid a newer and more
unconventional life, and hence one favourable to the poetic
temperament, he has sought matter, and not without finding
it ; and our American poets are well represented. His industry is beyond praise, and the result of it is a charm of
song for the elevation and instruction of devout minds.'

IRISH MONTHLY : 1894.

'It is good news to hear that "Carmina Mariana" has
within a year reached a second edition, though it is a portly
volume, and the first edition was not limited to a few hundred copies. This noble Anthology of the tributes that have
been paid in English verse to the Blessed Virgin Mary, both
within and without the Catholic Church, is due to the per-
severing zeal of Mr. Orby Shipley, who has devoted to
English hymnology the studies of many years. Probably in
no language is there such a glorious tribute paid to the
Madonna as here in this heretical English language, which,
alas, began to be the interpreter of genius chiefly when in
its insular jealousy it dared to usurp the office of the uni-

versal language of the Universal Church. We can but
notice some mechanical improvements in this new edition
of a great book which will be "a joy for ever" to pious
hearts and to many hearts that might disown that epithet.
The table of contents is improved, but even still the alphabetical arrangement that runs through it is not sufficiently
clear. However, this lack is supplied in the next pages by
an index of authors, comprising 204 names, besides some
thirty anonymous or unknown. Often, in glancing down this
list, one says, "what can he have got from *him ?*" and turns
to the page referred to. At the end of the volume, after an
index of first lines, Mr. Shipley has enriched this edition
with an interesting selection of criticisms passed on his work
by twenty-seven critics in England, Ireland, the United
States, and Germany between May and September, 1893 ;
and he names seventeen others which he does not quote,
though probably laudatory : for he abstains from citing
general expressions of appreciation, and he does not confine
his extracts to a fragmentary phrase, but he makes this
Appendix a really interesting piece of literature, a study in
comparative criticism, by giving at considerable length
coherent judgments from current periodicals. . . . The
minute accuracy of Mr. Shipley's editing may be illustrated
by the line prefixed to Judge O'Hagan's poem. "Translated
(1874) by John O'Hagan, 1822-1890," giving the year of his
birth and the year of his death, and the year in which he
published this translation in "The Irish Monthly." So, too,
at page 293 : "29th Ode of Petrarch, 1304-1374, translated
by C. B. Cayley, B.A., 1823-1883 : from 'Sonnets and
Stanzas of Petrarch,' 1879." Do we habitually think of
Petrarch as so long before Shakespeare, with his year 1600
in round numbers ? We are grateful for the condensed information given here about the translator of this magnificent
Ode, which most fitly is preceded by one worthy even of
such company—by Coventry Patmore. . . . In these selections Mr. Shipley lets us know the favourite pieces singled
out by the different reviewers, and the variety of tastes is not
a little curious.—M.R.'

To the above may be added the following extract from a
Letter, written in May, 1893, from Francis T. Palgrave,
sometime Professor of Poetry in the University of Oxford, to
the Editor, published (1899) by his Daughter in the Life of
her Father :
'I have delayed thanking you for your gift of "Carmina
Mariana" until I had gone through it. You may remember

that I feared the book would be too scrappy, too loaded with translations, too much like a *Lexicon Marianum*. It is therefore a real pleasure to me to find these fears not realised ; and that although edification has been your primary aim, yet that a good standard in poetical merit, and hence in power of holding the reader, has generally been reached. In short, if I may without the air of conceit pronounce such an opinion, the book seems to me a real success ; and such, I hope, it will prove with many readers. Should a second edition be called for, I think an error exists (which the writer corrects). I have observed no other erratum ; but I think you might much improve facility of reference by paging the poems individually in the Table of Contents. (After a few critical remarks, and some suggestions for the improvement of the Contents, Index, &c., the letter continues thus :) Of course, in such a book there must be a considerable uniformity of thought and imagery ; it is hence best read, like a set of sonnets, discontinuously. But I find many pieces new to me, of much grace and depth of feeling or thought. I have not kept a list, but I may name Sir J. C. Barrow's "Birth and Passing of Mary," pp. 51-55 ; Caswall's "Mary's Song," p. 93 ; Dunbar's "Ballads" (E. M. Clerke), pp. 128, 129 ; Maurice F. Egan's "Sonnets, Ode and Nocturne," pp. 134-139, of which is very striking,

Alone : who is alone ? The criminal dying,
Though steeped in shameful crimes all through and through,
Will leave some heart that trusted, spite his lying—
Some loving heart that, spite his sins, was true.

Father Bridgett's work is very successful, "King Solomon's Mother," pp. 72-78. Father Russell's rendering from Dante, his "Prayer to Our Lady" (Paradiso, xxxiii), I also like, p. 339 ; and his thought from Cardinal Newman, p. 341—I wonder you have nothing from himself. . . . Verstegan's lovely hymn, "Our Ladie's Lullaby," p. 406, in one way interests me most. I lately found the first four stanzas only (out of twenty-four) given as a whole poem, and anonymous, in a reprint of a Music-book of 1620 (Pearson's "Private Music"), and reprinted them with delight in the "Golden Treasury." I shall, if I can, restore them to the author ; but my book is stereotyped. I am very sorry I did not know of the whole poem when making my "Sacred Anthology," in 1889. . . . I feel proud to have been allowed to aid—ever so little—in such a valuable addition to our Anthologies.'

In addition to the above Estimates, Reviews or Notices of the First Series of 'Carmina Mariana' have also appeared

in the following amongst other newspapers and periodicals :
Bookman ; Bookseller ; Bristol Mercury ; Church of England
Quarterly ; Colonies and India ; Daily Telegraph ; Derry
Journal ; Freeman's Journal ; Globe ; Inquirer ; Irish
Catholic ; Irish Ecclesiastical Record ; Ladies' Pictorial ;
Leeds Mercury ; Liverpool Mercury ; Newcastle Journal ;
Queen ; Record ; Scotsman ; Speaker ; Truth ; United
Ireland ; and Westminster Gazette.

LIST OF REVIEWS QUOTED.